La Petite

C000148452

By G. La

Copyright © Gemma Lawrence 2016
All Rights Reserved.
No part of this manuscript may be reproduced without
Gemma Lawrence's express consent

For my sister Shani, and my brother Jamie,
For being not only my siblings, but my friends;
For your weird and wonderful humour and your guidance.

And for Petra Osterberg
For the miles we walked from Hever to Penshurst;
For the sandwiches eaten in the moat of Eltham;
For walking the steps of Anne Boleyn with me.

"Defiled is my name full sore,
Through cruel spite and false report,
That I may say for ever more.
Farewell my joy, adieu comfort

For wrongfully ye judge of me,
Unto my name a mortal wound,
Seek what ye list, it will not be;
Ye seek for that can not be found."
Robert Johnson

"Oh Death, rock me asleep,
Bring on my quiet rest,
Let pass my very guiltless ghost
Out of my careful breast.
Toll on thou passing bell,
Ring out my doleful knell,
Let thy sound my death tell,
Death doth draw nigh,
There is no remedy."
Anon, attributed to Anne Boleyn

Prologue

17th May 1536
The Tower of London

Circa Regna Tonat

I am not alone. Ghosts and spies surround me. I cannot run, nor hide. Shapes seem to move in the darkness about me.

The walls of this, my most opulent prison, are filled with the ghostly faces of those who were here before me. Their hollow faces stare out at me, watching me, from between golden thread and white plaster. I see them with but the edge of my vision, yet I see them.

Their ghostly forms shift and bend, flitting in and out of sight; they are behind the painted wall covers and tapestries, they move through the streets below and the towers above. From the window I see these shades mingle with the living, unseen by the crowds of people and peasants that amble through these palace streets about their daily business. I see ethereal rich clothing billow in winds that move through the paths and walkways. I see their phantom faces look up at the windows of my rooms. I hear their step behind me, close to my heel and when I turn, I see them disappearing once again.

I am haunted by their faces. I see those who died long ago, and those who have just passed. They are legion. How is it that no one else can see them?

The living do not see the dead; they do not feel it when their shoulders brush against these ghosts. But I can see them now, now that I am so close to becoming one of them.

Today, my brother's face has joined them, staring at me blankly from the walls; he no longer smiles. Does he, too, blame me for his death?

The others are also here; More, Fisher, Norris, Brereton, Smeaton, Weston. They join the other ghosts: murdered princes, murdered kings, dukes, ladies and common men. They all lurk beside me in this great palace, watching and waiting for me to join them; their silver fingers reach out from the walls to touch me, and I shiver to feel them close.

Some of them are men I condemned to die here, if not by my hand, then by my will. They wait for me to die because I was the author of their deaths. As Queen, I might say it was my right to remove those who threatened my power. But as a mortal woman sat awaiting death, I now fear what these shades will have said to God on my behalf.

Soon mine own ghost may wander with those shades and shadows I see before me. Is this place lost to God? Is that why these shades linger here? Am I, too, lost to God and to salvation? For what crime? For what sin have I been cast here, other than never showing to the King the humility of a true wife? God alone will know if I was guilty of enough to be brought to such a terrible end. I am innocent of the crimes I have been accused here of, and the Lord of Heaven must know this… but are there other sins I will be held accountable for when I face the gates of Heaven? What will these shades which walk at my side accuse me of, before the light of God?

I have much in my life to be sorry for, and yet of none of what I am accused am I guilty. Yet we all come to think on our sins when Death lingers at our side.

Empty darkness stretches before me in my dreams, when I can dream, when I can sleep. There is a chill running through my blood not caused by the cold stone of the Tower. The fire before me brings no warmth. Winds bay in the darkness of the night, howling about my windows and doors. The winds shriek at me, startling me from staring through this window, startling me from my dreaming, my wonderings... bringing me back into this unrelenting nightmare.

I cannot move, I cannot run. I am trapped. I have no control.

Finally, I am the true subject of the King.

I am his prisoner now, subject to his will. This was what he desired of me in life: to have me, to hold me, to control me, to command me... It was the spice of such a chase, such a challenge, which first awoke his interest in me, and what kept him chasing all those years. To have a woman, any woman, refuse him was almost unimaginable to him when we first met. They all said that his love for me would die in the long chase... that he would cast me off... that he would go back to his first wife... and yet, he did not. It was not the chase that he tired of, but the capture. I could not hold him, once I had become his wife.

But now, I am truly subject to his will, and now his will is my death.

I see the ghost of myself, just a few short years ago, glowing; dancing and prancing in these chambers for joy, laughing with friends and playing with her courtiers, smothered in jewels and furs, diamonds choking her slim neck, her hands weighted down in gold and emeralds. I shiver to see that ghost of my foolish self as she glides past me, glowing with exultation and pride, snapping her bold fingers at those who would oppose her, thinking she is safe, safe forever in the love of the King... my husband, *finally* my husband! After all those years I had him, at last. I was so happy that day. I remember it so clearly. My triumph, my crown, my England, my King! I shone that day; beautiful and adored, with my husband the King looking on, his love lighting my triumph like a wild flame; I was Queen. I was *his* Queen. I had ascended.

I was a fool; dancing, prancing and prattling my way to death.

And now, it is that same long-fought-for husband, that same handsome, glorious king who holds my doom in his hands. It is my husband who will have my death.

My throat feels constrained, tight; the hands of Fate are pressing on its slim and elegant bones. Breath after breath comes painfully, but that will all stop soon. There will be no more breathing; there will be no more singing, no more dancing, no more laughing… no more living. The wolves of court have caught their prey and now they close in for the final blow. Will there be peace for me finally, at the end? Perhaps a peace I have never known in life. I long for it now, now, now, now. Not to wait more hours and more minutes and more days, but just to come to the end now. Waiting for an end one cannot escape… this is true torture.

They sent Cranmer to me; Master Kingston brought him in. I clasped the hands of perhaps the last true friend I have in this world and felt tears come to my eyes to see the soft sorrow in his. He thought to bring me hope; that if I agreed that my marriage to the King was no true marriage, that if I had indeed been pre-contracted to Henry Percy, oh, so many years ago, then even now, the King might show leniency, send me to enter a religious order, rather than take my head on the block. I looked at my friend, and I almost smiled.

"He wants to be rid of me," I said softly, looking down at my hands; they shook slightly as I thought on his words. "He will re-write all that has happened, and cast me from his memory. As if I was never his wife, as if none of this ever occurred."

I smiled at Cranmer's grave face. "You think to bring me comfort, old friend," I said softly. "But the King, and his men… Cromwell… they will not let me go so easily, not now." I looked up at him, shaking my hands at my sides, as though I could shake the fear from them. "If the King will agree to watch over our daughter, even if she is declared a bastard, if he will agree to be still a father to her, if he will protect her, then I will agree to these things put here before me."

Cranmer nodded; I knew that he was thinking that he was unlikely to have trouble in convincing the King to agree to such a small request. To accept a daughter the King already knew was his, in exchange for writing Anne Boleyn out of his life, out of history... this was a small request.

Cranmer nodded to me, and I agreed to all he said; that I was pre-contracted to Percy, that my marriage to the King was no true marriage, that I was not the wife of Henry Tudor, that I was not the Queen of England... that my daughter was a bastard.

I told lies for the pen and ink of man and law, for my daughter, for Elizabeth, in the hope that this last sacrifice might allow him to reconcile himself to her, to remain as a father to my daughter. Katherine's refusal to do the same as I did now only led to her and her daughter being hated and ostracised by Henry. If there was anything I could do now, to ensure that the same fate did not touch my own daughter, then I would do it. The last act I could perform, to try and protect my little girl. The last act of a mother, trying to ensure the survival of her daughter.

Cranmer heard my confession that night, but it was a simple one. I told my old friend the truth, as I told it to God; I had ever been a faithful wife to the King, I had not tarried with other men, or wished or plotted for his death. I had not always shown humility or graciousness to the one who raised me up from noble seat to throne of royalty, but I had not committed the sins for which I was to die. Cranmer expressed no surprise at my confession; he knows as well as I that there are other reasons I am to die. The life of the court is a game of power, a game I was most skilled at... but I have lost this final hand to another player, and now I am in his way.

Cranmer left me that night, my lies walked beside him to the King. With the coming of the morning, my brother and those men accused with me for adultery and treason walked out to their bloody deaths. I watched them die. And I sit still staring from this window. Unable to sleep, haunted by the ghosts of the past and the wind outside these walls. My fears surround me, my impatience to die fights with my will to live. My head is filled with thoughts and memories, with regrets and yet with memories of sweetness too; perhaps it is this way for all who know their end is coming.

The dusty platform on which the final moments of my life will be played has been built. The swordsman from France will be here soon; they have prepared a stage upon which my life will end with the sudden sweep of a sword. I will never see my daughter again. I will never see my husband... and he will never see me again; that is what Henry does when he disposes of a wife. He leaves and she is forgotten. I will become a myth; vilified and tainted. My name will be spoken as they speak of cursed women of the Bible, of spiteful faeries, or Arthur's Guinevere. I will become a story used to make children behave, eat their dinner, or go to bed. I will become a demon; the Evil Queen Anne, the betrayer, the traitor, the whore, the witch. They will not remember me truly. They will not remember my charity, my loyalty, my desire for reform. They will not remember my love for my family, for my daughter, or my love for my husband.

It was a love that made the Church tremble. A love that made England roar. It was a true love, an equal love, a mighty love. It was all-powerful... once.

But people will forget these things, especially Henry. I know him too well to doubt it. His courtiers will tell him pretty lies to justify his wishes; they will paint me as a witch, as a whore. It is easier for Henry to believe that I deceived him in everything I ever did, in everything I ever was, than to believe that he wishes to get rid of me for the satisfaction of his own desires. He cannot believe bad of himself, he never could. To believe these lies of me will make it easier for him to kill his own wife, his once true love. Henry was always happy within a world of fantasy; now, in this tale, I am the evil harpy sent to lead him astray, but he is still the good knight, the virtuous prince. I will be killed and my name defiled, but he will live on as the great King who triumphed over evil.

The people will believe his stories of me; I always had fewer supporters than Katherine. I was never liked by many of the common people; they resented me, resented my rise in fortune and power. My temper and my arrogance helped little to win people to me, but my temper always had the better of me. I learned self-control far, far too late in life. But the common people blamed me for things that Henry too was a part of, acts and actions he took of his own accord. They blamed me for everything which happened in Henry's rule; for Katherine, for Mary, for England, for the reform of the Church, for the dissolutions of the monasteries. Henry will get away with killing me; there are none left now who would risk themselves to save me. Not even my father.

But there are those who will mourn me. They will mourn my death in secret, but there will be some in this world to sorrow at my passing.

And what of our child… my poor Elizabeth? Will Henry truly be kind to the daughter of a demon? When I think of my child I fear I shall truly go out of my mind; the thought of Elizabeth makes me sick. I cannot run to her as I wish to, I cannot protect her, I cannot hold her. She will be made a bastard, no more a princess… stigmatised as my daughter. But she is still the daughter of the King, and he cannot deny her that. No, he cannot deny that she was the true fruit of our love. She is the very image of him, with that red hair aflame with the fire of the Tudors, her pale skin and the little mouth which pouts when she is thwarted. Oh yes, she is Henry's daughter and none could claim otherwise. But the eyes in that little face are mine, those dark deep black pools; when I am gone, my eyes will still look on the world from within her face.

In Elizabeth at least, something good of me will continue to live in this world. I wish I could explain to her what is to happen, but she is only a babe. If she is clever, she will not seek to mention my name as she grows, but I hope that she will remember something that is good and sweet about me. I hope that she will live to see a better life than her mother's. I pray to God that she will lead a quieter, happier life than mine.

I cannot rest; I am plagued with thoughts that have no sense, no linear sense. Images and broken fragments of conversation flit through my mind, perhaps I do start to lose my mind, as so many have done in this Tower.

But a month ago, I had thought that there was little that could threaten me for my position, power, or my place in his heart; and now I am to die at his pleasure. There was so much time waiting to be his queen and such a short time *being* his queen. Three years. That is all my reign was. I could not hold it once I had it; his love, the crown, my power... it has all slipped through my fingers.

Henry has a tested method to discard unwanted wives. He has practised it well and often now. That Seymour creature will need to be wary... Will she succeed where Katherine and I failed? A matter of chance is all it is; produce a son and your position is safe, fail to do so and become the next wife to be shut in a castle, awaiting death at the King's pleasure. He did it to Katherine; waiting long years until she wasted away, her heart broken but her pride still intact, but for me there will be a quicker solution, a faster removal. Henry does not often make the same mistake twice. He is getting better at his own game.

I cannot hold only Henry to blame though. It was not all his fault. There was also me; my pride, my harsh tongue, my reckless, careless mouth. There were the long weary years of waiting for an annulment from Katherine that took such a toll on us both. There was my refusal to become what he wanted in a wife; my reluctance to relinquish the power I had over

Henry as his untouched mistress. There was my failure to conceive a son for him. My womb became as barren to his seed as Katherine's had. I think on Katherine and her daughter much now, for only now do I understand their pain, the pain that I helped cause. I understand it, because that same pain is now mine. I too am now imprisoned, held and captured, my daughter kept from me, abandoned by the King. God shows me now, at the end, the pain I caused to others. He grants their pain to me. These are harsh lessons to learn.

I think of the past as this night draws on, I cannot sleep; these are precious few hours I have left. My friends, those men who courted me as the Queen of their realm and hearts lie cold in the ground. My brother is dead. My daughter is kept from me. My Boleyn family is lost to me. I know not whether those left yet living are safe or not. My husband wishes my death and the platform for my execution is ready. The dust from its construction scatters gently in the night's wind. The fire burns in the grate and the winds whisper around the Tower. The skies are ominous, but there will be some sun to light the skies tomorrow.

The maids are all asleep around me on their pallets on the floor. They are not my women, but are sent as agents by my enemies to watch me. I will not wake them, for it will make their masters angry that they did not watch me all night, and there is enough humour left in my breast to find that thought amusing. My wakeful mind does not rouse them from their slumber.

I will not die as my enemies wish me to; my life has been carefully planned and played out in all I have ever done and now, at the end, I will not let all that is Anne Boleyn slip away from me. I will not walk out with my head hanging or scream and struggle in fear at the face of Death. I will die well and gracefully, just as I have lived. And this night, I will make my peace with God and the ghosts of my past.

I will not let my mind linger in this prison. There are other paths I wish to wander, this night.

Chapter One

1505

Hever Castle
Kent

The first memory I have is of my mother. It is the memory of a child, but I know not how old I was when it happened. There are feelings that lock hands with it in my heart; strong and sharp, of love and longing, of comfort and safety, which sing to my soul.

My mother stands in the rose gardens at Hever Castle; she is surrounded by the beautiful, sweet-smelling roses which she loves so much. She is the one who grows them, tends them, watches over them, as diligently and as lovingly as she watches over her children. Her fair hair is swept up in a hood, of the old gable fashion, but wisps of it have come loose and they tease lightly at her beautiful face in the sunlight, fluttering like the soft wings of butterflies. It is high summer; the crackling grasses in the meadows are almost ready to be cut for hay and straw, and the birds sing as they gather foods and show their young how to fly. The air smells of dusky, sweet spices from the kitchens, of the heat and sweat of the land, and of crisp, dry apples, pears, quince and medlar being made into pies, sauces and vinegars. There is singing and laughter far off in the fields where men and women work and toil on the land, our lands; these are the lands of the Boleyns. It is almost harvest time; a time of plenty, always a season for merriment.

My mother's sparkling eyes are blue and bright; they mirror the skies. Her pale cheeks are flushed with the pleasure of the day; she is young and she is beautiful. I remember looking up at her, suddenly struck still with admiration for her beauty, but then I am roused from my daydream as I hear her laugh at my wondering face. Suddenly, she runs from me, fast and wild, her scarlet gown billowing behind her like the great sail of a ship. She turns at the end of the grassy path, lined on either side with her rose bushes, and she beckons to me, her blue eyes sparkling with a naughty shine. I run to her, laughing, for I know this is but a jest. My legs are little and fat, and I trot after her as fast as I can, but with a swift and graceful curtsey at the edge of the path, she is gone, and I am alone in those gardens. The roses tower over me, red and white and beaming in the sun.

I stand alone in the gardens. I listen breathlessly for a sound of her. I am not afraid. I was ever bold and brave even on my tiny legs; ready to fight and roar like a lion cub. I will find her, I think silently. She will not escape me.

I see a flash of crimson cloth through the green stems of the roses and I run, as fast as I am able, after her. My eyes search through the gardens; I peek through bushes of lush green leaves and red-brown thorns, jumping to try to see through the web of flowers. I can hear her laughing softly, somewhere nearby, hidden by the flowers. Suddenly she is upon me, grasping my small body in her arms, lifting me into the air and laughing merrily as she hears my squeak of surprise. Then my cry of laughter mixes with hers. There are kisses in the warm sunshine for me, her youngest daughter, and perhaps, her favourite child.

It is a good memory… a good place for my story to begin. For at Hever was where all our stories started.

My mother would tell us stories, my sister Mary and me, before bed and when we wandered in the gardens. I learned later that she was a most attentive mother to us. Many noble ladies were not as interested in spending time with their children as our mother was. Many simply visited them from time to time to check on their progress in the schoolroom, but our mother was often with us, teaching us, guiding us. We were fortunate indeed to be her children.

As we passed through the generous herb gardens, our mother would pause in her stories of knights and kings and ask us to identify the sweet smelling tansy, borage and lavender for remedies and unguents; the parsley, sage and rosemary, the rue and juniper. We would tell her what each plant or berry or leaf could be used for, and she would tell us yet more uses, for every woman must know these things for the time she became a wife. Every wife should be a physician to her family as our mother was to us, for even if doctors could be afforded, it did not do to waste money for lack of knowledge ourselves. We must learn all we could, she told us, so that we might be of good use to our families and husbands, to our own children when we had them. And when she was satisfied in our knowledge, she would continue to tell us her tales of kings and queens, of saints and sinners, of knights and quests… of the court. Our mother told us of the world we lived in; its history, and its present, through stories.

She told us of our King, Henry VII, who had united our torn land. She told us of battles that had rent our country asunder before we were born… of how the King had won against the usurper, Richard III, and married the beautiful Princess Elizabeth of York. She told us of how she had once served the Queen Elizabeth, before that great Queen of the House of York had been taken from this world. Our mother mourned the death of her beloved Queen Elizabeth long after the official mourning period had passed, for she had admired and loved the Queen for her strength and her loyalty, for her love for her children and her husband. Elizabeth of York had died in 1503, of childbed fever, trying to offer another male heir to her husband, King Henry VII, upon the death of their heir, Arthur, Prince of Wales. But that last act of loyalty to her line had cost the Queen her life, and her babe had died too; no further heirs of the royal house of Tudor were born, as the King did not replace his beloved wife with another after her death.

But we had yet princes and princesses still living of the line of Queen Elizabeth and King Henry, our mother told us. Fine, strong and handsome Prince Henry, the second son of the house of Tudor and now heir to the throne, and the beautiful princesses, Margaret and Mary, who looked so like their good mother. Our mother's stories taught us of the greatness of the country in which we lived. She taught us our history in those beautiful gardens of the handsome house of Hever and the flowers themselves danced with the vibrancy of her tales.

My mother's eyes would shine when she described the Court of England, the games of courtly love; of poets who had written lines for her and the other beauties of the court. She talked of dangers, of men who stalked the corridors; their aims were not always as honourable as they might profess to a maiden, and women did well to be careful for their honour. She spoke to Mary and me of dances and pageants, of games and hunts; she was animated and happy when she spoke of the court. It made me long to go to court before I was aware of what and where it really was. To me, as a child, it was a fantasy world of heroes, of ladies, of princes and of gods.

I think Mary felt the same as I. When our mother spoke of the gallants and of the admiration that they could bestow on a lady through poetry or by wearing her colours at a joust, Mary's eyes would sparkle. Mary longed for such admiration as I did.

My sister looked like our mother; the same fair hair with a just a touch of the red fire of the sun. Her wide-set gold-brown eyes and full dusky-pink lips were pretty even when she was very young. Not much later, when we two had bled and flowered, her figure would grow full and buxom, and she would fill out her dresses with a more womanly figure than I ever had. Mary matured early and knew the effect she could have on men early, too. Later in life, she could stop a man speaking with but one bold glance from behind her long lashes. But for all her earthy wiles, she was sweetness itself, my beautiful elder sister; there was nothing in her that was mean.

When we were young, Mary was always the popular one with the servants and the guests to our house. She was pretty, and, at least outwardly modest and well-behaved, but there was always a sparkle of mischief about Mary. There was always a game and a laugh to be had when my sister was near. There was a twinkle in her eye that I could catch and I would feel my heart skip to know that Mary was planning something, and that I, her little sister, might be allowed to join in.

Sometimes her game was to steal sweetmeats or marchpane scraps from the kitchens, other times she would have us dancing in the newly built and stylish long gallery at Hever. We danced with imaginary courtiers and princes admiring us. Mary would take pretty things from our mother's room and would share with me pins and ribbons she had 'borrowed'. We tied the ribbons through our hair; hers a blonde-red shining waterfall and mine a mane, a mass of midnight black. When the sun shone on it, my hair would show hidden colours of reds and even blues… like the wing of a raven.

Our days were filled with lessons and with learning; this, Mary did not take to so easily as I. Although I was younger than her, it was soon clear to our parents and tutors that it was my mind that was the quicker, at least for the lessons they wanted to have us learn. Mary was easily distracted, and her lack of attention to detail angered our tutors. She was often beaten, but it did no good. She would howl and cry, but once the beating was over and the cuts had healed so that she squirmed no more upon her seat, she would return to her daydreams and our tutors would sigh and reach for the stick again. I was beaten too, but less often than Mary. Our tutors believed that a certain amount of pain was required to instil any learning in a child. But I loved to read, and learning was never a chore to me. It came as easily as breathing. I just seemed to remember all I was told.

Books were not all we learned, for there was dancing and music, riding, hunting and dinner graces. We attended Mass daily, either in the church at Hever or in the private chapel in the castle. We learned French, as it was the language of the court and sophisticated society, but we had some tutoring in

Latin and Spanish too. Our father was a formidable master of fluency in many languages, and since we both admired and feared him in equal measure, all of us sought to learn our languages well. We learned to eat with grace, to curtsey with fluid elegance and to converse with temperate, learned tongues. We were told that we must be beacons of loveliness, paragons of beauty and charm; an honour to our house and our name.

There was much to be learnt if we were to be allowed to enter the glittering English Court that our mother spoke of, and enter it we must, to fulfil what we were born to do. We had a great task to undertake; this was made clear to us from the very start of our lives. We must be ornaments to our family in all ways; but yet we must shine out from the hordes of other women brought to the court and be admired as the *most* beautiful, *most* virtuous and *most* courtly. We must be able to attract great and powerful husbands not only through the name of Boleyn, but through our many personal charms and accomplishments. If we succeeded, we would then advance our family's fortunes through our influence and station. When we were married, we would secure the future of our house by producing sons; brave lords of England, the power of the future, the security of our house and lands. We were to be the best of daughters, the best of wives, and the best of mothers... by becoming the best of ourselves that we could be.

These were the lessons we learned from our mother and father; our destiny was clear to us from the beginning.

There were three of us children left to my parents from the many my mother had borne. Our brother, George, was the youngest, born the year after me. He was the only male heir to survive childhood and therefore always the most important child, to our father at least. George would be the one to inherit the estates of the Boleyns and any titles that our father left upon his death, and it would be up to George to lead the family once our father was gone. It was a weighty responsibility for the youngest of the family to carry.

My mother had given birth to two other boys, but these brothers of mine I had never known for they died either when I was very young, or before I was born. No one told me which, and I never thought to ask. I had seen their graves in the churches on our estates; one brother rested at Blickling Hall in Norfolk, the seat of our grandfather until his death, and one brother lay near Hever. Since I was four years old, when my Boleyn grandfather had died, our family had lived at Hever Castle in Kent, and our Boleyn uncle, James, inherited Blickling Hall. My mother had taken us to see our brothers' graves, and that too of another sister, also taken by the Lord. She was sad when she looked on their little graves; sorrowful and beautiful, looking at the last resting place of her dead children.

Once, when we stood at the graves of my dead siblings at Hever, I looked up at her and told her that we were still here with her, George, Mary and I, and we would make her proud of her children who lived. Neither she nor our father would regret the choices God had made, of who amongst us children was to live and who was to die. She smiled at me strangely when I said that, and touched my face with her soft hand, lifting my chin to make our eyes meet in the quiet graveyard.

"You are such an old soul, inside such a young body," she said, smiling at me. "You speak the comfort of a woman grown, rather than the words of a child."

She paused and we listened to the breeze drifting through the yew trees that hugged the edges of the graveyard; there was a faint whistle as the wind blew through their sharp green leaves. Their red berries bounced cheerfully in the little breeze, happy in the knowledge that none should pick them, lest they court Death.

"I am glad that God gave me *all* my children, and that he let me keep some with me in this world," our mother said softly. "I love all my children, even those I never had time to know before they slipped from my breast, into the arms of God. But I doubt not that those still left to me in this life will make me proud."

Then she took my hand and led me silently back to the winding earthen path to the castle of Hever. I thought then, with my tiny hand held in hers that above all things I should like to make my mother proud of me, so that she would not feel sad for her children who were lost to her in this life.

George had a different tutor to Mary and me; as a boy and the heir to the family fortunes he was treated differently to us mere girls. But our education was far superior to those of other girls of our station. That was due to our father, the ever-ambitious Sir Thomas Boleyn. My father was a distant figure to us as children. It was only later, when we were fast becoming adults and were of proper use to him, that we grew to know him well. Whilst we were children he was only concerned that we be prepared well for the life that awaited us. He was often at court, or sent on missions in foreign lands by the King, but in all things he did, he worked to advance the interests of our family and our status at court.

Our father oversaw our education, hiring the very best tutors he could afford, and calling us to him to perform our growing skills whenever he was at home. When we were brought before him, we knew that to perform badly would be very dangerous. We all earned beatings by failing to live up to his high expectations, but fear of him taught us to excel at our lessons.

Our parents worked in different ways; our mother taught through love and our father through fear. Each was as effective as the other, although I believe that the fear of our father was certainly a *quicker* teacher than the love of our mother. Whether fear was a better tutor in the end, only time can ever tell.

Chapter Two

1507
Hever Castle, Kent

As I grew older, I often wondered why it was that Mary and George should look so like my mother and I should look so like my father. Surely, I reasoned, it would have been better for George to look like my father, for in men, dark colouring was fine and bold. In girls, the golden-red hair of my mother and sister was considered most comely and becoming. But I had none of that fortunate colouring. Being a girl, I felt I had lost out on the beauty in the family by taking after my dark haired, wiry father.

Like my father, my hair was black; but though his curled slightly, mine grew long and straight. It was thick and often unruly when I was small. The wind seemed to take hold of it no matter what I did, and twist it into knots which made my eyes water to have combed out at night. There was just the barest hint of red in it, perhaps a gift from my mother, whose red-gold hair had bred so true in George and Mary. Mary often compared my hair, unthinkingly and hurtfully, to a horse's mane, which gave me much upset. I did not want to be the horse-haired girl in the family.

My skin was pale, although not as pale and pretty as Mary's milk-like complexion. I caught the sun easily and my complexion darkened, too, with ease. I had to be careful to wear a veil when I rode in the lands of the Boleyns for I did not want to look like a peasant woman, with browned and ruddy skin.

Although I had my mother's wide, large eye sockets, the eyes that flashed out from beneath my thick black lashes were my father's; black, deep and dark depths that masked the thoughts that raced behind them. I came to rely on my eyes later in life, but when I was a child I disliked them. They were not a beautiful golden-brown like Mary's or the warm hazel-brown of my brother's eyes. No, my eyes had none of such warmth… but when I was excited or angry, my eyes sparkled like our fish ponds in the moonlight.

I had the high cheekbones that we all three had inherited. My face was oval and my lips full and deep pink. My hands were thin and graceful, much like my mother's; my long fingers made me naturally a better musician than my sister. Later, people would say that I had another finger on one of my hands, which proved I was a witch. Strangely, that was one of the slanders about me spoken by the common people which upset me the most. My long, elegant fingers were the loveliest things about me in my eyes; and I only ever had eight fingers and two thumbs.

My limbs were strong and I was to grow to be middling tall for a woman, with a willowy look about me. I was not an un-pretty child to be sure, but I always felt lacking when I stood near Mary, whose beauty shone clear and true. There was always something in my features that seemed to me unfinished, something that you could not quite make out about me. This queerness I knew people felt as they looked me over, and as time went on I realised that glances would return to me and linger long after they had taken in Mary's obvious charms. I was something of an unknown, something made those glances return to me, and keep watching, as though no one was sure what I was; whether I was beautiful or not, whether I was intelligent or not. When I caught my mother watching me in such a way I pouted, feeling that of all people, *she* should not watch me so. She smiled and stroked my face with her gentle hand and wondered aloud if I had been given to her by the faeries.

"For they say the faeries are small and dark like you, Anne," she said.

I did not want to be a faerie, I told her, for they lived in the mounds of the earth and I much preferred our comfortable house and the softness of my down-stuffed bed. My mother then let one side of her mouth curve up and lifted one of her eyebrows.

"Then you show good sense child, and reason far beyond those years of yours!" she smiled at me and leaned in to whisper to me. "I'll wager that Mary would be a faerie as soon as she was offered, eh?"

I smiled too, for Mary was always indeed ready to enter into any new adventure, something that our mother would come to despair of later in life.

"Mary!" our mother called across the gardens. "The faeries have offered you a place at their court; what say you to such an offer?"

Mary came bounding over, her face alive with the idea of living at the Faerie Court. I sniffed at her as she laughed with mother; I did not like attention to leave me for so long.

"Then you are a *fool,* Mary," I snapped with my long black hair swinging by my face and my dark eyes glittering. My temper was easily riled.

"*Anne!*" my mother reproved me and slapped my hand; it was not like a lady to speak so. Mary looked hurt. Like a rose, she bruised easily.

"She is *so,* my lady mother!" I went defiantly on, my wild voice ringing. "For much better than the *Faerie* Court would be the *real* court. The Court of England. The real court with the King would be much better than one made of earth and dirt. Think of how dirty all our dresses and hair would be! We would grow worms in the place of our hair!" And with that, both my mother and Mary laughed and I was forgiven for calling my sister a fool. I had a gift for outrageous behaviour, but could often soothe it with laughter.

My brother George was usually somewhat apart from our games. George was handsome and always bold; he had the look of my mother in his face but it mingled well with the strength of our father's features. George had well-defined cheekbones, a good leg and later a strong athletic figure. He had our father's strength and our mother's warmth. It was a good mixture.

Despite being younger than me, George was my hero when I was a child, and he was my friend ever after that time. He would boldly climb trees and steal birds' eggs. Mary was so upset at the thought of the baby birds being stolen from their mothers that she ran away, but I loved to stroke the shells of those beautiful eggs; some mottled blue and white and some with creamy shells dotted with brown spots. George let me keep one of them in my room, as my very own. He called it 'the spoils of war' and even allowed me for a while to be his second in command. I was supposed to be a man in those games, as women did not command armies, or so George said. But I knew my lessons better than George…

"Isabella of Castille commanded armies, Joan of France led men into battle," I would say with my hands on my hips and my dark eyes snapping, and then George would threaten to expel me from the game if I did not play his way. Although I knew I was right, I had to give in; I did not want to lose the honour of being George's right-hand commander.

We were happy in childhood, Mary, George and me, sometimes visiting our uncle at Blickling in Norfolk, yet spending most of our days at Hever in Kent. We were very close in ages, each having been born almost a year after the other. Later people would say that I was a commoner, an upstart, raised above her natural station in life, but my family was descended from great houses of English nobility. Our mother, Lady Elizabeth Boleyn, was of the direct line of the ancient King Edward I and had been the Lady Elizabeth Howard before she married my father. The Howards were a powerful family; her own father was the present Earl of Surrey and her grandfather had been the Duke of Norfolk.

Our mother's father had been held in the Tower of London following the Battle of Bosworth Field, where he had fought on the side of King Richard III, who had lost. His own father, our great-grandfather, had been killed in the battle. The only reason, our mother told us, that her father had fought on the wrong side was because of the great loyalty the Howard family had to the throne. The Howards had pledged their loyalty to Richard III as King, and so, had fought for him.

After Bosworth was won by King Henry VII, our grandfather was held in the Tower of London for some years until the King had released him, knowing well his worth and loyalty as a soldier of the crown. Now, our grandfather was in high favour once again at court; he was the King's great general, and was sent to suppress rebellions against the crown in the north of England. My mother's brother, Lord Thomas Howard, was even married to the sister of the dead Queen Elizabeth, the Princess Anne of York. We were well favoured and connected at the court of Henry VII.

"People still whisper about the loyalties of the Howards," our mother told us. "But people always seek to destroy those who are raised higher than them, those more favoured than them. You must never forget the greatness of our family," she told us. "And never forget that that greatness comes from the favour of the throne and the talents of those clever enough to use them."

Our father, Sir Thomas Boleyn, was a younger son of a family descended from the Earls of Ormond. As a younger son, he was fortunate enough to marry an heiress of the Howard family, but he was a rising star at a court which valued his natural talents. It was due to my father's cleverness, and eventually mine too, that the Boleyns would rise beyond the gifts that heritage and wits alone had given us, and into the circles of greatness.

Our father was often away from home, at the English Court; he was an intelligent and useful man who made his way through his own brilliance. Later, people would whisper spitefully that Thomas Boleyn only got advancements through the open legs of his daughters, but this was not so. Our father would have been valued for himself even if his daughters had not caught the eye of the King. Our father was a great scholar and a modern man; a follower of the New Learning and of *humanist* thought. The New Learning was a great revival of the works of Greek, Roman and other ancient cultures, and appreciation for classical architecture, design and styles. Scholars were interested in learning Latin and Greek, so that they might revisit the works of ancient philosophers and also learn to read and interpret the original scripts of the Scriptures themselves. Some saw the New Learning as sacrilegious, as the word of God had long been the office of the Church, with her priests alone authorised to transcribe and translate the word of God to the common man. But our father was a keen scholar with a sharp mind and he, like many others, believed that man should be able to read the word of God for himself, and take part in the New Learning.

Our father's interest in humanism and the New Learning was also a likely reason for our excellent education. Humanists believed that members of the elite should be educated to a high standard, to prepare for a life where they would serve the common good of all with their knowledge. Humanists taught that men should learn to master all of their God-given gifts and talents, so that the nobility could take care of the needs of the poor and lowly. They also believed that peace was preferable to war. Whilst many of these goals were, particularly in the case of everlasting peace, seen as lofty and unrealistic, there were many amongst the high and the noble in courts all through Christendom who followed humanist teachings. In our father's case, however, I believe that the excellent education he supplied us with came about as much from a desire to have children who were of great use to him, as from his humanist beliefs. Perhaps the one desire fed the other, or the first interest sparked the second... one never knew with our father.

Thomas Boleyn was not just a man of intellect, but also one of action. He spoke many languages and was a useful ambassador, sent on countless diplomatic missions during his lifetime. Desiderius Erasmus himself, that great philosopher of our times, would compliment and praise my father after meeting him in France. But our father was also an excellent jouster and sportsman; something which would endear him to the lords of the court and would eventually spur on his advancement still further. For much as kings love men with a mind inside their heads, they, like all men, love to be with those whose interests mirror their own.

Thomas Boleyn was an accomplished courtier who knew well how to play the games of politics and power. He was a man to be greatly admired in many ways, but he could also be ruthless, ambitious and dangerous.

George idolised our father when we were young, and we all followed our father's lead more often than not when we were grown. Thomas Boleyn was the head of our house, and we owed loyalty to him. Our father and mother gave us grand ideals to follow from an early age, and we wanted desperately to prove that we were worthy of being their children. George often boasted that he would marry an heiress and become a Duke, a star of the jousting field and a hero of war. Although he was chided for this boldness and arrogance, I think George's boasts were close enough to what our family was expecting of all of us, and especially of George as the heir; advancement and greatness. In our education and our accomplishments our father meant to give us the best start he could; his children were destined to further his dreams and lead our family higher still in society. This is what he polished us for; and we wanted it... we were eager for it.

We would surprise even our ambitious parents in how high we would eventually rise.

In the day, we trained in dancing, music, the classics and languages; I loved to dance and to sing and I had a sweet, clear voice that could make people shiver with enjoyment. I was proud of my voice and sung often. Mary and George had fine voices too, and to hear the three of us sing together was something beautiful. We would learn and sing old songs which our mother taught us, songs of valour and sorrow, of love and of loss. One of my favourites was the song of 'The Three Ravens'. With one of us singing the principal part, and the others singing in a round at the refrain, George, Mary and I could make this song of sorrow and loss into a work of prettiness:

There were three ravens sat on a tree
Down a down, hay down, hay down,
They were as black as they could be
With a down derry, derry, derry, down, down.

The one of them said to his mate,
Where shall we our breakfast take?
Down a down, hay down, hay down,

"Down in yonder greene field,
There lies a knight slain under his shield"
With a down derry, derry, derry, down, down.

"His hounds they lie down at his feet
So well they can their master keep"
Down a down, hay down, hay down,

"His hawks they fly so eagerly
There's no fowl dare him come night"
With a down derry, derry, derry, down, down.

Down there comes a fallow doe
As great with young as she might go

Down a down, hay down, hay down,

She lift'd up his bloody head
And kissed his wounds that were so red
With a down derry, derry, derry, down, down.

She got him up upon her back
And carried him to earthen lake
Down a down, hay down, hay down,

She buried him before the prime
She was dead herself ere even-song time
With a down derry, derry, derry, down, down.

God send every gentleman
Such hawks, such hounds and such a leman
With a down derry, derry, derry, down, down.

We were often called upon to perform for our parents, and any visiting courtiers to the castle of Hever. Our young voices matched each other so well that we sounded quite angelic, even if many of the songs were of death and love and loss.

Mary was not as good at learning her instruments as George and I were. We were clever in ways that she was too flighty for, but all of us deeply loved music. George would write songs and poems and give them to Mary and me to sing; soon he would give them to me to put to music, also, as I started to play with making my own tunes and songs. We were precocious in our musical talents I think; there are many others I have met since who played well enough, and could copy the tunes of others, but yet never experienced the joys of *creating* music for themselves. Since music and singing were accomplishments greatly admired at court, we were much encouraged in our studies and experiments in the musical arts.

We were allowed to play and work in the schoolroom or the long gallery at Hever. Of the two, we liked the long gallery better; it was newly built and made in the modern style. We could dance and sing in there whenever there were no visiting courtiers who might wish to use the passage for walking or talking on days where the rain drove them within the walls of the castle. Hever was close enough to London that our father could ride back to visit with ease and keep an eye on his growing family. Our mother visited court with our father at times, and then there would just be us children and the trusted servants that our family kept at the pretty castle. At those times, we would have the long gallery to ourselves and the walls would echo with the sound of tiny feet as we practised and practised the dances that our dancing master put before us to learn. We got used to the bruises and the blisters from hours of dancing the same steps and our feet hardened through our laborious practise. The sound of the lute and the harpsichord often filled the upper levels of the house. I remember the sound of Mary's happy laughter as she succeeded in completing a complicated dance without fault, and George and I applauded her. We were close, we children, locked away from the world in that little castle amongst the forests of Kent, which shone beautifully in the light of each dying day.

As we grew older I found that it was I, more so than Mary, to whom the adults turned for an opinion or an answer. I was checked often for boldness, and beaten, too, for what my mother called "*sauciness*". I did not mean to be saucy, even though at the time I hardly knew what it meant other than it was something naughty. It was just that I knew so often that I *was* right when I spoke, that I felt that I should speak first. Although my parents had me beaten for such behaviour, they did not discourage me entirely from boldness. I think my father liked my confidence, and saw a certain usefulness in it. My mother, I think, worried more that with such spirit I should never find a husband who would keep me, or that I would get one who would beat the insides from me once married. But my father and others saw that this confidence could be useful and encouraged it.

"After all," he said to our mother when they thought I could not hear, "she is to go overseas if I can manage to arrange it; she will need some spirit if she is to stand out."

Mary, too, saw that the adults were thinking differently of our futures, and perhaps this should have made her jealous. But there was little bitterness in Mary; she seemed not to have room for it in her heart. She would shrug off her troubles, and carry on as she was. But she confided in me in whispers when the tutor had fallen asleep, which happened often in the sultry summers locked in our room... then she would tell me of her thoughts for her own life.

"*I* shall make my own way," she declared daringly, sticking her chin into the air. "They expect I am good for nothing but marriage to a rich man, but I will marry where I choose... *I* will marry for love, be he rich man or poor!"

I would gasp and stare at her in admiration for this audacious and, ridiculous, statement; no one married for love. People married because their families wanted it. They married to advance their own wealth, title, or property. Love was something that grew once a couple were married and children were born; we knew this was the way of things from the start. To marry a man without fortune or title would be impossible for us; our father would cast us out and skin us alive, not necessarily in that order, if we dared go against his wishes so. So, whilst I listened to Mary's daring words with the round-eyed admiration of a younger sister, secretly I knew well enough that there was no such room in our lives for such ideas. Our parents were quite clear that what they expected of us was what would happen to us.

George had his own tutors, but he shared some lessons with Mary and me. Many outdoor activities such as archery, hawking, riding and hunting we did together. We shot at the archery butts in the park at Hever. We rode through the woods surrounding the castle, learning to control our horses and master our own bodies in the chase. We were taught the rudimentary skills of hunting with the hawk and hound in the marshlands at Hever, which was fertile country for the pursuit of wild game to bring to the kitchens. Sometimes our mother would invite others, the children of other noble families, to come and visit with us. It was another part of our training for court; we needed to know how to get along with others, how to charm and how to make friends with ease.

A neighbouring noble family at Hever, the Wyatts, were our most frequent visitors. Thomas and Mary Wyatt were the children of Sir Henry Wyatt, a Privy Councillor and advisor to King Henry VII. Mary Wyatt played with Mary and me and Tom Wyatt spent time with George. Little Tom Wyatt already considered himself a great hunter and commander of armies, just as George did. The two boys trained in the arts of war together, riding at the rings to prepare for the honour of the joust, learning to wrestle and to hunt like valiant young men. I often wished I could be at their side, rather than having to behave myself like a lady should, as I played with Mary and Mary Wyatt with our dolls in the gardens. We would all ride together, always accompanied by our elders or servants, and when I rode in those groups, I was always trying to out-best the boys. Sometimes, when I managed to outstrip them, I would look back on them with a pride-filled face flushed red with happiness and exertion. But often, the boys would surpass me, and when they did so, they hardly bothered to crow their victory over me, making me feel even less interesting than I felt already. I wanted their attention. I wanted to feel as though I were a part of their lives they could not be without. But I was not… not then.

George and Tom liked to boast to us girls that they would be ready to go to war immediately, should the time and the need arise. For it was not so long ago that our country had been torn apart by the houses of York and Lancaster fighting for the throne. Then, when those wars ended, the victor, King Edward

IV, had died suddenly. The throne had been usurped by the evil King Richard, who had murdered his own nephews, Edward V and his brother Richard, the little Duke of York. Our King, Henry VII, had fought Richard at Bosworth, and had won, freeing England from the tyranny of evil.

That was the way our history was taught to us when we were small. As I grew older, I found there were other views on the righteousness of Henry VII's slim claim to the throne, and even a few who believed that Richard had not been so very evil after all. These things were little spoken of unless in whispers, for to talk of anything other than the glory of the King of England was dangerous. Still, there were whispers. There are always more ways than but one, to see the path of history and how men made their way upon it. These were things though that I learned as I grew older, not things I knew then. To the imagination of a child, there is good and there is evil, and there is little in between the two. We were taught in terms of black and white; Richard III had been evil, and Henry VII was good. Good had won over evil, and so all was well in our land of England.

And, should the glorious hero of Bosworth need them, George and Tom boasted they would be ready to fly to his side at a moment's notice. It was a good story, a fine bold brag for little boys to make, but I shuddered when I thought of those days of war which I had never known, of family set against family, torn by their loyalties to the houses of York or Lancaster. I remember thinking how marvellous George and Tom Wyatt were for being so brave, and how sad I should be if anything happened to them.

Tom Wyatt was a handsome little boy. When he came to visit us, he and George were often too busy about their own business to pay attention to the girls in the family. But Tom's glance sometimes lingered on Mary, even though we were so young. Sometimes he would pluck a flower from its stalk and present it to her with a flourish like a court gallant. Mary would blush rosy and beautiful and mutter something in thanks to him with a curtsey. I could see that Tom liked the confusion and stammering that his gifts created in her, but I could not help thinking that Mary looked beautiful, but foolish, when she accepted his flowers.

If *I* were given a rose by Tom Wyatt, then I swore that I should look him back in the eyes, curtsey gracefully, as I had practised so often, and thank him curtly for his present, before sweeping off slowly and elegantly back to the house without looking back.

But Tom Wyatt gave his flowers to Mary, not to me.

I was not the one he saw then. I was not worthy of much notice, being little, young and dark. But I longed for those flowers, as I longed to be the one who was noticed, the one who was seen… the one who was beautiful.

Chapter Three

1509
Hever Castle, Kent

When I was eight years old, the old King, Henry VII, died. He had been ailing, our parents said, for some time... even since the death of his wife Elizabeth in 1503. Now he was gone. George seemed particularly sad, even though he had never met nor seen the King, for Henry VII had been the hero of his childhood games. The victor of the Battle of Bosworth Field, the man who united the torn lands of England... he was gone now from our lives but never from our games. A hero lost to life, after all, remains forever a star emblazoned on the skies of the imagination. He becomes more righteous, more perfect, more holy than he ever could have been in life. In death, our heroes become saints. That was what Henry VII became to George, in the years of his childhood; an image of perfection, the warrior King. With my sharp ears, however, I heard things of the dead King that George would never wish to hear.

Henry VII had been, I heard it whispered, an obscure claimant to the throne, the last tenuous heir of the house of Lancaster. It sounded so romantic: *the last heir of the house of Lancaster*. It fired my imagination thinking of him; his years as the outcast, living as an exile in France for fear of his life, then to return home at the head of a great army and to defeat Richard in battle, proving that God was at his side! How glorious! As a child, I always imagined Henry VII must be like one of the knights of the fabled King Arthur's court. But I also heard the servants whisper that the King had been miserly, suspicious, closed-mouthed and mistrustful. Although his people might have respected him, they had not loved him. I thought often it was a good thing that George had not heard these things of his hero, for they took a little of the shine from the armour of our dead King for me.

George and Tom Wyatt would often play at being knights at the Battle of Bosworth, but neither could agree to fight for Richard, so they would both fight on the side of King Henry VII, slaying imaginary foes as Mary and I looked on in sweeping admiration; we would be their prizes when they won. Tom loved to play Henry VII so that he could claim Mary as his new wife, Elizabeth of York. I was never allowed to be Queen Elizabeth; I had to be another lady of the court, often nameless. I was *always* the lesser prize. I became used to being overlooked, since Mary was the one with the obvious beauties; but I still did not like it.

After the death of Henry VII, his son and heir came to the throne. The new King was proclaimed on the 22nd of April 1509; St George's day. Given all that we would come to hear of the new King, it seemed most fitting to us later that he was proclaimed king on the feast day of this heroic saint and warrior of God. In June, King Henry VIII ascended to the throne. There had been a gap of some months between Henry VII dying, and his son's ascension. The new King had been just a little too young to claim his throne under the terms of his father's will, and so England had been ruled for a few months by the Prince's grandmother, the pious and formidable, Lady Margaret Beaufort, as regent.

Our father rode home from court after Henry VII was laid to rest and he had done his last duties to his former master. During his brief visit, our father informed us that we were all to travel to London to see the coronation procession of the new King. We were so excited at the thought of this that we barely slept. All games from that day, to the day we left for London, were of the coronation and court. Our father was to travel ahead of our family party, as he was to be made a Knight of the Bath at one of the ceremonies of the coronation; a prospect that excited George's imagination in particular. Our family party, led by our mother, and protected by trusted servants, were to follow our father later. We would not see the actual coronation, as only adult nobles were to be there, but we were to watch the eve of the coronation procession as it rode through the streets of London, which was quite enough to have us excited to the tips of our toes. We had never seen London, never seen the great city. We had never thought we would be honoured so by our parents as to be taken close to the glittering world of the court whilst we were still children. We were all determined to excel ourselves in good behaviour, lest we be stripped of this, the most exciting prospect to ever appear in our little lives.

Finally the day came; we were dressed in our newest and finest clothes. My smock and hose were fresh laundered and clean. My gown was a deep and beautiful green with a kirtle of crimson underneath, which could be seen through a slit in the outer skirt which ran up the front of the gown. My sleeves matched the colour of my gown, but had edges of crimson to match my fine kirtle. Mary was in crimson with a kirtle of green and sleeves of scarlet with green edging. We were opposites of each other; the one mirroring the other's style and beauty. The bold green looked well on me, and the bright crimson accentuated Mary's golden colouring. We had worked on much of these items ourselves, with our mother's maids keeping a close eye on our sewing and stitching.

Our hair was not loose around our shoulders as it was on normal days, but gathered behind new, fine gable hoods made especially for this trip to the city. The hood stood near the front of the forehead and from the back of it hung dark-coloured silk which covered all our hair. We looked most adult in our new clothes. Our hoods were decorated in fake, paste-made jewels, but they looked so real that we felt very rich and grand indeed. Paste-made jewels, after all, were not cheap to make or come by. My mother braided our hair under our hoods to keep it under control, and gave us one piece of her own, real jewellery each. For Mary there was a jewelled brooch which decorated the centre of her crimson gown. For me there was an enamelled tablet that was worn around the waist, with a circular pattern of knots held with a gold chain that accentuated the slimness of the waist and the wealth of its owner. I loved that little tablet dearly, and eventually, yielding to great persuasion, my mother allowed me to keep it as my own.

George's doublet was a tawny red and glittered with gems and little seed pearls, all real ones, since he was the heir. His legs were clad in close-fitting black silk hose and his hat was the same colour as the doublet, but finished with some beautiful white feathers that swung out from the ridge of the hat elegantly.

I gaped, open-mouthed, to see him looking so grand, and then I laughed and clapped my hands together when I saw that he, too, was staring in deep admiration at Mary and me in all our finery.

It was very early in the morning when we mounted horse and rode the long miles to the river; we were to use the river to reach London itself. Our servants carried tapers to light the path as we rode; our shadows looked like giants riding monsters into battle.

It was still quite dark even as we reached the river, and started along it to London on our barge; it was quicker to travel into London by river, the roads were not always good and were to be packed with people crowding into the city for the celebrations. There were sometimes bands of robbers, too, who might prey on a party made of women and children, even guarded by servants. So by boat we travelled most of the way.

The early morning light turned grey and silver and blue. The air was still and although birds were singing their morning song, there was yet a great peace in the countryside. I was taken with a feeling that something of great importance was happening this day; the coronation was more than just a king coming to the throne. There was more *expectation* than that in the air that surrounded us. It was as though the whole world were holding its breath at this moment, waiting for Henry VIII to take his crown. As though something was about to occur which would be remembered for all time.

I did not know it then, just how important this day would be to my life in particular, but at that time, dressed in my finest, my dark eyes shining in the dawn's light with excitement and anticipation, I seemed to have some sense of the significance of the day. Although the river was already busy with boats of both rich and poor, we were all quiet on our barge as we moved up the river towards the great city. The White Tower of the Tower of London shone out like a beacon to greet our arrival; I believe that all of us felt that something momentous was in the air that day…

For this new king was young and generous, where his father had been old, and some said, mean, although they would have not dared to say that in his lifetime if they valued their heads. This new king had the blood of both the two royal houses that had split the country for so long with civil war. Henry VIII's veins ran with the blood of both Lancaster and York; he would unite the country just as the two houses had united in his blood. The new King, it was said, was most handsome, resembling his grandfather Edward IV much more than his own father; he was generous of spirit, and learned in the new teachings of humanism. This new king was a scholar, fond of books, poetry and learned talk, but he was also a man of action; he loved to ride and joust and play tennis. He was both athletic and academic. In fact, it seemed from the way that everyone talked of him, that he was all good things and none bad; he was all virtue and his vices were shrugged off amicably as nothing but the healthy faults of a young gallant.

He had lately married a princess of Spain, Katherine of Aragon, who had languished alone and abandoned until he swept through her castle doors and claimed her. She had once been the wife of his elder brother, Arthur. But when Arthur died early in their marriage, she had been left in England, much alone. Her father, King Ferdinand of Aragon, had not wanted to pay for her return to Spain, and had desired his daughter to marry yet into England's royal house. Some even said that Ferdinand had wanted the widowed Henry VII to take his former daughter-in-law to his bed. I know not if the old King ever considered this, but he never took up the offer if it was made. Henry VII had turned shy about marrying his sole remaining heir to the forlorn princess... He had begun to think there might be a greater marriage prize to be had for the hand of his remaining heir. There was another reason too... which people always seemed to have forgotten later on. There were concerns raised of a match between Henry VIII and Katherine due to a passage in the Bible, in the book of Leviticus; a man should not marry his brother's widow, lest the marriage be cursed in the eyes of God and remain childless. Concerns of both canon law and political advantage kept Henry VII from marrying his last-living son to the daughter of Spain. And so, poor Princess Katherine had languished, stuck between two worlds, floating in an earthly purgatory. Her own father had sent no money to maintain her household from Spain, and her once father-in-law, Henry VII had wished to spend no coin on her either. The young Princess had been forced to pawn her own jewels and plate in order to pay her servants, and to buy food. For a long time it seemed as though this poor girl might have faded into obscurity, abandoned and forgotten by her family and her country. But this had all changed when Henry VIII came to the throne and decided he wanted to marry her; now Katherine had her hero, as perhaps we all did. She was brought out of her castle, as the new King swore he would have her as a wife and no other. A dispensation was issued by the Pope to allow the match, on the grounds that Katherine and her first husband, Arthur, had never lain together as man and wife, for Katherine swore she was an untouched virgin. If such was true, then the warnings of Leviticus would not apply to this match between England and Spain. And with such dispensation in place, the two were married to one another.

Riding in to rescue a princess from a life of neglect and distress was something typical, we would come to find, of the character of Henry VIII. He loved the old ways of chivalry and courtly love, and could never resist placing himself into the part of a knight. Pageants and entertainments at court were often created around stories and ideals such as this, and Henry VIII was an avid participant.

To us then, with the stories we were told, Henry VIII was romantic and chivalrous. He was a knight *and* a prince; he was a scholar, a man of God and a warrior; he was the greatest king to ever have been offered to us. People said that his reign would be the coming of a *Golden Age* of England. We were blessed with such a king to rule us.

Mary, George and I were captivated by the image of perfection that we held in our imaginations. We longed to see this great king and offer him our allegiance with all the others flocking to London on this goodly day.

Chapter Four

1509
London

We reached London by the afternoon and were to stay in rented lodgings that our father had provided. There would be great celebrations and the eve of coronation procession would pass right by our rooms. We were to watch the King and Queen passing by us on their way to the Chapel of St Stephen, where they would undertake the customary vigil before their coronations the next day in Westminster Abbey. Mary, George and I were so excited by the prospect of seeing the King and Queen that we found it difficult to compose ourselves and behave in the manner expected of us, but a few cold, harsh glances from our father on our arrival helped us in that respect. There was a long balcony that stuck out into the town from the second story of our rented town house. It was from here we could watch the celebrations and the procession.

How can I describe London on that day to you? It was the day before this young gallant of such promise was to truly become *our* King, in the eyes of God. There was such excitement in the air; it seemed to crackle like thunder in the skies in summer before a storm breaks. I had never seen the city of London before, none of us children had. The great, imposing buildings were so vast and so numerous that I felt I should be swallowed whole by the city, if it were not for the skies still stretching above me. I have seen other cities since that day, but then, I had seen nothing so vast, so unwieldy, so glorious. My eyes were overwhelmed with the sights and sounds of London.

There were so many people about us, and so many smells; many of them awful, many wonderful. There was the scent of horse sweat, stale ale, and earthy mud; the rotten smell of waste, pig's blood and urine, which ran down the streets into the fetid gutters. Those smells mixed with the fresh, mouth-watering scents of herbs, fresh laundered clothing, baking bread, crisp rich wine, spices frying, meats roasting, and pies crisping from the many kitchens, all preparing feasts to celebrate the coronation. Everywhere there were people on their way to somewhere else. Everywhere there was noise and smells and talk. I felt so overpowered that I knew not what to think. All I could do was to stare, my young eyes wide and goggling at every sight and sound. The city was busy with life, and life *owned* that city. Life ran through its veins and filled even its shadows with sparkling wonder. People were busy everywhere; servants running across the crowded streets, people standing, talking and gesticulating on the street corners and everywhere, everywhere there was the loud babble of conversation and of laughter.

London was ready to embrace the season of frivolity that had descended upon it as the young King Henry emerged to take his throne.

George, Mary, and I watched from that balcony and we watched with round eyes all the comings and goings on the streets. There were wonders to behold at every glance. Wine flowed from fountains in the street where there should have been water; some was red as blood, red-rich liquid flowing into waiting wooden cups, and some was white like fine diamonds, shimmering clear in the bright, cool sunlight. There were sweetmeats, fine blocks of hard marmalade and sugared almonds for us to nibble on as we viewed the crowds from our vantage point. We sipped small ale and watered wine as we watched lords in bright clothing and ladies in fines dresses. Litters flanked by running servants ran the course of the muddy streets, lords talked and jested together, their servants always close-by awaiting orders for more wine or food to fill their master's stomachs. Men pissed against walls, women sang in the street, merchants stalls creaked, weighted down with fine cloth, meats or spices, and doxies plied their wares from the shadows at the side of the streets. Merchant's children played with balls and bats, peasants begged for food or coin, young scholars walked side by side in dark clothing, great horses trotted along the damp cobbles with brightly-dressed lords upon their backs and everywhere was noise; honking, snorting, baying, shouting, jesting, talking and laughing... all mingled together like the strangest choir ever heard on earth!

The streets were hung with cloths of red and white and green, the colours of the royal house of Tudor. The houses of the streets of London looked as though each layer had been stacked upon each other with little planning, and every house, no matter how mean, had some form of decoration dangling from its windows or doors. There was cloth of gold and of silver, and even whole tapestries hung from the richest houses in honour of the coronation. The streets were decorated all along the route to Westminster Abbey and up to Westminster Palace where the new King would take up his seat as crowned and anointed sovereign of England on the morrow. We were too young and too unimportant to join the service at the Abbey, but we should see the royal couple today. Our father had already left us to ride to the court; he was to be made a Knight of the Bath this night, a great honour for our family, and for him. The Knights of the Bath was an ancient and prestigious order; the new knights would enter a ceremony of cleansing, then rise from their baths before the new King, who would anoint them in their new titles as they stood naked before him. It was a great honour to be chosen, and a mark of our father's rising position within the court. We watched him leave us to take his place beside the King in the procession with eyes wide with awe. Our father was a grand noble indeed, we thought, on that auspicious day.

The procession of the eve of the coronation started out later than expected, most likely due to organising the huge numbers of people assembling for it. It was a fine, bright, evening and was quite warm, but we children were having some trouble containing our excitement. We stood with bated breath waiting for the first signs that the royal couple were to come. When we first heard the procession coming, we thought that it would be with us in moments, but it was a good hour or two before the first of the grand convoy rode slowly into the streets near us. There were many entertainments, small plays, choirs and masques for the King and Queen to admire along the way to the Chapel, and they stopped to hear and see them all. They knew that their people had gone to great efforts to honour them, and they wanted to reward them with their attention.

George and Mary and I itched with anticipation and excitement, struggling to obey our mother's commands to remain still and be patient.

As the first column of the King's procession approached us, I gasped, and I was not alone. It was as though a *wall* of gold and silver were coming towards us. The great clothes, ornaments and canopies that were worn and held aloft by the King's vast procession were overwhelmingly bright and stunning. For a moment I thought that the sun had fallen from the skies and had landed in the streets of London. Faced with such magnificence, at first, the crowd was silent in wonder, but then there was a great cry, as joy and admiration burst forth from the mouths of those around us in a tumult of deafening cheers. It was as though a mighty dragon had lifted its head and roared. We three children added our voices to the thunderous cries, as did our mother and the servants standing behind us. Our hands lifted above our heads, waving in excitement, our voices deafening even the storm gods of old.

We claimed the King for ourselves in that moment. He was ours, even as we were his.

And there in the middle of this vast retinue of richness, was the one person we wished to see above all others. I shouted in excitement as I spied the golden head of the new King himself. Mary and I grabbled at each other, bouncing up and down in excitement, caught in the thrill of exhilaration. George continued to roar, trying to emulate the knights and lords in the crowds; too much of a man to scream and squeal like his sisters. Our mother put a hand on our shoulders to quiet us, but she was smiling at us, even as she reminded us to act as ladies should.

I could see him now, I could see the King; this great man of whom we had been told; a new king for a new England, where goodness and chivalry would overcome poverty and evil. He had been made a knight when he was but a babe, had been a prince since he came forth of his mother's womb, and now he was eighteen years old, and the King. And what a king he was! It was almost too dazzling to the eyes to look on him!

He wore his crimson velvet robes of Parliament, lined at the collar with ermine over a coat made of dazzling cloth of gold. He was tall and proud, but friendly and affable, for he lifted his hand often to acknowledge the roar of the crowds. His rings of gold and precious gems caught the light of the afternoon sun as he waved. There was a great collar about his neck that shone like red fire, made of great ballas rubies and gold. His beautiful horse, covered in cloth of gold like its master, and walking under a canopy of yet more cloth of gold, moved with him seamlessly, unperturbed by the cries of the hundreds of people around him. The horse was as calm as if it were simply taking a walk in the open country. It trusted its master well. The King and his horse moved as though their minds were one. Henry was, all his life, a great and gifted horseman.

Ahead of the King, marking his path, rode the Duke of Buckingham, wearing both rich clothing and a sour expression that I did not understand at the time; but many did, and noted it. For in Buckingham flowed the blood of royalty too, he was descended from kings who had ruled England before the Tudors. In Henry too, through his mother Elizabeth of York, this blood flowed, but yet some would always say that in Buckingham the blood was purer... and none believed that more than Buckingham himself. An accident of history and of birth had seen this man of royal blood born to the ducal position he held now, rather than that which some said he longed for instead... to be the King himself. And so, that tart expression, which Buckingham seemed unable to hide, perhaps graced his face for the simple reason that he believed he should sit where Henry VIII did now. These were dangerous things to think on... they could be the last thoughts any man dared to consider.

But such thoughts of treason and usurpation were far from most minds that day; we were suffused with the glory of the procession.

The men who were to become Knights of the Bath rode behind the Duke, our father amongst them. Their robes were blue as the skies in summer, with white laces on their shoulders. Our mother told us that they must have these robes taken from them by a lady once they had completed a feat of arms to prove their honour, and at that point, open-mouthed and full of wonder, all three of us children felt our father was not only a knight, but a hero. For to complete a quest, for his own honour and the honour of a lady of the court, made him as one of Arthur's knights in our eyes. But all these other men, even our own father, were truly but distractions; for it was the King we leaned and strained over the balcony to see. Although we could not see him well from where we were, we were told of his handsome face; we were told of his magnificence and his easy, friendly ways with noble and commoner alike. We could see the adoration of the crowds. We could *feel* the pleasure he gave.

Henry VIII, Henry *Octavus* shone like the sun. He warmed the hearts of his people with his presence. He was followed by banners showing the arms of royal saints; St Edward, St Edmund, and St George. At their back came the arms of the royal houses of both England and France. If anyone had required an indication of the intentions of this bold young king, there it was, fluttering in the light breeze at his back as he rode to take his crown. The titles of the King of France had long since, the English believed at least, been theirs by right and this young king rode to his coronation displaying the arms of France as his own. In time we would come to see that this daring young man would indeed seek to reclaim his hereditary titles as King of France, but sadly for Henry, the days of English military glory on the shores of France, were all but gone. We did not know it then, nor did he... but he would never become the lord of war he so desired to be... unlike his father.

Knights and lords, stars of the court and of the jousting fields followed in the wake of the King. He was surrounded by the love of his people. He was *ours*, our King; our future. I had never seen anyone or anything as magnificent as he.

As his procession tailed out of sight, and we stretched and craned our necks to see the last glimpses of his golden head, and golden cavalcade, I felt a sadness so acute that it wrung my young heart quite inside out. This great man was gone, and I longed to see him again. When I could see no more of the King's procession, I sat back on my heels and felt my heart drop within me. Although I longed to continue to cheer him as others did, I felt so sad not to have him within my sights any more that I thought I might never know what it was to be happy again. Such are the emotions of the very young; we bleed so easily, and yet recover with equal speed from our sorrows.

The Queen's procession came after that of the King. After Henry's entry, the Queen's arrival was never going to be as brilliant or thrilling; nothing could be, after all... but it was beautiful too, if more sedate. Besides, we too wished to see this princess who had been saved by our new hero-king from her life of loneliness and misery and made a queen. She was a romantic figure to us all, I think.

Queen Katherine rode in a horse-drawn litter, dressed in purple, cloth-of-gold and rich furs. She was young, pretty and flushed with happiness, her auburn hair loose about her shoulders and a simple circlet of silk, gold and pearls about her head. The crowds adored her. Of course the crowds loved her! They loved her for the same reason we wished to see her. She was the tragic, romantic figure who had languished in relative poverty and obscurity for years. Until, that is, our new handsome King swept in and married her. It was a role that we all found Henry rather enjoyed, playing the hero knight, wanting to be seen to rescue princesses and maids at all turns. The reality would turn out rather differently to these child-like imaginings. But now, our new queen was a pretty young woman, recently married to the most handsome and gifted king in Christendom. She was the Queen of a great land, taken from her neglected palace and raised high.

Katherine was so happy then. She had a world of possibilities before her. And all who ever knew Henry's love, basked in its warmth… while it lasted.

It was as Queen Katherine's procession passed below us that a sudden darkness gathered in the skies above. There was a great cracking sound above us and, as if from nowhere, the heavens opened and a fierce shower of giant raindrops burst down upon the street.

The Queen's retinue was suddenly soaked. Her weighty canopy, dressed in thick threads of gold and silver and decorated with jewels suddenly threatened to smother her as it grew heavy with water, flopping on her and about her like a great sea monster intent on swallowing its prey whole. We were hauled back into the house away from the downpour, under deep protest, as our new pretty queen had to take shelter under a humble draper's stall.

We wondered if it were an omen; such a sudden storm on an otherwise perfect day… a tempest of rain falling on the procession of the new King and Queen. It could be a herald of some doom to come, or so the servants whispered. But the shower passed as quickly as it came and soon the procession continued. The talk of omens turned to the sudden, quick shower of rain as a happy omen; perhaps it meant that any troubles would be ended as swiftly as the rains had, for this lovely young couple. The happiness of the crowds was infectious and no one wanted to see anything wrong with this day. Gaiety was resumed and there were cheers again as the water ceased to fall. The Queen resumed her position under her rather wet canopy and waved, smiling bravely to the crowds once again. She shouted something out to those nearest to her, and my mother smiled and laughed, clapping her hands together in approval. I asked her what the Queen had shouted to her servants. My mother smiled and said that the Queen was wise, for her words, as she laughingly went back to her triumphant procession had been: "In the skies of life, some rain is bound to fall!"

The procession continued and again the crowds roared in support. Katherine was glorious; bright and attentive to the crowds. She waved happily as she passed and even offered a wave up to us, three wide-eyed children leaning precariously over the balcony, waving back to her with all their might.

She did not know then how much sadness those three children were to bring to her life. She did not know that one, the small dark-haired girl, waving to her with lively hands, was to become the author of her destruction.

But these things were of the future; we did not know what was to become of us then.

We were so excited to have glimpsed even this fleeting image of the King that we were to talk of nothing more than that for a long time afterwards. Later that night, we were allowed to honour the new King and Queen, cheering their names and calling blessings on them, as we drank wine at our table within the rented house. From outside, we could hear the joy of the people. Great bonfires burned in the streets of London and lit the skies. All through the streets there was shouting, drinking, the squeals of wanton women, singing and bawdy laughter. For tonight was not only the eve of the coronation, it was Midsummer's Eve, a night when many had been known to undertake a risky adventure in the name of love.

George and Mary and I were awake much later than normal and for a while it seemed almost that we may be allowed to be up all night, as long as we did not alert our mother to that fact. Our father was keeping his knightly vigil near the King in St Stephen's Chapel and our mother was merry and lively with her servants. We feasted and sang and danced in the chambers of that joyous house in London. No one spoke of sending us to our beds, and we did not seek to remind any of the lateness of the hour. But soon enough, the excitement of the day overtook us children with weariness, and the lids of our eyes grew heavy as our mother told us stories by the fireside. I fell asleep in my chair and knocked my fine cup across the floor, which awoke me with a start. George, who had also been secretly half-slumbering, fell from his stool swearing oaths for which he was reprimanded. That was my mother's sign to put us to bed. We clambered in between the fine, cool sheets of linen, with warm woollen blankets over the top and lay back in pallet beds on two layers of mattress, one stuffed with hay and sweet-smelling lady's bedstraw, and then one of soft feather-down on top. In such warm and comfortable beds, even with the excitement of the day still wending through our blood, we began to dream; to dream of this new era, this new time. A great time was here, and we would be able to see it all. We thought ourselves the most fortunate of all the peoples of the earth, to have such a glorious king ascend to the throne of England.

I drifted to sleep that night, listening to the noise of the streets of London as the people celebrated.

This was a good time to be alive, I told myself as sleep took hold of my mind; this was a *great* time to be alive.

The next day the King and Queen walked on foot to Westminster Abbey and were crowned in that great place of God. They had prayed all night for guidance in their roles as leaders of the country, and after long hours of prayer, promises and vows to uphold the Church and protect the people of England, they were anointed and crowned, and then took to the Palace of Westminster. There, they started the courtly celebrations which marked the start of their new reign.

We were too young for such ceremonies; our mother and father went to take their parts at the court celebrations, and we were left in the charge of the servants. But from the window, we could see the bonfires and hear the carousing of the people continuing into the night once again. Mary, George and I danced to music played by our servants, sung together and talked happily of all we had seen. All about us, London was vivacious with joy for her new King. Never again have I seen a city so full of happiness and delight.

Chapter Five

1509
London

We were in London for some weeks after the coronation; our household stayed in the rented rooms from which we had watched the procession. Our father and mother were expected at court daily to attend the joyous new King at his active and already splendid court.

Henry VIII was busy handing out favours to his new officers, and our father was not one to miss any of those. He was eager to attend the King in order that he might become more advanced still; the King was happy and exuberant in his new role, and eager to gain supporters and friends. Our father would not be disappointed; he was rewarded by the King greatly over the coming years and would eventually become a Knight of the Body as well of the Bath, Keeper of the Exchange at Calais, Constable of Norwich Castle, ambassador to the courts of France and Austria and Sheriff of Kent. All of these titles he would gain by his own cleverness and because of the King's love for him. The King loved men who were like himself; jousters, hunters, riders, sportsmen... but he also admired thinkers and poets, wits and lovers of jest. There was a great deal of advantage in being a man who could boast some or all of these qualities within him, as our father could. The King was enamoured of poetry, and snippets of the verse he would write later in life were passed down to us. King Henry's poetry was often filled with the virtues of chivalry and love, and more than one of his verses were written for his Queen. There is one I remember well:

Green groweth the holly; so doth the ivy,
Though winter blasts blow never so high,
Green groweth the holly

As the holly groweth green,
And never cheangeth hue,
So I am, ever hath been
Unto my lady true.

Mary and I were especially enamoured of the new King, for we longed to have such words written for us, as he wrote for his Katherine.

Our mother got on well with Katherine, and there had been talk that she might be offered a place in the household of the Queen. Our mother had served Elizabeth of York, the previous Queen, and so was used to the offices and duties of serving royalty and now it seemed she would serve Queen Katherine too, although perhaps not as one of her permanent ladies, since our mother had a household and children to manage. Our mother was to become a personal servant and friend to the new Queen; our father was favoured by the new King. The Boleyns were rising high, so we children thought.

Our parents would return to us every few days to tell us of the entertainments and banquets, of the pageants and plays performed each night, and of the jousts that took place during the days. Our father rode in the jousts and completed his feat of arms before many other new Knights of the Bath; this only served to increase our great admiration for him. One day, we were allowed to attend one of the tournaments with numerous other nobles.

The joust was a violent but noble sport that George longed to be allowed to ride in. Although he, as a noble man's son, was already training in some arts of war, he had never been allowed to take part in an actual jousting competition. Instead he was allowed to run at 'the rings' as it was called, where young boys practised riding at a target, getting the end of a lance through a ring of cloth and thereby showing proficiency for the sport of jousting, which was, after all, all about hitting a target truly, whilst in motion. Our father was a keen and skilled jouster on the tilting field and he was keen for George to follow his footsteps... but not yet. Even our father, however ambitious he was, was not going to let George, at seven years old, joust properly. It was a dangerous sport, even for adults, and men had died in pursuit of glory in it. That was what made it exciting. Our wily father was not about to risk his only son by placing him in a real contest, even against other boys. George would have to wait to prove that he could be a knight like his father. It rankled with him, but he had little other choice than to obey. In some ways, the experience made George feel as though he had something in common with King Henry, for his father too had forbade him from jousting properly, for fear of his life. Henry VIII disbanded the edicts which his father had set up to stop royalty competing in the lists almost as soon as he had the crown on his head, and after that time, there was little to ever stop our new King mounting horse and charging the lists. Henry was a fierce and talented jouster, and it was truly his boundless enthusiasm for the sport which fired its intense popularity at the Court of England. The King was never happier than when he was in a saddle, lance in hand, charging to clash against the strength of another knight.

The joust we went to see was magnificent and it was clever, for rather than just being a match between the knights of the court, it had a theme. The court, as we learned later, was much like that. An event could not just be an event, it had to be something outstanding.

Mary and I gasped in admiration as we watched the ancient goddess Pallas Athene walk out to present to the crowds her knights of wisdom, matched in a fight against Cupid's knights of love. *Wisdom* was to fight *Love* before our very eyes. Breathless with excitement we watched the teams of knights fight each other, both in the tilt and matched in pairs to fight with the sword. Shaft of lance broke against armour and sword bashed with ringing tones of steel against shield. Men fell on the dirt before us with groans and cries that struck terror, fascination and, excitement into my heart.

George had never been before, and never was again, as quiet as he was that day. He was struck quite dumb with concentration on the glory of the knights. Mary and I, however, chattered and talked with gay abandon. We swore we were in love with each and every knight who came to the field; we avowed our hearts and gave intentions to marry many different men, changing our minds with heartbreaking, excited shallowness. We loved *all* those knights who rode, and all those who fought, and to choose between them at the ages of eight and ten was an impossible task. Our father ignored our prattling, until it grew too loud for him, and then we were silenced with a single dark look.

As we stood watching the joust, from the crowds of nobles and their servants came a dark-haired, dark-clothed man with merry eyes. He walked by and stopped to talk with my father who was observing the jousts with a more critical, experienced eye than his exuberant offspring were presently capable of.

"Sir Thomas Boleyn!" The man greeted my father with some degree of formality, but also an air of friendliness. He bowed, inclining his head in greeting.

"Master Thomas More…" My father greeted him back, turning towards More's happy face and returning a short bow.

"This is a fine day, my Lord, and fine times we have before us," the man said, clapping my father on the shoulders as he spoke. The gesture of affection was a little hard and exuberant, but our father was a solid and sturdy man. More's enthusiasm did not catch him off-guard. My father moved not an inch when he was struck on the back by this strange, dark man. But I sensed that More had perhaps wanted to catch our father off-guard, and wondered why. There was a sense between them that I could feel already, of competition and rivalry.

"It is indeed, Master More," my father replied, limiting his words. Our father was usually quite easy in conversation with the lords and ladies of the court, and yet now he was reticent; another thing to ponder, I thought.

"Now we shall see the people released from their slavery of ignorance and folly, and embraced by the liberty that this king shall bring us!" More's eyes were upon the distant figure of the King. "He shall wipe the tear from every eye, and put joy in the place of our long distress," the exuberant man continued, turning back and smiling at our father. Although many were speaking in enthusiastic terms of the new King, More's face and eyes shone with an ideal that, I fancy, only he could really see.

"Indeed, Master More," my father replied calmly. "This is truly a time for great rejoicing".

My father's voice was measured. He did not allow the contempt that I could feel under the surface of his speech to show in any way that More could discern. My father was a gifted courtier; adept at saying one thing and meaning quite another, but I who knew him well could tell that he found Master Thomas More rather trying. More, however, didn't seem to notice the underlying hostility of our father, and clapping my father on the back again, he walked on through the crowds of nobles, stopping to congratulate those he knew on the happy times before us.

My father allowed his lip to curl into a slight, contemptuous sneer at More's back, before turning back to the lists with a grunt.

"Who was that, my lord father?" I asked gently.

He looked at me for signs that I may have read him rightly, but I kept my little young face blank and open. I could learn these tricks too.

"Master Thomas More," he said without a trace of anything resembling emotion in his voice. "He is a lawyer and a writer. The King likes him."

I gathered from that short sentence that as much as the King liked More, my father did not. I wondered why, but such heavy thoughts passed me quickly that day and my father was not one to reveal much of his private thoughts, unless there was good reason.

The fast ailing and then death of the King's grandmother on the 29th of June brought the celebrations of the coronation to a somewhat abrupt end. Although after the official mourning period was over, the celebrations continued, they were a little more muted than before. The passing of the fierce matriarch of the Tudor line, Lady Margaret Beaufort, seemed to define the end of an era; England seemed to pass into a world of new possibility and opportunity from amongst the last threads of the influence of the civil wars. The King was now freed of the rule of his past; his father was dead, as was his grandmother, and whilst he may have mourned them in part, he was probably also rather keen now to rule without their guiding, and, some said, overbearing, hands. The King was eighteen, and he was now in control of his own realm and power.

We stayed in London for some weeks and then returned to our lives in the school room and nursery. I awaited this golden age, this *great change* that all said would occur with the coming of our new king, but our little lives returned to much the same as they had been before we went to London to see the coronation.

After some initial disappointment, I settled back into my life quite easily; reading, learning, riding the beautiful new horse, that had been presented to me by my father. Mary and I were instructed in how to brew simples and to manage household accounts. We continued our learning of French and Latin; translating texts and great works in the hope that one day we should learn to speak these languages as well as our father. There was dancing and table manners, needlework and dressmaking, learning to make shirts for a future where our work would adorn our husbands and of course, the making of beautiful altar cloths for the church on our lands. The hands of the Boleyn daughters would grace the tables of the Church and the altars on which the blessed Mass would take place. Our mother imbued us with a sense of humility in these tasks; to honour God in our every day work was a great achievement, she told us.

We were busy enough, to be sure, but I wanted more… although at that time, I could not think of what more there was to the world than what I already had.

Chapter Six

1511
Hever Castle, Kent

It was when I was ten years old that a great prince was born to the King and Queen of England. The Queen had suffered two failed pregnancies before this; both bringing forth dead children from her womb that had dashed the hopes of the country and the King one after another. In her first pregnancy, they said that she had lost one child first, but another was believed to still linger, yet alive, within her womb. In time, this second child seemed to die, too, and there were mutterings about the country as to the fertility of the new couple. But almost immediately after this first disappointment, the Queen was found to be with child once more. On New Year's Day of 1511, the Queen gave birth to a healthy, strong boy; a prince... for the King, and for England.

Christened Henry, for his father of course, the Prince was introduced to the world with a deafening salute of guns and cannon at the Tower of London, and the raucous sound of elation throughout the country. The little boy was immediately given the title Duke of Cornwall, and would one day become the Prince of Wales, and then the King of England. Such titles for such a small babe to wear! Our father was called to London to be one of the attendants to the King at this glorious hour. At Hever there was no less celebration, as the household feasted and made of good cheer through the night of New Year's Day and beyond. In the village near the castle grounds, the people danced about bonfires whose smoke plumed into the winter's air, and were sent the leavings of our great tables of feasting, so that they, too, might indulge in celebrating this joyous news.

It was a glorious time, for the succession of the Tudor line was now assured. With a strong prince as heir to the throne, our country was made more secure, we were told, for it was he would carry on the line of kings and lead our country. When such things as the line of kings were in doubt, then troubles came to the country, as they had done before we were born.

Our mother told us again of the horrors of the civil wars again; old men in the stables and mews, too, spun stories of the unrest that had torn the country end to end. They told George of the battles that they had fought in. But now times were good and there would be no more war in our lands; a living prince meant that God was watching over England with loving eyes and we were in His favour. Peace for England, and prosperity for the future was assured. We were all safe, and all because of this tiny baby boy.

Mary and I played at being Queen Katherine; looking softly on to the figure of a wrapped doll playing the part of the Prince. One of us would be the Queen and the other our mother, the Queen's attendant. We would assure each other of the greatness that this son of England would bring forth. His father had brought in a golden age, and now *his* son would continue that goodness.

We were not so much older than the new Prince; I was ten and Mary almost twelve, so at times, we played at becoming the wife of this prince in the future. One of us would be the Prince, discovering the fair maiden of his dreams quite by accident in some leafy glen, or rescuing her from bandits; one of us would be the blushing maid. King Henry VIII, who was perhaps twenty-one at this time, would come to us as a figure of our imaginations and tell us of his happiness that we had caught the love of his son. Queen Katherine would press gifts into our hands, and welcome us as her own daughters. Those little games… I remember them so well. It is strange to think on them now with all that came to pass.

The celebrations lasted through January and into February and our mother was often called to court with our father; in the second week of February, our mother returned briefly from court to regale us with tales of the jousts that had taken place in the Prince's honour that week.

"The court is at Westminster, still near to where the Prince was baptized in the Cathedral," she said as we sat next to the roaring fire in the great hall at Hever which kept off the chill of this bitter winter. Snows had come early and stayed late through this season of wind and ice. The offerings of the tables of Hever Castle to the villages and tenants of our lands had to be increased this year, for it was a hard winter. But within the castle we children were warm and comfortable, our lives never being as hard as those of the lesser orders.

Our mother stared into the fire, cupping her warmed, spiced wine in her hands. Servants were cleaning the tables of the feast that we had just eaten well of: spiced pottage made with leeks; haddock in white pepper and ale sauce; leeks and sops in wine; little lampreys fried in butter and parsley; *sallets* of boiled vegetables and fresh herbs; herb-stuffed trout from our own stock ponds, followed by small pies of thick custard, marchpane knots and spiced honey custard. It was a Friday, and on Fridays, as well as Wednesdays, Saturdays and during Lent, for the grace of God, there was no meat in the house. I was full from the leeks and sops, of which I had eaten a great deal, although always taking care to leave some of the feast within the shared messes on the table, so that it might be shared with the people of the Boleyn lands. To eat all that was set before you when dining alone, or at a feast, was considered not only greedy, but un-Christian, as what was left over at the table of a noble house was always shared between the house servants and the people of your own lands. I had to try very hard not to eat all of the leeks and sops for they were my greatest test; white lengths of slippery, soft leeks cooked in olive oil, pepper and salt, covered with white wine, then poured onto crisp bits of toasted, fine-grained bread. The dish was rich and sweet, earthy and filling; a particular favourite of mine.

With full bellies and the warmth of the fire on our faces, George, Mary and I were happy to listen to our mother's tales of the enchanting court. Her eyes shone warmly in the light of the fire and the crimson of her gown with its beautiful golden embroidery of violet flowers on the sleeves reflected the light of the red fire, making her look as though she was a part of those gentle flames. Her long, elegant fingers, so like mine, gripped the pewter goblet of wine she held, and she sipped as she talked.

"The whole court is *alive* with pleasure; there has never been a happier time. People call to each other in the halls and in the gardens; there is jesting and laughter everywhere." I noted that as she spoke, the servants in the hall were clearing the tables very slowly, anxious, as I was, to hear the latest news of London and court. Our mother must have noted this, but she seemed to understand in her good humour, and did not reprimand them for their slowness. My mother's maid-servants sat near to us sewing, with their eyes on their work, but their minds completely on her words.

"The King is like a boy on New Year's Day who has been given all he could ever wish for! He jests and rides with all his men all day. Your father is much in demand as he is one of the greatest huntsmen of the court, and the King is most bountiful to us in his happiness." She smiled proudly at the thought of her husband, a rising light of the court. "And the Queen is so serene in her happiness, such a good example of a Christian queen. But you can see the happiness and pride that she seeks not to show to us. She is worried, you see… anxious to be a good example to her servants and to the country, not wishing to exalt overly, even in her triumph. But she deserves to be happy. She has lost children, yes, but she has now given His Majesty a living and strong prince. God willing, other children will follow too, but this prince is the most welcome babe that there ever was."

Our mother sipped her wine and leaned in to us. "Two days ago there was a joust where the Queen presided as the

Queen of Hearts," she said. "The King, wanting to surprise her, disguised himself as a foreign knight, the *Sir Loyal Heart*. He came up and asked to ride in the tournament for her honour. The Queen was surprised, but she could hardly deny him. He rode for her in the lists, and won, and then the King swept off his disguise and uncovered his true identity to all in the crowds. There was much laughter then. The King is such a boy at times. Your father rode also, and won every match but one, for he lost only to the King, dressed as *Sir Loyal Heart*."

"Did father know it was the King when he rode against him?" George asked eagerly.

Our mother smiled with a fond, wry smile. "Well, George, of course, we all *knew* it was the King. His Majesty does not fade easily into the background. He is so tall and well-built and handsome... and he has an air about him that even in disguise you know who he is. But it does well at times to pretend... to go along with His Majesty's entertainments and jests. He likes to surprise the court by dressing as a stranger, and then to amaze us all by showing at last, after performing feats of brilliance, that he is the King. For you see, he wishes the court to admire his *own* talents. He wants his people to applaud the man he is, and not just the crown he wears. This is why he disguises himself, so that people may see his true talents first and *then* see the crown."

Our mother shook her head and smiled. "There is so much false flattery given to kings. King Henry knows this well enough, and he would have admiration for his own, real talents, of which he has many. But really, he could not ever hide his grace well enough that we should be deceived entirely." She laughed then... Warm and joyful, her laughter rang softly around the stone walls and tapestries that shone red-gold in the fire's light.

She shook her head at our confused faces. "I laugh only because Her Majesty, Katherine, is so much better than the rest of us in her pretence. She always knows it is the King when he comes to her in disguise, but she never shows it. You can see his eyes searching hers for a glimmer of recognition and yet, somehow, she masks all this from him and pretends he is just another knight welcome to court. She is a good wife to him because she understands him so well. It is a good lesson to us all."

"What happened next at the joust?" George asked anxiously and restlessly; he did not want to hear of the life of married people, even if they were the King and Queen.

"Patience, George," our mother reproved sharply. "Show respect for your elders and be not so impatient or else you will wait another night, in punishment, to hear my story."

"*No!*" Mary and I cried together in horror, and George shut his mouth quickly in the fear of losing the story altogether. My mother laughed again at our combined horror. Her good humour restored, she continued. "So I must give you more detail of the joust then, George?" She smiled as she was rewarded by a furious nodding from the desperately silent George.

"When the King was dressed as *Sir Loyal Heart*, he came to the Queen to ask for her favours; the colours that he would wear and honour her with if he won. The Queen looked around for her husband, but was told by Sir Charles Brandon, the King's great friend, that the King was late to the joust and had requested that she honour another knight in his place. The Queen pretended to be sad that her husband was so far away, and gave her favours to the new knight, *Sir Loyal Heart* instead.

"Then the lists began; knight after knight tore through the dirt of the jousting ring with the power of the horse and the crash of lance against armour. Your uncle, Sir James Boleyn, was thrown clean from his horse by the knight *Sir Loyal Heart* and the crowds were much amazed to see such prowess from an unknown knight, for your uncle is no mean jouster in his own right. There were whispers, from those who had not seen the knight up close and did not know the jest, that this must be some foreign prince in disguise. Charles Brandon, the King's great friend, rode against your father and the crash of their lances made such a deafening noise that I flew to the edge of the Queen's seating area to watch in horror, for I thought that your father might have been thrown... but no! Each knight was still on his horse and laughing with pleasure, for they were so well matched. They rode against each other many times that day and yet neither could unhorse the other. Your father won the match against Brandon in the end though, for the points he scored were higher than Brandon's. Your father honoured our name greatly, for none could unseat him but the mysterious *Sir Loyal Heart*. The other knights know your father is a man to be feared when drawn against in the lists. They dread the coming of his name against theirs. The King loves well those who triumph in the jousts; this week has put your father in better standing than ever before, as the King likes to be surrounded by those who love what he loves. He calls for your father often, to talk of jousting and to go out hunting with him." Our mother smiled with pride and sipped at her wine. We all leant forward more, longing for her to continue speaking her tale, but not daring to say a word, lest she stopped. She continued,

"At the end of the joust, when *Sir Loyal Heart* had distinguished himself above all others, the knight rode to the side of the Queen. She congratulated him on his prowess and mourned aloud that her husband the King was not present to greet such a distinguished, valiant knight. Suddenly, the knight swept off his helmet and there!... there was the laughing face of the King! The company, the Queen included, gasped and bowed as the King roared out his great laugh. His laugh... it only seemed to grow louder as it spread over the jousting lists. It is a good laugh, for all who hear it feel they are included in his humour and friendship. Then those in the stalls around understood the jest, and laughed also. The King has such brilliant blue eyes, and he was so merry, that none could resist that laughter.

He gave Katherine's colours back to her in honour and I heard him whisper quietly to her, "you knew not it was I? Come Kate… was there a slight doubt?"

"But the Queen assured him that she was amazed at the trick, and he believed everything she said. She was so pretty in her happiness there…. My girls, I would wish each of you the joy in marriage that Queen Katherine has. She is blessed amongst all women in her husband, and he has never been happier or prouder of her than now with the birth of their son." Our mother's eyes glowed, perhaps with memories of her own triumph in giving a son to our father, as she thought on the happiness of the Queen, and then she went on with her tale.

"On the second night of the great tournament of Westminster, the King wore a coat of purple satin, adorned with golden badges of H and K; his initial and that of the Queen. Some of the courtiers did not believe that the King's badges were all made of gold, and so the King invited each of those who doubted to pull one from his coat and keep it for his own. Such is the present joy of the King! It brings out such generosity and boyish play in him! As more and more people came to claim a golden badge, the King was quite beset by all the court, who pulled not only the golden badges from his coat, but started to divest the courtiers about him of their jewels too! There was much commotion; the King was stripped down to his very doublet and hose, as were many of his men. Sir Thomas Knyvet was stripped bare of *all* his clothing and had to take refuge by climbing up a pillar in but his undergarments for safety from the hands of the people about him! The King's guards had to come and pull the people back, but the King laughed well and hearty for all that had come to pass merely because of his people's excitement!" Our mother laughed again and lifted her goblet to her mouth. "These days are filled with such glory, my children! I shall never forget them."

She drank deep of her wine as she finished her tale and then, smiling as she looked at our glassy eyes, our mother ushered us to the servants to be put to bed. Before they themselves retired, she and her maids whiled away a few more hours in the company of the fire and told tales of romance and of love to each other.

For many days to follow, there was nothing we would play or talk of but parenthood and princes. George would boast that he was to be placed in the household of the new Prince. He would become his best friend, just as Charles Brandon was the best boon companion of the King now. George would awe us with stories of how he and Prince Henry, Duke of Cornwall, would take back the lands of France that rightfully belonged to England. How the Prince would favour him above all others; how they would go jousting and hunting together. Mary and I listened, eager too for this future. Little did we know that this dream was soon to be crushed under the heel of Fate.

Chapter Seven

1511
Hever and London

It was the morning of the 24th of February, when news was brought by a fast riding servant sent by our parents to Hever; the infant Prince had died on the morning before. He was only two months old.

The hope of the country died as so many babies did; blue and cold in a cradle without any explanation as to why God had called him from us. Mary wept; her soft heart was always ready to mourn for the sorrow of others. George was solemn and disappointed at the death of his future best friend and I felt a hollow form inside my own heart in sorrow. Our happiness, our play, our dreams had been so entangled with this prince. A baby I had never seen... but now that he was gone from us, I felt as though he left a gap in our lives that should never be filled. Everyone had been so happy, and now everyone was so sad.

Our parents were attendants at the funeral of the little Prince. We, too, were taken to Westminster Abbey to stand outside with the families of the nobility of the country and mourn the Prince's passing.

They carried his body from Richmond, where his household had been stationed, by boat to Westminster and from there the peers of the realm lined the roads behind the tiny coffin as they walked the Prince to the Abbey. There he should lie next to the most honoured of his ancestors, the great kings of England. The dead Prince Henry Tudor, Duke of Cornwall, would rest on the left-hand side of the altar, close to the tomb of Edmund Crouchback, the youngest son of Henry III.

Three hundred yards of black satin cloth were draped over the tiny coffin. The whole country seemed to have become silent as we young Boleyns stood in our new clothes of expensive black velvet, watching the very hope of the country die, as the procession wound its way to the final resting place of the little Prince.

Mary, George and I were not taken inside the Abbey; we were but children, after all, and there were many more important than us to line its walls and watch the priests perform their last sacred tasks for Prince Henry. We watched the coffin procession as it passed us in silence. The choir sang sacred songs to the glory of the Prince and to God. The voices of the choir were achingly beautiful. They spread across the silence of the great country; they rang with all the pain and sorrow of that day. And yet there was the beauty of God in their song too, and the knowledge that He had called our Prince out of this world for a reason. That reason was not ours to question. My heart shivered with the sweet voices of the choir. I was lost in the beauty of the hymns and in the sorrow of the solemn day.

We were guarded by the servants of our house. They wore Boleyn livery, but with bands of black cloth on their arms to show respect. They guarded us children in the crowd of nobility, as our mother and father were attending the wants of the King and Queen in this time of their sorrow. Our father had been chosen to help carry the little Prince into the chapel and to his final rest. Even in this dark time, it was important to remember that our father was receiving honours important to the advancement of our family at court.

We could never really put that out of our minds; it was repeated to us too often.

As I stood there in the great crowds, I noticed another small girl, to my left. She was dressed in her finest, attended by servants and standing by a woman whom I took to be her mother. That great lady wore a rich gown of black velvet and satin with an impressively-sized Spanish farthingale. Her hips looked enormous because of the dress. The woman's clothing was just slightly overdone, and looked a little ostentatious for the occasion, even by the standards of the court.

My mother had taught me well in the art of dressmaking and styles of courtly dress for court, so that even at the age of ten, I was becoming quite a critic.

The little girl seemed less interested in the procession than she was in playing with a ribbon that had come loose on her dress. She was younger than I, perhaps the same age as George, or a little younger. She was obviously distracted by her black ribbon, and not paying attention to the funeral procession. Suddenly, the older woman's hand flashed out without word of warning, and struck the girl hard across the cheek. The child looked up at the woman in horror, her lips trembling. But before her pretty almond-shaped green eyes could fill with tears, before a protest could emerge from that full-lipped mouth, her mother gave her such a look as would have chilled the bones of angels. She looked like the devil as she glared down on her daughter.

The small girl gulped back tears, obviously knowing that there was worse to be had if she did not control herself in public. She fixed her glance towards the Prince's coffin as it entered the Abbey. Green eyes full of tears that dared not fall, she looked ahead, her face pale and her visage ghostly. She looked tiny, so small to look so very afraid.

She caught my eye as I watched her, and I tried to give her a smile of support. But she took her shining green eyes from my black ones, jutted out her chin and looked resolutely forward at the procession in solemn dignity. Remembering myself, I too looked back to the funeral of our prince and sought, for the rest of the lengthy and tiring proceedings, not to look at the girl for whom I felt so sorry.

We were all very tired when it came to the end of the ceremony. Our young legs wobbled like thick marmalade with exhaustion and our minds were drained. It was also cold outside the Abbey and the chill of the air had seeped into our bones. As we left, I quietly asked one of our servants the names of the woman and her green-eyed child who had stood near to us. Mistress Maude was our mother's maid and was often at court with her, so she was well-placed to know who was whom at court. Maude looked where I had indicated, at the still steel-faced child and the stony-eyed woman. They had now been joined by a handsome, hawkish-looking man in great robes of black silk; they stood in silence together as the crowds dispersed.

"That's Lord Morely, Sir Henry Parker," Maude said. "And there is his wife Lady Morely and their heir Henry." She spoke of a boy standing with them whom I had not noted.

"What is the little girl's name?" I asked Maude.

She shrugged. "Why would that matter, Mistress Anna? I think there are two daughters in the family called Jane and Margaret, but I know not which of those she is. Come now, we must get you all back to our lodgings before the evening closes in, or I shall answer for it."

Darkness was indeed falling upon us; the freezing cold of the winter lapped at our heels as the coming night brought forth a deep chill. Our noses were red-tipped, our fingers ice-cold, and George sniffed loudly as we walked back to the boat to take us to our hired lodgings, causing Maude to reprove him stiffly, saying that gentlemen wiped their noses clean and did not sniff. Our lodgings were the same rooms we had used on that glorious day of the King's coronation. It now felt like a life-time ago. Such is the nature of sorrow; it steals time from us along with joy.

Mary looked up with a pale and sad face, made red with crying and with the cold, and her brown eyes were flat with unhappiness. My sister was made for happiness; sorrow made her ugly.

The winds whipped the empty branches of the trees and even the waters of the great Thames were grey and dull in the falling light and the grief of the country. I looked again at Lord Morely's daughter, as she and her family walked their way to their boat. Her solemn face was to stay with me perhaps even more than the funeral of the little Prince on that day, although I knew not why. I just felt so sorry for her. My parents and tutors certainly beat us at times, but her mother's slap had seemed cruel, heartless. She had only been looking at a ribbon after all. I wondered then, that the lives of other children might not be the same as my own life. It was a revelation for a small girl.

I wondered, too, if she had mistaken my smile to her, misconstrued my intended support, perhaps, for smugness at her punishment. But there was nothing I could do now to explain. We were worlds apart then, even though one day, much later she would become very close to my family.

You see, there would come a time when the name Lady Jane Parker would mean a great deal to my family. There would come a time also when that name would spell doom for the lives of two of the children standing in our party by the freezing waters of the Thames on that terrible day.

Chapter Eight

1512
Hever Castle, Kent

The country was quiet after the death of the Prince, even after the official mourning period had passed. It seemed as though a stillness had come hand in hand with the sorrow of the Prince's passing and it would not relinquish its hold on the country for a long while hence. The King had assured his councillors and his country that he and the Queen were still young and had much time left for more princes to be born, but there was an air of sorrow still in the country. Mary sighed often as we sat in our lessons, frustrated. She wanted to be merry again. I know that she thought it, as I did, but we had to be good and respect the feelings of others. George, too, grew restless in the sadness of the country about us.

In April of that year, a huge fire broke out at Westminster Palace and destroyed much of the grand halls in which the coronation celebrations and entertainments for the birth of the Prince had occurred. It seemed as though God was putting a final end to those pageants of joy for reasons none could really understand. The King was hardly short of palaces, and used Greenwich, Eltham, Richmond, Windsor and Lambeth as his residences. Rich and comfortable though they were, many of these palaces were too small to accommodate both the King and the court, and some, like Windsor were very ancient and rather out-dated. Whilst he ordered new apartments built in the Tower of London, it seemed the King did not care to stay there often. Perhaps the death of his mother in that palace had marked it with too much sorrow for him, or perhaps it was simply, as he said, still too small, to house all his needs. The court was a large body of people, and moved palaces every few months, since the smell and the waste produced by so many soon became quite unbearable. The court would relocate, allowing the last residence to be cleansed, then on to another and another, and so on, making for a veritable round of movement and cleaning which never ceased. When the court moved, all the furniture, all the bedding, clothing, tables, servants and nobles would move with it. Those who lived at court became very adept at packing... or at least their servants did.

I believe that the Westminster fire became part of the reason why our king came to love architecture and building; finding his other palaces to be either too small or ill-equipped for his needs, he strove to improve them, building on ancient foundations and modernising tired palaces. Later he would start to build not only new sections of palaces, but whole *new* palaces. There was no king before Henry who was so passionate about building perfect palaces, and I doubt there will come any to rival him in the future.

Our lives at Hever went on as though nothing would ever change for us. But I began to suspect that something was about to occur, even if George and Mary were unaware of it; there was something in the looks that our father and mother gave us from time to time that made me think that change was on its way for us. I was not wrong. It was our father who revealed to us the next step in our lives. It was the largest step we should ever make, and it would take Mary and George and I far away from each other and from our parents, for the first times in our lives.

We were leaving home.

I was twelve years old when one day, our father tore our small world asunder by announcing that we had all gained placements in other houses, and would be leaving for our continued education soon. It was usual for children of noble standing to enter other, more noble, households to complete their educations and perfect courtly graces before entering court life as adults. It was usual, and I had been expecting something to happen, but it was still a shock. We would be leaving behind everything familiar, and the security of our family, to enter the world alone.

For George, there was a placement as a page in the household of Edward Stafford, Duke of Buckingham. The Duke had recently become our kinsman through the second marriage of our uncle, Thomas Howard, to the Duke of Buckingham's daughter, Elizabeth. The household of the Duke was most important, for he was the only Duke in England at that time. He held a great many lands and titles, was a member of the Privy Council and he was often at court. The Duke also had royal blood in his veins and in his descent. George would be joining a household of great importance. His new position would place him at court much of the time and allow him to socialise with other young nobles of his age in service to the Duke. He would polish the many skills of courtly graces, dinner service and carving, the classics of literature, sports, and the arts of war and politics. He would also attend Oxford when not at his duties to the Duke, and learn to be a scholar there. George was excited by the prospect. It was a fine one, after all.

For Mary, there was a place with our mother's brother, Thomas Howard, Earl of Surrey, in the household of his new wife Elizabeth. Elizabeth Stafford was only a year or two older than Mary, and our father hoped that this placement would lead, in time, to Mary rising to a position in the household of the King's sister, the Princess Mary Tudor. Elizabeth Stafford was to be one of Mary Tudor's ladies and so *our* Mary would come into contact with the Princess often at court. Mary Tudor loved merry conversation and ladies with sweet voices who loved poetry, dancing and lively activities. Our father thought there was a good chance that our Mary might impress herself on the sister of the King by gaining access to her through a position with one of her ladies-in-waiting. It was a plan typical of my father; always looking three steps ahead to advance the family position and influence. Mary must prove herself useful, modest and lady-like. She was almost fourteen, a goodly age to take on the duties of a maid-of-honour, and train to be a lady-in-waiting. My sister was so excited that she could barely speak. She was to go to court, to the English Court... that place we had heard tales of, had dreamed of, all our lives.

All I wanted to know was my own fate. I listened with excited envy to the positions of George and Mary and barely noticed the drawn, sad face of my mother as her children were taken from her and placed in other houses. I wanted such a grand fate as my sister, and my brother too. Surely, they would not leave me here alone at Hever?

But no... My father had secured a place for me at one of the most glittering courts in Christendom. I was to go the farthest of all of us. I was to travel to another country. I was to go across seas and travel over foreign lands.

My father had been granted a place for one of his daughters at the Court of Burgundy, to enter as a *fille d'honneur* into the household of the Regent of the Low Countries, the Archduchess of Savoy; daughter of the Emperor Maximillian I, Margaret of Austria. Margaret's court in the palace of Mechelen was where I was to learn how to be a lady; I would learn styles and graces, polish my French and my other talents and become a brilliant ornament for my family. I would return to the English Court with time, and be greeted by the King and Queen, our father told me. I would earn a place in the household of Queen Katherine as a lady-in-waiting, eventually, through honing my accomplishments abroad.

I sat stunned, staring with open fascination as my father told me of how he and the Regent Margaret had met and become friends when he was on a diplomatic mission there; how she had offered him a place for one of his daughters in her retinue of eighteen *filles d'honneur* and how I, his youngest daughter, was the one he had chosen to go.

"For in you, there is the most potential for what the Regent Margaret is offering," he said cruelly in front of Mary, whose face fell as he spoke. "George would not learn what he needs to know to be a lord there, even from a woman as gracious and great as Margaret, and Mary will do better in England. Her French is appalling."

Mary blushed in chagrin at this insult. Her eyes searched the floor and her cheeks shone red. Her French was not as bad as our father said, but, being a great linguist, he saw many more faults than others did in her pronunciation and articulation of the French language. I shot Mary a look of support behind our father's back as he turned to talk to George and she smiled warmly at me, her flushes of mortification fading. Mary was not one to linger on disappointments. She later confided to me that the idea of travelling so far away was terrifying to her in any case, and she was happier staying in England and learning how to be a great lady here instead. So perhaps our father had chosen well after all.

I was dumbstruck with excitement, trepidation, happiness and fear. To go so far from all I knew for such a glittering prize was much for my small mind to take in. At last, after many moments of silence, my mother prodded me quietly to remind me to thank my father for the wonderful place he had won for me. I stammered my thanks and his cold face looked momentarily softened. "Let us see what you can do with the opportunity," he said, nodding to me.

A few days before I left, I found my mother standing amongst the roses. They were bare and empty of flowers now in the spring, although small leaves were starting to return to their stems. She was sadly stroking them with her fingertips, never catching her skin on the thorns for she knew each of them so well. She was sad to see us leave her.

"We will return, mother," I said to her, taking her hand, feeling her smooth and delicate fingers thread through mine; we walked together in the gardens in silence for some time, hand in hand.

My mother's hands were lovely; slim and white and elegant. I had hands like hers; when we were apart I would sometimes look down on my own hands and they would remind me of her. I would feel comforted; as though she was now and always would be a part of me.

"I always knew you would all have to leave and I am happy that you have been found such great opportunities by your father," she said and sighed. "But I shall miss you all. Mary and George I will see still quite often, but you…" She trailed off, and I knew she was thinking of the miles of land and sea which would stand between us; it might be many years before she and I stood together like this again.

We were quiet for a time. My heart beat with sadness, and found an echo of that same emotion in hers.

"Learn well, Anne," said my mother quietly. "There are not many who are given such a chance as this. The Regent Margaret is a learned woman who follows both the new humanism and the classical learning. She is a careful woman, a modest, yet cultured, queen, and a good ruler; follow her example and you will do well. You must please her and take in all you can. When you return to us you will be a woman grown and ready for a great marriage. That will be your purpose; a great marriage, a comfortable life, and the advancement of your family through your talents."

She held me at arm's length, and looked into my eyes. "But be careful. There are men and women who would seek to ruin you for no reason other than that you might stand in their way. This is the darker side of all courts, for power is an addictive thing. Be careful of your virtue and your name at all times. You are young, and there may be those who would seek to take advantage of that. Do not allow yourself to be alone with any man, and seek the companionship of only those who are good and moral. The court is a great place, but it can be a dangerous place, too. Trust sparingly and wisely. Use your good sense and curb your tongue; too much of your sauciness and you'll be sent straight back here in disgrace, and your father will marry you off to whomsoever he can get for you. Do not let this happen. Do me proud Anne; come back in glory!"

I nodded gravely, tears in my eyes; I had never wanted anything more than to make my mother proud of me, especially at that moment. I swore to myself that I would succeed at all costs.

Chapter Nine

1512
The Road to Mechelen

I was twelve years old when I left England for the shores of other lands, and I had little idea then that I should be gone for as long as I was. On the crossing, aboard a ship for the first time in my life, the rising of the waves and the salt air of the sea made me think that I might die. I made my peace with God several times over; begging him for the forgiveness of my foolish childhood sins, before realising that it was, in actual fact, a peaceful enough sea I was crossing with few storms that would endanger our lives. But to me it felt horrific, and I was pleased to place my feet once more on the solid earth of the world. My escort was headed by Claude Bouton, Seignior de Courbaron; a Flemish nobleman of the court of the Archduchess Margaret. Bouton had been secured by my father to take me to my new position; he was a trustworthy nobleman of good name and family.

We travelled with guards, servants and a maid to help me personally. I had not realised until that time that the world was so very vast. Claude smiled occasionally at me when he saw my great dark eyes take in the new sights with amazement. I must have seemed amusing to an older man who had long since lost his wonder at the world. Claude did not say a great deal to me; my French, which I had thought so proficient before we left Hever was, as it turned out, crass to an accomplished ear. This worried me a great deal, as I must be able to speak French well. Not only was it the language of the civilised, sophisticated world, but it was the language of the court I was entering. Not being able to speak French well would make me a disaster at court, and bring shame to my family. And I would be rather alone if I had no one to talk to. I imagined all this with abject horror, thinking that perhaps the

Regent Margaret would speak but a few words to me, and be so disgusted by my coarse accent or pronunciation that she would send me straight home. I had terrors of the imagination to haunt me on the road to Burgundy, thinking of my mother's eyes riddled with humiliation and my father's face cold with that distant lack of compassion that always signalled his disappointment.

Sometimes these fears would find their ways into my dreams. I would see myself cast off, unwanted and rejected by all. I dreamt I was locked in a tower, a prisoner held for her failure and disgrace. One morning when the sun was not quite in the sky, I awoke sweating, shuddering and muttering from such a dream, and made up my mind to learn French at every given moment there was; I would not be sent to that tower in disgrace. I would not be cast off. I would not shame my family.

Claude Bouton was resistant, however, to teaching me French... or for that matter, from engaging with me a great deal in any way. He had been enlisted and paid well to take me to Margaret's palace at Mechelen, nothing more. But by troubling him politely, yet persistently, with questions about the landscape and the places we passed, I learned more as we travelled. I pointed at objects and animals which were unfamiliar to me in French, and he repeated the French words to me. I tried hard to listen to his accent and imitate it. He was kind enough to me, although seemed to find me rather trying.

As we passed through one town, I noted there were rough men standing about a set of cages, each holding hawks and falcons. The birds were perched close to each other and as I looked closer at those magnificent creatures, it seemed to me as though they were almost dead. Rigid on their posts they sat, unmoving and unblinking. It was only when I had come much closer that I saw the dark threads that bound their eyelids shut. I gasped in horror to see those birds, blinded, as I thought they had been. Falcons and hawks were beasts for nobles and for royalty, so why had their senses been dulled so? The child I was, I thought it monstrous. I was lost in my thoughts, staring at the birds as a hand alighted on my shoulder, and made me jump, startled. I looked around and up, and there by my side was the rueful face of my protector, Claude, who had obviously worried as I had wandered off slightly from the main party.

"Why are they blinded so, Seignior?" I blurted out before he could reprimand me for wandering away from his guards and servants.

He gave me a puzzled look and then glanced over at the birds and smiled at me with the weary smile of one who is not accustomed to the continual curiosity of children.

"You have never seen such a thing before?" he asked slowly and then shrugged. "But, why would you, of course?" He seemed to be asking this of himself rather than answering me, but I waited patiently for an answer.

Claude looked down at me kindly. "They are not blinded, Mistress Anna, only *seeled*. Their eyes are sewn with one small stitch, so that when they travel they will not panic to see all the people and the things around them. They see nothing and therefore they are calm. Were they to travel without being seeled, then they would panic at every new sight, do damage to themselves or fly away, and lose good coin from the purses of these men who would have to replace them. This is how such birds are moved from their native lands to the homes of nobles, like your father, for use in hunting. They are well treated, fear not for them. The birds sense and see no danger, so they are calm and placid in the hands of their masters."

I shivered. I understood what he meant, and that he meant to reassure me but I liked it not. The birds could see nothing of the vast world around them. They could not see danger should it arise through the sewn lids of their eyes. They were at the mercy of those that bore them from town to town. These birds were capable of such freedom, flying into the winds of the world with their graceful bodies. And yet, here, they were captives in truth, at the mercy of others, unable to sense or see for themselves.

"I would rather see," I said to Claude and he smiled.

"But you, my lady, are a person. Not a flighty bird. God has given you different gifts. This is better for them; they are well cared for, I promise you."

Bouton nodded to the men who guarded the birds, and they smiled at me, bowing their heads and touching their forelocks. I nodded, but still felt sorrow in my heart for the birds with ugly stitches covering their beautiful, noble eyes. I would not like to be treated that way.

As we travelled, I saw poor peasants and townspeople. They were much like the people in our village at Hever, they dressed the same, although to my mind many of them looked a lot hungrier. My family, my mother in particular, was generous with the leavings of our table and the giving of alms to the poor at Mass. Some of the common people I saw on my way to Mechelen were in far more desperate straits that the people who lived in the lands of the Boleyns. But I learned that other masters were less generous to their tenants and farmers than my mother was, and the people suffered for it. I had been given money of my own for the journey and for use at the court of Margaret of Austria, but what I had been given to dispense as alms for the poor, I gave. There was little more that I could do, but on that journey I found within myself the first small threads of what it meant to give Christian charity to others, what my small coins could buy a family to eat. And although I had been told many times that God chose where to place his children in the order of the world, I could not help but think there had to be a duty to care for those who were less fortunate than others. My mother believed this, and so now I came to understand why she insisted so on ensuring the bellies of our people were fed. It seemed that not all lords were as keen to preserve Christian values as my mother was.

We stayed in inns on occasion on that long journey, but more often at abbeys and at the houses of nobles along the way. My father had arranged a great many families for us to stay with along the road to Mechelen. Sending his daughter, even one as young as I, was a good way to start a friendship with other courtiers. I had become an ambassador for the Boleyn family it seemed. I ate with many noble families and made sure I did not disgrace my family with my conversation or table manners. My father was never a man to waste an opportunity to advance the Boleyns. I felt also as though I was being tested somewhat by him. In some ways, I *always* felt as though I was being tested by him. It was his way. But I was learning much. This first trip also prepared me for the constant travelling of the courts at which I later lived. Both the French Court and the English were forever on the move; I learnt to find a home wherever I was, and to converse easily with strangers. These were good things to learn early in life.

And soon, we came to Mechelen…

The Hapsburg Court of Burgundy was, at that time, one of the most cultured and romantic courts in Christendom. We arrived after perhaps a month of travel, for it seemed my father had arranged for me to meet and dine with every noble house from Hever to Mechelen, and so our pace had hardly been ferocious. My eyes and my mouth were struck dumb with awe and wonder when we arrived into the gracious buildings of the court. There was never such a place as grand as this in all the world, I thought. If the saints themselves and all the apostles had arrived to greet me I could not have been more amazed, or more humbled. There were so many people and so many buildings. The main court itself resided in the palace of Mechelen, but there were outside buildings, vast sprawling estates and structures that had other functions that were kept separate from the court.

The kitchens, for example, were one of these. Kitchens were always so noisy and full with the smells of cooking that it is sensible to keep them apart from the living areas; one likes the smell of delicious cooking on the table, but not on one's clothing, after all. There was also of course a risk of fire. So distantly, there were the delicious smells of pottages simmering, meats roasting and sugared, spiced pies baking, but only distantly, to encourage hunger but not advance the lingering bad smells that cooks often have around them.

Mechelen was a beautiful palace; tall elegant towers of white-washed plaster reached up to the blue Hapsburg skies. The Regent Margaret was at that time still building and adding to her beautiful palace, but what later became known as the southern range, and the Palace of Margaret of York, the present regent's grandmother, was where we *filles d'honneur* came to live.

Mechelen had long galleries, some with comfortable window seats open to the fresh outside airs, which lined the upper floors of the palace, providing a beautiful place to walk or converse, and a sheltered place to sit in bad weather. There were gardens, done in knot styles where flowers stood to attention in neat and formalised rows and hedges were clipped into forms of fantastical beasts. Moss-covered seats of stone sat in merry cherry-tree groves filled with blossom, and the soft sound of water, falling over stones and from statues of cupids and ancient gods lingered in the background like music. The sounds of tree leaves brushing against each other in the gentle winds mingled with the sounds of voices raised reciting poetry and singing songs. These gardens were made, structured and constructed as an extension of the glory of the court.

To my eye, though, these gardens, however beautiful, were still nothing to the simple, somewhat wild beauty of my mother's roses. Sometimes, when I walked amongst those gardens with the other maids, I would think of her and my heart would ache for her presence.

The court itself was huge. When I first came to Mechelen I felt as though the court were a whole city unto itself; swarms of richly, brightly dressed noble men and women filled the halls. Ladies-in-waiting in their beautiful gowns and fashionable French hoods, dark silk streaming over their hair, looked like the many flowers of the gardens. Servants ran this way and that in their various liveries, consumed by the tasks of their masters. There was richness all around me. Everyone wanted to show how much coin and lands they had, and what they were able to do with such possessions. People's clothing, as I came to realise, was part of the grand show at court... part of expressing who you were, where you came from, and the power you had to wield. It was fascinating and there was so much to see.

Margaret was regent for her nephew, the young Hapsburg King Charles V, who was around the same age as I, and therefore still too young to rule alone. Margaret was the ruler therefore, and the centre of the entire court about which her people fluttered as butterflies to flowers.

The palace itself was dressed splendidly inside as well as out. There were tapestries of many-coloured thread hanging on the walls and marble on the floors. Rushes and sweet smelling herbs, like lavender, thyme and rosemary lined the floors of the palace, so that when you walked upon them, the herbs were crushed under your shoes and released their fresh scents. Margaret was fastidious about the changing of the floor mats, after some days they could become befouled with the scent of the dogs and mud and people. So she insisted that the rushes were changed frequently, at great cost. The chambers too were hung with tapestry or painted cloth and dark wood panels in the lesser rooms; there were great sculptures in the walkways, and glass windows in many of the rooms. Carpets were a great luxury, kept only on the floors of Margaret's own chambers, but the heady scented-rushes did well on all other floors.

When I arrived, I longed to be a part of such glamour and wonder. It was as though all these richly dressed, elegant people were additional decorations to this beautiful work of art that Margaret had created. Everywhere we walked there were the distant sounds of music. Music was a passion of Margaret's and she encouraged her courtiers to practise this skill. It was a good substitute for some of the activities they could have got up to instead, after all. Music kept the fingers limber and the voice pleasant, the mind occupied and the spirit lifted. One thing I remember the most about the Court of Burgundy was that everywhere I moved, I was followed and haunted by the sweet sounds of the lute and the distant voices combining in harmonies together. It was a world of song and music; a glittering palace of romance and harmony. It was truly a place of magic, especially to the eyes of a young girl who had seen but little of the world.

On that first day, I wandered behind Claude Bouton into the palace with my large eyes bulging from my face. People seemed to teem out of the very walls. Everyone seemed busy and everywhere there was a rush and a flurry of activity. As Claude guided me through the palace, I stared at the people around me, I could not help it. One young man raised his eyebrows at my bad manners, as I stared openly at the furs and shining jewels on his fine coat. I blushed, lowered my eyes and he laughed at my discomfort; turning off down a passage-way with his friend, laughing at the newest naïve addition to the court. I was overcome with shame, thinking that I would have to face him again sometime in the future, but whomsoever he was, I never saw him again. The court was so large and the movement of people through it was so swift, that you might never meet the same person twice if they moved not in your circle. Some people were permanent residents at the Court of Burgundy, courtiers who placed their future on the favours they might win there. Others merely visited, riding in and out for a day or two upon some business. At feasts and on special occasions there were more people than a man could count in a day, and even when the court was somewhat at rest, there still were swarms of people milling the halls and buildings, like a million tiny ants in a nest.

As Claude guided me through the halls, I saw a man swiftly reach out and catch his hand to the underside of a laundry woman's dress. In one quick motion he clapped his hand on her bottom and laughed, leering at her. She blushed and hurried away, somewhat more frightened than flattered by his lewd attentions. He and his friends laughed, slapping one another on the back, as she scuttled away, looking behind her to see if they were following her. They did not. Feeling well-pleased with themselves, the young men went about another task, heading through the corridors still laughing, but I watched, feeling wary. Even though I was young, I understood that there were some men who were not knights in the romantic sense of the words. My mother had warned me to be careful of such people, and careful I would be.

Claude and I had arrived a little late for dining in the great hall, and so our party were instead shown to a small chamber, and sent some rich pottage made with oats, roasted venison with spices; capons in a wine sauce with lashings of hot pepper; pies stuffed with pork and rice and fine, fluffy manchet bread. The pottage was very fine, much richer than some of the more standard fare we had tasted along the way, and I had not eaten manchet bread before, as it was considered expensive and too rich for children. But I was no longer a child, I realised; I was a courtier, or soon to be one. Courtiers ate manchet and other fine foods. I ate that white bread daintily with my pottage, thinking myself very grand indeed. I had a new jewelled eating knife with a pretty pouch that attached to my waist-band and I was proud to use it for it was most handsome. I ate my first meal at Mechelan most fastidiously; taking care to spoon only what I needed from the shared messes, wiping my fingers carefully on my bread and swallowing my food well before taking any drink, so as not to leave stains on the costly pewter tableware we were given.

There were also some small sallats of delicate leaves with the meal, flavoured with oil, salt and sweet-sour apple vinegar, and afterwards, delicious, hot, moist, spiced and sugared pears and slices of marmalade with crisp, sweet wafers to eat.

There was small ale for us to drink and eventually, and to my utmost relief, there was a bed in a shared dormitory of Margaret's *filles d'honneur* for me to climb into.

Although I was so tired that I thought I should never waken again if I slept, I laid awake much of that night in my excitement and happiness. I should have been scared, but instead I was thrilled from my little toes to the ends of my long, dark hair. I never wanted to be anywhere else, or go anywhere else, but this breathtaking, sparkling place.

But eventually, there was another reason why I restlessly shifted in my soft feather-stuffed bed in the dormitory where the other handmaidens of the Regent slept peacefully. Fears started to cloud my mind in the darkness of the night. For tomorrow, I was to meet the great Archduchess, the Regent Margaret, and tomorrow I should find out whether I was to be sent straight home in ignominy as an uncouth, badly spoken disgrace to my family, or allowed to stay and bask in the glory of her beautiful court and palace.

Chapter Ten

1512
Mechelen

The first time I was presented to the Archduchess Margaret of Austria, Regent of the Low Countries, I was so scared that I thought I might piss myself like craven men before a great battle.

Although I had been to the privy many times before entering her presence, I still thought I should disgrace myself in more ways than one when I came to her presence. How I wished then for the beauty of my sister Mary to impress the Regent with! How alone I suddenly seemed to be with no father or mother to tell me how to behave in front of this eminent woman and ruler! I felt like a foolish child, but I steeled myself to feel courage, like a warrior. After all, Isabella of Castille had led men into battle; I was merely facing an audience with a great queen... should it be that Mistress Anna Boleyn had no courage in her? I thought not, and I steeled my heart to feel courage even as I shook in my fine new shoes.

Margaret was in her private chambers when I was presented, her ladies all around her like a flock of gorgeous brightly coloured geese. The Archduchess was seated on a sumptuously embroidered, cushioned chair, and they on the floor, on cushions made of brightly coloured silks. They were all older than I and very grand. Their gowns were beautifully fashioned and elegant. Gems glittered from their sleeves where they had been sewn into the plush fabric; some ladies wore fur trims that likewise glittered with jewels. Their dresses shone in shades of scarlet, blue, pinks and gold made from velvets, satins, wools, and cambric, depending on the rank of the wearer. Their necklines were low, exposing the fronts of their chests and showing the fine lace edges of their chemises, but not so low as to appear scandalous. A fine linen lawn lined their gowns and their cuffs, just visible at the edges of their clothing; gold chains with pomanders hung from some of their waists, giving off heady scents of solid perfumes. Precious stones and pearls glittered from the beautiful hoods that caressed their heads and foreheads. Hoods in the French style were worn at Margaret's court; exposing more of the hair than the gable hood which was so popular in England. Everything here was as the French did, as they were the leaders in style.

French ladies would allow a little hair to show from under their hoods, teasing, sensual, but not scandalous. The hoods themselves were made of silks and velvets, lined with jewels and made stiff inside with bone. There was one lady whose dark hood was lined over the crown of her head in glimmering pearls; that was the most beautiful hood I saw that day and I longed for one just like it. The hoods' linings were made of silk; mostly of black silk, which was the most expensive colour. The black silks streamed over their hair and left them with an elegant sheen of silk richness instead of their actual hair. Although my own hair was covered in a hood, I knew it was not as flattering as their styles were. My hood felt bulky and crass, made in the English gable fashion; it sat far forward on my forehead and seemed to have no subtleties at all. Although, as with Margaret's ladies, silks streamed down over my thick and lovely hair, I felt that mine did not look as pretty as theirs. I intended to acquire such hoods and clothes as theirs as soon as I was able, for I had some money of my own, from my father, and was to take a small allowance from serving at the court under Margaret. I did not want to always seem as provincial and backwards as I felt now. The ladies in Margaret's retinue were all pretty creatures, and well-polished in their clothing and manners; I felt like a sack of wool standing before brilliant peacocks.

Most of them sat around Margaret, working on sewing for an altar cloth and talking gently. One lady was reading aloud from the Book of Psalms in Latin. When I was announced and allowed to enter, the reader looked intently at me but she did not stop in her recital until Margaret held her hand up for silence. I learned that was how Margaret was; she needed nothing more than a slight gesture to bring the whole court to her attention. I swept to the floor in the most elegant courtesy I had ever performed until then, and, as my skirts swept the floor gracefully and I held my position, I felt relieved that I had managed my curtsey without falling flat on my face, as I had feared I would in my dark imaginings of the night before.

"So, you are Mistress Anne Boulain?" Margaret said to me slowly in French. She pronounced my name a little differently to way the English spoke it, and suddenly it sounded all the more exotic and pretty! I was so relieved that I understood the Regent that I just gulped and nodded; but eventually, under her amused but not unkind eye, managed to answer back in French.

"Yes, Your Majesty."

She smiled at me; her face was as kind as it was beautiful. I felt such relief flooding through me that I feared I should faint away in front of her. But I did not. I held my deep curtsey to the floor, speaking sternly to my legs and arms to hold their graceful pose, until she asked me to rise, and I was pleased to see her look over me with satisfaction. I had practised that curtsey all the way here, for months. I had not disgraced myself, nor the name of Boleyn. That thought gave me heart.

Margaret took me in; she looked over my dress, which although was my best, felt homely, drab and unsophisticated next to these scintillating women. Margaret herself was dressed in black velvet with a black hood and white silk lining that flooded her pale and beautiful face with light. Black was the most expensive dye there was, and to construct a whole dress of the finest velvet, dyed black, was to be truly wealthy. Many princes and queens would shine in clothes of gold and silver, but Margaret looked like the centre of the world dressed in simple, but outrageously expensive, black and white.

But she did not let her passion for apparent simplicity overcome the need to look like a queen. For in the folds of the black velvet, diamonds and pearls winked out at me. Everything she wore was beautifully made; some embroidered by herself and her ladies, but most made for her by gifted tailors and seamstresses. A great pearl surrounded by diamonds and smaller pearls hung by a chain at her waist. On this chain she also carried a little inscribed and illustrated prayer book. It was covered in velvet and decorated with silver and purple hearts-ease flowers. She would show me such books later; their beautifully delicate writing, the edges of the books lined with illustrations and engravings. Such books were only available to the very wealthy.

I loved books for their own sakes, for the words or the stories, for the knowledge within, but the little books that Margaret carried on her waist at all times were true works of art. In time, I would come to own and treasure my own miniature books of prayer; less for their physical beauty, and more for their words, from which I drew comfort in difficult days… although it must be said, that when I first acquired such a volume, the admiration was very much the other way around. Such is the nature of young girls; we love to see a little sparkle in the world around us.

Margaret was a beautiful woman; her skin was pale, clear and fine. She smelt of jasmine and sage, heady and voluptuous scents that floated from the heat of her body. Her eyes were large, warm and brown with an element of merriment behind them, and her mouth was full and sensuous. Her bottom lip was fuller than the top giving her an expression that was slightly petulant. It was not entirely an affectation, as she would have everything her own way, but her lips also gave her a deeply sexual look; there was promise in her face. I would come to see how she used that to her advantage, and to learn from it. But there was nothing improper about Margaret. She was known for her intellect, her goodness and her chastity. Perhaps all this goodness and purity, wrapped in a figure and face such as hers, was the perfect allurement, and the reason why so many young men of the court wrote verses to her, all exclaiming their endless devotion and love.

She was eminently desirable and completely unattainable; the very vision of a queen of courtly love.

Her ample figure was wrapped in black also because she was a widow. Official mourning for her last husband should have ended long ago, but perhaps she felt the guise of the widow earned her more respect in her position as regent; there were many who did not believe that women made suitable rulers for countries, or for men. But a woman ruler was always more acceptable when she ruled in the stead of a husband or a relative. She wore her widow colours to remind people of her previous state as a wife, and she wore the power of her regency reminding people that she ruled in the stead of her nephew. In these ways, she commanded the respect of those who would say that a woman had no place ruling over the lands or souls of men. And in her own calm and considered self, she won the respect of her people. She was a just ruler, a fair mistress, and a good woman in her heart.

Margaret looked at me as her hands played idly with the jewelled cover of the book at her waist. Her hands were pale and had the flexible, long-tapered look of those of a musician who practised constantly. Simple rings of gold and jewels shone on her fingers. At her wrist there was a bracelet of gold with small diamonds imbedded along its edge. She was beautiful, sophisticated and intelligent, and I was at once terrified and fascinated by her

She looked me over. "We shall have to call you *La Petite Boulain*," she jested lightly, looking me up and down. Margaret's ladies giggled as I flushed slightly. "How old are you, child?" Margaret asked.

I replied that I was almost thirteen as best as I could in French; feeling somewhat reassured by her gentleness, although still with the sickness of terror in my stomach in case I was sent home upon failing her inspection. I could see the eyes of her ladies upon me and could feel them thinking; she is but a child! They were dismissing me as a rival in the games of courtly love.

When Margaret bade me look up at her, I saw her start slightly at the sight of my great eyes; when I was excited or afraid they glittered. When Mary was angry at me she would tell me that my eyes were the devil's; black and evil. Just as when she told me that my hair was like a mare's mane, those words hurt me. I looked into Margaret's own beautiful eyes and hoped that she, unlike my sister, might see that there was no devil in my eyes; I hoped she would see something good within me.

Margaret reached out, held me softly by the chin and looked deep into my eyes; hers narrowed, and she said with admiration, "such eyes… for such a young maid!" She shook her head slowly, thinking as she looked at me, and I felt my heart tremble. Perhaps she, too, saw evil within them.

"There is something… so *old* inside these eyes," she said, letting go of my chin and sitting back in her chair. She smiled at me. "Such eyes will bring the world to your feet, once you learn to use them… *ma Petite Boulain*."

Margaret nodded approvingly, and smiled at me again. I thanked her, not knowing what else to say. Margaret was looking at me speculatively; she shook herself slightly as though removing herself from a dream, and spoke.

"Your duties as one of my *filles d'honneur* will be light, *ma Petite Boulain*," she said. "But this is only as you are still young enough to be taught in the school-room. Your father and I have agreed that you are to learn the arts of the court and of a lady-in-waiting; but you are not to abandon your studies, and here you will receive the best education I can offer you, the best in Christendom. You will repay me by being modest and clever, by learning all you can quickly and well.

My court is one of gentle behaviour, of Christian behaviour, and I will not have any who are lewd or coarse here."

She looked me over and her stern expression softened. "But I am sure you would not be given to any such bad behaviour naturally, in any case," she said kindly. "I have a high respect for your father and he, being such a lord and gentleman, would not have brought his daughter up to be anything less than virtuous and good. Mind that you remember all I have said… and be well and happy at my court. I shall see you often."

All I could do was nod and try to reassure her in my imperfect French that I would do all I could to repay her kindness, and my father's ambitions for me.

Margaret gestured that I was to leave, and breathless and quivering, I stepped backwards from her presence and back into the outer chamber. Although it was such a relief to be able to breathe again, I suddenly wished that I could spend all my days with her, like those beautiful women, all day and every day. I thought she was the best, greatest and kindest, of all the women I had ever seen.

Chapter Eleven

1513
Mechelen and La Vure

My education at the court of Margaret started immediately, and I loved every moment of it. We spent much of our time in the palace of Mechelen, but Margaret was fond, too, of her residence of La Vure and the islands of Zeeland. But wherever the court was, it centred around the Archduchess Margaret. Margaret hosted dances and pageants and masques where the women of the court would play ancient goddesses or represent virtues or vices in acts and scenes played out for the entertainment of the court. Inevitably, the virtues would be rescued from the vices by young gallants. Margaret's entertainments were the height of sophistication; even the French copied the diversions she thought up for her court. Poetry was read aloud in the warm gardens, where we sat in the shade of bowers to protect our complexions from the sun, and the Bible was read aloud to us in Latin as we sewed gowns or altar cloths on rainy days. I moved in circles of elegance, wit and sophistication. I was taught to dance, sew, hunt and sing by the greatest teachers in the world. It was the most wonderful place I could have imagined, and I was not quite thirteen years old.

And then there was the food. I had thought my father's table to be a wealth of finery, but I knew nothing it seemed of food at all, until I came to Margaret's court. Margaret's tables were full of foods which were a wonder to the eyes as well as the belly… pottages of beef or pork; stewed conyes; dishes of roasted venison or boar hunted by Margaret and her huntsmen from her own parks, beef pastries and chicken *mortis*, which the French called *mousse*; roasted pigeon; peacock in ginger sauce; dressed crab or chickens in golden almond milk. Then followed grand *sallats* made of herbs, with marbled eggs and brightly-coloured preserved flowers coated in sugar. When these creations were brought out and placed before the court, our tables looked like a beautiful garden. On Fridays and Feast days, we dined on fresh fish; carp, river lamprey and trout, which were brought to the court alive in great barrels of water so they could be killed in the kitchens and roasted fresh, stuffed with herbs or swimming in onion sauce. Herring, mullet and turbot were brought salted from the coast, along with sea creatures such as puffin and seal, which the Church also permitted us to eat on Fridays and the days of the saints. Little scallops and hard-shelled molluscs drifted in creamy pepper sauces and oils with lemon and vinegar. Whole roasted fish stared blankly at us from beds of roasted herbs before being carved and served in delicate portions on our plates.

We were sometimes honoured enough to finish a feast with a private banquet of sweets held in Margaret's own chambers, or in small towers built for such a purpose about the gardens. I was not invited to such intimate occasions all the time, but when I was I felt as though I might burst for the honour being offered to me. Within those little towers we would think ourselves most favoured and fortunate as we supped on jellied milks, suckets, and pears poached in fine wine and draped in syrup with ginger. Sometimes great castles, knights or dragons would be made of jellies and brought wobbling to the table to great applause. Margaret was fond of cooked fruit pastries, and I found fruits on my table that I had never seen before, imported from the ends of the earth. Oranges were made into marmalade, cut in thick slices and served on knotted sweet biscuits made of wheat and almonds. More than anything I loved the sweet, fresh taste of the cherries and strawberries grown in the groves around the court and made into delicate pies with crumbling, buttery pastry.

I learnt the tricks of the etiquette of court eating, building on the knowledge I had when I left home; to take the salt delicately from the salt cellar with the edge of my knife and put it in my plate, to drape the napkin over the left shoulder and to take only small, delicate portions from all the numerous dishes on the table, so that I might enjoy all that Margaret's bounty had to offer, but not appear greedy, uncouth or uncharitable for leaving nothing for those of the lower orders to share after a feast. I learned to converse easily about current news, about the foods before me, about hunting and jousting or the latest styles in dance, thought and clothing. I discovered that I had a natural quickness and a sharp wit that was only just starting to emerge. As others enjoyed my little quips and laughed with me, I found the confidence to use that talent more and more. I was learning fast and well and I was surrounded by elegance and opulence. I was overjoyed and proud to be a part of such a wonderful court. Small and insignificant though I was, I was still a drop of this great and spectacular ocean.

In Margaret's court I believe I learned all of the most important lessons of my life; all the lessons I learned after were merely extensions on what I had taken from her court. In her schoolrooms I learned my lessons. At the feasts of the court I learned to open my mouth and converse with ease. In the halls of her palaces I learnt to speak French properly, elegantly and with a true accent which eventually made me sound like a native speaker.

When I first arrived at the court, I wrote to my father in French to let him know I had met the Regent Margaret and to thank him once more for the position he had gained for me. I knew that he wanted for me eventually to gain a place at the Court of England, and so I wrote with that in mind, hoping to please him by being capable of seeing the target he was aiming me for.

"Sir, I understand by your letter that you desire that I shall be a worthy woman when I come to the English Court and you inform me that the Queen will take the trouble to converse with me, which rejoices me to think of talking with a person so wise and worthy. This will make me have greater desire to continue to speak French well and also spell, especially because you have so enjoined it on me, and with my own hand I inform you that I will observe it the best I can. Sir, I beg you to excuse if my letter is badly written, for I assure you that the orthography is from my own understanding alone, while the others were only written by my hand. Semmonet tells me the letter but waits so that I may do it myself, for fear that it shall not be known unless I acquaint you, and I pray you that the light of it may not be allowed to drive away the will which you say you have to help me, for it seems that you are sure you can. If you please, make me a declaration of your word, and concerning me, be certain that there shall be neither thanklessness nor ingratitude which might check or efface me in your affection, which is determined to prosper as much unless it shall please you to order me. And I promise you that my love is based on such strength that it will never grow less. I will make an end to my letter after having commended myself right humbly to your good grace.

Written at La Vure, by,

Your very humble and very obedient daughter,
Anna de Boullan."

I shudder now to think of how awful that letter must have sounded to my father when he read it. It must have grated upon his very spine to see his daughter write in such a halting, clumsy way. But I was improving now, all the time. The *Semmonet* I spoke of in the letter was a tutor who was granted to me and some of the other *filles d'honneur* who were not natives of France, and therefore were lacking in true skill at the language. Despite the evidence of my first letter, which might give weight to ideas to the contrary, I had my father's ear for languages and each time I saw Margaret, or *Madame* as we called her, she would comment that my French was becoming most skilled. Since there was no one who really spoke English at the court, aside from ambassadors who would not have stooped in their dignity to converse with me, I had no choice but to learn fast and learn well. My father could not have chosen a better place for me to learn to be a linguist.

I continued to learn Latin also, for all religious volumes were in Latin at that time and if you could not read it, you could not read the words of God unless transcribed by a priest. There was new interest in learning the languages of Greek and Hebrew at Margaret's court, to better understand the Bible in its original form. Learned men and women of her court read and discussed the subtleties they found by studying the word of God in that way. I was not taught these languages then, as there were few tutors available for these lessons, but I did listen to many of the discussions with great interest. Although I loved learning Latin, questions always nipped my heels which were only encouraged by the atmosphere of knowledge which presided at Margaret's court.

I had never understood, for example, why God should choose to speak to his people only in one language, in Latin, a language that many people did not understand, especially if they were not noble. Early on, when I was still at Hever, I had asked my tutor why it was that God did not speak in a language which we could all understand. God must be able to understand and speak all languages, and if common people did not understand when God spoke in Latin, how were they to know what He wanted of them? My tutor had been rather shocked; he told me that what I spoke was *heresy* and that I needed to be more guarded in my speech. God spoke to the *priests,* and it was they who translated and transcribed what was intended for the common people by God through the teachings of the Bible. Many common people would not be able to understand what God meant, my tutor explained, as they were both badly educated and naturally stupid. They needed to be led by those with better understanding and intelligence. It was for the priests to determine God's will on earth, for the priests to tell this to the people and guide them, and for the Pope to oversee all that was done on earth in God's name. That was the natural order of things, and to question that was to speak *heresy*, to go against the will of God on earth.

Since I was frightened to be called a heretic, as I knew that they burnt at the stake and went to hell, I said no more to him then of my thoughts. He watched my silence with narrowed eyes, and then nodded, looking satisfied that he had answered my questions and perhaps saved me from the fires of hell for my ignorance. I understood then, perhaps for the first time, that it was sometimes dangerous to voice one's opinions aloud. But I could not help but wonder; what if the priests translated wrongly for us? What if the Pope got something wrong? Who was to help us then, if all of the people of the Christian faith were reliant only on the skill of the clergy to transcribe the will and wants of God? Would God punish us all if the priests transcribed his wishes wrongly and we all fell into sin because of it? Would it not be better if all people could understand the word of God in the Bible, for then all people would be responsible only for their own actions and translations of the word of God? These thoughts worried me from time to time as I listened to the Mass. It made me wonder if there was not another way for everyone to understand God for themselves.

But although I worried on these matters, when I listened to the verses read out loud from the Bible in Margaret's chambers, when I sat and knelt at Mass, or when I read my own little Book of Hours and prayed alone, I could not feel afraid of God's will. I knew in my heart that He was just and fair. He had sacrificed His own son to save us from sin, and so He must love us. I hoped He would not punish us for trusting so much in the priests that He had apparently chosen as emissaries of His words.

But the nature of thoughts is that once one comes to your mind, others are bound to follow in its wake. My first fledgling thoughts on the nature of the Church's control over the people of Christianity were already growing feathers and getting ready to fly. Just where those wings of thought would carry me I knew not then, but there were others who had begun to question, as I had, the authority of the Church, and the nature of Christian worship.

I did not speak these thoughts aloud at Margaret's court. There were many there who believed in reform of the Church, of changes to various corrupt practises of priests and the clergy which, I was coming to learn, were many and various. Many did not like the Church's practise of selling pardons and indulgences; little slips of paper allowing forgiveness of a sin or time removed for a soul in purgatory, which could be bought for a goodly amount of coin. There were, too, those houses of religious orders which had to be investigated or closed down for being rife with corruption and sins of the flesh. And now too, with the advent of the new interest in humanism, there were many new scholars seeking to read the Scriptures for themselves, in the ancient languages they were originally written in, and these new studies of the word of God were raising new questions and interpretations themselves. It was an interesting time to be introduced to religious theology, and I listened avidly to the talk of those around me.

But I was yet young, and my opinions were not well-formed in my own mind then. As I did not wish to be branded a heretic and sent home, I was quiet about my doubts, but I also listened carefully to any argument on the subject. I continued to wonder on the idea that perhaps God *had* intended for all people to understand His words; perhaps their remaining in Latin was not God's intention… Perhaps the priests *had* made a mistake, as it seemed, from some of the stories I heard, that they were far from infallible, or incorruptible.

I learnt, of course, to dance at Mechelen. It was one of the most highly valued skills of any lady or court gallant. As I grew, my figure became elegant. I was not made of the same meld as beautiful women like Margaret, with fair hair and full figures; my body was long and slim, my breasts were not large, but they were budding under my clothes. My waist was like a wasp's and my legs were strong, shapely and slim. I was growing to be middling tall for a woman, and my face was pale like marble with strong, high cheekbones and the flashing eyes that I was becoming known for. Clothes hung well on me and I was elegant when I danced. I knew this by the admiring eyes of the dance tutor and the jealous glances of the *filles* I practised with. My feet found the steps of all the dances quite easy to perform; all those hours of hardening my feet in the long gallery at Hever now came into good use.

I glided like the wind through dances that others would stumble through. Half the reason I was good was because I practised more than the others, but the trick was to always *appear* as though your dancing was good through natural talent, rather than hours of arduous practise. But for me, dancing was a pleasure, and I sought it happily, no matter how many blisters it granted me, nor how many times I had to soak my feet in herb-infused waters to draw the ache from them at night.

I could sing well and hold tunes truly. I had known this at Hever, but here at Mechelen I was given such songs to sing! I had not realised that my voice could produce such sweetness until it was so trained and tuned. My voice became an instrument to entertain the court, and Margaret was thrilled with me in this respect. Margaret was a wonderful musician in her own right, and to find that her court's newest acquisition was gifted with a raw but certain talent was a joy to her. She would go over books of songs and music with me and was working on expanding my skills to include proficiency in all the instruments she considered appropriate for a young woman at court. I still remember the joy in my heart to hear her praise, and the determination that sprung forth from that joy to do better and to please her more. I started to collect my own favourite songs and music in a book all of my own, and carried it with me wherever I travelled from that day forth.

Margaret would sometimes request that I read to her in Latin from her books of devotion, or sing to her in the evenings when she held court with her favourites in her private chambers. We would listen to others as they read their poetry and as they sang, and then she would ask for me and the other *filles d'honneur* to perform. Although my heart beat so loudly in my chest with fear at performing before so many people, I would swallow that fear and stand with the others and sing, lifting my voice to follow the lute and the haunting beat of the hide drums. When I closed my eyes, the song would take me away; I was not singing in front of so many people then, I was singing alone, and I lost my fear.

"*La Petite Boulain* has a true and sweet voice, do you not think?" Margaret would ask her courtiers, lounging on the cushions of the chamber as they drank their wine and talked of the matters of the day... and they would smile and nod to their mistress, agreeing with her as they did in all matters. "You sing well for God and for us," Margaret would praise me, often singling me out from the others in my group. This sometimes caused resentment from the other *filles*, and would make me blush, letting a little flattering colour creep through my pale cheeks, but I cannot deny that it pleased me.

Margaret's palace was a haven for music and for musicians. Her court organist, Henri Bredemers, would have died at her feet should she have asked him to; I am sure he thought her an angel sent forth from heaven for her generous patronage of him. I was lucky to be able to learn from him, for he was a genius. He was also a perfectionist who rapped hard on my knuckles and fingers with a thin wooden whip whenever I stumbled on a note. When he caught the edge of my little fingers I would have to use all of my self-control not to swear as I had heard the men do in the stables and the mews, and to put myself to the task of learning my lessons better, so that I did not receive more strikes of the whip.

But aside from the heavy hands of my tutors at times, the Court of Burgundy was a wonder to me. Everywhere I went there was a song in my throat and a tune in my fingertips. But I only sang in public when I was called to by my mistress. Sometimes in her chambers or at court events, Margaret herself would play for us; there was nothing more beautiful. I felt my performances, proud though I was of them, shiver into insignificance next to the beauty that poured out of Margaret's mouth and her skilled fingers. Not a wrong note did she make, not a touch out of place; her voice was delicate and yet strong. Bredemers would stand to one side of the gathering listening to her, his eyes closed and a look on his face as though he stood at the gates of Heaven, listening to the music of the angels.

Chapter Twelve

1513
Mechelen

We *filles d'honneur* at the court of Margaret were most often in the company of our mistress, or watched over sharply by the eyes of *la dame d'honneur,* one of Margaret's ladies-in-waiting given the task of ensuring our lessons were learnt and our behaviour was irreproachable. Also under the governance of Margaret though were her nephew, Charles, later to become Charles V the ruler of the Hapsburg Empire, and his sisters, Eleanor, Isabelle, Catherine and Marie. These young children had been born of the union between Margaret's brother, Phillip the Fair, and his wife Joanna, Princess of Castile, whom some called "The Mad". They had come under Margaret's care when their father died. Their mother, who had shown signs of a malady of the mind long before the death of their father, had seemed to grow ever more unstable after the death of her beloved Phillip, refusing at first to bury his body, and instead keeping his corpse enthroned as though he still had life within him. Margaret was therefore chosen as a more suitable guardian for the heir to the Hapsburg Empire, and the young Charles and his sisters came to Mechelen.

Charles was then perhaps fourteen years old, just a little older than I. He was a spindly youth, with the large Hapsburg chin which jutted out before him as though it wanted to take part in a conversation before his mouth could open. He had a habit of tilting his head, which only served to accentuate his large jaw, but he was a goodly young prince surrounded by a court all his own of young gallants from noble families from throughout the Empire, all wishing for advancement by gaining friendship with the heir. His sisters were all beautiful, perhaps Eleanor, the eldest, in particular. I believe I paid the most note to her because she was a talented musician, and Bredemers was almost as in love with the ability of her swift fingers and keen ear as he was with Margaret herself. The youngest daughters were most often in the care of the nursery, but on occasion we would see them brought out to celebrations.

But if I was not in the company of the most prestigious people of my own age group, I was far from being unsatisfied with my life. As well as the many and varied lessons in dancing, languages, court etiquette and manners, I was learning much in the way of how to make the best of my own appearance… a skill that can be taught, but can only be honed by an honest realisation of one's own natural attributes and advantages. Margaret and her ladies designed clothing for themselves and I learnt to do the same. I had a natural artistic flair that Margaret encouraged, but my clothing was designed by me, *for* me. I was not good at designing clothes which suited everyone; Margaret was talented enough to do this, but I could design for myself and that was all. Bold, bright colours accentuated my pale skin and dark looks and I learnt quickly to find the styles that suited my long and slim frame.

Margaret taught us how to preserve and protect our complexions from the dangers of the sun and the dangers of the body. She taught us to wear elegant plain masks when out hunting or riding. We sat under the shade of welcome trees to avoid the crude brownness and redness that the sun should bring on our faces. She taught us to make infusions of sage to wash our mouths with, and lozenges of mint and lemon balm, which made our breath sweet. We learned to make our teeth white with mixtures of burnt alum, honey and celandine water, and to pick stray foods from our teeth with elegant little tooth picks made of silver. Margaret taught us remedies for rheum of the head and for soreness of the body, much like those cures my mother had taught us at home, and how to tend to the female body when it was sore during monthly bleeds. Some of her women used belladonna drops to make their eyes bright and wide, but my eyes needed no such treatment. Margaret taught me to darken my eye lashes with compounds of kohl, and to pluck my eyebrows gently and carefully so that my eyes, always my best feature, shone. She instructed us to bathe in boiled water infused with rose petals and jasmine so that we smelt clean and sweet; to wash our faces and hands each morning in freezing cold, herb-scented waters, and bathe our complexions with mixtures of camphire, vinegar and celandine water to prevent unsightly redness or pimples. If you looked at Margaret's complexion you would never have doubted her knowledge on the subject of the tending of beauty; we followed her advice then, and I still do now. No matter how cold the day, I have washed my face every morning in the coldest waters I could stand, and my complexion has remained ever as beautiful as hers.

When I washed in those waters, the memory of my mother came to me with the scent of the rose petals; thoughts of her comforted me each and every morning. I remembered my promise to make her proud. I was learning all that I might need to care for myself and for my household when I was older and would marry. And I was also learning how I might attract a husband to me through my own person, rather than through my name, dowry or house alone.

Mechelen was a court that operated through the ideals and games of courtly love. It was copied throughout the civilised world and all courts, the English Court included, tried to live up to its ideals of chivalry and elegance. Perhaps the only court to rival Margaret's was the French Court. When I heard people talk of the French Court, I could not quite believe that it could be greater than Mechelen, but then I was so taken by this court that I could bear no other being held up as it's equal or better. For the first time in my life, I had fallen in love, and it was not with a man; it was with the Court of Margaret of Austria.

All the games of courtly love revolved around Margaret; she was the object of most of the poetry and music written at Mechelen and she was the one who controlled the games so that they remained elegant and did not become unruly. Young men were allowed to perform for the women of the court and to Margaret; they would write songs and poems extolling the virtues and brilliance of their subjects, or they would ride for them in the joust or spar at the sword for them. These poems, songs and feats of arms celebrated the talents of these men and placed these ladies at the centre of this intellectual adoration. And it was *intellectual* adoration, as the women would never give in to the pleas of the poets or the fearsome strength of the warriors. The men would call them *the mistresses of their hearts* and the *loves of their lives*. The women would smile and receive such attentions publicly with pleasure, but always express disbelief in the honesty of the protestations of their admirers, causing the game to continue to higher levels and greater feats.

The poetry and the songs were beautiful, but the game was power. We all knew that if the women truly gave in to these advances and protestations of devotion, then the men would tire of them quickly. And Margaret would not suffer her women to debase themselves in such a way; if a woman was found to be dallying physically with a man then the pair would find themselves quickly married, not always to each other, and often banished from her court. I could not imagine a worse punishment than to be banished from her world, and so the first impression of the *value* of virtue was made on my heart.

Courtly love was a game of power; as long as the women withheld their physical bodies from the men who worshipped them, then they kept the power, if the knights succeeded in seducing them, then they won. Courtly love maintained the romantic atmosphere of the palace and it gave young men a way to advance themselves through their intellect and skill or through war-like talent or sportsmanship. Young men, eager to advance at court, could rise high with generous patronesses amongst higher born women who enjoyed their poetry or their feats in jousting. High-born men, already established as lords and knights, or even princes of neighbouring lands, paid court to women who were not their wives in order to demonstrate their sophistication to the world. The object of the game was actually rarely about true seduction. It happened of course, but most who played it understood that the real object was to advance within the court, by display of natural talents, or by being the object of desire.

Young ladies who had been singled out as objects of devotion became more desirable as matches in marriage, and men could become renowned for their talents and prowess. It was a dance we all performed with each other, and at the centre of the performance was Margaret. She was the highest in the land, and to acquire her patronage through poetry and feats of bravery was the goal of many of the young men sent to her court. The same game was played at other courts about Europe too, but here in Mechelen, unlike other courts we heard of, the game was kept strictly intellectual, rather than physical. Margaret was most stern on that point; her maidens must be beyond reproach, for their behaviour reflected on her.

Margaret was still very young when she first felt the fickle nature of men's promises in her own life, and perhaps that early experience was why she was so stern about the rules of courtly love within her own kingdom. When she was three years old, she had been promised in marriage to the Dauphin of France. In accordance with the treaty that had sealed this match, she had been sent to France to live in the royal nurseries there, and to be brought up as the future Queen of France. Even at the tender age of three she was married to Charles the Dauphin, and called Queen of France, although due to her extreme youth, the match was obviously not consummated. After ten years, and when she was finally of an age to marry him in truth, Charles, now King of France, had broken his promise to marry Margaret. Charles wanted to marry Anne, Duchess of Brittany, for the greater wealth and lands that this heiress would bring to him. Poor Margaret, young, beautiful and rejected, was kept as a prisoner by the French, continuing to live in a court she had once been destined to rule, and now was kept within as a political bargaining tool.

France had long desired to take its neighbour, Brittany, as part of its territories, and with the sudden death of Francois II,

Duke of Brittany, his daughter, Anne, became the sole heiress to that state. At the age of just eleven years old, Anne showed courage beyond her age, and sought to marry Margaret's own father, the widower Emperor Maximilian, as a way to ally herself with another neighbour, and protect her country from the French. Anne and the Emperor were married by proxy to unite their countries, but it was not a match to be consummated either, due to the youthful age of the bride.

Once Charles had broken his promise to Margaret, he waged war against Anne and her country. French troops invaded Brittany, taking the little Anne a prisoner and forcing her to repudiate her unconsummated union with the Emperor and marry Charles instead. It was a great scandal. There was even an investigation by the Pope to determine whether or not Charles had forced himself upon Anne to compel her into marriage. Anne capitulated to the demands of her new husband, seeing no other way to escape, and became his wife. Margaret, still a prisoner at the French Court, begged to be released, saying that she would even flee Paris in her nightgown if it would ensure her liberty from this place of her humiliation and disgrace. Eventually, Margaret was set free, at the age of just fourteen, she rode home to Mechelen.

Although I could not help thinking that Margaret had had a lucky escape from marriage such a brutal animal, I knew that she harboured deep feelings of bitterness towards the French because of this past rejection and shame. She would purse her lips slightly whenever France was spoken of, and her hard policies towards them throughout her later reign spoke of the hurt and humiliation she had felt as a girl of fourteen, riding slowly out of the land that she had grown up in and that she had thought she would eventually rule at the side of the King. Perhaps that was why her court sought to shine so brightly and why she was so proud that other courts sought to emulate hers; every word of praise that her court received was another loss that the French Court could have had, but rejected.

Charles did not last long on his throne; he died soon after becoming King of France. If she had married this man, she would not have been Queen for long. But even so, I burned with anger to hear her sad tale. How could anyone treat the wonderful Margaret so badly? At night, in my dreams, I sought to avenge her wrongs by the sword, but in the day I would say nothing about this sad tale. I would never do anything that would hurt this great lady.

Poor Margaret had seemed doomed in marriage. After being rejected by Charles of France, she had been married to Juan, Prince of Asturias and Infante of Spain, the heir of Ferdinand and Isabella of Spain. It was at this time too that the match between Margaret's brother, Phillip the Fair, and Joanna of Castille was arranged; as the ships came to leave the Spanish Princess with Phillip, so they turned around and took Margaret to Spain. On the voyage there, the storms of the sea were so dangerous that Margaret and her maids wrote their own epitaphs. Margaret's, writ by her own hand, was:

"Cy gist Margot la gentil' Damoiselle,
Qu' ha deux marys et encore est pucelle"

Or

"Here lies the gentle lady Margaret,
Who had two husbands and yet remained a virgin"

She landed at Santander, and Juan rode out to meet her. All who had seen the young couple agreed that they had never seen two people more in love. But it was not to last. After only six months of marriage, Juan fell ill. His illness was kept from Margaret by King Ferdinand, as Margaret was pregnant, and it was thought that this news might endanger her child. But as Juan grew worse, Margaret had to be told. They brought her to his chambers where he entreated her to love and care for their unborn child. Margaret was suffused by grief, crying at his side. When she lifted her head and put her lips to his, she found that they were already cold, and had to be carried from the room, screaming for sorrow at the death of her beloved young husband. She lost her child less than a month later. Now, the heir to the throne of Spain was dead, as was his unborn child.

The strange-minded and slippery Ferdinand sent word to his wife Isabella, telling her that *he* had died rather than their son, believing that to find her husband still alive after such awful news might mitigate the pain she felt in losing her only son. Ferdinand was much given to ideas of this sort. At first, the eldest sister of Juan was made heir to Spain, but when she and her infant son died, so Joanna of Castile and her husband Phillip the Fair, became heirs to the throne of Spain and the Empire of the Hapsburgs.

Margaret stayed for some time in Spain after the death of her child. The people loved her and she was popular at court, even teaching French to the young Princess Katherine of Aragon, for the time when she would be sent to England to marry Prince Arthur, the eldest son of Henry VII. Margaret returned home when she was twenty years old, and spent two years at her father's court in the Low Countries before accepting another union of marriage. Despite offers from Poland, Scotland and even an enquiry from Henry VII of England on behalf of his son Arthur, who was supposed to be engaged to Margaret's sister-in-law, Katherine of Aragon, Margaret chose to marry Philibert II, Duke of Savoy, who was known as "The Handsome". They were married in the same year that I was born. He was tall, strong and exceptionally good-looking. Margaret's grandmother, the English Princess, Margaret of York, accompanied her to Geneva where Margaret's new husband met them and gave Margaret a heart made of diamonds and surmounted by five giant pearls; an ornament she would keep with her for the rest of her life.

But again, God seemed to have reserved only sorrow for sweet Margaret. After three years of marriage, Philibert was one day hunting boar with his men. He arrived at the fountain of Saint Vulbas in a fine mood, and ordered a feast to be served on the floor of the forest. Soon after eating, he fell into a sudden chill and then a fever, with great pains in his side. He was taken to Pont d'Ain, to their castle where Margaret tended him, even giving pearls from her personal jewellery to be ground into dust to make elixirs which the physicians thought might save him, but to no avail. He died one morning in September in 1504, he was but twenty-four years old. The sounds of Margaret's sorrow could be heard echoing throughout the castle from the forest outside.

Margaret was sought as a bride many times after that. She was only about twenty-six when Philibert died, and was still a young and desirable woman, with a fabulous dowry. But she wanted no more matches which would steal her heart or her dignity only to grant her sorrow. When she left France she carried a device of a mountain with a hurricane about its summit, with the motto *"Perflant altissima venti"* meaning *"the winds blow and change"* which spoke of her treatment at the French court. When she lost Juan, her device changed to a tree laden with fruit, struck in half by lightening, and the motto *"Spoliat mors munera nostra"* or *"death takes our gifts"*. When Philibert died, she took on a new motto, which she kept until the end of her life, and was reproduced all over her palaces. It read: *"Fortunate, Infortunate, Forte, Une"* strictly translated, this meant *"Fortune, Unfortunate, Strength, One"* which made little sense, but it was understood that Margaret held the meaning of her obscure motto within herself. Some said that she meant that she was a *plaything* of Fate, or that she was *unfortunate* in Fate, but I believed that she meant it to be a message of the changing nature of the world. That one might be fortunate or unfortunate by turn as Fortune's wheel rotated, but what we needed to face either fate, was the strength within ourselves. That was what I believed the "Forte" and the "Une" meant.

It seemed for a while that Margaret might spend the rest of her days in the lands of Philibert, hiding from the world, but in 1506, Margaret's brother, Phillip, died. He had been King of Spain for just two months, and was only twenty-eight years old. The heir to the Hapsburg Empire and Spain, Charles, was but six years old, and with concerns rising about the sanity of his mother, Joanna, Margaret's father, Maximilian appointed Margaret guardian of her nephew and nieces, and eventually made her regent for the young Charles. Margaret was brought back from Savoy and took on her new role as the guardian and guide of her young wards. She had missed out on being a queen twice, and had never held a child of her own, but now she had a nursery full of children. She took to her new role with a renewed happiness in a life which had dealt her so much sorrow. Margaret was twenty-seven when she became the governess of Austria, and from that time she refused any further offers for her hand, even from the most persistent candidate, Henry VII. When his wife died, Henry VII apparently tried for many years to get the beautiful Margaret to marry him, but she always refused, accepting instead a match between Mary Tudor, daughter of Henry VII and her nephew Charles, an engagement which greatly terrified their French neighbours, perhaps to the satisfaction of Margaret.

And so she continued within her palace at Mechelen; this young widow of such sorrow and loss who had faced all that life had given her and taken away, and yet still remained a gracious and sweet lady. You might think that after so much loss in her young life, that Margaret would not be a bitter woman, marked and bowed by the ravages of grief. But she was not. All her sorrows had delivered her but to another position in life, she said, and they had brought her to become the guardian of her nephew and nieces, whom she loved above all things. She could not be a mother to children of her own, but she became a mother to her brother's children, and to the countless hundreds of young women who passed through her service as *filles d'honneur*, as I did.

I admired her greatly. I don't think I can tell you the effect that hearing her story had on my young heart. I thought of all that she had faced and I thought of her present kindness and sweet disposition. I wondered if I could ever be as great as she; for to face such trials in life and to yet retain hope and courage… that is a true test of the mettle of a soul.

It was her first experience of the frailty of men's promises in France, which, I believed had cemented her ideals of the rules in the games of courtly love. All her painful experiences had contributed to her wisdom, but Charles had been the only one to discard her and that, she could never entirely forgive. She maintained a great deal of hostility to the French, even though Charles himself had long since died, and she made sure her court glittered all the more brilliantly to out-do the French Court.

Margaret, then, had real experience that men's promises could be as empty as Charles' had been, and she made sure her maids were aware of it too. Sometimes courtly love, of course, could lead to real love, but this was rare. The world of the court was not a place where true love and true feeling were easy to find. All was for show and for advancement. Margaret had advice for her maidens that she wrote in verse and made us all learn by heart:

Trust in those who offer you service,
And in the end, my maidens,
You will find yourselves in the ranks of those
Who have been deceived.
They, for their sweet speeches, choose
Words softer than the softest of virgins;
Trust in them?
In their hearts they nurture
Much cunning in order to deceive,
And once they have their way thus,
Everything is forgotten.
Trust in them?

Margaret also instructed her maidens in the method by which to play this game and to win at it. For the lady, victory in the game of courtly love was to be admired without ever being captured, and perhaps win a greater husband than her birth may have allowed, by being honoured by the gallants of the court. But a maid had to be careful, for to encourage some men too much was to entice danger to come near. Margaret taught us that there was protection against the advances of men in a maid having a ready tongue and a ready wit to defend herself with:

Fine words are the coin to pay back
Those presumptuous minions
Who ape the lover
By fine looks and such like.
Not for a moment but instantly
Give to them their pay-
Fine words!

So we, the ladies of the court, were taught to rebuff the advances of these gallants with our wit. They would protest their love, and we would protest their lies. They would sing our praises, and we would shake our heads and smile in mock-disbelief. We knew that most of their protestations of devotion were false, and they knew we would not surrender ourselves to them. And so the game was played. Although I was young, I too had my share of admirers amongst the young men. Under Margaret's tutelage my tongue became well-trained. I learned well and quickly that the successful maid at court was adept at both encouraging *and* rebuffing suitors without injuring them. Some women were too cruel in their wit and the men would become angry and remove their praise. Some were too soft and the men would think they were easily won, losing interest in them swiftly. One thing I learnt quickly was that the more *unattainable* a woman was, the more desirable she would become. That was Margaret's secret. She was beautiful and accomplished, but what made her more desirable was the simple fact that she was the Regent and could not be touched. Men fell for Margaret and they would never recover their footing. She was the Queen of the court, and the ruler of their hearts.

I burned to be so admired.

I was so busy at court that I did not think often of home, or of my mother, although I wrote to them as often as I could. I was learning so much and yet there was so much yet to learn. I had little time to wonder what George and Mary were learning, or if my father was doing well in the English Court. As a dutiful daughter, I should have thought more about them, but the truth was that I was so caught up in the wonder of the new world I was discovering that I could not spare them room in my head.

We maids were taught to shoot with a bow and to handle and train hawks. We were taught using little merlins in how to train and fly a bird in the hunt. Merlins were not big and not much use for hunting, but they were good enough for us to train with. I had a great fondness for birds of prey and found that I could train and look after my own hawks as well as any falconer in Margaret's mews. The Master Falconer, Paulo of Castile, thought I had a natural flair for understanding those magnificent birds. Once I had trained with the tiny merlins, he allowed me also to fly the falcons and sakers that Margaret kept in her mews. The falcons were my favourites; such beautiful silvers and browns on their feathers and they were such clever birds. But the sakers, too, were interesting, for in them there seemed to be such an impulse for freedom that I could not help but admire them.

"The saker is a pest of a bird," Paulo said ruefully to me as he held a beautiful female on his leather gauntlet. "For if she sees the sun in the sky then off to it she will fly, and once she is gone… poof!" He made a gesture with his free hand. "Then she is gone, and will never return to your hand again. With a saker you must always know that she is bound to the sun and he, he is her only master, the only one she will truly follow and obey." He shook his head. "We have lost more good coin on the loyalty of sakers to the sun than on any other bird in this mew."

I gazed in wonder at the bird on his glove. Although I understood why Paulo was pained by a bird for whom the risks of losing her was even greater than normal, I felt a great respect for a bird who obeyed the master of her own choosing. The saker was no slave. She had no master but the sun. She was wondrously free in a world where all men had many earthly masters. All common men were ruled by nobles, all nobles were ruled by dukes and earls. Even kings were the servants of the Pope. But the saker was not ruled by any man. She chose her master herself, and was ruled only by the sun in the skies.

There were also sparrow hawks in the mews, used to hunt smaller birds and gyrfalcons and lanners; huge birds that brought down herons and cranes. They could carry whole hares and rabbits in their sharp beaks. These beautiful hunters of the skies stared out from the mews with a lust for the freedom of the air; I understood them well.

Hunting birds with hawks was a sociable affair at court and one that ladies were often involved with, especially when we moved to Margaret's residence at La Vure, or hunted in the forests of Scheplaken, Groenendael or Boisfort. We would rise early and dress quickly. The sun would not yet be up as we quietly mounted our horses in the strange silver-blue light of the dawn, our birds and our sacks brought out by the huntsmen set to accompany us into the forests. Through the royal parks the company would move with our spaniels lolloping along by the sides of the horses, the feet of the falconers and valets pounding on the wet grasses. Drums sounded as we set out; the feet and the hooves and the drums beat out the rhythm of our excited hearts in the grey-blue light.

In the vast forests of Margaret's lands we would wait for the sighting of the game by the huntsmen, whilst breaking our fast on bread, cold roasted meats, cheese and small ale. Then the signals would come and we would send up our birds; the most important noble of the party would try first and then by turn, the rest of us flew those great birds against the game of

Margaret's parks. The birds would find and hover over targets hiding in the bushes and marshes, or catch little birds from the skies as the beaters moved though the undergrowth with drums and whistles to flush out partridges and heron. The dogs would pounce upon the fat birds taken from the skies by the swift feathers and sharp talons of the hawks that flew under our command. Each dog brought a prize back to a rider and each new, fat dead bird was tucked with laughter back into our saddle-sacks to take home to the court. We were not quiet or silent hunters on these trips, for making noise only encouraged the wild birds to flee before us into the talons and claws of our waiting hawks and eager dogs. The spaniels were not much use for the stag hunt or the boar hunt, but they enjoyed this social hunt; bouncing and slobbering on us as we left the morning behind in the pursuit of our quarry.

When we returned to the court, we would eat the birds we had caught: herons roasted whole with their beaks pressed into their breasts; pheasants cooked in a glaze of sugar and mustard; vast crusty pies made from the delicate flesh of many little birds that were too small to roast, where sparrows and thrushes would wallow in wine and spices making thick rich gravy. Woodcocks stewed in ginger and pepper and mallards in onion and mace. We would rest and eat happily, knowing that our efforts had brought these delicious delicacies to the table of our mistress. Our hunts would fill the kitchens with good food for the table of the court. We provided food for the hundreds of courtiers and servants who lived there, and for all the servants who came with them. The leavings of the tables would be given to the poor who came begging at the gates of Mechelen, or La Vure, and to those tenants who lived on the land about the court. Our excursions into the forest fed many bellies.

I loved the hunting birds housed in Margaret's mews, and whenever I was allowed, I would take them to the fields and practise with them. Although it was not unusual for a woman to hunt so much with the bird, I was becoming as good as a man at it.

At the bow, too, I was skilled. I could shoot as straight and true as any, and my eyesight was sharp and keen. Soon, Margaret said, I should be able to accompany her and her huntsmen on a bow and stable hunt for hinds. The season was due to start on the feast of the Holy Cross in the autumn, and I wished to be ready for it.

Chapter Thirteen

1513
La Vure

To be allowed to hunt with the full court was almost too exciting for me. I felt as though I had been accepted as an adult, as a courtier, and this pleased me. The court was at La Vure, Margaret's summer residence which was also a goodly place for hunting excursions.

The night before the hunt, the huntsmen came to the great hall and ate with the company on great tables which lined the main hall. Afterwards, as the tables were packed away by servants, and courtiers danced, the huntsmen sat with Margaret and some of the court nobles at a side table, passing around small, dark pellets which they lifted to their lips to taste, and to their noses to smell. When I asked another courtier what they were doing, I was told that Margaret and her men were examining the *fumays*, the droppings of the hinds that we were to hunt on the morrow. The valets of the hunt had been out questing for the signs of the deer that would lead us to them. I watched as Margaret lifted a fumay to her nose, sniffed the scent of the deer's droppings and crumbled it in her elegant, white fingers to see the insides.

A hunter must know her prey.

That night there was dancing and celebration for the start of the season of the hind, but all night Margaret and her huntsmen sat pouring over maps and discussing the hunt.

We started very early; I was roused from my bed in the shared dormitory of Margaret's *filles d'honneur* in darkness and stumbled into my clothing, my body still longing for the soft, warm bed it had left reluctantly. Soon though, the cloud of sleep was lifted from my head with the growing realisation of excitement. In the courtyard there was a great clatter of people mounting and riding out of the castle walls to group together outside in the forest. The air was dark and fresh in the glittering grey of the morning's half-light; the calls of people shouting to one another were infectious in their expectancy. I mounted my great horse and smoothed his dark neck as he snorted mists from his nose.

"Hold on to me, good friend," I whispered to him. "I do not fear to fall, but I fear to shame myself before so many." He nodded his head and snorted, as though understanding me.

A lady by my side gave me a roguish smile in mutual anticipation of exhilaration. She was older than me by some years; very beautiful with beautiful long fair hair and snapping blue eyes. Margaret had already ridden far ahead to the assembly point in the woods, and I knew but few people in the crowds. In the throng, I recognised the back of Claude Bouton, my travelling guardian, and some of Margaret's ladies-in-waiting. The woman who had smiled at me leaned forward on her horse.

"You are *La Petite Boulain*? Ward of Her Majesty, the Regent Margaret, Duchess of Savoy?" she asked.

"I am, Madame," I said politely, bowing my head to her as I could not bow my body.

She gave me another smile, "I am Lady Etionette de la Baume; I am of the Lady Margaret's household. She asked me to find you in this crowd and to make sure that you come to no harm on your first hunt with us." She grinned at me. "I feel I should have known you anywhere," she said with a laugh. "You are so petite and dark, just as my mistress said."

I nodded gratefully, although felt a little discomforted at her condescending tone. Etionette was a stunningly attractive woman, especially in the saddle; her fine figure hugged its riding clothes with slashed stripes of silk in pearl grey on her sleeves against brushed red velvet. Her face was flushed with the early morning airs. She nodded to me to follow her, and we clicked our tongues, making our horses walk on through the courtyard and outside of the castle walls towards the forests.

As we cleared the castle of La Vure itself, suddenly she kicked her horse and spurred it on. In a slight panic, I kicked my own horse to action and forced myself to keep pace with Etionette as she raced to join the faster riders at the front of the party. I was a good horsewoman, although not as good as the Lady de la Baume. She flew with an effortless grace as I struggled and fought to hold control of my horse at such speeds and over such rough terrain. She looked back and saw me keeping pace with her and laughed happily.

"You *are* a hunter, Mistress Boulain!" she cried, her words giving courage to my heart. As I rode behind her I felt the fierce elation of the horse's churning hooves beneath me; the thrill of the wind in my hair and on my face.

We reached the assembly point in the woods and dismounted our frothing, sweating horses, handing them to servants to be looked after and watered well. I patted my friend on the neck as he was led off. "Thank you for keeping me on your back," I whispered in his ear. He snorted a little at me again and pressed his nose against my neck. It seemed we understood each other well.

Etionette and I joined a throng of excited people pointing at maps of the area and breaking their fast with meat, shavings of hard cheese, bread and small ale. I gulped down a fair amount of small ale as I arrived, as chasing my 'protector' Etionette had made me thirsty. I felt no resentment for her having ridden so. Although it had scared me at first, it had been so thrilling that my whole body was still resonating with pleasure.

Margaret came and found me deep in conversation with Etionette and others about what to expect from the day's hunting and nodded to me as I happily curtseyed back.

"You shall be in with the hunters with the bows, *ma Petite Boulain*," Margaret said in passing to me. "We shall see how you have improved and if you shall, perhaps, bring down your own hind this day."

I nodded and wished more than anything to make her proud. It was unlikely that I would be able to take down a deer today; I had only shot at much smaller targets. Etionette was to stand with me and show me the lay of the hunt. She seemed impressed that I had kept pace with her in the chase to the assembly and was being a little less patronising towards me as she told me what to expect and how to shoot.

"Do not aim for the hind itself, but a few paces before it," she said. "The deer is running fast, faster than you can imagine, and if you aim for the hind herself, then by the time your arrow reaches its mark she will be already further ahead, and you will miss her. Aim for the position the body *will* be in. A hunter must always think ahead of the game itself, *Petite Boulain*."

I listened avidly; the deer were to be driven down into a long valley by Margaret, her huntsmen and their packs of running-hounds. Etionette, I and others were to take standing positions along the valley where we could best see and shoot the deer. Running-hounds, mastiffs and valets were to take position at the end of the valley to bring down the deer that had been shot.

"The deer will not stop running unless you take its *heart-bone* with your arrow. Until that time it will continue to run with all the courage and fire it has," said Etionette. "Not all shots are so successful." She smiled at me pityingly, as if to think that such a feat for a child like me was impossible. Her glance made me all the more determined to shoot straight and true.

Our arrows were dipped in different coloured dyes so that we should know which hunter had taken which deer. We hunters with our bows took to our positions in the woods after the great assembly was done with. We were each given a huntsman to take care of us in the wilderness.

We waited.

It was still early in the morning and although the sun had now risen, the forest was cool and quiet. The birds had started their erratic morning song, but the world felt so still, so calm. I felt peace descend over me; the feeling of being so removed from the noise and the clatter of court, of being removed from the world. There was no talk here in these woods, no chatter, no prattle. The trees seemed to whisper in the autumn breeze and a light chill crept over my alert form as the damp of the forest made itself felt, even through the warm lining of my furs and my heavy velvet gown.

In the distance, I heard the hunter's horn sound, cracking through the still calm of the air. Other horns were raised in song behind the call of the first. I knew that Margaret and her huntsmen had found the quarry they sought, and had started to drive the hinds towards us in the valley. I readied myself, but the noise of the first hind that flung herself desperately through the undergrowth was such a sudden shock to me, that rather than shoot my poised arrow at her, I just stared dumbly. Her magnificent form cast itself furiously through the woods, plunging away from the terror of the hunters behind her who wanted her life. I watched her fly through the woods, darting past tree and branch and disappearing into the dripping darkness of the forest. She would not be a meal on any table this night.

The huntsman beside me urged me to ready myself for the coming of another deer. Suddenly, as though God himself were walking over the earth, there was a great noise of hooves and horns as four deer at once came careering down the sloped path towards my arrows. I saw the arrows of the other archers flying true and straight into the path of the charging deer.

Abruptly my fingers seemed to move of their own accord; arrows flew from my fingertips in a great torrent. I was barely aiming, but doing as Etionette had told me and loosing my arrows ahead into the furious flight of the desperate beasts. This way and that, the deer turned and dodged. Their bodies moved faster than anything I had ever seen in the intricate steps of the dance of their own death. Their black eyes were wide with fear and their breath was like smoke rising. They ran for their lives, reckless, beautiful and powerful.

On and on my fingers flew to their position on the bow, releasing an arrow then grabbing another from the sheaf on my back. The forest was but a blur and the deafening noise of the hunt, the hooves and the shouts of the other hunters rode my heartstrings like the intoxication of a fine wine.

I had never felt so alive in the face of so much death around me.

My servant was clapping his hands in excitement as he shouted to me over the noise of the running deer that he thought I had shot one of my own. A feeling of pride and excitement filled me at the thought. Perhaps Margaret would have another reason to praise me this night.

Quickly he re-filled my sheaf as the hunt continued. Deer after deer were being flushed and herded down that ravine by Margaret and her clever hounds. At the bottom of the pass, I could see the shapes of the running-hounds and huntsmen as they stalked the wounded hinds. Some of the charging deer flew past the men at the base of the hill. Not every one was caught. The thought pleased me in some indefinable way. They had fought so bravely to live, that I was glad that some of this herd still would remain to walk the forests again.

That afternoon, we counted and took credit for the game we had caught. My servant was right that I, on my first hunt, had succeeded in wounding a deer unto death and bringing her to the table for Margaret. I looked on the dead deer lying on the forest floor with my arrow buried deep in her withers. Her blood was clotted down her beautiful neck and her once-bright eyes were dull with death. I felt a little sad that I had been the one to take the fire of life from her eyes. But my youthful heart, too, felt pride at bringing down such a trophy on my first hunt. She was a large hind, and would feed many people of Margaret's court.

Etionette clapped me on the back and laughed at my pride-filled face, dirty with sweat and with the dust of the arrows. "Your first kill, Mistress Boulain!" she said smiling at me. "I knew when I saw you that you would be a dangerous woman to know."

I laughed. "It seems to me, my Lady de la Baume, that you are more dangerous than I, for you were my tutor in killing."

Etionette gave me her roguish smile once more and touched my face with a glove that was smeared with blood and dirt. She stared into my eyes. "A dangerous woman is really the only type worth knowing, *La Petite Boulain,*" she said. "I think you know that as well as I."

She laughed again, moving away to mingle with the nobles of the chase. Her smear of blood and dirt was upon my face, as though I were marked as her protégé.

The hinds were unmade and then the dogs were given their *curee*, a reward for their work, from the bellies of the hinds. Fresh blood and bread was mixed together with cheese from our packs, and meats roasted from the hinds on great bonfires lit in the forest. Lymers and mastiffs were fed separately to avoid fights, but the running-hounds were allowed to stick their famished heads into the belly of a fallen deer as a pack; a feast of blood and bone and gore, all wrapped inside the blood-rich scent of one of the great deer that they had helped to drive and take down.

The dogs were then as wolves in their reckless hunger for the blood of the hind. Their lips smacked, their jaws snapped; the noise of the clotting blood of the hind being lapped by their eager tongues echoed in the air. The snarls and whimpers of the pack as they shared their rewards were satisfyingly gruesome sounds of victory and appetite. When the hounds were sated in their hunger, and the company had drunk well of spiced wine heated over the bonfires, the hinds were hauled up upon great ropes and hung from lengths of wood to carry home on the broad shoulders of the huntsmen.

Our horses were brought to us by the servants of the court, and we mounted them laughing and talking gaily together in the common, weary, pleasure that filled our tired bodies. Then, in a last gesture, Margaret again lifted her horn to the skies and blew, to recall us hunters home; the last cry to return us to the civilised world of the court, leaving behind the dual nature of the peace and the viciousness of the wild.

We rode in happy, tired groups back to the castle to enjoy the feast of the first day of the season of the hind, and all the attendant dances and entertainments. I was the youngest noble in the party, and, felt I could truly celebrate this festival as I had helped to bring food to the table. That night we feasted on the flesh of beasts we had brought down with our own arrows and each bite of the tender flesh of the fat hind was as sugar in my mouth as I ate with pride and happiness.

Margaret lifted her goblet to me during the feast. From my place on one of the many tables lining the great hall, I blushed and lifted my goblet to her, feeling the honour of being so noted, by such a great lady, in public.

Chapter Fourteen

1513
Lille and Tournai

During my stay at the court of Margaret, the King of England visited. He was busy with waging war against France at the time and keen to encourage allies amongst the Hapsburgs, such as Margaret and her father the Emperor Maximilian. In July of that year, Henry and the Emperor laid siege to Therouanne and routed the French at the Battle of Spurs, which claimed its name because the French had retreated so fast from the English forces, leaving the English with only a glimpse of their French spurs shining in the sunlight, as they urged their horses away from battle.

Sadly, glory did not come without a price, especially for my family. My uncle, brother to my mother, Sir Edward Howard, died in an attack on the French Fleet at Brest. I wrote to my mother when the news was sent to me, trying to console her in her sorrow at the death of her brother.

But truly, having little known my uncle, I did not sorrow long. The court was caught up in watching for the arrival of the King of England, and I became caught like a fly in a web within that excitement. Since my father, too, was present in the English forces riding with the King, there was also a certain sense of trepidation for me as the party of the King came to Margaret's court.

At the time, though, I was most excited to see once again this great king whose coronation procession I had watched all those years before. The other *filles d'honneur* questioned me on what he was like, and I delighted to tell them of his handsome face and magnificent bearing.

King Henry VIII was twenty-three years old when he came to Margaret's court. I was thirteen. With the other *filles,* I watched from the windows when his party arrived. We all looked amongst the crowds of men and jewels and horses to see the King of England in the clamour of their arrival. In the years that had passed since the coronation, he had grown in reputation; it was widely said about the courts of Europe that he was the handsomest prince in the world. His height, strength and prowess in sport and hunting were talked of avidly, but also his desire for learning, for languages and for music. A lot of flattery is gifted to princes and kings, but in many ways, Henry was all the things they spoke of him. We *filles* were eager to see him, and to judge for ourselves how much that was spoken was true.

From those great stone windows we spied down upon the party of the King riding into the courtyard at Lille. We were not meant to be watching Henry's arrival, but were meant to be sewing demurely in Margaret's chambers. But the event was too exciting for us to miss. Each of us *filles* had sworn to the other we would not tell, if they did not. The ladies of Margaret's entourage were already at her side, and *la dame d'honneur,* our overseer, was amongst them. The servants were as eager as we were to see the arrival of the King, and so there was no one who would tell our mistress that we were not where we should have been, on the day King Henry of England arrived at the Court of Burgundy.

They came in a great rush of people, seemingly unplanned and impulsive, but at court there was nothing truly left unplanned. The crowds thinned out amongst the rush and the bustle of their arrival, and then I saw him. There could be little mistake that he was the King. Although the others were dressed richly, he was the most stunning. Cloth of gold and silver mixed with bright and royal reds and purples on his tunic; gems glowed from amongst the rich folds of velvet and silk. His fingers glittered with gold and jewels. There was no understatement in this king; he wanted all to know who he was. His hair shone golden and red under his black velvet cap. He was tall and broad and muscular. His body was toned and strong. He swung down from his horse with the ease of a true horseman and he walked with the grace of an athlete. His face was indeed most handsome, and I could see it much clearer this time than I had at his coronation. His eyes were blue and clear, his beard fashionably short and golden, and his laugh, which seemed to ring out against the stones of the courtyard, was hearty and warm.

My breath caught in a little gasp at the back of my throat. He was the most handsome man I had ever seen, and Margaret's court was full of handsome men. There was something so likeable, so young, so magnetic about him that all of us *filles* leaned forward. There was something in him that drew attention, that drew you towards him, and it was not just because we knew he was the King of England. He was compelling, charming… captivating, even at a distance. It was there in the ease of his manner and the grace of his movements. It was the way he moved, it was his voice that sung with both friendship and command. It was his laugh, which boomed about the palace walls.

No, it was not just the crown that made him attractive; after all, although he was a rich king with all the money his frugal father had left him, he was not as powerful as the King of France, or the Hapsburgs. No, it was not only the King I was interested in, it was the man. We *filles* started avidly at him from that window. It was something in the man himself that called to me so powerfully, so… tantalisingly.

As I watched him through that window it suddenly occurred to me that he was the King of *my* country, he was *my* King! I had been at Margaret's court for so many months that I had almost forgotten that my home was England and that this magnificent king was the ruler of my true country. My eyes scanned the strong face that beamed down on those around him. He put his arm around another man who was so like him in hair, stature and appearance that they could have been brothers. The other man said something that made King Henry laugh again. This then, must be Sir Charles Brandon. I had heard of him before. Brandon was the King's favourite; he was not of very noble stock, but his father had been King Henry VII's standard bearer and had died for him at the Battle of Bosworth Field. Henry VII, this King's father, had wished to reward his loyalty and had taken the dead man's son into his own household. Brandon and Henry had been raised together, had shared lessons and sports. Now that he was the King, Henry VIII wished to reward his friend and companion and had raised him up to be a great noble. Rewards were heaped upon Brandon. This was the way that such a king treated his friends; they were rewarded for loyalty and devotion to him, rather than just for being noble.

This thought gave me such a rush of admiration that I blushed suddenly, my face feeling hot and my hands cold. As I looked at this king, on his manner, on his handsome face and broad shoulders, on his boyish ways, I felt my inner thighs begin to ache with a feeling that I had not experienced before. My loins tingled, teasingly, and I felt excitement sparkle through my blood. My breathing quickened as I felt moisture rush softly between my legs.

I felt desire for this man… and it excited me.

One of the other *filles*, Elisabeth of Brittany, turned to me and saw my flushed cheeks and glittering, glassy eyes fixed on the royal party. She pounced on the opportunity to catch me off-guard.

"Mistress Anna Boleyn!" she whispered, loudly enough for the others to hear. "Are you lusting after the King… or the handsome servant of the King?!"

The other *filles* burst into giggles as I turned to them, flustered and caught. My heart was throbbing in my chest and I felt the quickening of craving lust in my immature body. My first true feelings of desire had been caught and exposed by my companions; I was confused and humiliated.

Suddenly, and before I could ready my tongue to whip back at them, the figures in the courtyard turned our way and looked up. Our giggles had attracted the notice of the King and his friend. The two great men looked up at us, shading their eyes from the sun, and other figures in the yard also began to turn our way. The sudden thought that my father must be amongst them made my heart quite stop within me.

Quick as a flash of lightening, and with a clearly audible, collective shriek, we *filles* dropped from our positions and ran the halls back to where we should have been all along, sewing in Margaret's private chambers. As we turned tail and fled, I heard that great laugh ring out again against the stones of the palace. The King of England, it seemed, was not displeased by the prying, lusty eyes of the court maidens shining down on him illicitly from above.

Fortunately, none of this was revealed to Margaret, and she was too occupied with the business of entertaining to pursue any rumour of her maids acting so immodestly. Fortunately for me, also, my father did not know the identity of the maidens who had fled from the amused eyes of the King.

Chapter Fifteen

1513
Lille

I was called to see my father shortly after his arrival at Lille. Although almost a year had passed since I had last seen him, he had barely changed. I found him in the gardens and as I walked towards him, stopping to curtsey as I approached the sharpness of his gaze, I saw him nod once in satisfaction. A little drop of the ocean of fear in my heart fell away as I noted that he was not displeased with my appearance or manners.

"Your mother has sent letters for you," he said as we took a turn in the gardens.

"I will be most pleased to receive them, father," I said, my now-much-improved French accent lilting pleasantly as I spoke.

"Your French is better," he nodded. For a moment I thought on the terrible letter I had sent when I first arrived at Margaret's court, and felt a little colour creep into my cheeks for shame. "You are learning well, and behaving modestly?" he asked.

I nodded. "*Madame* is most careful with her *filles*, father," I said. "And in any case, I would be a fool to not take advantage of all that you have secured for me here... I will be forever grateful to you for this opportunity. The court of the Archduchess is a place of wonder and beauty."

He nodded to me, apparently satisfied with my answers and my deportment of myself. Our meeting was short, as he had many more important matters to attend to, other than simply seeing his daughter.

My father simply wanted, in that brief meeting, to assure himself that I was behaving well and taking advantage of the opportunities he had gained for me. Perhaps I should have been upset at the brusque nature of our meeting, after being apart from my family for so long, but I was not. My father had ever been a distant figure to me, since I was a small child. I was more pleased to find that my audience with him was brief since it shortened the time I would have to live in fear of making a mistake before him. Besides, my time was much occupied during the visit of the English King, since there were many entertainments whilst dignitaries visited, and we *filles* were called to perform for the King and his men during the few days they were with us. There was much to distract us in the games of courtly love which unfolded during their visit. Sir Charles Brandon was a very handsome, but, I began to think, a rather foolish and somewhat easily-led man. He flirted with Margaret outrageously, rather beyond what we had come to see as the general bounds of decency in the game of courtly love. He was crass with his attentions to her, although she pretended not to notice. I believe that he thought her rather in love with him. He was sadly mistaken. Margaret could not speak English, and Brandon's French was quite terrible, so often their games were conducted through translators, which only made the whole spectacle of Bandon more and more awkward and somewhat amusing to us *filles*.

At court we had become used to gentle attentions and to cultured lines of verse offered in praise. Brandon offered none of this, but rode in many tournaments for Margaret, which he always won unless he was matched against King Henry. But in his attentions to her he was quite ardent. I believe at some stage he really thought that Margaret might forget herself and marry him. But she would never have lowered herself so. I think the game amused her and although she certainly found him attractive, she was not fool enough to enter into a marriage or affair that was so beneath her. The game of courtly love was most often played to gain a richer and more powerful patroness, rather than a lover in the real sense. Brandon, I am sure, would have loved to marry so much higher above himself, but he was happy to settle for a patroness as rich and influential as Margaret.

The King, Henry, was adept at this game, much more skilled than his friend. He was most quickly enamoured, it seemed, of another of Margaret's ladies, my own companion in the hunt, Etionette de la Baume, daughter of the Lord of Chateauvillan. It was not unusual for a man to be married and to have a mistress in the games of courtly love, but this affair, it seemed, was more than just a game of love. A year or so later, when she married, Henry wore black in mourning for *"the love of a lady"*, as he said, which, it seemed, may have been Etionette. The thought made me a little sad, even though I had no real cause to be. I did not like to think of his admiring Etionette so. With the foolish wants and wishes of a child, I yearned for the King to notice me.

I was too young, too unimportant to have attracted his attentions then. I was a child even if I believed in my heart I was not. But even as a child I watched him... watched him with a growing longing in my heart, so strong that I thought it should burst. The love of the young is so violent and simple. I would let no one know of my desire for him; I was learning to keep my emotions and feelings secret from the other *filles* who served Margaret with me. After that first embarrassment, I swore I should never be humiliated in front of others again. My feelings were my own and that is how they should stay.

So with the other *filles* and court ladies I watched Henry the King. Admired him, talked of him... but no more than the others did. I watched him, usually from a distance, as I was rather young still to be involved in all the events and entertainments. When I was involved, I was usually in a throng of many maids and the chosen group that he moved in was far away and above my social standing.

At times I bristled with indignation to be still restricted, for after all, I was of an age to marry and therefore of an age to attend all the entertainments, surely. But Margaret had promised my father that she would protect me, and I realise now that I was still not ready or equipped to defend myself as the older women of the court were able to. There were dangers at court which I was to truly learn of later. The protection of Margaret at this time, as I realise now, was a true blessing.

Henry did not come with his Queen Katherine, as she was in the latter stages of pregnancy; a condition that she seemed to perpetually be in with no viable result. After the death of the little Prince when I was ten, there had only been more failures and no living children to show for all the sorrow the royal couple undertook in trying for them. He still, though, held her in high esteem; Katherine was acting as his Regent in England, a position of true authority and trust. Their marriage was rumoured to be strong despite his occasional discreet affairs, and what man did not have affairs? It seemed that there was genuine affection in this royal marriage, a rare thing indeed.

Katherine was defending the borders of England against the Scots who had taken the opportunity to invade when Henry had headed off to war with France. The *Auld Alliance*, as it was called, meant that France and Scotland were bound as allies, and whenever the English thought of waging war on their neighbours across the water, so would conflict follow from the lands of the Scots. My own grandfather, then the Earl of Surrey, was a general in those wars, along with my uncle Thomas Howard. Katherine, Queen of England, with the aid of my family and others, was in time to quash the Scots. In September of 1513, the Scots' King James IV, the husband of King Henry's older sister Margaret, was killed by the armies of the English at the Battle of Flodden Field and the Scottish attempts to invade England faltered and failed. The crown of the Scots went to the heir to their throne, James V, a babe in arms, little more than a year old, and the threat of the Scots to England was much diminished. Katherine was so excited by her victory that she wanted to send the corpse of the King of Scots to Henry; his own brother-in-law's corpse shipped as a trophy of war! But the English nobles, my uncle and grandfather amongst them, thankfully thought the idea too horrific and so Katherine sent the Scottish King's bloodstained shirt as a ghastly trophy to her husband instead, to use as a "*banner of war*" as she reportedly wrote to him.

People talked of Katherine as a most gentle and humble Christian lady; but there was always the spirit of a ruthless fighter there. She was, after all, the daughter of Isabella of Castile, the Queen who had rode to the frontline of her troops whilst heavily pregnant, and had raised many of her young children on campaign with her. Katherine was never such an unassuming, meek creature as she was made out to be by those who supported her in her later troubles. And, I doubt, had she been so, whether Henry would have found her interesting enough to remain at her side so many years. Although some of his mistresses had been obliging, quiet women, for the most part, he liked his loves to have a little fire within their spirit… He tired of the fire only later in life.

I was vastly proud of the valour of my mother's kinsmen who had fought, died or won in the wars against the Scots and the French. My mother wrote to me in glowing letters of the accomplishments of her father and brother against the Scots, and I showed the letters to Margaret, who praised my family. She said to me that she was sure my grandfather would win back the titles of Duke of Norfolk now that he had proved his loyalty and valour to his king in feats of arms. I shone with pride at the thought of calling my grandfather a Duke. This happened as Margaret had foreseen; in 1514 my grandfather became once again the rightful Duke of Norfolk and my uncle Thomas, now a man of more than forty, inherited the title of the Earl of Surrey. My grandfather was given, too, the honour of being allowed to display the royal arms of Scotland alongside his own, with the Scots lion impaled with an arrow, to signify his part in having brought the King of Scots to his death. My mother's family was amongst the most important in the land of England once more.

In the amusements planned for the visitors, there were hunting excursions, dances and pageants; I enjoyed hunting fairly often now, but was not chosen for these parties due to my youth. I was skilled at archery, but those hunts that Margaret and Henry and their retinues went on were for boar and stag. *Par Force* hunting required different skills and was much more dangerous than bow and stable, or hunting with hawks. I was too young and not of sufficient rank to accompany them, and therefore I was left out of those hunting parties. I watched the heart of the court return from their day of game with their trophies of dead boar and hart, and I felt a pang for being so left out of all that was exciting and interesting... all, in fact, that was anything to do with Henry Tudor. I longed each day to get a glimpse of this hero who had ignited my imagination and my female desire. There were other *filles* who joined me, also seeking to steal a glimpse of the most handsome King in the world, from the great stone windows of the palace.

The pageants, however, *were* for the maids and youths of the court, but there were special seats in galleries from which we could watch. This was so that we could be taken away should the entertainments go beyond our years or understanding.

Always in the centre was this man, this golden king, so young and so handsome; I believe that most of the court ladies, not just Etionette, would have been open to him both in the game of courtly love and in the realities of physical love. He knew the effect he had upon women and he loved it. To see their blushes when he talked to them was a drug to him. Through the nights Henry would dance with the ladies of the court, even once throwing off his doublet and shoes to dance with further vigour. In the days he would ride in the joust, only seeming to grow more vigorous with every lance he broke. He went to bed late and rose early, and all the courtiers were amazed at his vital and unrelenting energy for life and pleasure.

He was cultured also; at night, before the dances would begin, he read aloud of the poetry he had written and although some of the praise was meted out for his position, some of the praise was also for the talented poet that he was. There was a certain naivety about his verse that fitted well with the games of Margaret's court; an honesty and a truth that fitted well. You could tell that he really did believe he was a knight of old; a protector of virtue and of love, or at least, he wanted to be. There was a story I heard later of the English King which spoke well of his attachment to courtly behaviour and love of the ancient ways of knights. One day, whilst travelling on a barge to Greenwich Castle, apparently to visit a lady with whom he was enamoured, King Henry challenged one of his men, Sir Andrew Flammock, to take up a verse which he would begin, and complete it. The King spoke the words:

Within this tower
There lieth a flower
That hath my heart…

To which, obviously in the throes of mischief, Sir Andrew continued:

Within this hour
She pissed full sour
And let out a fart.

The King was so offended by this, that he shouted at his man, "begone, varlet!" and ordered him from his sight. Henry adored the old ways of chivalry and courtly love; he did not like coarse language or impolite ways. This reflected in the manner in which he chose to approach women of the court, and the words of his own, more cultured verse. One of his poems, I remember well:

Though some say that youth rules me,
I trust in age to tarry.
God and my right and my duty,
From them I shall never vary,
Though some say that youth rules me.

I pray you all that aged be
How well did you your youth carry?
I think in some worse of each degree.
Therein a wager lay dare I,
Though some say that youth rules me.

Pastime of youth some time among –
None can say but necessary.
I hurt no man, I do no wrong,
I love true where I did marry,
Though some say that youth rules me.

Then soon discuss that hence we must
Pray we to God and St Mary
That all amend, and here an end.
Thus says the King, the eighth Harry,
Though some say that youth rules me.

As a youth myself, I felt I understood his words well, and when he spoke them, smiling slightly in the light of the torches and candles at night before the court, I felt my blood swim within my head, for I felt as though he spoke to me alone. Such was the magnetism of Henry; he could speak to an entire assembly of people, and yet leave you feeling as though you had been his only care.

At night I dreamt of him and would awaken with that same ache in my thighs that I had felt when first I saw him. I longed for his touch, longed for his gaze to rest upon me. I thought of what his lips might feel like against mine. Sometimes I was distracted during the day, drifting into daydreams, imagining his body and his hands moving against my skin, although in reality I knew nothing of love-making. But I could imagine kissing and caresses, and I imagined them well... and often. He was the first man for whom I had ever felt the stirrings of desire, the first lord for whom I ever felt I might have lost my heart. None knew it, of course, for I was careful with my feelings. But I loved Henry of England truly before he ever knew who I was, and before I knew him at all. I loved him as so many of the young love; I loved an ideal, a wish, a paradigm. I thought him all that was good, because I had fallen for his handsome face and charismatic ways.

I performed for him within in a group of *filles* when he was at court. On the last night of Henry's visit, after a great feast, Margaret called for her group of *filles* to sing, and asked me to take the premier role in the song. I flushed instantly, thinking that perhaps the King might recognise my face from the balcony when we *filles* had been almost caught watching him, but of course he had seen nothing but many maids rushing off, obscured by the glaring sun's light, and I was but one amongst them. I was just one tiny member of a huge and glittering court. I was but one more face in a sea of so many people. I was nothing to him… then.

He looked over us as we stepped up beside the lute player; his eyes roamed our young figures discreetly, but noticeably. I saw him enjoy the flush upon our cheeks that this intimate attention caused. My flush was added to by the intense rush of passion I felt for this handsome prince. I was embarrassed, and aroused in public. I steeled my heart to behave itself.

I went to close my eyes as usual, to block out the court as I sang, and dispel my nerves, but this time I saw Henry's eyes, clear and blue, watching me. He was watching all of us, but his eyes came back to me more than once. Boldly, I kept my eyes open and turned them to him from time to time through the song, catching his gaze and holding it. Margaret was pleased with us. Her smile gave me courage and I sang well; my sweet high voice turned the corners of the song and lifted the melody of the lute with ease. The others joined and our voices reached to the ceilings; reverberating keenly around the great hall, caressing the stones of the walls and lifting the company. Our subtle voices blended together in harmony; we were careful and had practised often. We didn't miss a note. We were haunting and lovely, sweet and smooth in our song of love and valour.

When I finished my part, I saw that the King's eyes were closed, and his hand poised where he had beat the tune softly on the table. Music was a great pleasure to him, and I knew by the way his sparkling eyes caught mine as I walked off to stand beside Margaret once more, that our song had moved him.

As we walked from before the court, our hands clasped before us in maidenly poise, I looked over at my father who was standing nearby watching. He gave one brief nod to me, and I felt a little pride enter my heart. It was the closest thing I had had akin to praise from him.

"Your court is full of the finest of musicians," I heard the King say to Margaret later. "I only wish that my court was so blessed."

"One day, my lord, it may well be," Margaret said, her eyes gleaming with his praise. "One of my song-birds is one of your own subjects; the granddaughter of your general Howard, daughter of Sir Thomas Boleyn who is within your company now. I call her *ma Petite Boulain*. One day it may well be that I will have to give her up to grace your court, but I hope you will be gallant and leave her with me some time yet."

When she explained which one of her ladies she meant he asked, "the little… dark one? I never should have known; she seemed like a French-woman born."

And that was all he said of me. But it was good enough to send me hugging my arms about my body for happiness when I was alone. To be thought to be a "French-woman born" meant that I was considered sophisticated and graceful. I treasured such short words and repeated them to myself each night before I slept.

Soon Henry and his friends rode away with their entourage and went back to their war. He would have more victory in France with the aid of his friends and advisor Cardinal Wolsey, although not as much as he would have wished for. We met up with his party once more, at Tournai, after another battle near that region, and there were more entertainments and diversions there.

My father came to see me, again, briefly, before the party of the King left Tournai. His instructions were concise; that I was to maintain a high level of pleasing and modest behaviour, to continue in my instruction in the French language, and to honour the opportunity he had gained for me by learning all I could. I agreed to do all he wished, gave him letters for my mother, and for Mary and George, and then my father left again. Were it not for the slight feeling of wariness which remained with me for days after his leaving, I would hardly have remembered meeting him again at all.

We went back to life at court as it had been before the English visit. Although the entertainments and daily life were no less than they had been before the King's party arrived, it now felt duller at Margaret's court, *reduced*. It was as though this king had taken the sun with him when he left.

I went back to my lessons in the school rooms and in the court; I went back to learning how to be a good court lady. I still dreamed of him at night and would sometimes awaken, moaning in half-asleep desire for the feel of his hands upon my young body.

But soon enough, this dream started to leave me and in a few months, with the cold-hearted resilience of the young, I barely thought of him.

At this time, after all, I had little idea that I should ever see him much again.

Chapter Sixteen

1514
Mechelen

It was August of the year 1514, when I received word from my father that he wished me to leave Margaret's court. I was to join the wedding party of Henry's sister, the Princess Mary Tudor of England. Mary was to wed the aged King of France, Louis XII, and she required ladies-in-waiting with a good command of the French language to help her as she settled into her new life as Queen of France. My father had put my name forward, extolling my proficiency in the French language, and it had been accepted.

Louis was the King who had come to the French throne after Margaret's intended suitor Charles had died. Louis of France had been married twice already; his first wife, Jeanne de France, was a poor cripple whom he had placed in a religious order when she was unable to give him an heir. Jeanne had agreed humbly to her retirement from the position of Queen of France, and the Pope had issued a dissolution of the marriage contract between them. Louis' second wife had been Anne of Brittany; the self-same bride for whom Louis' predecessor, Charles, had rejected Margaret. Their marriage had largely been one of respect and love, a rare enough thing for arranged marriages between royalty. Anne of Brittany had died, leaving Louis free once again to marry. Anne bore Louis two royal daughters, Renee and Claude, but no sons. I think he was hoping Mary Tudor would help him with that matter. Due to Salic Law, the throne of France could not pass to a woman, and so if he had no son, then his throne would pass to the nearest prince of the blood royal, François de Valois, a man whom it was rumoured that Louis held no love for.

Mary Tudor, Princess of England, was reputed to be the most beautiful princess in Christendom. I am sure Louis thought he had made a fortunate match to be married, at his great age, to her.

My father wrote to tell me that my name had been accepted because of his position at court, and for my fluency in the French language observed on his visit to Lille and Tournai, but there was another reason that he wanted me to leave Mechelen. The wars between the French and the English were now over; the two countries were uniting together and cementing that alliance with this marriage. This meant that the Hapsburgs were not as strongly allied now with the English as the French were. Indeed, the marriage between old Louis and the fresh young Princess Mary, had only come about by Henry VIII breaking Mary's previous engagement with Margaret's nephew Charles. Margaret was already outraged that her previous ally Henry would so quickly break the future match between her nephew and his sister, for the chance at making his sister a queen, now.

Relations were therefore growing frosty between England and the Hapsburgs; it was only a matter of time before that chill would spread. In such circumstances, it would be improper for an English lady such as I was, to stay at Margaret's court. If I left now, before diplomatic relations suffered further, then I would be in a position to link our family with the new power in France. I was to leave this great and romantic court that I loved so well, and travel to another that I had never seen… all for the whim of politics.

Margaret was not pleased at all that I was going to leave her for France, for the very court that had so rejected her, and to go to attend on the Princess who was supposed to be marrying her own nephew! She was also aggrieved, I think, to lose one of her favourite *song-birds*, so she called us. She stalled my leaving for as long as possible, telling my father in correspondence that she could not do without her *Petite Boulain* and wished to keep me with her until the last possible time that she could. I flatter myself that much of this was born of natural affection for me rather than just for my voice, for she had grown fond of me and happy to have me ornament her glittering court.

To own the truth, whilst I understood my father's reasons for extracting me from Margaret's court, I was deeply unhappy to think of leaving. Even though the prospect of joining Mary Tudor's wedding party was certainly exciting, and I had never seen the French Court, despite hearing much of it, I still felt my heart wrench inside me whenever I thought of leaving Mechelen. It had become more to me than a palace of rich and varied pleasures; it had become my home.

At the time, however, I reasoned that once my duties were done in France, and once political relations had become warmer with the Hapsburgs, then perhaps I could return to Mechelen. The friendships between kings and countries were as fleeting and transitory as the weather along the English coast; they could change at a moment's notice. Perhaps in time, I could come home once more, to Margaret.

Margaret delayed for as long as she could, but she could not keep me against the wishes of my father forever. Eventually, she gave me permission to go. Before I left, Margaret took my hands in hers and bade me promise to return to her one day.

"I will follow news of you when I have it, *ma Petite Boulain*," she said warmly, releasing my hands from her grip. I took her hand and kissed it, looking up at her with eyes shining with tears.

"Thank you for all you have done for me, Your Majesty," I said, "and all that you have taught me. I will never be able to repay such beneficence."

"Come *back*, *ma Petite Boulain*, and sing for me," she smiled. "Then you will repay my kindness to you."

"Whenever my father allows, *Madame*," I said, "I will return to your side."

Margaret nodded to me, and I left her presence.

Margaret's court had been everything to me. I had grown in body and in mind under her tutelage. Leaving Mechelen was even more painful than leaving Hever had been, and in the nights that led up to my leaving, I cried often into my pillow in the shared dormitory of Margaret's *filles*. But there were other thoughts which lessened the sadness somewhat. My father wrote to me that he would be in the wedding party as an ambassador to the French Court, and my sister Mary would also be there, as she was now a lady-in-waiting to Princess Mary Tudor. I was happy to think of seeing my sister, but I could not help but raise an eyebrow when I read that; my father's plan had come to fruition as all his plans seemed to. Mary had done as had been expected of her and moved from the household of Elizabeth, wife of our uncle Howard, to serve the Princess of England. How did he seem to know what would happen, with the right person positioned in just the right place? It was a gift.

So it came that one day, feeling both excited and sad in equal measures, I rode out from Mechelen to join the wedding party in France. My belongings were brought by cart and I was given a guard to take me safely to the Court of France. I thought fondly of returning to Mechelen after my duties to my father were done; but this was to prove an idle fantasy. I had not realised that the treaty made between England and France, and the turning nature of Fate, would prevent me from returning to Margaret's court. I never saw the Court of Burgundy again, but I always remembered it with love in my heart.

Chapter Seventeen

1514
France

The Princess Mary Tudor of England was one of the most beautiful women I had ever seen. Erasmus himself had described her as *"a nymph from heaven"* adding that *"nature never formed anything more beautiful"* than her, and I could not disagree with this report of her beauty. Her face was lovely, her eyes large, dark blue and doe-like, and her lips pretty and dusky pink. Her skin was clear and creamy like new milk. Her figure was perfect; just the right amount of breast and flesh to it without ever looking too ample or too spare. She was eighteen and her hair was the same hue as her brother's, golden and red. There was dragon-fire in the Welsh blood of the Tudors and it shone through in their hair and in their spirit.

She was also the most singularly unhappy bride I have ever seen, and at the various courts I came to live in, I saw many.

Louis XII was fifty-two, an old man by the standards of our time, and he looked old and smelt old. He had lived a quiet life of near retirement with his previous wives. His court, although beautiful and rich, was nothing to the splendour and sophistication of Mechelen. Courts tend to reflect the personality of their ruler; Louis' court was good, and rather dull. The French might be the leaders in style, but this was not brought about by the example of their King. The once-greatness of the French Court seemed to have dulled in the twilight years of his reign, and I wondered to myself how anyone could have thought that this court compared in any way to Margaret's in Burgundy.

The common people loved Louis, partly because of his frugality. To his people, Louis was *"La Pere de France"* as he imposed few taxes on them and did not waste the money he did take from them. His nobles hated that quality in him, feeling that a king should make more show of his magnificence, not only to his own people, but to the world. It was the way rulers imposed on other rulers how superior they, and their countries, were, after all... For the nobles, a king should be easy to find in a crowd; he should be the richest and the most noticeable of men. Louis often seemed more like one of the servants than a true son of France. He went to bed early and rose early, he was careful with his money, staid in his appearance. He was not fond of dancing or hunting and preferred his books to the companionship of his nobles. He was, in short, an old man, already retiring from the world.

Whilst I could see why the common people loved him, I could also understand the fear Louis' nobles felt at having a king who was so very dull, aged and ordinary. It did not set them very high in the stakes of the courts of Europe.

But this was all to change when Mary Tudor arrived! The old man who went to bed early and rose early, who was frugal with his money and appetite was suddenly invested with a bride who loved everything he shied away from. Unhappy though she was to be placed in a match with an old man, Mary Tudor was fond of the many pleasures that her new position could afford her. She wanted endless rounds of dances, feasts, hunting and masques; she was as elegant and refined as a princess should be, but it was obvious from the start that the court was about to change.

There was a new power in the Court of France. But the Queen's reign had not started smoothly.

Before I arrived in France, and a few weeks after they were married, Louis had both surprised and outraged his new bride when he sent almost all of her waiting women home to England and replaced them with French attendants. Although this was not an unusual occurrence in royal marriages, the young Tudor bride was deeply offended. As with all the Tudors, friendship and her own pride mattered to Mary a great deal. Louis had injured both her feelings of loyalty to her friends, and her Tudor self-esteem... a dangerous mixture.

Louis had to work hard and provide many very costly presents to make the hurt up to her. He was entirely spellbound by his delightful new queen, and although he would not have the Queen of France surrounded by English women, he *did* want to be on good terms with her. I imagine he found her bed to be rather more exciting a prospect than those of his previous two brides.

But all princesses must send home the women who accompanied them to their new court and country; it is the way of things. No king wishes to have his court awash with creatures of another realm; therein lie far too many opportunities for crafty spying by kings of other nations. A handful of English attendants were left to her from the many hundreds who had accompanied Mary to France. Out of the few that remained behind to serve the new Queen was my sister, and I soon arrived after Mary Tudor's coronation.

The removal of Mary Tudor's English attendants had left her with few people that she could converse with easily. Her French was not unaccomplished, since she had the education of a princess behind her, but she longed to speak English, perhaps out of a feeling of homesickness. I had been selected to act as the Queen's lady-in-waiting, but also as her translator, if required, and something of a tutor to her in the French Court. Mary, my sister, had no real gift for languages, although she muddled along well enough, but she was allowed to remain mainly due to the affection that Mary Tudor had for her sweet lady-in-waiting. My sister Mary had made an impression on Mary Tudor, and our father had done everything he could to ensure her position with the Princess.

Mary Tudor greeted my arrival in France with some relief. Her own tutor, whom she had selected to accompany her to France, was named Jane Popincourt, but Jane had apparently not been approved to accompany the Princess from England to France due to a lack of proper morals. Whispered to have been a mistress of the English King, Jane Popincourt was not considered to be a good example of a modest lady to accompany a princess. And so the English Princess was left without her tutor, and whenever there was a post which needed filling, our father seemed able and willing to mention a name to fill it to his advantage. Mary Tudor had been somewhat offended to receive notice that one of her ladies was not considered worthy to accompany her, but Louis started as he meant to continue, before the match even took place, he sent his bride-to-be a fabulous jewel to appease her, a vast diamond adorned with a pendant-shaped pearl, named the "Mirror of Naples". He was to lavish many and various gifts upon his princess whenever he came to upset her.

Mary Tudor was not ignorant of the French language; ignorance would have been difficult since French was spoken often at the English court. But she worried about her accent, whether it was refined enough, if it seemed crass… much as I had done when I came to Mechelen. If there was something this fiery Princess would not suffer, it was looking or feeling a fool in front of others; her pride was strong. And with that pride came the opportunity for my entry to the Court of France.

I think that many of the French Court, along with Louis, were hoping that a son and heir would soon follow this marriage. The French crown could not, by law, pass to a woman, or through the line of a woman, and so Louis' daughters could not inherit their father's throne. If Louis died without an heir then his throne went to the young François de Valois, Count d'Angoulême, the nearest male relation to Louis. François was married to Louis' daughter, the Princess Claude, perhaps as a way for the old King to ensure his bloodline still reigned after his death. But not-so-secretly we all knew that Louis despaired of the idea of handing his throne to the young, bold and rather licentious François. Louis had apparently said of François: "*this big boy will spoil everything*". Louis was hoping for a son to come from his loins and grow in the belly of the fiery Princess of England. Whilst it was certainly not impossible for an old man to conceive a child with a young pretty princess, the task was not one Mary Tudor warmed to. Although Louis was captivated with her beauty from the first moment he saw her, glowing and beautiful on her horse as she rode into Paris to meet him, the feeling was not reciprocated by the Tudor Princess.

She had had another groom in mind for her hand, even before her marriage to Louis had been decided.

Princesses do not choose their princes, not unless they are very fortunate. And this princess had set her sights on a rather lowly match. Mary Tudor had fallen in love with Charles Brandon, now the Duke of Suffolk and her brother's best friend. This was the same man who had visited the Court of Burgundy with King Henry when I was there, and made a fool of himself over the Regent, Margaret. Whilst Mary Tudor's brother was aware of her feelings for his friend, King Henry was not one to let such a trophy as his beautiful sister throw herself away on a match with a mere English subject. To have his sister installed as the Queen of France was a much better use for her, so away she went; to marry an old man and to bring further glory to the country of England.

So you see; it was not only my father who was happy to use his family to advance his own interests. It was the fate of all nobles and royalty to marry where they were told, not where they desired. Perhaps that is why the history of my life is in many ways so remarkable... for eventually, I was to do just the opposite of what was normal.

I joined the party just after the marriage had taken place; Mary and Louis had been wed by proxy before the Princess had set out to France. In order to make the match legal before the couple had even met, a noble member of the French King's court had symbolically consummated the union. Before witnesses, the Duc de Longueville, the representative of Louis, had climbed into a royal bed with Mary and touched his naked thigh against hers.

Thus was a binding contract of marriage, an allegiance of countries and peoples made, between her thigh and his.

Once I had settled in my apartments that I shared with some other ladies in Mary Tudor's retinue, I sought out my sister. Mary was now sixteen to my fourteen years and in the time that we had been apart she had grown taller and more beautiful. Her figure had filled out; her breasts were ample and on easy display for admirers in her low-cut gown. Her clothing was of the best that our father's money could buy, as were mine, but she wore the English styles which were not as sophisticated as the clothing I had learned to design and make myself at Mechelen. Her gowns were all much lower cut than mine, and I noted that I was not the only one to see this; the young men of the court were most appreciative.

When first we saw each other we rushed together and were breathless in the pleasure of seeing one another again. I saw her eyes travel over the fabric and cut of my dress and I took a little pleasure in seeing envy creep through her clear and wonderful eyes.

"You are so grown!" she said to me as we walked through the beautiful gardens of the court. "You are very elegant, my little sister, and you seem as old as me now, perhaps more so," she said with a giggle.

"At Margaret's court, we were taught so," I replied, smiling at her as I twirled a jewelled ornament on my belt. "We were instructed to walk with elegance, to sing and dance well. I learnt also to design and make my own clothing," I gave a little shrug. "I am no more elegant than all the women who are there, and any elegance you do see is due to the graciousness of the Regent Margaret, not I."

Mary smiled and looked around her. The gardens were full of courtiers wandering and taking the air. "Shall we have much pleasure here, do you think?" she asked with the naughty look

I remembered so well. "There are many handsome men to be found at this court."

"Are *men* the only pleasure to be found then?" I asked with a short laugh. "Then our pleasures shall be short-lived indeed! If all there is to amuse us is the prattling of young gallants then I shall become most jaded!" I raised one of my eyebrows at her. "I shall wish for some dancing, some singing and music; you shall have all the young cockscombs you wish for."

"Oh Anne, I intend to!" she said, and smiled saucily.

Suddenly I understood why the young men looked her over so boldly. There was a promise to Mary, no mystery or challenge... there was within her smile and her way of moving an absolute *promise* of pleasure. She was a sensual creature. In some ways I felt the same within my own blood, but there was something so open about Mary's attention to pleasure, and her desire for it, that it chilled me. There would be no challenge with her, no chase. If Mary liked a man and he liked her, then there would be no obstacle put in his way; he would simply beckon, and she would come running, with her arms and legs open wide.

I seemed to see all this in an instant, and I felt cold. It was as though my older sister did not understand the rules of court life, or the game of courtly love. She did not seem to understand the need to save herself for marriage, the need to *value* her virtue. If there was an opportunity for a liaison with a good-looking man, then she would take it. There was no subtlety; there would be no clever play at the game of courtly love to be the mistress of a man in name but not in practise. Mary was as open in her heart as she was in her words and that was not the way that things were done at court. To become a mistress in the *game* of courtly love was one thing; that was respectable and admirable. To become a mistress in the *true* sense was something else entirely. If that came to happen, it was not accepted publicly unless the man chose to acknowledge his mistress, and that only happened if the man was important and powerful. Even then, the woman would be recognised as morally deficient and earn the disapproval of many. The refusal to allow Jane Popincourt to accompany the Princess Mary was a good example. The men in these affairs, of course, received no censure, or very little. The rules of morality were different for men and women, it seemed. Women suffered in reputation by indulging in the sins of the flesh, whereas men were but considered normal and healthy for doing so. I had learned that there was a value to remaining a maid. Mary, however, seemed to set little store by the rules of morality, or the rules of courtly love.

I would never be that way, I swore then, for at Margaret's court I had learnt to take pride in myself, in my virtue and my accomplishments. I was worth more than to waste myself, my name and my future prospects on a fleeting affair. I was not merely the plaything of any man to be picked up, used and cast away when he wished. My sister's open desire for affairs of the heart left me cold. That was not the life I wished for, for myself.

I had learned well at Margaret's court that the promises of young men are not to be trusted, I wondered if Mary had learnt the same. Soon, I should find that Mary cared as little for the promises of young men as they did. She would pursue a life bent on happiness, and she would pursue it often without reference to or regard for the rest of our family. Although through most of my life I abhorred her selfishness, as I thought it was then, I can see now that perhaps my appealing sister, who sought a life of personal satisfaction and contentment, may well have been the wiser of the two Boleyn daughters.

That first meeting with Mary after almost two years certainly opened my eyes. I had thought that perhaps all women were raised to see the world as I had been at Mechelen, but the houses Mary had lived in had given her different ideas. She had certainly not picked up these thoughts at Hever from our mother; Elizabeth Boleyn would have been entirely shocked with the idea of her daughter speaking so. Mary had formed these ideas somewhere in the time which had passed between our parting and our reunion. But for now I wanted to be happy merely to be with my sister again, no matter how worried her attitude to men made me.

Our father, too, was in the entourage, although I barely saw him between his other responsibilities. When I first came to his rooms, he was busy with papers; the King of England had plenty of work for a useful man such as our father and Thomas Boleyn was advancing well throughout the court circles. He had been appointed ambassador to the Court of France and was handling further negotiations between the slippery King Louis and Henry, King of England.

He, like Mary, looked me over when I arrived. I felt suddenly as I had on the first morning I had met Margaret at Mechelen; that sudden fear that I would be found wanting. But when he had looked me up and down, he grunted in approval, nodding to me, and I was relieved; he was satisfied then with what I looked like and how I held myself. I dressed now in the French fashions, to fit in at court, although I still gave every dress my own twist and style. My hair was gathered under a French hood adorned with simple but beautiful pearls. My velvet dress conformed to the fashions of the French Court, but my richly embroidered sleeves, tended to by my own needlework, were longer and wider at the ends than generally seen, giving my figure an elegance that went beyond my years.

I had started to work on this new style of dress which accentuated all my best features at Mechelen; long-hanging sleeves, which widened at the end, accentuated the slimness of my young waist and the cups of my growing breasts. My clothes were of bright colours that I could carry well, being so dark of hair and pale of skin. I could look exotic in bold colours where pale, fair beauties looked washed out. The insides of my sleeves were red as was the kirtle I wore, which could be seen through a long slit at the front of the dress. My outer gown was a deep, forest green. The confident colours contrasted well with my black hair and set my eyes to seem darker and more sparkling. Golden and silver rings were placed on some of my long fingers, and a golden chain held a little Book of Hours and a pomander at my waist. My complexion was clean and fresh, and I held myself well. I was no true beauty, unlike my sister, but I knew well by this time how to make the best of myself and *seem* like a natural beauty. In my darkness and my dress, I stood out even amongst the many glorious women of the Court of France. I was far more sophisticated in my appearance even than the last time he had seen me.

I saw him look me over and take in all my physical attributes; my father was a man of business, after all, and having a daughter who could make herself seem more beautiful than she was, was a good investment to own. He seemed satisfied with me... on the outside, at least.

So far, so good; I had passed the first test.

Now there would come the testing of my other accomplishments. In some ways I realised that I was an *instrument*, a *tool* that my father wished to use, but this was not as much of a sadness as you might think. My family was important to me and I wished to help in our mutual advancement and greatness. This was partly why my suspicions about Mary's intentions at court were such a worry to me. I did not wish us to be disgraced in any way.

I looked back at my father, wondering if there had been changes in him since the last time I had seen him. His black curling hair had started to grey slightly in strands all over his head, but his hair was still quite dark in general. His face was more worn than when last I saw him, but there was still that grim fire of ambition in his eyes and energy in his movements.

"Duchess Margaret the Regent has spoken well of you," he said, speaking to me in French; it was a test that I recognised immediately. I almost smiled; he would see now how far I had come since Lille.

"The Regent Margaret was ever-gracious and good to me, father." I replied in perfect French. My accent was unimpeachable, impeccable; I might have been a natural born French woman for how fluidly and beautifully I spoke the language now. "I was sad to leave such a gracious sovereign, but grateful to have another opportunity granted to me... by you." I sank to the floor in a graceful curtsy, holding my elegant position with firm poise and grace and looking up at him with sparkling eyes.

Thomas Boleyn smiled; a wide, proud smile, and he laughed shortly. It was like a bark. I rose, and smiled at my father.

"They have taught you well, then." It was a statement and not a question. "You have become an accomplished lady, so Margaret tells me. The Archduchess was most displeased to lose you from her household, which pleases me... It means that you have learnt well. Let us hope that some of that can rub off on your sister," his face darkened slightly.

I knew what my father meant. Beautiful she might be, but Mary was not likely to become a great courtier, as I was perhaps destined to be. I felt pride swelling in my heart and then I was suddenly ashamed of it. I was determined never to crow over my sweet sister as my heart had urged me to then; those feelings were not only un-Christian, but they were also not the attributes of the person I wanted to be.

"What of your music and singing?" my father asked, going back to business. "I heard one performance of your voice, which was pleasing. What of your knowledge of the lute and other instruments?"

Our short meeting was comprised mainly of my stating and briefly performing my varied accomplishments for him. I understood why; he wanted to know how he could use me in our family's advancement. Even if we brought nothing else, Mary and I should attain husbands that were cultured and wealthy. But I am sure our father hoped that we would also bring other uses to him. Having two daughters at the Court of France could be useful, as secret ambassadors, as gatherers of information for English interests, or to bring new contacts and friends to the family. He wanted us married well, but that could wait a while, until he had found the matches he thought were the best we might achieve. In the meantime, he wanted us to reflect glory onto our house and his name. Although I understood all his ambitions, I could not help but feel a little like a horse at market during that brief reunion with my father.

Chapter Eighteen

1514
France

The Court of France was much changed with the arrival of Mary Tudor. She was not one for quiet needle-work and devotions, although she performed those duties with suitable well-played aplomb when they were required of her. She loved more to ride and hunt in the forests by day and to dance through the nights. She was young and beautiful, and as fresh as the spring. The court felt as though it had suddenly had a great jolt from its sleepy existence and now was in a high bustle of activity and excitement. As though some wind had swept through the halls and chambers of the palaces, and swept out all the old ways along with the dust. King Louis did his best to keep up with this young bride who had turned his life upside down, but it was clear from his drawn face at the dances, and his pale visage by days, that this wife was draining the very life from him.

This was, perhaps, just what she intended.

It is hard to blame her, for she was forced to spend the night with this old and smelly man for whom she held no desire. She had to subject herself to the debt of marriage whenever the gouty Louis was able to manage it; hardly a task to strike passion into the heart of a young girl. We maids giggled to see him present her with jewel after jewel to win her favour and affections; each gem was more fabulous than the last. We tittered heartlessly into our sleeves to see Mary prance and twirl with the other men of the court as Louis sat in his chair, unable to dance due to his swollen limbs and crumbling bones. Mary Tudor was exhausting his already tired strength day after day and after a while we all wondered, how long can he last? Does she really seek to tire him out, so that she might be free to marry where her heart led her?

There was a rumour that Mary Tudor had forced a promise from her brother King Henry before she wed Louis; that she would marry dutifully where her brother and King dictated *this* time, but the next time she married, her husband would be of her own choosing. Clearly, Mary Tudor did not believe her first husband would be her last, or her only. I could imagine that our passionate princess was more than capable of making such demands; she had more spirit than many women I had met. Whether her brother had agreed to her terms, or intended to keep any promises he made to her, would have to be seen.

It was an exciting time to join the court. My sister, Mary and I were busy most days helping the Queen, performing the many tasks that were made for the waiting women. We helped her to dress, bathe, and tend to her complexion, we kept her company, attending Mass and prayers with her, dancing with her in her royal chambers, or playing at cards. We were her constant companions on the hunt, or riding in the forests. We were her entourage for court dances, her servers at feasts, and her confidants in privacy. We sewed, made, embroidered and mended parts of her fabulous dresses, admiring the soft and expensive fabrics that Louis had bought for her. We helped her at her toilet and took turns to sleep in her chambers at night so that she was always guarded. We fetched and carried, tidied and cleansed. We were her hands in all the tasks she wished to accomplish. This is the place of a servant to a queen.

As ladies-in-waiting, we had been given shared apartments at first. At Mechelen, I had shared a room with seventeen other *filles* and in the first days in France, our sleeping arrangements were much the same. But I was fortunate enough to be eventually placed in a chamber with just my sister Mary, when we were not called on to stay with the Queen in her chamber. Our standing was higher than mine had been at Mechelen, and with that standing came certain benefits. Sharing a room with many others had not been abhorrent, but it is pleasing to have more privacy. It was a rare thing at court, to ever be truly alone. Mary and I could talk each night of the court, as we rested upon our beds, and we grew closer at this time.

This was also how I knew that my sister was not always in her bed when she should have been.

The first night I discovered this, I awoke having had a bad dream; there was a room in which I sat that overlooked a great palace. The palace had seemed beautiful at first, with great white turrets and gracious gardens, but as I looked closer I saw that the walls were running with bright red blood. Deep, dark red globules of blood gathered in pools around the windows. The walls shone crimson in the sun with the sheen of blood. I cried out and clutched my hand to my face, clawing at my skin and eyes to make the horror disappear. But instead, my clawing fingers tore delicate, paper-like skin from my face. I screamed; turning to a mirror I saw in the place of my own face a skull staring back at me. I fell to the cold floor, crying, hysterical, grasping at the bits of skin that I had torn from my face as they floated away from me on a light breeze. The walls of the room were now running with my own blood, seeming to come forth from my veins without show of injury, just flowing from my skin. I tried to stick my skin back on my face, but it would not stay. I tried to stop the flow of blood from my skin but I could not. As I fainted to the ground, my head bounced off the hard stone floor.

In my dream I heard the laugh of a woman, shrill and shrieking, sound about me, as I passed into unconsciousness.

I awoke with a start from that terrible dream to find my sister sneaking into the chamber. Her gown was awry, her hood in her hands and her face was flushed. There were red marks on her pale skin about her shoulders and neck. My first thought was that she had been attacked, and I rushed out of bed to her side. Then I saw the look of sated pleasure on her face and smelt the smell of sweat and something sour I did not recognise on her body, and her breath. She smiled languidly at me, and pressed a finger to her lips. It was then I knew that she had been with a lover.

"Where have you been?" I cried, my voice not under control, mostly due to the dream I had just had, but partly because I was shocked to see her thus.

"Shush!" she said, looking about her with fear in her voice. Then she giggled softly and ruffled her shoulders at me. "I have been out dealing with important matters of state." Mary smiled again. Her sensual lips curled up at one side and her loose hair fell over her face; she was very attractive in this dissembled manner. "Or, at least," she said saucily, "dealing with *one* important matter of state."

Mary began climbing into bed and winced visibly as she closed her legs together. She turned her head to me and smiled again... Her lover had obviously been rough with her, but it did not seem as though she was unhappy with this. She sighed happily once she was comfortable.

"Who?" I asked, my voice full of shock.

"Why? So you can run and tell our father?" she asked, laughing. "Not a sinner's chance in hell do you have of me telling you this, Anne. I saw the prudish way you looked at me just then, and if you don't want to join in the diversions of court then leave me to enjoy them."

She lay in bed, staring at the ceiling, smiling softly. I climbed back into bed; the chamber was not warm enough to stand around in one's nightgown.

"What if you are found out? What if there is a child?" I whispered.

She sighed, my questions taking her from her memories of her lover. "There are ways and means around all things, little sister. You think *you* have all the learning from your stay at

Mechelen, but there are things that *I* have learnt too, like how to prevent a babe being born when one is not wanted. The offices of Mistress Rue and Juniper are not only those our mother taught to us, you know. Now," she said with purpose. She leant over in bed and propped her chin on her hand as she spoke to me.

"Our father needs to know nothing of this; eventually I shall marry like a good daughter to provide him with noble grandchildren and many means of furthering our family. I shall be dutiful and obedient. I shall be a humble and good wife to whomsoever he chooses to buy my hand. But before I am sold off to the highest bidder, I mean to have a little life, a little *excitement* before I must settle and marry where I am ordered. There are plenty at this court who do as I do; men and women alike. As long as father does not know, then it does not matter. Do you not wish for a little diversion too? Just look around you, everyone is doing it. There is no reason why we should not *each* have a little excitement here, is there?" She eyed me speculatively with a wanton face; she looked beautiful and somewhat dangerous to me.

"I can think of reasons," I said, feeling my heart sink as she talked, and feeling anger at her. Partly I think I was jealous of her wild recklessness, but partly I was also shocked that she would stray so far from all that I had been taught was right by Margaret in Mechelen. I could feel disaster threatening my sister, and she would do nothing to stop it. Keeping something like this quiet and out of the ears of our father, I was sure, would not be as easy as my sister thought. I sat up too and looked at her.

"You do as you wish Mary; our father shall hear nothing from me, but leave me from any hint of inclusion in your pleasures. This is not the way I have been taught to behave. The risks are so great, Mary! Too great! I do not wish to give birth to a bastard, to be sent home in disgrace, to have all men know me for an idle plaything, to have my chances at a high match in marriage damaged for an hour's idle pleasure. You do as you wish, but I shall do as I wish also. My honour will remain intact until I marry."

Mary laughed at me. "Your *honour* shall remain intact?" she mocked. "Do you think that any truly have their *honour* intact when they come to the bed of their spouse? If there are any who come so, they are few and far between. Come, sister, do not be so naïve. Life is for taking pleasure where one can find it. Who knows what your husband might be like? If our father has his way then we shall find ourselves married to very old, very rich men. And most likely our father will choose a *succession* of old rich men for us to marry, who we will have to submit to and then outlive. The wealth and treasures of our dowager lands will flow into our father's coffers, as he sells us off to another and another, bearing children for as many as we are able before we come to our deaths at last. If you do not take pleasure in life now, then you may never have another chance."

She smiled, and lay on her bed shaking her head at me. "If the rest of my life is owned by my father, and I end up saddled with a husband I love not, at least in my long evenings by the fire, I might stare into the flames and remember what passion once was mine, what freedom was once mine." She looked up at my grave, pale face and laughed lightly again. "But by all means, Anne, keep hold of your *honour*. I am sure when you lie in your marriage bed suffocated under the weight of an old fat man, it will be of great comfort to you to know that you were always *honourable*."

I lay down in the bed and felt anger flow through my veins, for a part of me knew that she was right. Most likely my fate *would* be to be married off to some old man I had no love for, much like our mistress Mary Tudor. A part of me almost wished to take my sister's offer, and run wild with the men of the court, too; there was a freedom in Mary that I envied. But at the same time, I did not wish to, no matter how much she made fun of me. I had learned from Margaret that there was great danger in a woman offering herself so lightly. I could not help but believe that all would go wrong for Mary here. And time proved me right.

Eventually the strain of having the young, vigorous Mary Tudor as a wife, combined the long years that he had lived, overtook Louis, and on the first day of 1515, in the midst of a great storm which battered the royal palace, he left life behind. His wife was not unhappy; I believe she felt some remorse in perhaps being responsible for hastening his end, but in true Tudor style she was more than able to push unpleasant thoughts to the back of her mind. We could already see her thinking on the happy times ahead, when she might be able to marry where she wanted. Before Louis was cool in his bed, I think she had already made her mind up on the subject of her next marriage.

When Louis died, as was the custom, Mary Tudor entered a world of seclusion in which she was to mourn in a stately fashion for her departed husband. This time was also used to check whether the Queen was carrying the dead King's heir in her belly. Although we were all quite sure that this was impossible, the rituals of royalty had to be observed. Mary may have hastened his end, but she would give all the show of a woman in the clutches of grief to the world; to do any less would show a terrible and un-Christian lack of respect.

So Mary entered her secluded world, dressed in purest white, the colour of mourning for French royalty. We, her maids, were allowed out and around the court in a modest fashion if our duties required it, but the Dowager Queen remained in her closed apartments, awaiting the time when she could leave and choose her new husband for herself.

It was around this time that Charles Brandon came to France. He had been sent by the King of England to negotiate the return of Mary's dowry; those properties and monies that had accompanied her to France. As a widow, those goods were now entitled to return to her family. Brandon was also sent to escort Mary home safely, once her time of mourning was finished. As it turned out, Mary had plans of her own for Brandon which were not quite as her brother might have imagined.

Mary was having serious doubts as to the worth of her brother's promise regarding her next choice in marriage. Stricken with fear upon hearing rumours that Henry intended to marry her off to a prince of the Hapsburgs, she took quick action. Enlisting the help of the new King, François, she laid her plans well.

Charles Brandon was a man of much physical strength but little wit or sense; Mary needed a husband as quickly as possible, and she had always desired Brandon, loved him even. Though I have not spoken of him very highly, I will tell you he was an attractive man. He was also rather malleable, which might have interested Mary; having a husband she could control was something she clearly had enjoyed in Louis. Mary seemed certain that if she could persuade Brandon to marry her, then eventually Henry would forgive them. Once she was married, there was no way her brother could send her off to another foreign match. She would be safe, and she could remain in the country of her birth, a privilege afforded to few royal women.

Mary was no fool in the games and arts of allurement, but she had help. François perhaps enjoyed the idea of flummoxing his neighbour King Henry almost as much as the romantic idea of aiding a beautiful princess in distress. He was happy to help the pair. Brandon, so easily led and impressionable, was perhaps already genuinely in love with Mary. He certainly must have been attracted to her, since all men were, but upon his arrival he was beset with an onslaught of her affections and love, with her weeping for fear of being sent once more to marry where she did not wish to, and their clandestine meetings were obtained in secret with the good will and help of the new French King. The Duke did not stand a chance. Like a knight in a romance, he was convinced to sweep in to rescue the Princess from a life of ugly husbands and loveless marriages… But in truth, if any one person was wearing the armour and carrying a sword in this tale, it was Mary Tudor. She was in control of this match, and she had all others dance to her tune.

Before he knew it, or had time to think on the dangers of such an imprudent match, Brandon found himself wedded, and bedded, with the slippery little Tudor Princess, thereby making it impossible to separate the pair but by death. As we all watched Mary wrap her beloved around her finger like a pretty ribbon, we took some time to wonder if she would have much time to enjoy that handsome face when they returned to England. King Henry might well have decided to separate the new groom's head from his shoulders; marrying a member of the royal family without permission from the King was an act of treason. The public feeling of the people of England was no less disapproving, as later, we would come to hear lines of verse which came from England to tickle our amusement concerning the match between Mary, the 'cloth of gold', and the upstart Brandon, the 'cloth of frieze':

Cloth of gold do not despise
Though thou be matched with cloth of frieze;
Cloth of frieze be not too bold
Though thou be matched with cloth of gold.

Mary seemed to think she could charm her brother into forgiveness for her rebellious act. The King of England, however, was simply furious to find that his sister, a precious bargaining chip in any foreign relations, had been married in secret to his best friend. Many of his councillors, particularly those of my family, the Howards, urged the King to have the Duke arrested and executed for treason. But Cardinal Wolsey, the King's greatest advisor, intervened for the couple, and thanks to this and to Henry's love for his sister and friend, they were forgiven… though not without a price. They had to pay the King a massive fine for marrying without permission, one that had to be paid in instalments, for it was so vast. Mary had to surrender to her brother all the jewels and plate she had accumulated in her marriage to Louis, and Brandon had to give up a rich ward to the King. When all this was agreed, the couple were allowed home to England, and were re-married once more before the English Court. François was not very happy when he asked Mary to return the 'Mirror of Naples', the hereditary property of the French Queens, and found that the wily Princess had sent it to her livid brother to help mitigate his fury. Henry would not return the jewel, and to the anger of his French counter-part, wore it openly on many state occasions.

When the time came for them to sail for home, Mary's face wore the expression of a satisfied cat at a fish market. Brandon's face, however, had a faintly puzzled look about it, as though he had put something down and forgotten where he placed it. All that had happened in the short time he had been in France had clearly been too fast for the Duke. I laughed to see the game that Mary had played with him; I thought Brandon a complete fool then, even more so than I had thought when he was at the Court of Burgundy, and my opinion of him did not get much better later on, either.

Whilst the marriage of Mary and Brandon might not have started auspiciously, theirs was a happy marriage, as marriages go. They had children and seemed to enjoy each other's company. Brandon took mistresses as most men do, but Mary ignored them, knowing her place was never at risk from his petty liaisons. In many ways, because she married beneath her station in life, she was always his social superior. When they were allowed to return to the English Court, she was always titled "The Dowager Queen of France" whereas Brandon would only ever be Duke of Suffolk. It must have been soothing to her pride to remember she outranked him. As the little verse said, she would always be the 'cloth of gold' to Brandon's 'cloth of frieze'.

Later in life, Mary Tudor came to despise me as an upstart, much to the appeal of irony, since she herself had married one; but in those days when I was her lady she was a kind enough mistress. Our troubles with each other came later. It can be unnerving for those in power to see others start lower than they and rise higher. It makes them uncomfortable and afraid.

But I am running ahead of myself, for there were other events in those first months of François' reign that shook me much more than the games of my mistress the Queen Dowager and her attainment of a husband.

These events concerned my sister.

It was during the time of François' ascension to the throne; Mary Tudor was at this time still voluntarily imprisoned in her mourning chambers, and my sister Mary and I were waiting upon her daily with her other attendants. One of our primary duties to her in those days of mourning was to keep her entertained. It is very dull waiting out months of official mourning in seclusion. If she had actually grieved for Louis then it would have been different; those months would have been spent with her heart aching for his loss and her mind finding ways to carry on without him. But she had not loved him, and therefore the waiting was dull, heavy and tedious.

We could not dance. We must wear insipid, plain colours. We played cards although strictly we were not supposed to, and we sewed altar clothes and clothes for the poor. I loved needle-work and was good at it; there is a certain type of concentration that the art requires which is soothing to the soul. I was, however, almost fifteen now, and although needle-work was one of my duties and not wholly unpleasant in itself, after weeks of it I was quite prepared to never lift another needle or measure another thread.

Life was becoming dull for us just when the rest of the court was becoming lively. François was a young, virile and engaging king; he loved to dance and to hunt, he loved art and music. Although François, too, was meant to be mourning Louis, there were suddenly a lot more entertainments occurring at court, and we were not in attendance. Mary and I found it most frustrating.

Hovering over us was also the question of what would now become of our positions when Mary Tudor returned home. My sister longed for England, but I still hoped that I might return to Mechelen. Although I had been away from England and the rest of my family for over two years now, I felt no desire to return. The Court of Burgundy was more familiar to me, it felt more like home. The Court of England could not be as grand as those I had seen now on the continent, and I was still learning so much. I did not want to return to that grey land over the waters, I wanted to see more of the world.

The new queen, Claude of France, came on occasion to Mary's mourning rooms. Claude was about the same age as I, a little older perhaps, and she had married François about a year before the death of her father. Claude was already pregnant, to François' delight, and her great belly swelled before her, making her rather ungainly. Claude was a plain-looking, rather stout young woman; she walked with a slight limp that had been with her since birth, and her body was twisted slightly, which meant she was unable to ride much or to hunt or dance. Claude was quiet and modest and seemed to have made up for her physical plainness by being especially attractive in character. She did many good works, she loved art and sculpture, she carried out her duties as the Queen and, later, as a mother, with dignity, love and grace. She turned a blind eye to all of François' affairs and was civil and attentive to his mistresses and to those courtiers to whom he showed favour. Claude was every inch a queen, raised to be one, born to be one. The people loved her, loved her for her deformities as much as for her kindness to them. Both my sister and Mary Tudor thought her awfully dull, but I rather liked her; she needed no one's approval although many were happy to give it, and she seemed as though she regarded the schemes of the courtiers as the innocent games of children. She appeared much older than my mistress Mary Tudor, and far older than I, even though we were almost of an age.

In my duties to the dowager Queen Mary, I often found myself serving Claude, too, and she noted my deftness and ability around the chambers with satisfaction. My sister, however, was less adept at her duties and often incurred a frown from Claude, which was the closest thing she had to anger in her.

But it was displeasure of my sister's activities from another source that was soon to bring a storm to our little world at the French Court.

Chapter Nineteen

France
1515

It was one afternoon when I was wandering in the gardens, enjoying the few times of exercise that we in the mourning chambers were allowed to take, when a lady-in-waiting to Queen Claude found me. She grabbed my arm with urgency as I was wandering past, and whispered to me that I must attend to my father's rooms immediately. I had met this lady when Claude had visited Mary. She was generally quite calm and dignified. From the look upon her face this afternoon, however, I gathered that something dreadful was about to happen, or had already happened. My father had a way of terrifying people.

I hurried to his fine chambers in the court circle. He was an ambassador and was kept in good state. Upon being ushered into his chambers by a rather frightened looking page, I found a strange scene before my eyes. My father stood, tall and terrible in the centre of the room; his dark eyes were black mirrors of coldness and his hands were clenched by his sides. There was a feeling in the air that he was fighting hard to restrain himself. My father had been a soldier and was an expert jouster; it felt as though he was reining himself in before flying at an opponent in war... As though he meant to kill someone.

Looking around, he saw me enter and his brow furrowed and darkened. I curtseyed to him and he laughed; it was not a pleasant laugh, but one filled with animosity and rage. Mary stood before him, terrified; her hands twitching at her sides, clutching at the folds of her pretty crimson dress. Her face was ugly with tears, and she choked as I walked in the room, looking at me with a horrible, pleading desperation, as though

I might have come to save her. Her eyes were wild, and she plucked at her dress as though a hole in it might provide some sort of magical escape route from the menacing man that stood before us. She looked ready to run, like a hind poised at the edge of a forest who sees the coming of the hunters. I had never seen my father angry, not like this. Usually he was cold and distant, controlled. Now he was a mountain of fire waiting to explode. My heart suddenly came to beat hard in my chest as though it meant to burst free from my body. I was scared. I stopped where I was, frightened to move any further into the room.

"Come here," my father said, with an awful coldness in his voice.

I walked forwards slowly. I was no fool; he knew about Mary's adventures at night. There could be no other reason for such rage to be within him. We had done nothing else which was capable of arousing such fury in our father. I was cautious, fearing his rage. My feet wanted to run. I made them stay where they were, steeling my heart to find courage.

He turned and gave me a twisted smile. "Did you know that your sister is a great *whore*?" he asked, noting with satisfaction that Mary flinched as he spoke. His voice was strange; it had a false lightness about it which I did not trust.

"The whole court but I knew of it, apparently," he continued in an almost conversational tone. "I have heard that she is a pretty mare; swinging her hair, and opening her filthy legs as far as she can, so that anyone and everyone who cares to ride her are able to."

He turned to me, looking into my eyes. I felt my skin tremble. I felt as though I could not swallow, could not talk. I looked at Mary, my terrified eyes meeting her swollen, tear-filled ones. Mary shook her head at me, behind our father's back. She must have tried to deny the accusation. I tried to think of what I should say to tame our father's temper, to diffuse the situation. But words did not come to me easily that day. My mind seemed to have gone blank.

"Did *you* know that your sister is a great whore?" he repeated coldly to me.

I was unsure of what to say, not wishing to insult my sister and not wishing to further anger my father. My mouth opened and then closed again. I could feel the blood draining from my cheeks.

"*Did you know that your sister is a great whore*?!" He shouted, advancing on me like a leopard rushing its prey. I stepped back in fright, my hands raised before my face, for I feared he would strike me. Mary sprung forwards, clutching at his arm.

"*Please Father, please!*" she pleaded, grabbling at him hysterically. I believe that she also thought he was about to strike me, and was seeking to protect me from him. But instead he turned to her. Suddenly, viciously, our father grabbed at Mary's dress; his hands were like claws as he ripped at her gown, shaking her, slapping at her face. He seemed to have lost all control. He yanked the front of her gown open to reveal her undergarments and her breasts. Mary screamed under the viciousness of his attack, and grappled with him, suddenly looking as though she were fighting for her virtue against one who would rape or kill her. Our father was incoherent with rage, stuttering at Mary in furious anger as he shook her and tore at her clothing.

"*Whore!*" he shouted, spitting the words in her face. "*Jade! Strumpet! Doxy!* Show off your wares, Mary! You don't want to miss a customer!" He grasped her by the shoulder with one hand, slapping his other palm over and over against her cheek; the noise of his hand on her skin made a great cracking noise through the chamber. Mary screamed and sobbed, but she could not move from his grasp, although she struggled against him, shrieking and crying, her hands flailing in front of her face.

I panicked, not knowing what to do; I threw myself at my father, grabbing at the backs of his arms, trying to pull his hands from Mary. With a strength that Mary and I did not possess, he shook me off, jutting his elbow into my middle and causing my breath to rush painfully from me. I fell to the floor, my arm bouncing painfully from the stone slabs under the scented rushes. I lay on the floor as I struggled to regain my breath. He slapped Mary again about the face, and then flung her, as though she were but a rag-doll, hard across the room. Mary wheeled and skidded on the rush-covered floors of his chamber and hit the fireplace with the side of her head.

She gave a short and soft grunt of surprise as her head cracked against the fireplace, and fell to the floor in a great heap.

Then she was still.

"*Mary*!" I screamed, my voice hoarse in my throat, scrambling along the floor to her side. I turned her over into my lap. For a moment I thought she was dead. Blood stained the marble of the fireplace and was running in a grotesque stream down her beautiful face. I pawed at my sister desperately, seeking for a sign of life as I cried over her, my tears falling, mingling with her blood. Then she moaned softly, her eyes opening, and relief flooded through me. The side of her face ran with blood and a large, ugly bruise of yellow and purple had started to appear on the delicate skin of her temple beside the red marks where our father had slapped her. She was white as a frozen pond and trembled in my arms as she awoke. Her dress was ripped and her breasts and chest were exposed. She looked down on her dress and flushed with shame; her hands shook as she tried to hold her dress together. She was crying quietly; saliva ran from her mouth where there was a small but deep cut, making her look as though her mouth was twisted in a terrible smile.

It was as though she had been ravaged by some beast. But this was done by our father.

I stared up at my father in horror and saw him staring down at us with nothing but disgust in his face.

"There, in the dirt, is where you belong, Mary," he said slowly, his characteristic coldness and control once again back in his voice and in his manner. "Why, you are even *dressed* for whoring now, with your filthy dukkys hanging out." He sniffed and re-arranged his doublet; Mary and I had pulled at it in the struggle and left him in disarray. "We shall have to get you a yellow cap, Mary, so that you can sell your wares at Southwick and at the Docks; then you'll turn us a pretty penny."

His lips curled in disgust as he looked on his crumpled, crying daughter. "Is that how you imagine you will turn the fortunes of this family? Through the pennies thrown at you in the gutters? Shall we shave your head and parade you through the town like you deserve, you *dirty little whore*?"

Mary flinched at his words as I held my dress to her bleeding head; there was a lot of blood seeping through the fine velvet cloth of my gown. Mary stared slack-jawed at our father as I did. Both of us appeared to have become like the marble statues of the palace. I had never known him to possess such ability for violence, not towards us. He was terrifying in his rage. I knew not what he might do next.

He turned to me. "Did you *know* that *your* sister is a great whore?" he asked again. This time it was careful and measured and cold. I nodded dumbly at him and instantly hated myself for betraying my sister, but I was afraid to say other than the truth to our father then. I did not want him to attack either of us again.

He turned his gaze to Mary. "Is *your* sister a great whore as well?" he asked her.

Mary shook her head and fresh, humiliated tears sprang from her eyes. "No" she croaked, "she is not."

Our father stared at us. "That had better be the truth," he said. In unison, Mary and I nodded our heads.

He breathed in, and then released a large sigh through his nose. "At least that is something, although it seems I have two daughters who are liars and one who is a *wanton whore*." He went over to his desk and turned from us.

"This will be the last thing that you ever seek to keep from me, Anne," he said calmly. "If I ever find you keeping anything from me again, lying to me, or that you have been up to the same tricks as your sister, then I shall do far worse to you than I have done to her, do you understand me? For then you will have betrayed me twice." He turned around and I nodded at him. Mary was clutching the sleeve of my gown as though I was a raft in a great ocean.

"You, Mary, will be sent back to England with the Dowager Queen Mary. Nothing shall be said of this between us. I believe that your reputation has already been ruined by your whoring, so we will have to act fast to reclaim anything we can of this situation. I shall arrange to marry you off as soon as I can to whatever poor fool will have you. Hopefully he will not know what type of disgusting baggage he is bringing to his bed, nor what foul poxes she may give him from her past career as a mare for all to ride. As for you, Anne…" I looked up at my father feeling my heart freeze within my chest. "You will enter the house of Claude, Queen of France, upon leaving the service of the Dowager. Claude has asked for an English translator to help her in her role as Queen, and has accepted you upon my recommendation. Let us hope that Claude will learn nothing of your sister's whoring with her husband, or she may feel less generous towards you. To both of you, if you ever disgrace me or this family again, I shall make you pay for it."

Our father's face seemed to darken like that of a demon and he walked towards us again. "If you betray my trust again, then I promise I shall find men to be your husbands of the worst kind possible; men who would force you in your own beds and beat you every night. Men to bring you home diseases from prostitutes that will eat your bones and decay your insides. You would never enter the courts again, but stay in foul and isolated country houses bearing child after child until death," he sighed, shaking his head at us. "I have worked long and hard for this family. You will not be the ones to ruin that for me. Now get out."

He turned to me again almost as an afterthought. "Anne... do not let anyone see your sister in that state," he said, and then he turned and walked from the chamber.

As soon as he had left we hastened to get out, too. I pulled Mary into an adjoining chamber to clean her wound and re-dress her. She was stumbling, crying and incoherent in her speech. As best I could, I cleaned her wound with wine and water, we pulled her hair a little more from her hood to try and cover the bruise. There were some ointments and cosmetics in our chamber that I knew we could use once we got back there. We could cover up the red marks on her skin with paint and powder, such as the older women of court used and she could wear a gable hood about the court to hide the worst of her bruise. But I needed to get her back to our chambers without anyone seeing her like this. If she was seen in this state then it would not do any good for her reputation, or for mitigating the furious anger of our father.

For now I sought to dress her again. Our father had torn her gown and kirtle, and ripped the ribbon-holes and the hooks for pins, but there was enough there to patch together a semblance of modesty. Whispering words of comfort to her, I urged her to hurry. We hastened through the back passages and corridors usually used only by servants. We raced past servants who looked on our presence there with interest, but happily without comment, and soon found ourselves safely back in our rooms. We would soon be late for our duties to Mary Tudor, but Mary was in no state to go as she was. I must say she was sick. Once I had dressed her cut and applied angelica ointment to her wounds, I put her into bed and placed a cup of wine at her side. Mary was still crying and shaking, curled up in her bed. I promised her I would be back as soon as I could.

Mary Tudor was concerned about my sister's illness. I convinced my mistress it was not serious enough to send a doctor, whilst managing to make it serious enough that missing her evening duties was required. The court was turning me into an accomplished and consummate liar. In practise it mattered little that Mary was absent, as I was more than capable of doing both her duties and mine; I was more useful and adroit in the chambers of royalty than my sister.

Once I had completed my evening's tasks for Mary Tudor and she was settled with her French attendants for the night, playing cards, I hurried back to our chambers. Mary was sitting in the little window seat, staring out at the great gardens lit in the half-moon's light. It was beautiful here in this palace. The knot gardens that Louis had worked so hard to maintain were symmetrical and measured, so that nature was tamed, controlled and bent to the will of man. The sheltered coves and crannies where one could shade oneself from the dangerous rays of the sun were hidden amongst the lilies and roses. Mary's eyes wandered over the gardens and out to the city beyond. Her lovely brown eyes were serious and speculative this night. She turned and nodded to me as I came in. She appeared, to my relief, to be over the worst of her fright from our father's attack on her.

"How did he find out?" I asked, pouring some ale from the tankard on the table and handing her a cup. I poured one for myself also and sat on my bed.

"Brandon made a jest within our father's hearing," she said. "He repeated that François called me his *"little English mare"* because he *"rode me so often"*. She shrugged a little. "I didn't know François called me such names," she said sadly.

"François!" I exclaimed slightly. I had not been aware who it was that my sister had been bedding until now. I realized our father had mentioned something of it as he shouted at us, but at the time I had been too scared to take much note.

"Yes... he has great charm," she said smiling. "And he taught me many things. He talked to me often of wonders. He loves humanism and art and music. He is a great man."

She paused; her look of admiration fell from her face suddenly as she continued. "But perhaps he only pretends to be a great man. After all, there is no knight who would say such things of one he truly loved, is there?" Mary seemed pensive once again.

"There were others, too..." she said staring from the window. "François was not the only lover I took. He tired of me quickly, but there were others who liked me well enough..." she trailed off, looking at the stars. "But the King was the best of them, in more ways than one."

I sighed, feeling too weary to absorb much more shock than I had done already this day. "You are too generous, Mary," I said. "You think that everyone is like you, that everyone is looking for love and happiness. Some are not..." my face darkened. "It seems to me that most are not. They want only what they can get. Love does not come into it."

"Yes," she nodded softly, and then turned to me with a little smile. "But perhaps the husband I will now have will not be so bad? Our father threatens me with horror... but would he really give up a chance of a grand marriage and alliance with a great family just to spite me? I think not; he will marry me as high as he can, and who knows?" She smiled wider, looking happier. "Perhaps this husband will be good to me... Perhaps he will be handsome."

Mary drained her cup and looked at me. "My elegant little sister," she said. "You have always been cleverer than I, so perhaps you will do better than I have."

"Perhaps, perhaps not," I replied. "I have wished sometimes that I had your freedom. But I do not feel as though men can be trusted, even when they say they love you."

Mary snorted slightly. "Well, I am not sure either now, when their mouths say one thing in private, but something else to their friends... But let not my experience prevent you from having pleasure, from having love, if you want it. They are useful for some things, you know." She smiled again, that old naughty smile I remembered so well. Mary's spirit was fighting back.

"I have had such pleasure that I would you could try, too," she said and then grimaced, touching her head where the cut throbbed with the pulse of her blood. "Although... Perhaps I had better seek to find that pleasure in the marriage bed now, eh?" We both laughed a little; it was more from relief that the encounter with our father was over, and that we had survived, than from real humour.

Mary left France soon after that with Mary Tudor and her new husband Brandon. I remained in France, with Queen Claude. I don't know if she ever did know of my sister's encounters with her husband, but if she cared or not or knew or not, Claude never breathed a word of knowledge to me on the matter. My father stayed on at the court for some time, sending for me but rarely, until he, too, sailed for England to arrange a match for his eldest daughter. He did not speak of Mary or of that terrible day to me again.

My sister was to go on to other adventures, but I never forgot that night. Although Mary and I were sisters, there were so many differences between our two characters. But she was my only sister. She was my blood. Whatever else she was and whatever anyone called her, she was always my sweet sister. Too generous in her love to hold it back, too honest in herself to ever change her true nature.

And I loved her, even though we were so very different.

Chapter Twenty

1515-1516
France

I entered the service of Queen Claude when my duties to Mary Tudor had ended. Claude's household was housed separately to François' and was quite different to his. Although later on, people would say that I had been an active and enthusiastic part of the most scandalous court in history, the court of Queen Claude was somewhat different, somewhat distant, and vastly more modest than that of her husband. Claude's court was filled with poetry and music, with devotional works and art. It was akin to the court of Margaret at Mechelen, although not quite as sparkling. François' court was filled with diversions. He was a modern man and had a great interest in and enthusiasm for religion, beauty and art, but his court was also filled with a great licentiousness of behaviour in both women and men that was led by the King himself through example. The King loved the beautiful in life, and encouraged his gallants to follow his example in enjoying both artistic beauty and female beauties. He saw women as wonderful adornments to the gracefulness of his court and on occasion bought costly dresses in the newest fashions to be handed out to his wife's ladies, especially on state occasions.

The two households of the King and Queen met and visited each other of course, and were as one court for entertainments and feasts. We were one court for public occasions, and for many of the duties of court life. But in truth, we were separate for much of the time. Claude's household was centred in the upper Loire, at Amboise and Blois. A lot of our time was spent in reading, praying, sewing for the Church and the poor, writing verse in the gardens and dancing with each other in the evenings; practising for the next courtly entertainment where we could demonstrate our talents. There were men in Claude's court, of course; all of the senior posts in her household were held by men, and there were courtiers who came to Claude in search of patronage and support. With these courtiers we would enter into the games of courtly love, all under Claude's guiding hands and watchful eyes. Our behaviour was always to be of the highest morality; our honour could not come into question.

Claude's court was as modest and as cultured as Margaret's, and I was content and stimulated there. After Mary's disgrace, it was soothing to enter a world where I felt I understood the rules once more. Claude and her husband had a stable and, it did seem, genuinely affectionate marriage. I don't know if in truth they loved each other, but they were good friends. She never expected him to be faithful to her and never mentioned his various and numerous indiscretions. She pleased him by doing this and with her like-minded affection for arts and cultured ideas. She remained almost perpetually pregnant and gave him many sons and daughters. They were polite and happy in each other's' company, but also she was perfectly content to rule her own court and life herself, not often interfering with politics of the country. It was a good marriage and a good life, and it worked for them. Claude was the same age as I, but somehow she seemed older, wise beyond her years. I learnt many things from her, but I never managed to learn her self-control; there were never cross words from Claude. When she showed displeasure it was only through brief looks that indicated disapproval, and that was always enough to stop whatever it was that displeased her from happening again. I have wished many times that I had her control. I never managed to cool my hot temper, never really managed to think before I lashed out when I was angry. She was a better woman than I, and I never had a gentler mistress or a kinder friend than this humble, good lady who was also the Queen of a great land.

Claude loved art and was especially fond of miniature paintings and portraits; her mother had also been fond of this art form. It was in Claude's household that I first had my portrait painted; at first I sat for a normal portrait, and then for a miniature, which she kept of me when I eventually left her service.

In 1516, the aged and renowned artist, Leonardo Da Vinci came from Italy to Cloux to retire at François' request and expense. François was anxious that his court be seen as the centre of beauty and arts in the world, and enticing the great Leonardo to his lands was part of that plan along with great new buildings, sculptures and apartments at court, all done in antique fashion to emulate the classical cultures of Rome and Greece. But despite accepting the offer of a comfortable life in France, Leonardo was not interested in a life at the court itself; he liked not the rush and the clamour of courtly life. When he came, François gave him his own residence, and came to visit him often. From here, the old artist, and some said genius, was to spend his time living at the expense of François, creating, painting and drawing. It was a happy retirement, I think. He was housed near enough to Claude's court that we could visit him often.

Claude visited Leonardo frequently; partly because she admired his beautiful mind and partly because to her, he was an old man first and foremost, alone and perhaps tired of the world. Claude was a kind and good woman who would not leave an old man to loneliness. I believe the two of them became good friends and she often returned from these trips both elated and saddened.

"It is sad that such greatness should eventually be lost to us, but he is so old that it will be a blessing to him to return to God," she said one day when she returned from visiting him. I think she found her visits both interesting and sorrowful, for she came to love Leonardo during his time in France, but knew that he would not be long for this life.

I would often accompany Claude to the house of Leonardo; we would sit in the beautiful rooms that François had chosen for him, and I would play on the lute, or sing softly as Claude and Leonardo talked. The great man rarely said anything to me or the other ladies, but he seemed to take pleasure in my voice. He was a great musician himself. The first day I came into his house, he spent a great deal of time staring at me, which I found strange. It was not that I was not used to men looking at me, but the unhidden manner in which he chose to stare at me was unusual if not a little unnerving. Claude smiled when I mentioned this to her. "When he sees a person with an interesting face, he does this," she said and touched my cheek. "It must be your eyes that catch his interest. Do not be worried, it is just his way. It is the interest of an artist, of a painter, and nothing more."

His presence was usually a soft and gentle one. There was great calmness in him, but he could easily become distracted and drift into his own world, becoming lost in his thoughts. There were days when he would lock himself in his workrooms, beating new ideas from his mind in furious bouts of energy. But when he met with us, he was more often languid and tranquil. Old men often become lost in their thoughts, but there was a sense with Leonardo that, when he was distracted, it was his genius mind that had taken hold of him, rather than the weak and doddering mind of an old and increasingly feeble man.

His house was filled with his works. His workrooms overflowed with sketches, maps and drawings; tables and tables of paper with diverse things drawn on them. Many pages written in what looked like a strange language, but in fact they were written in Italian or French in a 'mirror' fashion, starting from the right side of the parchment, and moving to the left. It seemed that these notes were intended for his own reading, for he wrote normally when the paper was intended to be read by another. There were so many ideas on those pages... It was as though his mind could imagine anything and everything; how a man might one day come to fly, the inner workings of the body, the beauty of the human form, machines made for counting, the make-up of plants and strange creations made for war. There was nothing above or below his intellect. There was nothing he was not interested in. He also would eat no meat, and sent his servants to the market place to buy caged birds, which he would then release into the skies of the estate François had given him.

I marvelled at a mind such as his; whilst he seemed so calm on the outside, his mind was ever-working, always running over a new thought or idea. I could not imagine what it must be like to have such a restless imagination. I imagine when Leonardo dreamed, he dreamed the thoughts of God.

Many of his works were brought to France with him, and François proudly displayed them at court. We were taken to court events to view these works; there was nothing like them, nothing I saw before or after that could compare to the brilliance of his paintings. I could tell you of the colours, could tell you of the pearl-cream complexion of his *Madonna and Child*, tell you of greens and blues, of yellows and gold and red. I could tell you of the wonder as your eyes opened onto his paintings to see people who looked as though they could walk from the frames of gold into the world of man. But none of that would ever tell you of the true experience of seeing his works. There was silence in the chambers where his pictures were displayed, because words became lost to all who looked on them. Spell-bound and breathless, I would look on his works with glittering eyes and wordless mouth. I felt as though I had come into the presence of God when I looked on these works. There is no other way to explain the awe that struck me dumb before the strokes of his brush. God had placed his hand next to that of his child Leonardo, and through his works, it was as though we could understand the beauty of the mind of God.

Leonardo was as much a holy man to me as any priest, more so than some who claimed to be holy, but in practise were not. Many in his lifetime, I believe, had thought him capable of evil, but I did not see that as the truth. No man who painted as he did could be capable of real evil. He did not even eat flesh or fish. He was like a monk; his workrooms were his Church, and his brushstrokes were the prayers he offered daily to God.

Leonardo died on the 2nd of May 1519, at the grand age of sixty-seven. I felt him leave this world with great sorrow even though we had barely ever spoken. I was not sad because I had lost a friend when he died; I was sad because the world itself had lost a great man.

Chapter Twenty-One

1516
France

During my time with Claude's court I came also to know a most fascinating woman who entered the Queen's service in 1516. The beautiful Lady Françoise de Foix became a good friend to me, and taught me many lessons in life.

Françoise de Foix was of noble, even royal birth; she was the second cousin of Anne of Brittany, the second of Louis' Queens, and therefore Françoise was a third cousin to Claude herself. Françoise had married Jean, Count of Chateaubriant, in 1509, although she gave him a daughter in 1508 when they were still only betrothed, to much scandal about the court. Françoise loved her daughter, named Anne, like me, but like so many noble women of the time, she had left her daughter at the country lands of her husband when she came to court to wait upon Queen Claude. The court was no place for children; the airs of the cities in which the court often stayed were considered dangerous to the health of children, and the morals of some within the court were perhaps more dangerous still.

François had requested personally that Françoise de Foix and her husband come to his new, vital court, and there was an obvious reason for this appointment. Françoise was beautiful, with long, lustrous, dark hair and flashing eyes. She was accomplished, being an excellent dancer and fluent in Latin and Italian as well as in her native French, of course. And she was sensual. Deeply attractive and engaging, witty and clever, she was quickly followed around the court by eager, captivated men, desperate to court her. The King was no exception to the strength of her charms. But it was to the household of the Queen that Françoise came, not the court of the King. Although he paid court to her at entertainments, during the days she was safe in Claude's chambers.

But it was not her accomplishments or her beauty that attracted me. She was a gentle and great friend to me, and her kindness, spirit and steadfastness satisfied my need for a companion in those days when Mary had left and I was once again alone. It was difficult to become close to people at court. In some ways this helped me to become independent and self-reliant; traits which helped me a great deal in later life. These were qualities which I believe, later, made me stand out at the English court. For it was certainly not that I was the most attractive woman at court that drove men to me, it was the difference between the other women and me that made me stand out.

Still, self-reliance and independence can be lonely; being surrounded by people and feeling completely alone is an isolated space to occupy.

King François started to chase Françoise in earnest later that year. He tried to pay the attentions of courtly love to her, and she was polite but cool with him. He heaped favours on her relatives in an effort to win her as his mistress, but Françoise was not willing to enter into the bed of the King for mere favours. She was clear in what she wanted; a secure position, and, more surprisingly perhaps, she wanted to feel that she was in love with the King in truth. Many of the King's mistresses would give themselves up to him just for the fleeting riches such a title might bestow, but Françoise was not made of that mettle.

Françoise was a complicated woman; she could be hot-tempered and bawdy at times, but she also was cultured and fiercely intelligent. If she was to take a lover, then she wanted one who could offer her stimulation in more places than just the bedchamber. The French were more open about this type of affair than their English cousins; official mistresses were as much a part of a king's life as were wives. But Françoise wanted to be more than just a diversion to the King.

François the King was a man of many faces and attributes. He was a polished courtier who spoke several languages; he was interested in humanism. He went out of his way to protect the free thinkers and reformers of the Church in France, and he loved art and sculpture. Many works of masters of paint and marble graced his court, not just Leonardo's. Paintings by Michelangelo and writings by Homer lined the walls of his palaces. There is a sense of greatness in a king who could so admire the works of these illustrious men that he sought to surround himself with them.

But François could also be crass and unfeeling. His behaviour towards my sister was one example, but there were many other times when this polished man suddenly seemed to lose his veneer, and become a crude fool like so many others at court. There were rumours, too, that he was not above forcing a woman should she prove reluctant to give in to his charms, although this, for reasons that may become clear later, I found hard to believe.

And then there was his desire for peace and the countryside. Often Claude's household would go to see him, only to find that the King had left court for hunting in the great forests. François would go for days at a time; disappearing from his life like a shadow in the sun. He was at once both very ugly and very attractive; his face and body were long and tall, his features, especially his nose, were large. His lips were sensual and full, his figure was broad and well-structured. Only his legs let him down as they were rather spindly at the calves. He was not handsome, and yet he *seemed* handsome for his confidence and his manner. His dark eyes were warm and clever; his mouth was full of wit and jest, he was a brilliant musician and a wonderful and energetic dancer. He could hunt all day without tiring and desired women like water; he was, by the opinion of the many who had spent nights and days with him, a great and exciting lover.

Yes, he was interesting, this King of France. He commanded such love and adoration from his subjects; not the least of them his mother and sister. Together, the three of them made up the 'Trinity'. Their loyalty to each other and their tight bond could never be broken by anyone. His mother, Louise of Savoy, Countess d'Angoulême, had worked her whole life to see him achieve the throne. Louise was a lioness who would give anything for her son. Nothing was more important to her than he was, not even her daughter, the great Marguerite d'Angoulême. No, it was François, her 'Caesar' as she called him, for whom she would give all. When Louis was still married to Anne of Brittany in 1512, Anne had borne a son, who died almost at the instant of his birth. During this time of sadness, Louise of Savoy was heard to mention that it was a good thing that the Dauphin had died so quickly, so that he could not "prevent the exaltation of my Caesar". This was the type of woman that she was; ruthlessly devoted, utterly and entirely, to her son, at the cost of all else.

It would have seemed possible that Louise's daughter, Marguerite, would have resented this special devotion, but no! For Marguerite was also one of the Trinity, devoted to the advancement and protection of François her brother. They were very close, and he valued her opinion on many things. He inspired such total devotion from the women in his life, and it was clear why. Despite all his faults, and there were many, François was a deeply charismatic and charming man. I found it hard not to like him, despite what he had said about my sister.

In 1516, François was in hot pursuit of Françoise; he lavished her and her family with presents and titles, he wrote poetry to her. He invented masques where she, talented woman that she was, could shine in the title roles he gave to her. But still she did not given in to him. Why? Because in truth she really was in love with him. This ugly, yet charming, king was blatantly offering her all she could want in money and riches if she would only lie with him. But she wanted to know that there was truth in his protestations of love, she wanted to know that she would not simply become another conquest to him. It seems simple, does it not? That a woman would love a man and look to him for security of his promises... But in reality, she was asking much more of him than all his other past and fleeting mistresses. She wanted his heart. She wanted security.

We had become friends, Françoise and I, and as we wandered the beautiful gardens of Claude's palaces, she often spoke to me of François and her deep attraction to him.

"There is something in me, something so powerful, that when he pleads for me to believe in his love and give myself to him...," she paused, her great dark eyes on the skies. "Ah!" she cried. "All I want is to give in!"

She laughed. "But he is used to women giving in, is he not? He is used to the easy conquest and he tires so quickly of them afterwards." She looked at me and shook her head. "Men like François... they are hunters. They want to chase and capture. But the quick and easy chase will not satisfy them; they will not come back for more if it is over too quickly. They will tire, they will wander, they will stray, and then what are we women left with but an empty bed and a name all speak whilst laughing?"

She smiled at me, her lips pursed in a saucy pose that was so characteristic of her when she was in a light mood such as this. "I shall not be the one to be caught with ease," she said, shaking her head. "I shall give him a good chase, and at the end, *he* will be the one who is caught by me. The hind will become the huntress, my friend."

I nodded to her. "My sister was easy prey to capture," I said. I had, against my father's wishes, told all of the affair of my sister to my new friend. But I trusted her to say naught of it. "And he tired of her swiftly. I think what you say is true."

Françoise nodded, biting her nail. "And you will learn from her mistake, and not do the same."

"I will be no man's mistress," I said haughtily. "There is no man that I will have but my husband."

"And who is he?" she asked, laughing a little. "I am surprised you have not introduced me... do you keep him in your cupboard or under your bed?" She laughed gaily and I could not help but join in. She was entertaining to be around, Françoise. Even when she said something that might be hurtful, she had a way of softening it with her wit.

"I understand your position," she mused as we continued to walk. "You value yourself highly, and your sister's example gives you no reason to think your opinion is wrong. But life, Anne... ah, it is never quite as simple as we imagine when we are young." She smiled at me; she was hardly old, but she had been married young and that certainly gave her more experience in life, and with men, than I.

"You may find, Anne," she continued "even if you marry happily to a man whom you love, that this may not give you all you want of life, or of love. After a while of being married, or even not that long, you may find that your husband no longer desires you as he did before you were married. You will become *familiar* to him, and the familiar is always less desirable than the unknown... to most at least."

She paused and sighed. "When we were first promised to each other, Jean was so energetic and powerful, so romantic. He and I rode for days in his lands, stayed in hunting lodges in the forests and made love for hours, for days. Sometimes we did not make it out of bed until long past noon. Our daughter was conceived in such love, and before marriage! Ah, there was scandal even though we had been long engaged. But that did not matter to me then. I thought then that we were destined to be together and what we were then, what we had then, would be forever."

She shrugged. "Back then, I would have answered as you do now; that I should be no man's but his. But now…" there was a silence as she thought and shook her head. "But now, Jean takes his lovers; they are younger and look at me with spiteful eyes. They are paraded before me, even within my own house. I can do nothing about it, and my tears do not move him as once they were able to. Before I came to court, I would cry myself to sleep because of his careless cruelty. I had become too familiar to him, and the love he told me of when we were first together has faded from his heart. But here, with François… I am the special one once more. When the King looks my way, it is as though all other people have vanished from the world. I am the one who is paraded and adored. Once more, I feel as though I am beautiful."

"No one could ever say that you were not," I replied hotly, frowning at her.

Françoise smiled. "Beauty is as much in the mind as it is in the body," she said. "If one does not think they are beautiful, then they can never truly become so. You must believe in *yourself* to be beautiful; you must know in your heart your own worth. I was losing that self-worth and so I was losing my own beauty. When Jean rejected me, I was downcast. But now I have a new love, and Jean cannot say or do anything against him, because this man is the King. If I choose to, I can have love and hope returned to my life. I can be beautiful. Or I can choose to be a good wife and return to my husband's cold and indifferent bed. What would you do?" She turned to me. "Would you be the good wife, no matter what the cost, or take love from the arms of another?"

"That is not a question for me," I shook my head. "This is your choice. I cannot tell you how to live your own life. We all make our own choices, and for good or bad they are ours."

"You are so clever for one so young, Mistress Boleyn," she said. "And your beauty grows day by day as your sense of self does. There is something in you that men will start to see soon; they are always further behind than us when it comes to women. With men, it is the obvious they see first, then, they come to appreciate the hidden. With women... we always see the hidden in other women first, especially at court. We always know when there is another to rival us; we can feel it in our bones. You must learn to watch like a serpent for the other women at court; they are the dangerous ones, not the men. I see in you such things that the men have not noticed yet, but they will. There is poise in you, there is power. You understand your worth and are not willing to barter. I am not willing to barter either, I hold my price, but my price is different to yours. You say you will be no man's mistress, but I am older and have learned my own lessons. I may live in a marriage without love, but I will find love too. Soon, if François is genuine in his attentions to me, I shall be his *Mistress en Titre*; his official mistress, and no one shall challenge my place in his heart. That is the price I hold out for; those are the terms I have given him."

I nodded; I understood her desire to be loved. She found it not in her marriage anymore. The position of the King's official mistress was one of great social standing in France, although not all, of course, considered it an honourable position. She would be recognised not as a plaything or mere diversion, but as a powerful member of court, one who had great influence with the King. But although I understood her price, I did not want the same as her. The position of a mistress was one that was never certain, not even when it was that of an official and recognised mistress. Men were changeable and the position of a mistress was to ever be entirely reliant on her lover. If he decided he loved her no more, then he could leave her without anything. She could become not only rejected, but lost to society and position, without money or friends. Most mistresses of the King were cleverer than that, however; learning to line their pockets well long before they came to be cast off. Many people looked down on them for being money-hungry whores, but really, when the option to abandon them was always there for a king, were they not but looking out for themselves, for the time when the fancy of their lover came to tire of them? Their reputations were always damaged, of course; a man might take a thousand mistresses and hardly be looked on with anything but a gentle smile of amusement, but if a woman took even one, then she was judged as morally repugnant, and disgraced.

With the bond of marriage, at least, the husband had an obligation in law and the eyes of God to his wife. Although this institution was hardly perfect either, it did not leave a woman open to attacks on her morals and character as being a mistress would. Perhaps my ideals were too simple, too high, but I did not like the idea of such insecurity in life. Forever wondering if I fell in love and gave my heart and body to a man, would he simply tire of me and move on to another, leaving me disgraced and alone? That was no way to live, for me at least. I was a sensible young woman at heart and I had learnt well at the courts of France and Burgundy. Mary's example had plagued me, and when I thought of the things which François had said behind her back, and the things people still called her, it made me feel quite ill. I was determined never to be treated like that, and to my mind, that meant never giving in to the false protestations of love which men seemed to make and break with such devastating ease.

Françoise gave in to François in 1518, but only after he offered her the position of his *Mistress en Titre*. She received apartments at his court, horses, servants, litters and other trappings of brilliance which came with her position. She was honoured at state occasions and was at the side of the King constantly. She had her own ladies and her own little court within his. She had come by greatness by setting her price, and demanding it of the King. And she had his love, then at least. Her husband could say nothing on the matter, he was granted titles and lands too, for the position his wife now held with the King. Even if Jean had objected, he had to keep his silence; the King's will was all that mattered, if one wanted to keep one's position and standing at court.

It was an example I was to follow well in later life; I had seen how this game was played by a master.

Claude never mentioned Françoise's position as her husband's official mistress and the two of them continued to be friends; Françoise often served at Claude's side at state occasions. Claude knew that François's affairs were inevitable; I think in her own way, she respected Françoise for holding out for so long. Françoise never pushed herself above her station with Claude, and this was probably another reason that she and the Queen continued to be close. Later, there were other women I saw both in France and England, who pushed beyond the realm of the discreet mistress into public notice. I myself was one of them. When I was in this position, of course, I thought myself justified in the love of the King and the great position I would eventually hold. When, much later, I saw others parading themselves before me, I would know the pain that I had caused to others. Françoise never did this to Claude.

Françoise was correct in her assumption that men would start to notice me. As was often the way, as the pursuit of Françoise by François became more obvious at court, courtiers began to ape the King in their own appetites. François' appreciation of the dark Françoise sparked a new interest; gallants began to fall in love with and court the dark-haired and dark-eyed women of the court. The general appreciation of beauty at that time had long been for women like my sister Mary, and like Mary Tudor; the sparkling fair hair, the wide set blue eyes and the full figure with ample breasts. But with the King's appreciation of Françoise, however, it suddenly became most sophisticated to court a dark-haired beauty, following the King's avid appreciation. Almost overnight, I found I had a volley of courtly appreciators all apparently desperate for my love and for my attentions. It was also considered rather intelligent, suddenly, for a man to prefer the mysterious dark beauty to her obvious fair counterpart. To the vexation and disgust of all the blonde beauties at court, we dark nymphs were suddenly most desirable. I was most pleased; the blonde beauties were not.

Françoise taught me well; I had retained the cold aloofness to men that I had learnt at Margaret's court, and it had built up within me in fear after my father's attack on Mary. I had felt that this coolness with men acted as a protective device, but Françoise assured me that this would not help me forever, and would act as a deterrent to marriage suitors, which would help my career at court not a jolt. I wanted to advance myself and my family; there were ways of dealing with men that I must learn. To master men, after all, was the only way that a woman could gain power or influence in this world. Men ruled the world, but if we could rule *them*, then we held power all our own. I must learn to attract myself a husband at some stage. If I wanted to have any influence in the life of the family I would eventually be mother to, I must learn how to work men, how to bend their wills to mine without their realising it. I learnt well from a consummate master, adding her skills to those I had learned in the games of courtly love at Mechelen.

The trick to dealing with men at court was to give them hope, but to refuse them at the same time. The *promise* of capture is always there, but it is dependent on being convinced of the worth of his words. That way, men of the court are encouraged to pursue a woman, but to never catch her.

The best way that a woman could keep her power was to refuse her love, in the physical sense at least, and thereby, retain control of the game. The game of courtly love meant that we women trod a thin line between flirtation and modesty, between the promise of affection and the withholding of that last critical barrier between us and men. It perhaps sounds cruel, but the men who played the game with us understood the rules as we did. Many of them did not truly love us. They could show their accomplishments through us, and we could advance in recognition through them.

There were great advancements too to be made by these artists and young talents by securing the patronage of a great lady such as Claude or Françoise. Such women had power, they had money; they had the ear of the King. They could hand out rich rewards to those they deemed worthy. And what better way to convince such a woman, but by playing the game the best, by showering her in verse and music, jousting for her in the lists, picking her out of the crowds of women and making her feel special? Courtly love made the Court of France sparkle. It was a brilliant and fascinating world to move in; a cultured and learned world. My love for France and all things French came from my time moving amongst the brilliant players and the wondrous creations that were brought about through the games of love.

Françoise and I would read the poetry of our admirers to each other. Since her primary admirer was the King, and he was a talented man, verses written to her would be of a much higher standard than those lines offered to me. But my admirers were not without talent. I started to pen my own poetry at this point. I showed it only to Françoise, who said I had some talent with words.

I learnt to use my skills at court to impress; I danced beautifully and carefully, played the lute and sang well, and this, as well as my growing, striking looks gained me more admirers. The ladies of the French Court began to ape my style in dress; copying the long-hanging sleeves of my dresses and little bands of jewelled velvet I wore about my long neck. As my collection of admirers grew, so did the number of people claiming to be my friends. Suddenly I had more influence at court. This was how one advanced. It was all a show, all a dance, all a game.

Françoise was the author of much of this; she was brilliant at court, she shone in her abilities. She spoke Italian, and Italian was seen as the height of sophistication at the French Court. She would read Latin from the Bible for Claude and Claude's other ladies, with her low-toned and husky voice. Her dancing was of the first degree; to see her measured and delicate steps, her body poised and held in elegant poses as she danced the *basses dances* or *pavannes*, was to see an artist at work. There was such passion and style in Françoise the dancer that I was ashamed to put my feet near her steps. But in this, too, she taught me all she knew and was not stinting in her advice. Many women may have been; wishing to retain their high positions by refusing to help another advance, but not Françoise. For one thing, she was so sure in her position now as François' *Mistress en Titre* that she feared no competition.

The dancing of the French Court advanced much whilst I was there, and went on to brilliance after I left. The few dances and entertainments of Louis' court had been lacking imagination and style. With the arrival of François, his accomplished sister Marguerite, and Françoise, the court started as though from a deep sleep into the wholehearted enjoyment of entertainments which forever after, would define the French Court as one of the greatest in the world.

Chapter Twenty-Two

1518
France

In 1518, a special entertainment was arranged to engage ambassadors of England. It was to be a great state feast at the castle of the Bastille to celebrate the coming of English ambassadors who were to negotiate for marriage between the Dauphin, who had been born in 1517, and the sole Princess of England, Mary, born to Henry VIII and Katherine of Aragon in 1516. Although both children were, as yet, infants, it was a perfect opportunity to ally England with France, and both kings were keen to take political advantage of their newly-born children.

I was chosen as one of the ladies to be in attendance. Claude was proud of me in her retinue, and, under the guidance of Françoise, I had come far in attracting attention to myself at court, in the right way. Even the King had started to cast admiring glances in my direction, but I was not interested in becoming the second Boleyn brought to his bed. Although I admired him, my sister's treatment at his hands still rankled with me. I was careful, never allowing myself to become into a vulnerable position with men, especially at feasts or the more intimate banquets that followed, when the wine flowed freely. There was danger in some of the men that made up François' retinue. Fortunately, the position of a lady-in-waiting to the Queen afforded some protection from this, but there was always the possibility that a man might forget his courtly veneer, and so a keen and watchful eye was important.

The King's wandering, admiring eye was also useful to me. François allowed me to partner him in dances, when he was not dancing with Françoise, and this attention allowed me to rise at court. I was enjoying my fledgling rise into prominence.

Amongst the English ambassadors to France was my own father. I was to be in the party that greeted and entertained him and the other lords of England. My talent for languages was one of the reasons I was picked, along with my rising prominence at court. I was more than a little nervous to see my father again; although his presence often brought up such feelings within me, they were now especially so because of the violent encounter that had taken place after Mary's disgrace. But despite some hours of worry on the idea, I should not have been so anxious; in the end, my father mentioned little of my sister at all, preferring perhaps to sweep old troubles from the door of his house, and not think on them again unless he had to.

The Bastille was a great castle; the state banqueting rooms were high up in the rooftops and could hold hundreds of people. The courtyard had been draped with an awning of dark blue cloth, on which was painted all the stars and heavenly bodies of the night's sky. Inside, long tables were set out around the hall, and musicians held a place in one corner. All the rich golden and silver plate of the royal family were put on display in cabinets around the hall, so that the guests could admire the ostentatiously displayed wealth of France as they ate. Gold and silver cups, plates, servers, and ornate salt cellars lined every wall in huge cabinets, winking at the guests in the torchlight. Venetian porcelain and rows of intricate glasswork, too, were displayed, with carpets of white and orange cloth lining the floors. True wealth was marked by a gentleman's ability to host a feast and use none of the plate he had on display, and for the royal house of France of course, there was plenty to both display and use.

As usual, there was to be a little twist in the play of this feast; this time it was to *almost* dispense with the rules of seating by rank, and instead to alternate the men and the women so that each man had a court beauty sitting at either side of him, to give an appearance of informality. The ladies, however, were consciously picked for their positions, so that their titles reflected those of the men they surrounded. So that is why I say rank was *almost* forgotten; it was never truly forgotten.

We ladies served the dishes of the feast to our companions on the stroke of midnight after much dancing. We gave the beautiful *sallats* the prime place on the table with their sugared flowers and peppery leaves. We put the ornate salt cellars near to the richest men we served, for their convenience. Then we took our places and began to spoon out delicate portions of almond milk and spice pottage, rich venison or spicy boar to the guests. Mushrooms swam, bobbing in deep sauces of ale and stock, salmon and pike lay roasted and garnished with herbs, tiny eggs and peppery capons set the taste buds on fire even before they met with the mouth. Apple pies, alive with hot ginger and nutmeg warmed the belly, and wine, rich with spices, flowed down the throat like nectar. Later, golden custard and rose water puddings glistened on the tables, along with huge subtleties of sugar, crafted into castles, knights and fair maidens. We even had goblets made of sugar paste to drink our hippocras from with little biscuits at the end of the feast. When you drank from such goblets, the sugar paste melted into the wine, sweetening it and making each sip taste different to the last. The feast was a dance for the senses. France understood the wealth and influence of foods.

As each dish came to the table, we women rose to serve the guests of the house of France like servants. At each serving, the English ambassadors were charmed by this homely appearance of lack of ceremony, and we were well-primed to charm them. We were under strict orders from Louise of Savoy, François' mother, to bewitch our important guests; and Louise was not a woman to be disobeyed.

François had bought gowns for each of us for the occasion, made in the new Italian fashion; they were simply the most beautiful gowns that the English could have seen, and the secret hope of the French was that the English lords would be quite overwhelmed with French sophistication. François had given us these gowns a few days previously to keep for state occasions. Visiting his wife's rooms to give us the gowns, he leaned in to me and whispered. "For the little Mistress Boleyn," he said with a strange twinkle in his eyes, "there is a special adaptation."

I had blushed a little to be so singled out, and curtseyed, thanking him. When I examined the gown later I found that the sleeves had been altered from the Italian fashion; my gown had the long-hanging sleeves that I designed on all my dresses, the very style which other women at court were starting to copy from me. But no other dresses had been altered in such a way as mine. Françoise's dress was of much finer materials than mine, but mine was different in design to all the others. It was an honour to be so singled out, but it also made me feel wary of the King's intentions towards me.

In everything we did in these games of court, we walked fine and delicate lines. It was of benefit to have small and careful feet, used to dancing, such as mine.

You would believe that Françoise might have resented François giving me a special dress. But it was not so. Françoise's heart was not like that. Françoise and François were so alike in person; as their relationship developed through the years if seemed as though they mirrored each other. If François took other lovers, then Françoise invited other men to her bed in retaliation. Françoise's protestations that she would take only one other man to her bed were proven untrue in practise, but she only had one love. When she and the King argued they would have the most unbelievable fights, which caused the palaces of the Valois to shake in their foundations. But they would always make up and be more enamoured than ever in each other. Then there would be poetry and laughter. Later, again, the King would be unfaithful, she would retaliate and they would fight again. But this was later. Her position was never threatened at this time; she was the master of his heart, although not the master of his will. They loved each other both with fire and with gentleness.

She was never worried that another might truly replace her in his heart.

So, the King was free to show me attention and I was free to receive it, but nothing more. And this was well, for I wanted nothing more of the King. After the feast, there was a grand entertainment where the noble lords of the court took part in a mock melee... twenty-four men on each side, with the King leading one of the teams. There was much cheering and shouting in this raucous match and the ambassadors from England seemed most amused. Once this entertainment was finished, the rooms were set once more for dancing, which lasted long into the night. As the dancing started anew, my father came to talk to me. We had not been placed together at the meal and I had not seen him for some time.

"Your dress is different to the others," he observed, looking me up and down once our formal greetings were done with. I smiled and looked around me.

The tables had been folded away to make room for the dancing to begin. The candles in their iron cages let out a soft, becoming light, and the wine flowed as freely as it had done during the feast. Music started, and some of the dancers had started to perform. I was softened by the beauty of the night, and happy to see that my father was pleased by me again. His violence towards Mary and disappointment in me had hurt me deeply and I longed to regain his approval. I could see by the manner in which he looked on me that he was satisfied with what he saw.

"The gown?" he asked impatiently, stealing me from my thoughts. I immediately stepped up to answer my father.

"The King showed me special favour," I said calmly. "He noted the style of gowns that I designed to wear at court, and noted that other ladies copied that style. When choosing the gowns to give as presents, he chose to alter mine to include the sleeves that I have made popular here in France."

"I take it that his favour is shown in these ways, and no others?" my father asked, raising an eyebrow at me.

I stared him straight in the eyes. "I am a maid," I replied coolly, "and shall remain so until I give that honour to my husband, when directed so by you, father. No man, King or otherwise, shall make me his whore."

My father grunted slightly and then looked over the dress again. "It is elegant," he said. "And it is good that the King notices you. Be sure to use that advantage wisely."

I nodded and took another draught of the good wine in my cup. I longed to dance as I always did when I heard the music at an entertainment. But I must wait for the invitation of a partner already in the dance.

"There is someone I wish to introduce you to," my father said.

I raised my eyebrows at him, but he did not explain. My father moved me gently by the elbow through the crowds to the seating area where François' sister, Marguerite d'Angoulême, was sitting. Although I had seen her often at court, usually with her brother, François, I had never been properly introduced to her. Marguerite was a royal princess and one did not simply walk up to royalty and introduce one's self. My service in Claude's household had kept us somewhat apart from François' main court and that was where Marguerite was always to be found.

Marguerite was pretty and witty and shone like a star at the court of her brother. She was learned, and interested in learning, most especially in reform and reformers of the Church. This was not strictly legal; many of those who dared to question the Church were viewed as heretics and could be arrested or executed. But there were genuine questions being raised on the indulgences of the Church, on the morals of the men who taught the word of God, and many thought these questions needed addressing. Marguerite was the King's adored sister, and therefore she was free to ask many of these questions, and meet with many who asked them, in safety. She was untouchable and beyond reproach, for she enjoyed the King's favour and absolute love. She was a powerful woman.

My father, I knew, was interested in the religious reforms which were being discussed in the courts of Christendom. Although some thought that any criticism of the Church was heresy, I was interested in this new thought, too. It did not seem un-Christian to me to seek to place ourselves closer to God through better understanding of his words, and better practise of his wishes.

As we approached the seated area where Marguerite and her admirers were seated, she let out a short quip that set her companions roaring with laughter. In the aftermath of their amusement, my father walked into her circle, hovering on the edge until the Princess noted him, and then he walked forwards, to introduce me to one of the most fascinating and powerful women in the world. She waved him towards her; a high honour.

"I am honoured to see you once more, Your Highness," my father said as he bowed low and gracefully to the Princess. Marguerite smiled at him, pleased to see an interesting acquaintance approach her.

"Sir Thomas Boleyn," she said happily, gesturing to him to rise. "I am so pleased to see you here again. There is always a good discussion to be had with you and as you can see, I am quite *starved* of intelligent conversation." She spread her hands about her as though despairing of her company and those surrounding her laughed again, knowing full well she made a jest; there was such merriment in her eyes that her seemingly harsh words turned to lightness. She was talented in making people love her; this I knew from one minute in her company.

"May I present to you my *youngest* daughter?" my father asked, clearly trying to distinguish me from Mary whose reputation was infamous at the French Court. "My daughter serves Queen Claude, and served previously at the Court of Mechelen with the Archduchess Margaret."

Marguerite raised her eyebrows with interest as I came forwards and dropped to a graceful curtsey before her.

"Rise," she said, and as I rose slowly and elegantly before her, she nodded to me with approval. "You are well travelled for one so young, Mistress Boleyn," she said. "And you are… most striking to the eye, as well as being obviously well-versed in the art of serving royalty." She smiled and waggled her finger at my father. "But rather like a man, you father has told us all about you and yet managed to forget to tell us your name." She laughed prettily. "We cannot have that… what are we to call you?"

I smiled back at her warm face. "My name is Anne Boleyn, Your Highness," I said.

Marguerite looked me over and smiled again. "I have seen you at entertainments, Mistress Anne; you shine well at court and you will sparkle further, I think. You seem rather different to your sister, whom I met briefly when she attended the Dowager Queen here."

I flushed slightly and cast my eyes downwards, expecting bawdy laughter to erupt from those around her, but it did not. It seemed that Marguerite had her companions well-trained to know when she was jesting and when she was paying a compliment.

"My sister and I are different, Your Majesty," I said, feeling somewhat like Judas but not wishing to miss an opportunity to better my own reputation. "I am more… wary with my love and friendship."

Marguerite leaned forward and nodded to me. "We think alike then," she confided. "There are many in this world that trust readily, and without reason. I am not one of them. I keep my own counsel. Perhaps, Mistress Boleyn, you and I shall meet again; we may find that our counsels are beneficial to one another."

I nodded to her. "I would like that greatly, Your Highness," I said, and curtseyed again. As my father and I walked back to the celebrations, I glowed with pleasure to think that such a great woman had taken the time to talk to me, although I did not really think that anything would come of it. Royalty was often given to making easy promises that were not remembered later on. Later that evening, however, as I was finishing a dance, I was given two messages by a servant. The first was from Marguerite, asking if I would join her and her party in the gardens the next day, if and when my duties to Claude allowed me.

The second note was from my father. He had left the entertainment already and would be gone on the morning's tides. He bade me remember my family and honour, and to continue to excel at the court. It ended with a customary goodbye, and his name.

That was all.

I sighed as I read it, for it seemed to me then that no matter how hard I strove I should receive little in the way of praise from my father.

In disappointment he was loquacious, violent, vicious… in approval he was silent.

Chapter Twenty-Three

1518
France

I was allowed to join Marguerite's party in the gardens late the next morning. Claude expressed some pleasure that Marguerite had noticed me, although there was a hint of worry in her pale eyes should her sister-in-law steal away one of her ladies from her retinue.

I found Marguerite and her company in one of the larger sections of the beautiful gardens; musicians were playing softly and there was a great deal of gentle talk and laughter. There were a lot of people there, some clearly in Marguerite's inner circle, and some who simply tried to be near her. Most of the party were seated on the soft grass, lying on rugs, cushions and blankets and there was a beautiful scent of violets and lavender in the air. Marguerite sat on brightly coloured cushions at the head of the group; in her lap was a book that her inner circle were clearly discussing avidly with her. The discussion was clearly lively and excited, but it was more serious than was the atmosphere in the rest of the company in the gardens, who were listening to music or chatting gaily of the entertainments of the previous night.

I approached carefully and softly, feeling shy in front of all these people. Marguerite looked up and around the garden whilst talking and saw me standing hesitantly. She smiled and beckoned me over to her; I approached sweeping to the floor in a curtsey as I did.

"Mistress Anna Boleyn," she exclaimed happily, "come and join this discussion we are having. Your father has a fine mind; let us see if it has passed to his daughter."

I walked over and smiled nervously at her as I joined the group. The others looked me over with interest as Marguerite introduced me as the daughter of the English ambassador, Sir Thomas Boleyn. The name "Boleyn" brought a few smiles which were quickly hidden in the sleeves of fine coats, and I spoke sternly to my cheeks to stop them flushing, for I was sure those smiles were to do with Mary and her reputation. I looked about me, hoping to distract my mind from such thoughts. I saw amongst Marguerite's companions courtiers who were writers of court entertainments, and some I knew to be poets and thinkers; this was an interesting group of people. My heart was hammering in my chest as I feared what I might be asked.

"We are talking of a new philosophy that has come to our interest," Marguerite said. "Some, who would close their minds to anything new, would say that it is a heresy, but I say that it warrants closer inspection. What say you, Mistress Boleyn?" She asked, and turned to me.

I shook my head a little, blushing. "I am sorry, Your Highness, but I know not of what you speak and without that knowledge I cannot comment on the nature of the subject."

She looked me over with seeming coldness. Suddenly I felt quite worried. "Some would say that the honour due to a princess of France should be enough to warrant *your* opinion to agree with hers, no matter what the subject," she said.

The others looked at me; for a moment I was afraid to speak, so changeable she appeared, but then I thought I could see a twinkling warmth in her seemingly cold eyes, and suddenly I knew this was a test.

"Some would say so, Madame," I said carefully. "But like you, Your Highness, I keep my own counsel; I wish to understand the matters of a discussion before I agree or disagree with its principals. I feel that this quality is more useful to a princess of

France, than a tendency to blindly agree to all that is said without once considering the truth of the matter."

I spoke boldly, but Marguerite roared with laughter as did those around her.

"You see?" she said happily. "I told you there was a missing member of this group that I thought I had met last night!" She smiled warmly at me. "You are welcome to always speak your mind in *this* circle, Mistress Anna Boleyn," she said. "There are few other places in the world where thought is valued as much as here, and few other places where it can be as protected. My brother values my thoughts, and I protect those I can with his love for me. I bid you welcome, as one of those."

I felt honoured to be so welcomed by such a woman as she, and eager to take part in the discussion with Marguerite and her companions. I smiled at the others and they back at me, as Marguerite steered the conversation back to the book in her lap.

"We are discussing the contents of this book that I have acquired," she said, tapping her finger on its sheets. "Some call it heresy and would have it burned along with the author, but I believe that it calls for a much needed reform of the practises of the Church within its many arguments."

I nodded as she spoke and she raised an eyebrow at me. "You have read it?" she asked, surprised. I shook my head.

"No, Madame, but I should like to, if it has your approval; I have long thought that certain areas of the Church need to be better regulated: the giving of pardons and indulgences, for example; the behaviour of some members of the priesthood." I spoke nervously and quietly; words such as these were not supposed to be spoken aloud.

"Fear not, Anna," she said gently. "I have said to you that in my circle, thoughts are to be spoken without fear. Although I would not encourage you to do the same in *all* company, you are safe here. It is interesting that you should speak of the scandal of pardons, for this is the main subjects of this book. It seemed that perhaps you are of a mind with the writer and with me. Shall I lend it to you to read? I have read it many times now."

I was speechless as she passed the beautifully bound book to me. The others in the group looked equally interested, as it seemed that Marguerite had taken to me a great deal.

"Do you think that the consideration of Church reform is heresy?" she asked of the group as a whole. "Should we dare to talk of the reform of something that God has given to rule our souls?"

"God gave us the Pope and the priests to aid us," Marguerite continued. "But the priesthood is still made of men, and men are fallible, unlike God. To seek to better the Church I say is not heresy, but our *duty* as Christian people."

We around her nodded with her. Only a princess could dare to go so far, but I agreed with her; there were parts of the Church that were shocking and illicit.

Quietly I said, "To love… is to be able to question."

She nodded at me, a sign to continue.

"Your Highness, I feel that in questioning something, we can also seek to make it better," I said, the words only starting to form in my mind as I spoke them. I struggled to bring together the frayed ends of my thoughts. "If we cannot question, if we are not allowed to question, then we are truly not a part of a relationship, and if we are not a part of it, then love fades from a partnership. If we cannot be a part of the Church, then we will come *apart* from the Church and since we do not seek that, we must be allowed to converse with the Church. We must be allowed to grow closer to God by better understanding his words and to understand, one must question." I finished then, feeling that I had not really expressed what I meant. Marguerite however nodded at me enthusiastically.

"Indeed," she said. "I see your thoughts. We must be allowed to question in order to understand. Only in *understanding* the word of God can there come true closeness to God. Only by working together with the Church to reform practises which dishonour our faith, can we become closer to God."

I smiled at Marguerite, thinking that she was blessed with a much better talent at expressing her thoughts than I.

Marguerite smiled. "Take that book, Anna, and read it well. But don't let my royal sister Queen Claude catch you reading it… You'll be sent to the priest to atone for such sins before you can say '*question*', if your mistress sees it."

The group roared with laughter again.

"I have no wish to upset my mistress, Madam," I said. "The Queen is kind and good to me; I will keep the book a secret."

Marguerite nodded and rose; the group started to get up also, as the party was clearly disbanded when Marguerite left it.

"You will join me in the hunt at sometime this week," she commanded. "I shall ask Claude to spare you from your duties for a day; the park is beautiful at this time of the year and I think that this merry band will enjoy a ride in the forests and a picnic in the woods. Do you know how to hunt with the hawk?"

"I love to fly the hawk, Madame," I said. "But I have none of my own here in France."

"Then you shall borrow from my mews," she smiled warmly. "And show me if you can cast birds into the air as well as you cast thoughts."

I bowed to her, pleased and excited by her attentions. I had never felt more exhilarated by talking to one person.

"And see that you read that book well, and swiftly and return it to me," she tapped the little cover with her fingernail and smiling. "For I wish to discuss it with you, and see what your mind made of it."

Marguerite touched my cheek and stared into my eyes; I tried to cast them down, but she shook her head and took hold of my chin, lifting my eyes once more to hers. "Those bright eyes of yours were not made for staring at the floor, Mistress Boleyn," she said. "Be not afraid of my company." She let go of my chin and shook herself. "Come," she said. "It is time to eat, let us go inside."

We followed her. I had never felt more youth in my veins or excitement in my heart; Marguerite's conversation was lively, witty and dangerous too. There are few of us who can deny that when we were young we loved the spark of rebellious thought, but some of Marguerite's talk bordered on the truly perilous for the Church did not take kindly to those who would question it, and the Church ruled the world. I slipped the book into the pocket of my dress, concealed by the folds of fine velvet and silks. That is where I kept it, hidden from my gentle mistress Claude, to read and absorb in secret.

The book Marguerite had lent to me had been banned in France... That I knew from the name of the author inside; Martin Luther. The book was a copy of a thesis that this friar had written the previous year called *Disputatio pro Declaratione Virtutis Indulgentiarum*, or *The Ninety-Five Theses on the Power and Efficacy of Indulgences*. The thesis largely questioned the practise of selling papal indulgences and pardons, but also contained many general criticisms of the Church. The thesis questioned whether bought pardons could ever truly compare to an act of penance for sins committed, or indeed real contrition. Many people, noble and poor alike, spent much money on pardons that were sold by the Church to alleviate sins or spend less time in purgatory. When they came to Church to confess their sins and receive absolution, they would present the pardons and indulgences rather than performing acts of penance. Many people, myself included, had begun to question this practise, for it seemed as though the Church would allow anyone to be freed of their sins, if they paid enough coin. It did not seem in keeping with the purity of faith for the Church to allow such practises to continue. Luther also questioned the right of the Pope to hold such vast sums of wealth, believing them to be better placed educating scholars or helping the poor. None of the challenges within the thesis were things the Church wanted people to be reading.

I had heard of the book, for it had spread through the courts of Europe fast, mainly due to it being, in many places, a banned book, but I had never seen a copy of it. It was not strictly illegal to be in possession of this title, certainly it was not something I ever wanted to be caught with by a member of the clergy. It was unlikely however that anyone would know what I was reading, or that the contents of what I was reading were so inflammatory. I did not wish to risk being caught, however, even though I wished very much to be able to read it. Marguerite had obviously gained a copy and kept it through the love and protection of her brother. I would have to be more careful than she.

To my mind, the fact that it was banned made it all the more enticing to read and the sanction of Marguerite made me feel that there was in fact much worth to be found in such a volume. I found a great deal in the book which I agreed with, and it was written with such fire! You could feel the passion of the author for his subject leaking through the ink of the pages. I became sure that Martin Luther had some very interesting ideas on the reform of the Church, and I also came to understand why Church leaders abhorred this text. It was dangerous to their positions of absolute power and it was dangerous to their coffers.

That book stayed hidden in the folds of my dresses; a small piece of original thought hidden under the skirts of just another court lady.

It was through Marguerite that I gained access to many books and ideas that I should not have done otherwise. She opened my imagination to the wonder of free thought and to the greater knowledge of God, through learning. I had held half-formed ideas on reform of the Church for many years, but through Marguerite I learned to formulate those ideas, hone them and mould them, until I understood my own thoughts with clarity. But I could not speak freely to others as I could to her; this world was one where free speech, especially from a woman, was not looked on with favourable eye. The idea of the reforms of which we spoke were causing great unrest in the Church, and many called for men who questioned the Church, like Luther, to be excommunicated or burned at the stake… or both.

No, there was a lot of caution to be observed for a lady such as I. Marguerite may have the protection of her royal brother for her and her circle, but that did not mean it was advisable to speak of these matters to just anyone. I had to save my ideas on any questions raised from those books for the ears of Marguerite alone.

Some would later say that Marguerite harboured heretical ideas, but she was as devout as she was clever. She was no heretic. This was why she enjoyed the idea that I put forward; that to love is to question and therefore understand. She believed wholly in God and the Catholic faith, but she also thought there was always room to improve anything. She did not accept anyone's words blindly, and that included priests, cardinals and the Pope himself. She was possibly, in her heart, the purest person I had known. She was not without fault, but her faults did not lie in heresy, rather in the other direction. She wanted so much to improve our relationship with God that she was willing to brave the displeasure of

Church leaders to bring forth new ideas. Her household became a haven for free thinkers and philosophers. Many in the Church reviled her for it; believing that any who questioned their power should be destroyed. They were the ones who sought to call this good woman a heretic; they were the ones who sought to blacken her name. Such is the lot of many good people who dare to question the power of the Church. Men who had become powerful because of their positions in the Church feared people like Marguerite. But if they had simply taken the time to listen to reformers, many things about this world would be different. Those who wanted reform wanted to work with the Church, not against it, at least to begin with... the changes and the fractures which would appear in the very fabric of the Church and its followers were already starting to show... they would lead later to much change in all of Christendom.

During my time with Marguerite, I thought often that it would help the Church as a whole if more of its priests and leaders read and conversed on books as much as Marguerite did.

Since the previous year, Marguerite had been largely concerned with the reform of convents in France; helping to mend the sloppy ways that had taken hold and turning the attention of the inhabitants back to the glory of God. It was her passion to ensure these convents were run for the glory of God, rather than as an easy resting place for lesser children of noble houses.

There was corruption in many spheres of the Church, but to Marguerite this was something to be addressed and changed, not allowed to stay and fester. It was this reform of convents that had led her on to thinking of reforms in other matters; she was a great asset to her country, being a wise physical and spiritual presence in the world.

She opened my mind to a whole new world of possibility and philosophy.

Chapter Twenty-Four

1520
The Field of the Cloth of Gold
The Val d'Or, Calais
Neutral territory between English held Guisnes, and French held Ardres

There came an event in this year that would never again be surpassed in greatness or wonder. It was a phenomenon of the modern world, a spectacle of magnificence; it was the physical manifestation of a battle of pride between two kings. It was the biggest boast of all time, made material and given physical form.

It came to be called *The Field of the Cloth of Gold*.

I, amongst others, was fortunate enough to be present at this event. It was a meeting of the Kings of France and England under a new banner of peace and friendship. The Kings were united in a declaration of peace; the French Dauphin was betrothed to the English Princess, and the two Kings were united as brothers against the Emperor Charles of Spain and the Hapsburg territories. They were sworn to protect each other's countries with fraternal love and eternal loyalty.

Of course, we all believed little of this grand talk, really. Many treaties were made and then broken from one country to another. But as the opportunity arose for King Henry of England, and King François of France to meet in person, they found they could not resist the idea.

The new treaty was merely an excuse for the two Kings, much alike in age and accomplishments, to finally see each other. Both were described as being handsome, learned and virile. They were but three years apart from each other in age. They were curious about each other, and that curiosity could not be sated by portraits, letters or dispatches. They had to see each other in the flesh, to compare themselves each to the other in person. Reports were given to us that the King of England had frequently questioned ambassadors on the physical attributes of the French King. One conversation was relayed to us in detail.

"The King of France, is he as tall as I am?" Henry had asked the court ambassadors.

The ambassadors had replied that there was little in difference between the two of them, both being tall men. This clearly had not pleased Henry, since he was often noted for his great height, for he then asked, "Is he stout?" the ambassadors answered that François was not stout, but lean and strong.

"What sort of legs has he?" asked Henry, seemingly desperate to find something to best his rival with.

"They are somewhat spare, Your Majesty," the ambassadors spoke truly, for François' legs were not his best attributes. At this, the English King had beamed, pulled aside the edges of his rich doublet and clapped his hand on his solid thigh.

"Look here!" the young King exclaimed, "I have a good calf to my leg!"

The ambassadors then apparently had to spend a while laughing, and admiring the legs of the English King. And whilst François might have bellowed with laughter to hear of the vanity of the English King, he himself was no less eager to compare himself to Henry.

Each King was simply dying to best the other, to out-do the other, and both were quite interested, obviously, to see how they compared personally to the other. In short, they were so close in character and accomplishments that they would become either the best of friends, or the worst of enemies. We would have to wait to see which would prevail.

And see we would, for this was not just a meeting of kings and a few attendants. *The Field of the Cloth of Gold* was to be a great coming together of two entire courts. François and Henry were both bringing thousands of courtiers, nobles and servants to the meeting. This was to be an event like no other; the greatest state meeting of two kings, two courts and two peoples for eons to come.

The meeting became known as *The Field of the Cloth of Gold* mainly because of the copious and profligate display of wealth that both countries brought to the field. Nobles attended the event only at ludicrous expense. Every lord and lady wore the newest and most expensive clothing at all occasions, and jewels were as common as pebbles on the ground. Good horse, rich foods, and tents made of silver and gold marked every turn of the event. Several of Henry's nobles bankrupted themselves in the effort to dress and entertain as their King expected them to. Henry of England had to cut his nobles vast breaks in their taxes to the Crown to allow them to recover from this ostentatious show of wealth. It took the royal house of France ten years to pay back all the bills incurred by the event, so, perhaps you start to grasp the scale of the occasion.

There was no palace or castle in England or France that could hold the sheer volume of people that were going to attend to this meeting. It was rumoured that King Henry alone was bringing a personal retinue of five thousand people, which we were much amazed at. François, not to be outdone by his rival, proclaimed he would bring as many attendants, if not more, and each Queen would have over a thousand attendants also. This was a meeting beyond any scale that can be imagined and the only way to accommodate all these people was to construct a camp for them.

We were to meet where the English territory of Calais met French territories. Neutral ground… in theory at least.

In some ways this would be like a military operation with all of the French, and English courts staying in tents. In other ways, since the tents were made of cloth of gold and silver, and were outstanding in their sumptuousness, it was nothing of the sort.

Louise of Savoy was busy choosing the best and the brightest of the court ladies to accompany Claude, herself and Margaret to the meeting. Whilst numbers clearly mattered, so did manners. None were taken who were not up to the challenge of out-doing the English court ladies in beauty, manner, talents and breeding. It was an honour to be chosen, as I was.

We were confident that we should dazzle more than the ladies of the English Court. But to be sure, we were all charged to make and order fine new clothes, to practise our music and dancing and to rehearse our English, so that we might charm our guests by speaking in their own language. French was often the language used at the English Court, for it was considered the more cultured tongue, but if we ladies of the French Court could turn our tongues to the language of the English, then we would have one more skill to set on a peg above the English Court. Seeing that English was not difficult for me, I spent some time tutoring other ladies who were not as proficient as a native-born speaker. We would out-do them; we were utterly determined to.

It did occur to me that I was in a unique position; as should the English outshine the French, I would be on the winning side since I *was* English. Something which, to be fair, I had almost forgotten during my time in France. Should the reverse happen, I should still be triumphant, as I was a member of the French Court. I liked that kind of wager.

The Field of the Cloth of Gold came into our sights as we rode towards it; gold and silver cloth stretching for miles before us so that the whole valley shone as though it held the sun within its depths. A field of gold indeed; where no wheat nor grain grew in the lush valley, but where richness and wealth were tended instead. It was quite blinding in the sunlight. The camp of over three thousand tents had taken weeks to construct. Hundreds of men had worked ceaselessly to bring about this wonder, and each king had poured more money than any man could count into ensuring that his camp was the most impressive. Even so, not all of those who followed on the tail of the Kings could be placed in a tent or in nearby castles and estates; some ladies and lords of the court stayed with farmers in the area, and some, whose titles did not buy them a bed in this vast crowd, laid their heads upon beds of straw and hay wherever they could find a space.

Tents and pavilions shone gold and silver in the sunlight, jousting fields with freshly painted poles glimmered white and green, blue and silver. Hundreds of beasts for feasting on were held in the farms and valleys about the camps and vast kitchens, housed in tents of red and gold, rang with the noise of the seemingly impossible task of making food for so many thousands of people.

We sat on our horses at the top of that green hill and gazed silently on the wonders that our modern world had created. This spectacle was the greatest I thought I had seen, until one in the Queen's party let out a short, surprised shout, pointing further into the mass of golden and silver tents. Beyond the French encampment was the English. We could see it in the distance. In amongst their tents of gold and silver cloth stood the impossible; a huge and beautiful castle! But there was no castle on this land, and there had been not enough time to build one. How had the English done such a thing?

Claude looked both amazed and somewhat amused. Her husband's tent was a huge and beautiful construction of gold and silver cloth, lined with tapestries, with many rooms; its roof was lined with blue velvet and silver stars, imitating the skies of the night. We had all seen the plans for it, it was a grand invention. But somehow the English had constructed a whole castle! This was a feat of greatness indeed and it was such a beautiful castle. Designed in the Italian style its face was red and white plaster, and turrets of black and gold and white stood upon it, stretching to the skies. The gateway was surmounted by the royal arms of the English, Tudor roses and a huge shining golden stature of Cupid. Great statues of noble beasts stood outside the castle, lining the route to its huge wooden gates upon giant poles, painted in bright stripes of green and white, the colours of the Tudors. More great beasts stood out, too, on the turrets of the castle and heraldic flags flew, billowing gently in the light breeze. Glorious works of decoration, knots and badges, devices of the English King and Queen lined the outside of the castle walls. There were the pomegranates of Queen Katherine's badge and the lions and roses of the Tudors entwined with the initials H and K. Here and there, the badge of the pomegranate was marked with an emerging symbol of a little rose, showing the addition to the English royal house of the living daughter born to Katherine and Henry. Whilst she was a princess, rather than a prince as her father so desired, at least she was a living child and heir to the English throne. Many worried that the royal couple had only a daughter to succeed them and there was much fear within England of what might happen if a woman came to the throne in place of a man. All in England hoped that the living daughter of the King and Queen may prove yet to foreshadow male heirs to come.

But we were not thinking of such things of the future then; we were staring at the castle.

The castle was a work of beauty, and shining huge windows of glass poured the light of the sun back towards us, as we stared in open-mouthed wonder at the brilliance of the English and their King. There was but one question on our lips... How had they managed to build such a castle so quickly?

No one said anything for a while, but we gazed admiringly on this palace. There was silence apart from the horses, who sighed and huffed, longing to continue on their paths. In the silence of admiration, I felt pride in my native country, once of course, that pride had made it past the sense of French resentment that also rose in my heart! Such complicated emotions came to me as I looked on this castle, along with great admiration for the English King who had brought such wonders to pass.

But how had the English done it? It was a simpler explanation than we imagined. For the palace that we sat admiring was not wholly made of stone. It was made of wood, timber and brick, but painted to look like stone and mortar. The walls were not as thick as they seemed and although stone chimneys graced the rooftops, most of the castle was made of wood; it was a lie, a feint, it was like a castle made for an entertainment or a pageant at court, just on a much larger scale. It was constructed to draw wonder and amazement, and it did its job well. I don't think any of us could have been more amazed to see such a wonder, and from a distance, you would not have been able to tell that it was not made of thick, solid stone.

Later, we were told of the trick, and some were allowed to see inside it. The palace had real windows and two floors. There was a great banqueting chamber and separate privy apartments for the English King and Queen and their young daughter Mary. There were chambers for entertainments and an alley for bowling, a sport becoming popular at this time; a chapel, and apartments for the Dowager Queen Mary, now Duchess of Suffolk, and her husband Brandon. There were more chambers; for Cardinal Wolsey, Lord Chancellor to the King, and housing for all his servants. The inside of the palace was furnished with carpets of Turkish work, tapestries and painted cloth, beds of estate, and great glass cupboards for the display of plate. At the front of the palace there stood two huge fountains that flowed with malmsey and claret wine, given freely to all who came to them with goblets eagerly in hand. It was a clever trick; one which Henry no doubt had great glee in devising, for the whole thing, this massive show of costly pageantry was of course planned and designed by him. It must have cost a king's fortune to construct and it was done in perfect secrecy.

We rode down the hill and the first meeting of the two Kings happened as though it was entirely informal. To the sound of ringing cannon fire, trumpets and drums, the two Kings rode towards each other and embraced as friends and brothers whilst still on horseback; we all applauded. Every eye was sparkling, for this was to be a time of great festivities and celebrations. Although we all knew that peace is easily made and easily broken between kings, we all entered into the spirit of happiness that was on offer. There were to be pageants and tournaments, there were dances, jousts and masques and each camp was desperate to outdo the other. Such a spirit of competition was exhilarating and intoxicating.

And for me there were yet more pleasures to be found, for amongst the English were people I had longed to see for some time; my father, my sister and her new husband, my brother, and my mother.

I had not seen my brother or my mother for almost five years. When I left them I had been but a child, and now I was a young, accomplished and elegant lady-in-waiting to the Queen of France. I was eighteen when I came to *The Field of the Cloth of Gold* and my family, even my father who had seen me fleetingly at various court functions, barely recognised me.

I went to them in their tents on the English side when Claude granted me time away. George was so changed I hardly knew him. He had grown into such a handsome and accomplished young man and I was so pleased to find that he and I had much in common. He had done well at court and was now a page in the King's household. George had been with the Duke of Buckingham for some years until the King had noticed him, enjoyed his humour and easy ways, and asked that he join his own household.

George was here as father's official attendant, but was also called upon to work in the King's household in the make-believe castle. George had become a gifted poet and we traded lines and wrote for each other. At first each of us was so polite that we got nowhere, but soon we were picking each others' lines apart and improving our writing to no end through careful and correct critique. George was also interested in theology and reform. We had many whispered conversations on the value of Martin Luther's arguments, as well as conversation on other banned texts. I was acquiring these volumes through Marguerite, and George was having them shipped to him secretly through our father's connections abroad. Our father, it seemed, was also of the same thinking as George and I; he believed in reform. It was fine to find, despite the distance between us and the time passed since we last met, that George and I were so close in our ways of thinking.

My sister had married a few months previous to the summit meeting, and was part of the party of the Queen of England, having become one of her ladies-in-waiting. Despite his threats, our father had taken his time to choose a match, and had married Mary well. Mary's husband was no mean catch, but a man much in favour with the English King. His name was William Carey; he was young, fairly rich and titled, and a gentleman of the King's Privy Chamber. This was a good position to occupy, as the ear of the King was the route to power and influence. William was related to the King's grandmother, Lady Margaret Beaufort, as William's grandmother had been her aunt, and so he was therefore a distant relative of the King of England himself.

Although distant connections to the King did not necessarily mean that favours were a given conclusion, it was still a useful connection. William Carey was handsome and well-built, and like all of the King's friends he was a fine jouster and a cultured man. I liked him well, and found him good company. Despite all this, Carey was not as highly born as I would wish to marry, and I suspect not quite as highly born as our parents had wished for Mary. Her time in France had done some damage to her reputation and, once tarnished, her behaviour would always be under some suspicion. It was important to rich, noble households that the offspring of their marriages should carry their own blood and not that of any passing man who happened to take a daughter-in-law's fancy. Blood was important to all families. This was another reason I did not wish to indulge in my sister's pastimes. I wanted to marry well, and well above my own station.

On the whole though, Mary had not done badly in her husband and she seemed pleased with him. He was obviously happy in his match with her, but it was not just her charms and beauty that he was pleased with. As I learned soon enough, my sister had a profitable habit of attracting the attention of kings.

My mother was as lovely as I remembered; although her face was older now and there were lines appearing where once there had been but smooth skin, she was still a fine beauty. Her long tapering fingers grasped mine as we embraced for the first time in five years. I felt my heart quicken and tears spring to my eyes at the echo of her heat beating next to mine as we held each other close.

She held me at arm's length and her eyes shone as she looked me up and down. I was overwhelmed to feel the love radiating from her.

"I am proud, Anne," she whispered as her lips puckered with happy tears. "So proud… and so happy to see you again. You have indeed become a fine lady, as your father has often told me."

I was overcome with tears and laughter at the same time. To think that my father had ever said something of such fulsome praise about me! And that it should take the reunion with my mother for me to hear of it! My father looked on our reunion with a little detached amusement, but I believe he, too, was happy to have our family together for once as well.

I was infused with joy to be once again with my family; after so long at foreign courts, I had forgotten the great contentment that one's own family, the roots of life, can bring. I wanted to soak up as much of them as I could to store with me in whatever should come next in my life.

Mary and I walked out together a few days later to see the great castle that the English King had built, and it was she who showed me the careful paint-work which had gone on top of the wood of the castle, making it look like real stone. Swan feathers had been used to drape mottled brown over white paint to create the look of marble. As I stood admiring the clever arts of the English, she told me that in addition to a new husband, she had a new courtly admirer.

I was not totally taken aback by this news as after all, I knew the ways of courts well by now, and I knew Mary. But I *was* surprised to hear that our father knew and had encouraged Mary to hearten the attentions of this new admirer.

"How can this be so?" I asked, remembering when he had found out about François.

Mary gave me that naughty smile, unchanged since our childhood days, and she laughed. "Because, Anne, our father appreciates that my new admirer may do much good for our family," she grinned. "Our father is somewhat like the Roman god Juno, Anne; he has two faces. What displeased him in my relationship with François pleases him in my liaison with another. It was not, as it seemed, the bedding that I took part in that was the problem, you see, it was the bed-partner!" She giggled again. "Come, can you not guess whom it might please our father that I bed at night, besides my husband?"

Mary laughed and cast her sparkling eyes up at the great palace, up to the Tudor roses which stood proudly over the gateway, and then looked back and smiled triumphantly at me. A sudden, and unexpected crushing blow of jealousy and pain hit my heart; I realised she meant she was the lover of King Henry of England.

Until that sharp and ghastly blast of jealousy hit me, I had almost forgotten those feelings I had once harboured for the King of England when I was just a girl. But upon hearing my sister's gloating pleasure at her new lover, I suddenly felt all those feelings I had once felt for him, that paragon, that knight of my youth, return.

My heart ached with sadness and jealousy. I felt sick suddenly.

I must have turned pale as she was looking at me strangely when I looked at her again. She frowned and gave a twisted half-smile, mistaking my pale jealousy for general disapproval. "Come, Anne, it is not a bad thing," she said. "The King admires me; he calls me *sweetheart* and offers me pretty gifts. He favours our father and brother and calls me to dance with him at the court. The King has me brought to his bedchamber often. His liaison with Bessie Blount is at an end; why should it not be Mary Boleyn who steps into her shoes, and her bed? If it continues, and if he likes me, I will have the ear of the King. I can help our family advance."

I drew myself up and looked at her stiffly. I felt as though my heart had been torn from my body and trampled upon.

"We advance then… not through ability." I said, chewing on my jealousy.

Mary laughed naughtily again and raised a questioning, saucy, eyebrow at me. "I wouldn't say that," she said with a throaty, alluring laugh.

I blushed, feeling suddenly young and foolish about this subject of which my sister appeared to be a master; I spoke again, my jealousy of her overwhelming me.

"You know what I mean; we advance as a family because you please the King in bed, nothing more. Kings are fickle creatures; what shall we do when you please the King no longer?"

"Bah!" she said dismissively, waving her hand. "Then we shall advance as we did before, slower and with less pleasant types of tasks!" She smiled and the sun beat down over her beautiful jewelled hood making her pretty eyes shine like gems.

We stood, we sisters, in the shade of that great palace, and I fought to reconcile my emotions. I had always felt... superior, to Mary, in so many ways. It was not a nice thing to admit about one's self, but it was the truth. I had always been the cleverer of the two of us, and I thought my morals above hers. But now, although I should never tell her this, I suddenly wished nothing more than to be in her place.

I had all but forgotten my childish infatuation with King Henry, forgotten the nights I had lain in my bed at Margaret's court wishing myself in his arms. But like so many things tainted by the brush of jealousy, this did not matter now to my heart. Mary had the admiration and desire of this great King who had once captured my foolish heart... Mary had attained the desire of the one man I had ever felt true desire for. She was the one who was better than I, for she was in a happier place than I could ever hope to be. Adored by a great king... desired by a great man... perhaps the best of men.

My thoughts were as rapid as they were foolish. My mind swam with images of the King; of his golden hair and his easy laugh, of his handsome face and blue eyes, of his poetry and his feats of strength in the jousting lists. I felt my heart beat no more with blood, but with the sickening, fast-pulsing slime of envy. It was all I could do not to strike my sister about her face, simply for having attracted the notice of a man I had once desired. I tried to fight the resentment within me, for how often had I said I wanted not the place of a mistress, and yet here I was, wishing I was in Mary's rich velvet shoes? A fine test for all my high morals and beliefs; that I should fall at the first obstacle, and wish to become the mistress of a king so quickly!

"Come, sister," she said, linking her arm with mine. "Let us think not of what will happen if I *fall* from favour, but what we can enjoy now whilst I am *rising* in favour. Our family can do well from my position. Both our father and my husband are happy that I please the King. I am discreet in my affair with the King, as he likes to think of himself as a moral man. This, too, pleases the Queen, who would prefer that if her husband must take a mistress it should not be one that flaunts herself about the court; and this will allow me to keep my position and my honour. You see? I *have* thought about these matters!"

She looked at me for approval and I could not help but give it, grudgingly. It did appear that for once Mary had given some thought to something she was doing. She could not know that I spoke not from real disapproval of her choices, but from the mouth of jealousy. Nor did I want to admit it to myself; we are all of us happy to make plain our talents and accomplishments; we are less happy to make our faults known to others. Brewing in my heart were dark and mean emotions. I liked not the feel of them sliding inside my skin.

"I am happy, Anne," said Mary. "I mean to make sure our family does well from this. I know that you have scruples about this type of thing, some do, but this is the great prize; this is the King of England. You will marry well, better than I most likely, because of your accomplishments, your wit and your looks; but perhaps my position with the King could help you also. If I please the King and become his long-term mistress, I may be able to advance you to a greater marriage than our station would normally allow. And all this from doing something that is of great, great pleasure to my own self!"

She laughed and broke free from my arms to prance on the grass before me in a well-executed twirl of one of the popular dances of the English Court. Some gallants near us looked on appreciatively at her boldness.

"All is goodness, Anne!" she exclaimed, and she was so happy I could not help but laugh with her too. Mary was infectious in her happiness. I took her arm again to stop her prancing more in public, and tried to quell the feelings this conversation had stirred in my heart as we continued to walk and talk.

Mary was right; her position as the mistress of the King of England could mean great things for our family and that was what I should be thinking of. After all, what was the King of England to me? What was King Henry to the course of my life? I would marry a noble man and hopefully live a happy life at court, in France, perhaps, or in England. I would serve Queen Claude or Queen Katherine, have children and raise them to become courtiers. I should be happy that my sister was in favour with the King of England; Françoise was powerful in France because she had the ear and other parts of the French King at her command. Why should Mary not enjoy the same position in England, and why should the Boleyns not benefit from that?

It was foolish to feel such jealousy and resentment of my sister's position because, after all, it was not one that I really wanted. Although I would have been happy to hold the desire of a King such as Henry of England, I did not wish for the fragile and precarious position of the mistress. Long had I known this truth, as I strove to remind myself. Mary's fate was different to mine, and however much I envied her such a lover as the man who had once stolen my heart, I did not wish to be a temporary distraction for him. If I was to belong to a man, then I wanted to be his only woman.

I realised then, with clarity, what it was that I wanted. I wanted stability and respect in a marriage. I wanted to be a cherished wife. I wanted to be loved, and to love my husband.

This was rarer than becoming a mistress, for happiness and love in marriage were a matter of Fate, not a rule of life. My sister was conventional in many ways; marrying for position and seeking love and pleasure outside her wedded bed. I should be different; I should be no man's lover but my husband's.

But yet, my heart still ached, as I thought of the man I had adored from afar. Whilst I wanted not Mary's position, I still envied her for her lover. Dual thoughts and beliefs can often exist side by side in one mind. I was torn between jealousy of my sister and my understanding that I wanted not her fate. My heart and my head were in conflict against each other, and neither had won outright by the time we finished conversing on that sunny day.

But now was not the time to dwell on such things. My head tried to talk to my heart to calm it; Mary was right and, once the jealous fires subsided in my heart, I would begin to think well of this match, I was sure. Henry was a discreet man in his affairs and he was hardly prolific in them. François was a lover first, and then a king, and he cared not who knew it. Henry was different as he really believed himself to be a morally upstanding man. He conducted his affairs quietly and carefully. He had, before this time, a mistress named Elizabeth Blount who had borne him a male child in 1519. She had done well for herself and the child, who was officially recognised by Henry, a rare thing for a bastard of Henry VIII. All knew that the King of England longed for a legitimate male heir. So far his marriage to Katherine of Aragon had produced but one living child, their daughter Mary, and countless dead babies. When Bessie Blount gave birth to a male child, who was hale and hearty, it proved that whatever the fault of fertility was in this royal marriage, it did not lie with the King. He was capable of getting sons on women other than his wife, so therefore the fault must lie with Katherine. Whatever happiness a living son gave the King, it could not be complete however, for the boy was, and always would be, a bastard. Without a legitimate male heir to his throne, the country of England would never be secure. With only the Princess Mary living of his lawful union to Katherine, there were questions about the future of the country which none dared speak aloud. If the Princess Mary became Queen, then her husband would most likely be a foreign king; would England become annexed by another power if she came to the throne? Would the people of England and the nobles ever even accept the rule of a woman over them? Would the country once more face the peril of civil war? No one knew, but all thought of the future with troubles in their hearts.

Henry VII had not failed in his duty to give England a prince to continue the line of the Tudors.; he had had two sons! It seemed inconceivable, perhaps especially to Henry VIII, that he could fail where his suspicious, miserly father had triumphed.

But whilst it seemed, indeed, that Katherine was the party within the marriage who brought its fertility into question, Henry had not yet given up on his marriage to Katherine. She was still his honoured wife and her connection to the royal house of Spain and the Hapsburgs was at times a valuable one. She was also a wise and learned woman, pious and God-fearing. She was well-respected in England and beyond and she was loved by the common people.

But we all knew that there was a problem when a king had no true male heir, and Henry was not the type of man to take defeat in any area lightly. There had only been one time in English history where a woman had sought to rule on her own; that woman was the Empress Matilda, granddaughter to the Conqueror, and her rule had been contested by her cousin Stephen, plunging the country into civil war for years. That period was known to history as "the anarchy" for the unrest it had caused in England. Since that time, although the laws of the English did not prevent a woman taking the throne as French Salic law did, no one had been eager to see the throne left to a female. Until this time, it had hardly been a possibility, for there had always been, it seemed, male heirs brought to the throne, either by right of birth or by conquest. Men ruled the world, and many of them feared that a queen would have neither the strength nor the intelligence to rule alone. And so, England required a male heir; for the peace and the security of her future. And the King, who seemed in all ways a paragon of knightly virtue and worldly strength, could not understand why God should withhold such a gift from his hands.

Henry's affair with my sister was just starting at *The Field of the Cloth of Gold*, and many, including my ambitious father, were monitoring it closely to see what they could gain from it. Mary was right; our father was a man of many faces. Her affair with François had angered him, but I realised now it was mostly because Mary had sold herself so cheaply and so easily to the French King that our father had become so enraged. He was not above bartering his daughters to kings, but they had to be the *right* kings, and they had to offer the *right* price. Under his guidance, Mary would not sell herself so easily this time.

Perhaps I should have felt disappointed with my father; perhaps I was, a little. But the reality of life at court was that the ambitious man must be ready to do anything to advance himself. And what difference was there really, between a father bartering for the best price for his daughter, within wedlock, or doing so without?

Women were for sale, that was the way of the world, and our father was a most worldly man.

As we walked back to the English camp and I left Mary and the rest of my family that evening, I was thoughtful. I did not want to be a mistress to anyone… on that I was clear. But what if someday my father should insist I became one? If Mary had resisted, would our father have insisted that she bed the King? I had always thought that our father would insist on my marriage rather than anything else, but clearly he was not adverse to the idea of selling his daughters in other ways. Should I have the courage within myself to hold true to my values and refuse if such a situation occurred in my life? It was a difficult thought.

My head was most full that night. I served Claude distractedly and she smiled at me, perhaps thinking my head was caught up with the excitement of the event.

But both my head and my heart were spilling over with emotions and thoughts that they were ill-prepared to reconcile. I was awash with sensation.

Chapter Twenty-Five

1520
The Field of the Cloth of Gold

As part of the celebrations of *The Field of the Cloth of Gold*, the Kings of each nation took turns to dine with the wives of their opposites. I had some doubts that Katherine, Queen of England would have delighted overly in her duties for her blood was of Spain, and now her husband was uniting with France against her own nephew, the Emperor Charles. But the lot of a queen is to obey the will of her husband, and so she had little choice but to entertain François and enter into the activities of *The Field of the Cloth of Gold* with as much dignity and graciousness as she could manage. Katherine was a skilled courtier and Queen, she did her offices well.

It was on these occasions, during the meetings of the Kings and Queens that each set of ladies on the French and English sides would try their hardest to outdo the other nation. Just as the knights riding in the joust sought to better each other with feats of arms, so we ladies of each court were set against one another too. In many ways the summit meeting was like a war rather than a peace, as each tournament and each festivity was a trial by courtly graces; we ladies fought each other not with the sword or the lance as the knights did, but with wit, with beauty, with dancing, with song and fine clothing.

Henry of England came to dine in Claude's tent several times. On the first night we, her ladies, danced for him dressed as the servants of the Gods of Love. We were the servants of Cupid and Aphrodite. We dressed in long robes made from cloth of silver, styled like the ancients, and before the King we danced a difficult dance symbolising how *Love* might create *Peace* from *War*. It was a beautiful dance and Henry watched our slow, controlled movements avidly. The dance and our dresses were designed so that some small, sudden glimpses of our thighs and legs showed very briefly as we moved; tantalising flashes of creamy skin beneath silver cloth.

It was cleverly choreographed; just as the watcher thought he had imagined this discreet flash of skin, there! There was another... as swift and pretty as if it had been done by accident. But nothing was ever done by accident in the French Court. It was done to entice and refuse, to show and conceal. And this unusual, elegant and discreet sexuality had the great King breathing fast and shallow as we danced, slowly and prettily, in front of his table.

Each lady was masked; our masks were the gentle faces of feminine love, but my brilliant eyes shone through the mask like no other's and caught his eye. My figure was long and slim, my breasts were full but not large; I had a fine and slender figure and I was skilled in the dance. He looked on me on that night as the candle-light danced over the enticing glimpses of bare, pale skin. He stared at me; my eyes shining like gems, and the movements of my willowy body sensual. I felt his attention bearing down on me and that attention encouraged my dancing to its finest.

He was as handsome as I remembered.

Once more, I envied my sister.

But on this night, I was merely a beauty behind a mask that bowed and exited when the music was finished, leaving the first of the court dancers to enter and start the entertainment in earnest. When we ladies of the pageant had changed into our fine dresses and returned to the entertainment, he was dancing with another. I danced that night with courtiers. Once, in the crowd, I saw *him* look over at me, his eyes narrowed to try and see me properly, but quickly the dancers moved on and in the swirl of people he was gone. Later I saw him dancing with another in Claude's retinue and his eyes were taken up with her pretty eyes and pretty face.

I knew not what it was that drove me to long for his glance upon my face. Perhaps it was that lingering sense of girlish desire that he had awakened in me so many years ago. Perhaps it was because he was a great king who built such wonders. Perhaps it was the jealousy of one sister for another sister in seeing her ability to bring such a man to her bed. I knew not... but I wanted to be seen by him. I longed for it, in the secret places of my heart.

There were others at *The Field of the Cloth of Gold* who had their own wishes, and wills to prove. Emboldened by fine Gascon wine one night, Henry challenged François to a wrestling match, King against King, before all of their courtiers. I do not know how it was that Henry's ambassadors had not informed him that the King of France was, in fact, an expert wrestler; but either Henry did not know this, or he assumed that he was better than François could ever be. I can't imagine that Henry would have made such a challenge, if he did not think he could win.

François took the challenge and the two Kings moved to the centre of the throng of guests and dignitaries. Claude and her ladies were not amongst those present, so I did not see the event myself, but my brother and father were both present to see the humiliation of the English King at the hands of the French.

For François was truly an expert wrestler. He threw the English King to the floor in the first minute of the match. Although Henry of England was tall and strong, although his legs were sturdier than François', there was great skill and wiry strength in François. He moved like a dancer and could throw a man like the Giant Antaeus of old.

What a humiliation for such a proud king!

Henry declared he would have a re-match, and challenged François again. But the French King declined, not wishing to cause further hurt to the pride of his brother and ally. Henry went back to his great chair red-faced and embarrassed. François was gracious in his victory, but I was sure that this was one event the King of England never forgot.

Although he later made both peace and war with the French for political reasons, Henry would always resent François for those moments when he lay on the floor, winded in the dirt; his eyes snapping like those of an angry child, helpless at the feet of the King of France, with all the court looking on. Always, he would remember that humiliation and burn because of it. His temper was always resentful, and he could remain angry for longer than anyone else I have ever known

That short wrestling match did more to confirm Henry's feelings towards François than did any treaty or pact of everlasting peace that the slippery Cardinal Wolsey could concoct. From that day forth, in Henry's mind at least, he and the King of France were to be above all else, forever rivals.

For François, I think the occasion was amusing and rewarding, but I don't know that he would have had any idea that the cultured and sophisticated King lying at his feet could have been such a child inside. François could separate political and personal lives; Henry could not. François would leave old grudges where they lay; Henry would nurture them and carry them with him wherever he went.

This was not so obvious when Henry was a young man, but it became more so as he grew older. I, who came to know him so well, sensed this of him even then. Henry and I were alike in many ways; humiliation was not something that was easily borne by either of us. My heart was sore for his pride when I heard that story. My brother told me of it, laughing, as he whispered the tale to me. Although I smiled at my brother's story, I felt sorry for the wounded dignity of Henry.

Within hours, however, it seemed that no one in the English camp had any memory of the event occurring. Although the French were laughing into their sleeves about the English

'*King of the Dirt*', the English seemed totally unaware that anything had happened. The event was never recorded in the English accounts of *The Field of the Cloth of Gold* either, although it was recorded with relish and zeal by the French.

Such is the nature of politics and advancement; we see, hear and speak of only what is advantageous. That which is dangerous to survival is forgotten… it never happened. The English King could not bear to remember his mortification and so his courtiers made it as though it had never happened. Only for a king would such a thing be done.

It teaches us all a good lesson; that the word of but one man should always be checked against the word of another. The truth may be found somewhere in between their accounts.

But then, it was the same for the French; the beautiful tent of King François made from gold brocade and decorated with silver stars was dismantled after four days, completely ruined by the weather. And yet it seemed that no one remembered that event at all on the French side. The English, with their magnificent and stable, purpose-built, false castle chortled loudly about it for the French to hear whenever they could.

So you see, even on the greatest of occasions and in the most genteel company, all men are still as children seeking to outdo and ridicule each other.

The morning after the wrestling match, we were to hear a strange tale. The King of France had risen early and against the advice of his men, who always suspected the English may harm their King, rode to Henry's wooden castle. Here, he had entered Henry's chamber before the English King had risen, surprising him whilst still abed. François had laughed at the astounded and somewhat suspicious expression on King Henry's face, explaining that he was there to but help his brother dress for the morning. Henry was so overcome by this overt display of brotherly affection that he declared, "Brother, you have played me the best trick ever played, and shown me the trust I should have given you. From now on, I am your prisoner."

François then performed the duties of a servant for Henry in the name of friendship; holding a bowl of scented water, that Henry might wash himself, and helping him to dress. The two Kings exchanged presents of fine jewels and embraced each other, coming out of Henry's chambers laughing and jesting.

What a display of brotherly love! The story roamed through the camps and was reported by all ambassadors who heard of it. But how much of this fine show was real affection? Afterwards, a Venetian ambassador was said to have commented, "These sovereigns are not at peace. They hate each other cordially" which to my mind was an apt description of the attitude that the two Kings held towards one another.

On the last occasion that Henry came to Claude's tents to dine, the Queen had sought to create a more intimate affair. We ladies of the court waited on Claude, Henry and his men, and served them whilst dressed our gowns of Italian style. The King was happy and laughed greatly when Claude jested gently with him. Claude was very good at handling people, whoever they were. They often came to speak of her with great affection, and none of that praise was due to the crown upon her head.

Later that evening, we pleased him greatly by singing a new arrangement of a song that Henry had written some years previously. It was called 'Pastime with Good Company'. It sounded well when sang with many voices, playing both high and low parts of the song. The English version was often heard with great ringing notes of battle in it, with drums and horn blasts, but we played it in a softer and more feminine style, using the lute and our voices to create a siren-like adaptation of his famous song:

Pastime with good company
I love and shall unto I die;

Grudge who list, but done deny,
So God be pleased thus live will I.
For my pastance
Hunt, song and dance.
My heart is set:
All goodly sport
For my comfort
Who shall me let?

Youth must have some dalliance,
Of good or ille some pastance;
Company me thinks then best
All thoughts and fancies to dejest:
For idleness
Is chief mistress
Of vices all.
Then who can say
But mirth and play
Is best of all?

Company with honesty
Is virtue, vices to flee:
Company is good and ill
But every man hath his free will,
The best ensue,
The worst eschew,
My mind shall be
Virtue to use
Vice to refuse
Shall I use me.

He sat very still when we first started to sing, and he paid close attention. He was a talented musician and this was his song; daring to perform a new interpretation of one of his own works was a risky gamble. To fail would be to bring shame to the Court of France. Louise of Savoy was there watching us; if any of us failed in our rendition of this song, we would be sure to be dismissed from court and never to return.

So, we were suitably nervous when we came to play the song, although no one would have known this from the poised and controlled manner of our bearing. I took up the lute, speaking silently and harshly to my fingers, telling them not to slip upon the strings. I had long forgotten the nervousness that had plagued me at Mechelen when I had first played before crowds. Now I was practised in this as I did it almost every day at the French Court. But playing for Henry of England was a special circumstance, not only because of the importance of the occasion, but because of my own feelings for him. I did feel my heart quicken in my breast as it used to when I was but a child, as we took up those first lines.

But I should not have worried so; our performance was beautiful, elegant and feminine. The rendition pleased him. I saw him watch me as I played and sang. My voice was one of the stronger ones, and it was high, sure and beautifully haunting. My performance of his song on the lute was pretty. I saw him looking at me as though he was slightly perplexed, and I knew he was trying to place who I was. Perhaps I reminded him of my sister? That thought made me blush. Perhaps he saw the eyes of the dancer whose legs and eyes had caught his attention before? Or perhaps, in the face of the woman before him, he recalled the features of a child he once heard sing before him at the Court of Burgundy? I knew not, but in my secret heart I hoped that he watched and admired me as I had watched and admired him.

At the end of the song I looked up from my playing and into his eyes. I could not hold his gaze for long. I blushed and lowered my eyes feeling like a foolish girl.

His eyes were clear, piercing, and blue as the sea.

Applause erupted around us as we rose to return to our duties serving the Queen of France and the King of England. The night continued with more songs and more entertainments.

Afterwards, Claude told me that Henry had asked who each of the ladies were. "He seemed taken with your voice, Anne, in particular," she said with a smile.

"Did he ask who I was, Your Majesty?" I asked quietly of my mistress. Claude nodded and smiled again.

"I told him you were the younger daughter of his own ambassador, Thomas Boleyn," she said. "And I told him that you had been with my court these past few years, serving me well. He jested then, that I must not seek to steal the beauties of England from his court." She smiled at me in the mirror as I took her head-dress gently from her hair.

I smiled at Claude and thanked her for telling me. My heart leapt foolishly to hear Henry had called me a beauty. I longed to ask more, but it would have not been proper to do so, and I was concerned at the idea of anyone knowing I was still infatuated with this King. But whilst I would show it to no other, I could not deny it to myself. I longed for his notice, however impossible, however inappropriate, however foolish.

I wondered what he had thought when he heard that I was the younger sister of his new sweetheart. The thought of him comparing Mary and me made me flush even in private. Eventually I had to shake myself from these thoughts. There were many beautiful women, many noble girls around him. He had liked my singing and thought me attractive that was all. I was a passing fancy for his eyes, as fleeting as any jewel he looked on that another might wear. He was enamoured of my sister. Nothing was ever going to occur between the King of England and me, so I should get used to that idea.

He will forget me as easily as he forgets every face here, I thought, willing myself to stop being foolish.

But I did not know how wrong I was.

Chapter Twenty-Six

1520
The Field of the Cloth of Gold

The Field of the Cloth of Gold went on for weeks. There were endless entertainments; tourneys, dances and jousts, eating, drinking; and from the grunting sounds outside the tents sometimes at night, there was much in the way of other adventuring also for some. But the greatest times for me were the pleasures of being once again with my family.

After years of wandering the courts of Burgundy and France, I felt almost rootless, but the presence of my family beside me now filled a hole that I had hardly understood was there. My heart swelled with the warmth of my mother's smile, my sister's naughty laughter, the calm control of my father and the wit of my charming brother.

It was George's company that I sought the most. Mary and I had known each other as adults already, and the love of a father or mother seems unquestionable when you are young; but George, I knew the least, and yet perhaps wanted to know the most.

Sometimes we would wander the grounds and see the tourneys together. George now rode in the lists and excelled in them. He was a handsome young man. The maids of the court watched him closely and it was a pleasure for me to sense their jealousy in watching us walking out together. It is always nice to be a little envied. For George, there was pleasure too, in having two sisters who were charming and attractive; he was somewhat careful of Mary and me around the other gallants, however. I think he wanted to feel as though he was protecting his older sisters a little, which was sweet of him, if unnecessary. Both of us had spent our entire adult lives at court, and, after all, Mary's new admirer was the

King of England. We believed we were easily capable of looking after our own selves, a belief that for me would come to be cruelly tested in the future.

George was a man of the world, learned and clever. He had a quick tongue, with a great wit and imagination. He and I conversed on many subjects, but religious reform came easily, if quietly, to both our lips. Happily, we were of one mind, understanding that reform was needed and that the Church had to accept this. We spoke in low voices on the subject, and always in private. Although I was not ashamed of my thoughts, and I believed in my heart we were right, it was still dangerous to be found talking openly of reform, to be found questioning the Church. This showed that the Church, as George put it, was insecure, blind to the corruptions being committed in its midst because it could not bear to face them. There had to be changes made. The works of Martin Luther had reached England as well as France, and many were questioning and discussing points of theology and religious change, my family amongst them. George assured me that our father and mother were also keenly interested in the subject.

"And Mary?" I asked with interest. George snorted and looked at me scathingly.

"And I thought you were the clever one?" he asked, with amused distain in his voice. "Mary does not think about such matters, as they are beyond her," he sniffed and smiled at me. "Mary thinks of Mary's pleasure, she is incapable of thinking further ahead than a few days; even then her mind is not filled with religious or weighty matters, but rather with the colour of ribbons and the set of her dress. She will die and go to Heaven no doubt, because she will never have entertained a bad thought in her life and any sins will be forgiven because she has never really understood that what she is doing may be regarded as sinful." George looked at me with sparkling eyes; although his words sounded harsh, his tone was anything but serious. "The truth is, dear sister Anne, that I have two pretty sisters and one clever sister. *One* clever sister is quite enough for any man to have to deal with. If we all had clever sisters then we should all have to marry clever wives and then what? The world would be in ruins!"

He laughed as my hand flashed out and struck him across the middle. A sudden flare of anger had hit me, but I could not help laughing at his outrageous expressions. I shook my head at him, scolding him for speaking as he did, both about our sister, and about women in general. I did not like to be so dismissed for my sex, even in jest.

"What do you think of this affair with the King?" I asked him as we continued our walk.

We were nearing the tourney fields and knights were out practising in the late morning's sunlight. Soon it would be too hot for them to fight in their armour, so the tourney would be abandoned to pursue other entertainments that did not cause a man to roast like a peacock. Gallants often found the afternoons were suited to lying in the shaded gardens with the ladies.

George observed appraisingly as we watched two knights fight at the sword. Although covered in heavy armour, they moved fast; striking and hacking at each other with their great swords. Flashes of steel shone like flames as the sun caught the sharp edges of the beautifully made blades. George smiled at me, and still watching the fight, he continued to speak.

"The truth is, Anne, that there are three ways for a woman to advance in this world, and two of them require the opening of her legs, whether within wedlock or without. A woman may marry well, or she may become the sweetheart of a powerful man. There are two of the ways. The last is for a woman to enter a nunnery and then she must do something truly spectacular to be seen at all past her habit. This world belongs to men, and women must please them to advance. They may be clever like you, or foolish like Mary, but either way, they need the pleasure of a man to become the key to their fortunes. Even your beloved Marguerite enjoys her position and favour through the position of her brother. Even the famous Isabella of Castile deferred to her husband. Women must make compromises, and if they are clever, they will learn to turn their men to their will. This is what we must hope Mary is able to do for our family; in the manner of your other friend, the infamous Lady Françoise de Foix, eh?" George gave me a leering glance and I went again to slap him, but he danced out of the way on swift legs, laughing at me.

"Come, *Anne*!" he laughed. "You are easily shocked for one who keeps company with the whores *and* the philosophers of France… what a mixture! Have you never thought of jumping beds like Mary and Françoise, or of entertaining love like the free thinker Marguerite de Valois? Do you know strange rumours abound about Marguerite and François? Some say that the love between them is not that of sister and brother, but that of man and mistress."

And with that jest, my temper snapped. I stepped forward, and my hand lashed out and caught him surely around the jaw. The sound of the slap rang out across the valley; a short, sharp snap. I leaned in to him. My eyes were fire, my hands were clenched, and I was ready to fly at him. George cupped a hand to his cheek and stared at me in horror.

"You will *never* breathe a word against the Princess Marguerite in my presence!" I snarled at the abashed face of my brother. "*Never*, do you understand me? She is a greater lady than any I have ever known. A greater mind than you can ever hope to understand. I may be a woman, but I will fight you as a man if you dare to insult her honour again."

George was a-taken aback by the vehemence of my anger and could do nothing but nod at me. I shook myself; the anger in my mind snapped at my heels to do more, to keep on screaming at him, to hit him again. I struggled to control it.

"She is a great woman and a great princess," I spat at him. "She is a leader of reform in France and those who speak against her are those who want to destroy reformers. The words that you have listened to are the words of those who would see corruption continue; those who would have the clergy as rich as kings, whilst the poor starve in the streets; those who would *buy* their passage into heaven and live in sin upon this earth. You have believed in the words of those who have grown fat on the flesh of their fellow men. Marguerite seeks to *heal* the Church, to bring the faith further into the lives of the common people. You should feel ashamed of the words you have spoken." I breathed deeply, trying to calm myself.

"And I know why it is that they say these things of her," I said. "Because of her devotion to her brother they say these things; and because of this…"

I pulled from my pocket a pamphlet that Marguerite had written. It was a manuscript she had been working on for some years and contained radical thoughts on the nature of spiritual love. It was part of a poetical manuscript that she would later publish under the title *Le Miroir de L'ame Pecheresse,* or *The Glass of the Sinful Soul.* Marguerite had given me some of the work to read over, trusting me with her thoughts. She had only shown it to a few, trusted friends, but even so, word of it had reached other courts.

It was a tract that talked of the relationship of every Christian to every other Christian. It proposed that we were all related to each other in Christ. It outlined a theory that all sexual unions were equally sinful, all guilty of incest of a spiritual nature, as we were all God's children and therefore all related. Those who were pure of soul could achieve consummation with each other through spirituality and learning. Abstinence from sex, and communion with God was the only way to be sure of this spiritual communion. Due to its radical nature, the work even in these stages of its infancy had excited a lot of scandal. But Marguerite's main point was that *abstinence* from sexual relations was required in order to allow spiritual growth under the guidance of God. Those who had taken her words as some sort of excuse for a hypothetical affair between her and her brother had entirely misunderstood the point. Marguerite was a free thinker, but she was also a devout and zealous Christian. Her honour was precious to her; this tract was an expression of her religious and spiritual ideals, not a crass apology for an incestuous affair with her brother. It was also a work that very much upset traditional ways of thinking, as it seemed to advocate a *personal* relationship with God, not reliant on the saints or on the Virgin, or on priests; something akin to the faith of the followers of Luther.

George took the book from me and looked over the manuscript. He whistled slightly as he leafed through it. "I have heard of this... How do you have this?" he asked, still reading over the scribbled pages.

"Marguerite trusts me," I said quietly. "I have become her confidante in many ways."

He whistled again. There was a bright mark on his cheek where my hand and its rings had struck, but he seemed to have forgotten this in the interest he had in Marguerite's papers.

"So you have the ear of the sister of the King of France, and you have the admiration of the King of France," he said, looking up. I went to deny this, and he shook his head at me. "Yes, you cannot deny it, Anne. I have seen how he glances at you. And our sister Mary has the admiration of the King of England."

He rustled the papers in his hands and looked out at the field again. "Our family was made for great things, Anne, or, at least, the women in it appear to be." George looked down at the precious papers that I had handed him. Although he was a gallant and a warrior, he was also a man of letters and new thought interested him as it did me; almost as much, it seemed, as gossip did.

He handed them back carefully. "I am sorry if I offended you, Anna," he said. "I intended to make you laugh, not to make you attack me." He touched his jaw and winced slightly. "I hope you do not plan to treat your future husband in such a way, or we shall have to find a larger dowry than previously planned by our parents to recompense the man for marrying with a Fury."

I reached out and touched his cheek with my cold pale hand, and tears of remorse sprung to my eyes. He saw them, and he smiled at me, the warmth returning to his eyes again. He put his hand over mine to hold it on his face.

"I shall have to remember that my nearest sister took all the spirit, when the older one took all the sweetness," he said ruefully.

"Spirit is somewhat more useful at times," I drew his hand to my lips, kissing it gently.

"Sweetness is what a man desires to come home to," George said warningly, but then she shook his head and smiled. "But spirit is what puts fire in the belly," he continued. "I doubt not that you would be the more interesting to chase of the two of you."

I snorted. "That is only because Mary is a lame hind, apt to fall at your feet before the hunter's horn is sounded!"

He laughed, and arm in arm, we continued our walk around the fields of contest, talking of lighter matters.

Chapter Twenty-Seven

1520
The Field of the Cloth of Gold

The last of all the great events was a Mass, presided over by the Cardinal of York, Thomas Wolsey who was also the Lord Chancellor of England and advisor to the English King. The Mass was to encapsulate all the promises of peace between the two countries for the glory of God.

The French lined one side of the make-shift chapel that had been created in the vast jousting arena of *The Field of the Cloth of Gold*, and the English took the other. I was placed on the French side near to my mistress Claude, so I was close to the front with other attending nobles; a place of honour. The service was beautiful, punctuated by singing from the Cardinal's choirs. When those boys raised their voices to the heavens, I felt as though God Himself were touching my heart, and I felt blessed.

Cardinal Wolsey was a fair, handsome man at this time; although later he was to grow fat and leech-like in appearance. On this day, there was the light of accomplishment on his face. Much of the preparations for this great event had been down to him, and he seemed well pleased with himself. He lifted his arms to God, and I could see him gloating on his success at this meeting. I wondered if perhaps he should have been thinking more on the glory of God and less on the glory of Wolsey.

Wolsey dominated the English Court and had the ear and trust of its King. He had risen high, from comparatively humble beginnings as the son of a landowner, to become the second most powerful man in England. Some said that in truth, he was the *most* powerful, for things had been said of Wolsey that his King was unlikely to care for if they were repeated to him. An ambassador once remarked of Wolsey that *"this Cardinal is King"*, for if a man or a lord wanted anything, especially in the first years of Henry's reign, they needed to speak to the Cardinal before they approached the King. Wolsey had made himself invaluable, and whilst Henry still held the reins of power, it was Wolsey who tended to take hold of all else for him. Henry was not a happy man when the chores of his kingship weighed him down. Wolsey was his man to take on all that the King loved not, and with that responsibility great power came too.

Some called Wolsey's father a mere butcher, and the term *"butcher's cur"* was often applied to the Cardinal behind his richly-dressed shoulders, but Wolsey's father had been a landowner in truth. Whenever insults are thrown at another, birth and virtue, it seems, are the easiest and most common ways to insult. We all think ourselves so special and unique, but the same things come pouring from our mouths, the same thoughts strike through our minds; we are often so much more alike, so less original, than we care to recognise. As women are insulted using virtue, so often men who rise through intellect are insulted for their birth… and the further one rises, the more people are willing to insult you. Wolsey was a clever man, a charming man, and a ruthless man. He rose high because he had the talent to, and the strength to hold his position. Henry was good at seeing usefulness in men, and in using it. Although Wolsey was no friend to my family and kept a wary eye on my father, since he disliked anyone who wished to rise high at court, seeing them as threats, it cannot be denied that he was an intelligent, wary man, and a ruthless opponent of all those who might challenge him.

But… these are reflections better kept for later in my tale…

Through scholarship and the Church, Wolsey had worked his way upwards to become the King's advisor, and then Lord Chancellor, and had been made a Cardinal by the Pope in 1515. Wolsey had a keen eye for money, and an able hand to grasp it; he dressed in the finest clothes and had many great houses and palaces in England, some of which, such as York Palace and Hampton Court, were said to outshine even the palaces of the King himself. John Skelton, a court poet, who had been Henry's Latin tutor when the King was a boy, was famed for his scathing, often scandalous verse on the court. Skelton was not overly fond of Wolsey, whom he saw as the epitome of corruption and vice at Henry's court. Of the Cardinal's palace, Hampton Court, Skelton wrote:

Why come ye not to court?
To the King's court, or to Hampton Court?
The King's court should have the precedence,
But Hampton Court hath the pre-eminence.

Wolsey had not been pleased at this poem when he heard it bandied about court, and Skelton narrowly escaped arrest by the Cardinal by seeking sanctuary in Westminster Abbey. I doubt not that the King intervened for his old tutor, although Skelton was not welcomed at the Court of England much afterwards. Such was Wolsey's influence that to offend the Cardinal was most often to be cast from the halls of power entirely. But the works of Skelton lived on. His play *Magnificence*, a satirical work on the life of a king who fails in his duty as he dismisses his servant *'Measure'*, and takes up with one named *'Liberty'* to the ruin of his kingdom, was often performed in houses where Wolsey was not a popular figure. But it was not performed at court whilst Wolsey reigned supreme.

Wolsey was fabulously wealthy, owning more land than any in England bar the King, and he received money from other countries too; pensions given to him to endear his favour. France was one of those countries that saw value in feeding the already heavy pocket of the Cardinal. When Wolsey rode out on his supposed humble mule, apparently emulating the figure of Christ, amongst the people, his saddle cover was crimson velvet and his stirrups were solid gold. He was ever surrounded by multitudes of servants, his path marked by silver crosses and sons of noble houses bearing the Great

Seal of the King, Wolsey's mark of true authority. The Cardinal dressed in ermine, silk and red velvet; he held fabulous feasts made famous for their sugared subtleties, danced with ladies of the court, and kept a mistress called Joan Lark, who bore him children. To the King, Wolsey was indispensable.

"*This Cardinal is King*"… a fitting thing to say of such a man.

This man, I thought as I looked upon him, embodies everything in the Church so desperately requiring change. How can a man with golden stirrups and coffers overflowing with money possibly be in communion with Christ; he who rode on a mule in sack-cloth and gave up his life for the salvation of his people? How can this man standing before me with such pride on his face, have a better understanding of God than I? Should he, a man of God, not give those stirrups up to feed the poor of his parish, or to better educate scholars? How can he hold a good relationship with God and help his people understand God when he spends all his time ruling in the stead of the King? He is supposed to be a man of God, to lead by example, in virtue and reason, and yet if we were to follow the example of Wolsey, perhaps we would all be rich as kings, caring nothing for the souls of others.

It was as I mused on these thoughts that a frightful event took place. We were only part way through the ceremony when a fearsome crash came from the skies above us. It was as though a thunder storm had broken, but there were no clouds in the pale sky that morning. Then, from above us, like some giant monster of old, there came a creature, hurtling through the skies… a great dragon! I saw it rear its head and seem to laugh at the Mass of the treaty of universal peace. I stared at it in frozen terror. All about me there was screaming and shouting as people pointed to the skies at the terrible creature flying above.

Then, just as suddenly as it had appeared, it was gone, and there was nothing but grey and black smoke billowing in the air. I looked around in wonder, fearing what such an omen may mean. I was not the only one; men, their swords half-drawn in their hands, looked around themselves in wonder at the dissipating smoke. Women, faces drawn with fear, clutched books of devotion in shaking hands. I heard the Kings of England and France talking to each other in animated voices; it seemed that each suspected the other of deceit.

But, as it turned out, it was an accident. Someone had accidentally let off a great firework, made to explode in the form of a salamander, King François' own personal badge. It was supposed to be ignited later, during the evening celebrations, to impress the English. It was a trick gone awry, although at the time, it seemed like an almighty omen of doom to us.

The company was settled by the guards and the reassurance of the Kings, and the Mass continued, although many people continued to glance suspiciously about themselves. Everyone tried to bring back the feeling of brotherly camaraderie, but it had been tainted by the strange events of the Mass.

I was furious when at the end of the Mass, a papal indulgence was given to all those present, allowing reduced sentences in purgatory. Time spent in purgatory was in the hands of God, not of the cardinals or the Pope; the Pope and his minions could not give souls time off from purgatory if we deserved that fate. There were other disapproving faces around me; my father's face looked somehow both blank and disgusted at the same time; but all were silent as we received this blessing. None spoke out, even if they did not agree. I saw Marguerite shrug in disappointment.

Change was in the air. The Cardinal may have been unaware of it, but it was on the move. There were many in that educated company who disapproved of the supposed blessing given to us by the Cardinal on us that day.

As we left the great Mass, I briefly joined my father and mother, who were standing with a handsome hawk-faced man and a proud-faced woman. I was introduced to Lord and Lady Morley, and their daughter, Jane. It took me a moment to remember that this pretty, green-eyed young woman before me was the same child that I had seen and felt so sorry for at the funeral of little Prince Henry so many years ago. Those green eyes, which I remembered so well filled with tears, were now bright, set in almond-shaped sockets of the attractive woman before me. Jane was now middling tall and slim, with the figure of a girl teetering on the edge of maturing into a beauty. I remembered her well, although the courtly smile she turned on me held no flicker of remembrance.

It was a brief meeting, and as we walked away, my father nodded to George in such a way as to make me suspect that this was no chance meeting. Instead, the meeting seemed to hold great significance for George; a potential bride perhaps? George nodded back to father in a nonchalant manner that held no real excitement. My brother was a young and handsome courtier; his wife would be, as so many are to their husbands, his wife, and nothing more. His would continue to choose his loves from the volley of attractive young women at court, with whom he was already popular. George was, it seemed, quite successful in convincing young ladies to abandon their reserve to him; he had already made his way through a fair few experienced mistresses of the English Court, so he told me. Men who find easy conquests usually tire of them with time… George was already reaching such a stage in his life. A wife, who was bound to obey and serve him whenever he wished, was unlikely to hold his interest long. I don't think he had any real inclination for a wife, but would marry where our father and his account books dictated. Once again, I found myself feeling rather sorry for green-eyed Jane, who walked away from us looking back slyly behind her for a further glance at my handsome brother. It seemed that if they were to marry, she, at least would be happy about it, for a time at least. George, it seemed, would match her interest with equal disinterest. A wife held no challenge for him, and therefore no interest.

Soon enough the events of *The Field of the Cloth of Gold* drew to an end. In no time at all those great tents were dismantled and flung to the floor like the skirts of great female titans dressing for bed. The jousting grounds and tilt yards became but dusty scraps of ground; the cook fires and banqueting tents could be found only by patches of heat-scoured earth and food debris; the places where we had danced through the night became but wisps of flattened ground on the horizon.

The great palace of Henry VIII of England, that wonderful invention that had so gloried and astounded us all, was chopped up. The glass was sent back to England, the great walls and turrets were burned in the bonfires of the final night's celebrations. Gone was that palace of pleasures. Gone was that momentous occasion. And gone were we; my horse saddled and my body dressed to ride, I said farewell to my family and they to me. My sister sat pretty and happy on her horse, jesting with her husband, her shoulders covered in a new fur-trimmed cloak, a present from the King of England. My mother, her eyes filled with tears, pressed a small jewelled book of devotions into my hands. My father clasped me to him in a cold hug and informed me of the dates he would next be in France. My brother, my new friend, gave me a ring, a simple golden hoop, which he said would sting the cheek of the next man I hit far less than the ones I wore now. But he said this in a whisper, so that our father would not hear that his daughter had been striking the heir to the family name. I smiled at George and promised him I would keep the ring with me always.

I still wear it now.

My family sailed out on the morning tide with the English convoy. I rode with Claude and her retinue back to the Court of France. There, across the waters, were my family and their lives, and here, I remained in France; in this land was the life that I loved and would continue to lead.

Chapter Twenty-Eight

1520
France

I lived in France for almost another two years in the service of Queen Claude. My days were full, for I served the Queen, and I was much in company with the Princess Marguerite and her circle. More and more, I drifted towards Marguerite's company, spending less time with Françoise. Although Françoise and I were still great friends, it seemed that we shared less in matters of thought and philosophy than we had before, and she was often busy with the King. My admiration for Marguerite and her circle grew day by day, as did my desire for new learning, for new thought, for reform and for knowledge of God such as Marguerite had. Françoise would often find me reading in some quiet corner alone, and would force me out to practise dancing with her; she would steal my books and run from me, screaming with laughter. She did not know that many of those books could have had me arrested, had the wrong person found them in my possession.

At court events, François would pay me special attentions. I believe that he wished me to become one of his lesser mistresses, but he had been warned by Marguerite that this position would not be acceptable to me. She told François that I valued my honour highly and did not want to become the mistress of any man. Whilst I think he might not have liked this, he accepted it from his sister and did not push or proposition me for sexual favours, though he still sought my company and hand in the dance.

You might think it odd that a sister and brother would talk in this way, discussing frankly such private matters. But they were very close, François and Marguerite. To Marguerite, it was the union of souls that mattered most in life, above all other loves, and this was the union she had with her brother.

They understood each other completely and worked together easily. They were, in fact, like two halves of the same book; it was impossible to truly understand the one without the other. I was grateful that Marguerite talked to François on my behalf; I had no wish to anger the King. I was happy that she had explained my feelings to him, and that she had obviously done it in such a way that François was happy to continue to offer me his attention at court events without expecting that I offer him anything but friendship in return.

There were, unhappily, other men at court who were not as sophisticated as their King. And it took one short and unhappy event for me to understand this fully.

It was one night at a celebration; Claude had given François another healthy child, a daughter named Madeline, and the whole country of France was alive with feasting and celebration. There had been a great tourney during the day and then a masque where all had worn masks and danced together as supposed strangers; the masks had been uncovered and we had eaten well in the great hall. Then there was more dancing. The evening turned into the early hours of the morning and no one noticed or cared.

The wine was flowing freely and I had drunk perhaps too much of it. The Rhenish wines were strong and tasty; their richness flowed down the throat like sweetened water but made the head giddy and the senses dulled. It was then that some of the party, specially invited by François, broke off to take part in a private banquet; a feast of smaller proportions and of sweet fare in one of the secluded banqueting towers in the gardens. Because of my friendship with Marguerite and my position in Claude's household, I was one of those chosen to attend to the banquet in the gardens.

My dancing partner, for most of the night, had been the same gentleman, a man called Charles, who hailed from Navarre. All night he pestered me to dance with him; he was handsome and a good dancer, so I had enjoyed the flirtation and the attention that he gave to me. I thought little more of it; every day and each event at court was very much the same. We all played around each other, flirted and danced, talked and amused. That was the normal way of the court.

After the banquet of sweets was over, many of the party broke down into smaller groups to wander in the gardens. For most, it was a chance for an intimate moments or a mild indiscretion, or in some cases, just a chance for friends to walk and talk together under the clear moonlight in one of the most beautiful gardens in the world. Charles asked me to walk with him; he had been gentle and attentive all night, and the August night was warm and inviting. I suspected nothing in a gentle walk at the end of an exciting day, to wind down the senses and become ready for sleep. There were plenty of people walking in the gardens. I felt no need to consider my safety.

As we walked, we talked softly of the court and of the newborn daughter of France. Eventually, I realised we had wandered farther from the main body of the banquet party than I had intended, and that were alone in the high hedges of the knot garden.

Charles turned to me and clasped my hand. "Now that we are away from everyone else, I can tell you; I have long thought you to be the most beautiful woman of the court, the most beautiful lady I have ever seen."

I smiled and inclined my head distantly; I was used to such over-blown phrases as these. It was all in the act of the courtier and all in a day's work for a lady of the court. Although I was flattered by these words that I often heard, I knew that in reality, they meant little.

"Ah!" he cried. "You shrug… but you must believe it to be true." He moved towards me and encircled my waist with his strong arm. "Come," he murmured, his voice husky and his wine-soaked breath suddenly very close to my mouth. "I shall show you how it is between us."

Suddenly his mouth bore down on mine and his arm became like a vice around my waist. Startled, I did nothing for a moment, and then, fearing the pressure of his body against mine and the sudden urgency of his desire, I flailed my hands against his face and shoulders, and when he would not let go, I bit the tongue that he rammed inside my mouth.

"*Bitch!*" he exclaimed, pulling his head back. Brutally he shoved a hand over my mouth, preventing me from screaming and almost from breathing. His other hand proceeded to try to lift my skirts up, even as he shoved me backwards. I staggered under the pressure of his strength, shouting against the hand that muffled my calls for help. My hands, all my strength, felt useless against him.

He is going to rape you, I thought. A strange, clear voice seemed to speak in my head that was somehow far, far away from the girl that was struggling with all her might against the strength of this man.

He is going to rape you and you are not strong enough to stop him.

He was forcing me backwards into an arbour where there was a seat. His eyes, so close to my face, were bloodshot, and his breath stunk as he pressed his mouth against my skin. I tried to call out, but his fingers were pushing into my open mouth and making me gag. How could I have thought him handsome? This was a beast, not a man. Tears sprung from my eyes. Wild, strange, deep noises came from my throat as his hand bore down on my mouth even stronger than before. He held me, struggling against him, under him, trying to undo his codpiece. I threw every part of my body into movement, struggling against his hold. I had never truly known fear until this moment.

His codpiece was unhooked and now he fought with his britches as well as with me. Swearing, and unable to complete his task with me flailing against him, he loosened one hand to try and avail himself. I could feel him, against my leg, hard as rock beneath his clothing. The feeling of his urgency was revolting, terrifying. Choked sounds of rage and terror sprung from beneath those fingers on my mouth. I was petrified. I felt both powerless and enraged.

But suddenly, the pressure of his hands upon me was lessened as he tried to get the drawstrings of his britches undone. One of my hands broke free from under his. With a strength that was not my own, I lashed out, my fingers like the claws of a lioness, and I scratched at his cheek and eyes with all the force I could exert. My clawed fingers went into his eye and I felt the soft flesh of his eyeball scrape under the nails of my fingers. He screamed, sounding more like a harpy than a man, and flung himself backwards from me, grabbing at his eye, allowing me the moment that I needed to fling my foot upwards, into the middle of his legs as hard as I could. As I ran from that arbour, skidding and stumbling, I heard, with terrified satisfaction, the soft grunt of him hitting the floor in pain.

I tumbled, heedless and petrified, from that arbour and stumbled headlong into another man. I reeled backwards, afraid that another man might do the same to me. I went to run in the opposite direction, but a hand, gentle and firm, caught hold of my arm and propped me back up to a standing position.

"Mistress Boleyn?" the voice was polished, somewhat amused, and familiar. I looked up into the eyes of François the King of France, and relief swept over me. Almost fainting, I burst into tears and threw myself to the floor before him. On my knees, I held out my hands to him and croaked, "Please help me, Your Majesty."

The amused expression that had touched his features when first I tumbled into his path turned to confusion and then darkened with anger as he saw the swearing shape of Charles begin to emerge from the arbour behind me. My dishevelled appearance, my white face and the tears of fear running down my face were enough to tell the King what had occurred here. He offered his arm to me and I rose, trembling. He guided me to his side, looked into my eyes and nodded at me. I had his protection. I could have fainted with relief. Looking behind him, he nodded to his companions to leave, and they wandered away, thankfully not witnessing me in the pitiable state to which I was reduced.

"Charles!" François said sharply to the humbled nobleman who stood glowering at me from the darkness.

"Your Majesty," Charles answered, attempting to bow, and doing so with little grace due to the pain coursing through his manhood.

"You appear to have drunk too freely of the wine, and you have fallen and hurt yourself," said François smoothly. "I believe it would be best if you go to your apartments and partake in no more moonlit strolls, where it is so easy to fall and do mischief to yourself."

François looked at me. "*I* shall see your walking partner safely to her chambers. I do not think that you should accompany Mistress Boleyn on such walks anymore; she is rather different to many court ladies and, as such, I should like to see her remain." He raised one eyebrow at Charles. "If… you understand me clearly?"

François' voice was all politeness, but underneath it there was iron. Charles nodded and mumbled "Yes, Your Majesty," before turning and limping away through the gardens.

"I would advise you to be more careful in your choice of walking partner, my lady," the King said to me, taking my arm gently and walking me, trembling, in the opposite direction. "Some men do not take *no* for an answer, even from a lady."

I nodded and fresh tears burst from my eyes, I tried to keep them under control, but the reality of the situation I had just been in hit me with all the might of a cannon ball. I could not stop shaking or crying. I felt weak and foolish. I felt dirty and soiled. There was nothing I could do to stop the shaking in my bones or my head. All I could hear were reprimands from my own self: Why did you walk out there? Why did you walk so far? Why did you not scream when first he put his hands on you? Why did you not run when you first were scared of him? Why are you such a fool Anne Boleyn? Why? Why? Why?

I noticed that François had led me inside the palace and was walking me, stunned and wordless, into the private apartments of the royal family. I stopped and looked at him questioningly, fresh fear flooding into my heart. Surely, after all I had endured this evening he was not expecting me to reward him for saving me, by undertaking the same act I had just almost been forced into?

François saw my expression and shook his head at me. "You need women now," he said, "not men." He smiled a small, sad smile at me, and continued to lead me through the halls. Eventually he knocked at a door to a private salon and inside, halfway through taking off her jewels from the night's entertainments, was Marguerite. She was alone; her servants dismissed to her outer chambers to guard her person yet afford her some privacy. I choked when I saw her, as fresh tears of relief flooded my throat, and I flung myself, heedless of rank and order, into her arms. She caught me, started and off-guard. Her beautiful violet eyes widened as she took in my face.

"Child?" she asked in wonder at my total lack of control. "What is it, Anne? What has happened?"

She looked sharply towards her brother who raised his hands to mimic self-defence. "Not I," he said to her questioning look, "but there was someone who knew not what a lady means when she says *nay*."

He sighed and shook his head at his sister. "I do not think she was hurt, just scared, but I thought that you were the one to care the best for her in her present state."

He turned as he walked to the door, and he said to me, "I hope you will be well-recovered from this malady, Mistress Boleyn, and that you shall find that not all men are as the one you found yourself in company with this evening."

With that, François, the King of France and my rescuer, left the room and left me to beat out the hard, dry sobs that rocked my body as I wept into Marguerite's breast.

She let me cry for a while and then pulled me back away from her. "Did he hurt you? Anne? Listen to me; did this man my brother spoke of achieve his purpose?"

I shook my head and gulped the painful sobs backward into my body as Marguerite breathed a sigh of relief. "Then he did not?" she asked. "You are a maid still?"

I nodded again, unable to speak and she propped me up in a chair and poured a large draught of wine which she made me pour down my throat. The taste for a moment reminded me of the fetid breath of my attacker, and I choked back a wave of nausea.

"You have been lucky, Anne," Marguerite said. Her face was as pale as mine and her eyes, although looking at me, were lost somewhere in the past. "Do you know why my brother brought you here?" she asked, pouring wine for herself into a fine silver goblet and taking a large gulp as she came again to my side.

"You… have been kind to me, Your Highness," I said wiping a shuddering hand over my sore and blotched face, red with crying, and white with shock. I was far from the elegant woman of court who had danced with such abandon and energy all night.

"That is one reason, yes," she nodded. "But my brother, who knows me better than all others in this world, also brought you here because he knew that I could help you where others could not. For I am well placed to understand your feelings at this moment."

I looked at her, the horror of my own night frozen suddenly by the encroaching feeling of horror for what she was trying to tell to me.

"You see, one night, many years ago, my brother and I were staying at a castle owned by friends. It was late at night and I had retired to bed. My ladies were dismissed to my outer chambers and I was alone; such is the privilege of a princess at times. A young man had broken into my bedchamber, unbeknownst to me, and was hiding under the bed, waiting for me to lie down to sleep. He emerged, much to my horror and surprise, and sought to make love to me. When I refused him, threatening to call my maids and guards, he leapt upon me, and sought to take me by force, violently and with great strength, he sought to take from me what I would not give him freely. He was no stranger. He was a man of the Court, a lord and a noble, in name at least. We had been dancing together all night and he had sought to be my courtly admirer for a long time. I liked him well enough… before that night. He was handsome and he had been gentle towards me. But I am a princess of royal blood and my honour is my greatest virtue. I did not desire him in the way he desired me. I thought that we could enjoy the friendship that can come of courtly love; I thought I was unreachable, that I was secure with my position. But I was not. I screamed and fought him, which he seemed to enjoy… but I did not. I was terrified and outraged. He was so much stronger than me that I suddenly realised that all women, even a princess such as I, are powerless under the fist of a stronger, brutal man. I struggled against his attempts to keep me quiet, I screamed, and my screams brought my ladies to me. He ran from the room. As I recovered from the violence of the encounter, I swore that I would have his head for the insult he had done me, for all that he tried to do to me."

She looked at me. I was marble, I was ice, frozen solid. Marguerite's dark eyes did not sparkle as they had done when I first met her. In her eyes was blankness, darkness. "Then one of my women said something to me that I will say now to you. For little as I like it, it is the truth. It is not justice, it is not fair, nor right, but it is the way that the world is." Marguerite breathed in, steeling herself.

"That woman told me that should I go after the man who attacked me and have him arrested that I may well gain his head in retribution, but I should lose my honour with it. For all had seen us dancing that night, and other nights, all had seen his attentions to me and seen me receiving them with pleasure. Even though it is part of my office as a princess to enter into the games of courtly love, and to be friendly with all I meet, my actions would still be held against me. In this world, there are few who will believe the word of a woman over that of a man, and none who would believe that I had not *encouraged* him to make love to me. *I* would be held accountable for him attacking me. *I* would be the one blamed and censured by the world. If I sought to take revenge on him, *I* would be the one to suffer."

She looked straight into my eyes. Her face was bitter, unlike I had ever seen her look before. Her lip curled in distaste. "There were none who would believe that it was not my fault in some way. I should have been ruined if I sought justice against the monster who attacked me. The world would not blame him for having concealed himself in my chambers and attacked me. The world would blame *me*. For *I am a woman*, and it seems that in the eyes of the world, women are held to blame for all that men do in matters sexual."

She took another deep swallow of her wine. "And little I like it, Anne, but that is the truth of the matter. If I had him arrested and the story was spoken, then men and women would have believed me loose of morals. There were none who would have taken my word over his; even being a princess, *I* would have been held as the one at fault, not him. I learnt that night that wisdom does not always come in easy lessons and justice does not always prevail. I learnt that knowledge is not all to be found in books and that the world is ready to believe the worst of women and the best of men. I learnt from that harsh lesson, as *you* must now. I had to see that beast every day at court, knowing every day that he had got away with what he tried to do to me. Every day, I had to steel myself to stop the fear in my heart pounding when I saw him. Every day I had to hold my head up as I passed him and remember my own dignity. And every night, I fought him, over and over, in my dreams."

She shook her head. "Anne, listen to me… You remain a maid; the man who attacked you, he has hurt you, shaken your trust, but he has not damaged your honour or your name, unless you let him by allowing this event to ruin anything further in your life. You will not speak of this matter, and neither will my brother; nor will I. It will become, as my experience did, something you carry within you, a warning to you, for the rest of your life. But you have been lucky, for he did not achieve his purpose. Do you think you are the first woman this has happened to? You think you will be the last? Through the streets of Paris, through the world, there were many such women as you tonight, some forced in their lawful marriage beds by their husbands, and some pressed to dirty floors by strangers. Those women would look on you and wish they had been in your place, rather than theirs. Men own this world and women do not. Perhaps this will be the only time you will face such a horror in your life, but perhaps not. Being clever or highly born will not protect you; you must be careful and you must have the protection of God and your wits if you are to remain chaste in this world."

She sat by my side and put a hand to my wrist. "Take from this experience and learn; be cautious in your trust. You must learn to keep a piece of you secret from others in your heart.

Do not believe the words of men who prance and prattle, but believe in the counsel of your own mind and that of God. You can trust few in this life, but *you* should be one amongst those you do trust. Trust your instincts from now on. If you feel that a situation is dangerous then it *is*, and you should extradite yourself. If you worry that a person is dangerous, then they *are*, and you should be wary. Do not suppose that your rank or position will ever make you safe, and keep your watch always for those who are your enemies. From now on, trust your instincts and use the lesson you have been given. For now you know that there is no justice for women in such matters; we will always be blamed for the actions and abuses of others against us."

She put her arms around my shoulders. I had stopped crying. I was staring at my beautiful friend in dazed horror. "You know now that people can wear two faces, Anne," she said softly. "You must learn to see the one that they do not wish you to know, the face of the beast inside. You must learn to detach yourself from people who are not worthy of your love; for only then shall you be safe. Trust in God and trust in yourself. No more can we ask in life."

I nodded dully. My mind was swimming with half-thoughts and I felt dirty and tired.

"Come," she said. "You shall stay with me this evening. I shall send word to Claude. You will be safe with me, but no more midnight walks? Not unless you have another maid with you."

Marguerite helped me undress as though I were the Princess and she the servant, and then she helped me into a pallet bed of soft feather and down on the floor of the chamber. I was exhausted, but fearful of sleep. When I closed my eyes, the face of Charles flooded my mind. I woke many times that night, starting from the scent of the sour wine on his breath and the feel of his hands pressing painfully on my body. But in the darkness I heard Marguerite breathing quietly in the bed above me and I knew I was safe. She was the kindest friend I had ever known. In the midst of my terror and fear, she had shared something of her own pain with me, and had taught me a terrible, yet valuable, lesson about the world.

I awoke the next morning a changed and altered woman. I bathed myself over and over in a bowl in my chambers. Scrubbing at my flesh until it was pink and raw. I felt as though I might never be clean again. But I was resolved.

From now on, the part of me that was real, the part that could be hurt and damaged, would be hidden behind the mask that was Mistress Anne Boleyn. I was a child no longer. I trusted blindly in the goodness of people no longer. Marguerite was right; I could not call this man to account for what he had tried to do to me, not without damaging my name, and my prospects in life. I would be blamed in some way for the abuse done to me, by him. I had to hide a part of my heart, damaged and broken, from the rest of the world, as I held my head up high before the court, and tried to leave the memories of that night behind me.

Chapter Twenty-Nine

1521
France

That spring we received troubling news from the courts of England. The Duke of Buckingham, that same Duke whom my brother had served as a child, was suddenly arrested, tried, and beheaded for high treason.

The courts of the world were shocked; the Duke held some of the last vestiges of English royal blood outside of the house of Tudor in his veins, and his trial and execution were almost unprecedented in the lands of Christendom. There were whispers of witchcraft, that the Duke had consulted auguries to divine the King of England's death, and wished to bring it about through the offices of magic. Whether these rumours were indeed true, we knew not, but the Duke *had* been found guilty of plotting the death of King Henry by mortal means; he had apparently mobilised a great horde of soldiers, perhaps in preparation for taking control of the country by force.

In May, the Duke was arrested, interrogated and then tried. Four days later, the Duke of Buckingham lost his head. Many blamed Wolsey for the downfall of the Duke, for it seemed impossible that the Cardinal could have been uninvolved in the fall of such an eminent member of the court. Many courts around the world were stunned by the news. Buckingham was essentially a prince of England… although not of the family who sat on the throne, his blood was seen as royal as theirs.

Charles V, the young boy with the large chin who I had known from afar at Mechelen had recently become the Emperor of the Hapsburgs. Charles commented that "*a butcher's dog has killed the finest buck in England*," and many others in France and in England too, were quick to lay the blame at Wolsey's door. But was the Duke brought to early death for rivalling

Wolsey's position at court? Or was the Duke done to death for having within his veins a claim to the throne which many thought more legitimate than that of Henry VIII? Was it the Cardinal who had wanted Buckingham gone, or the King? None could say for sure.

François was shocked and grieved, as he had known the Duke personally. And, I think, he had liked the proud man. Marguerite whispered to me that she believed the Duke had been too close in blood to the throne to remain comfortably near to Henry, and that this was, perhaps, the real reason for his removal.

"Your Tudors are a great family," she said to me, shaking her head. "But they are new to the throne, new to power. Buckingham was of the old blood, too close to the throne to remain alive. This killing, they say, was done because the Duke was plotting the King's death. It could be true… it could be a lie. We will never know." She looked at me and raised an eyebrow. "But what we do know is that he was too close to the throne to stay alive."

I shivered, despite the warmth of the day. As I reached adulthood it seemed that the world became more and more dangerous; even the blood in your veins could be the author of your death.

My father, however, benefited from the fall of the Duke. Upon Buckingham's death, his property was divided between the courtiers upon whom the King of England felt he could depend. Although Henry kept the lion's share for himself, courtiers such as my father received new lands and titles that had once belonged to Buckingham. Penshurst Place, a grand house near our own Boleyn estates at Hever was reserved for the King's use, and my father became its steward. I wondered if this house was in part reserved for the King of England so that he could meet in secret with my sister whilst she stayed with our parents.

It was also in this year that Henry of England published a scathing attack on the works of Martin Luther, that same author whose banned works I had admired. Henry's book, *Asserto Septem Sacramentorum adversus Martinus Lutherus,* or *A Defence of the Seven Sacraments against Martin Luther*, was a virulent attack on Lutheranism, a belief fuelled by Luther's works and that of others like him. Lutheranism proposed that a man should adopt a more personal approach to faith than that taken by the Catholic Church. Martin Luther's philosophies and pamphlets were setting all of Christendom afire with talk. Luther espoused that the faithful could pray directly to God Himself, that they needed not the priests or the Pope to intercede. Lutheranism did away with the need for intercessors such as the saints, or Mary, the Mother of Christ. For Lutherans many priestly offices were made redundant, which the Church found threatening and sacrilegious. Luther's followers had even started to challenge the transubstantiation, the act in which the bread and wine of Mass literally became the body and blood of Christ. Luther taught that this act was merely symbolic and to believe otherwise was to become lost in magic and superstition, rather than in the true light of following the word of God. To the followers of Luther, faith alone was the force that men needed to be good Christians.

It was revolutionary thought, dangerous thought. Martin Luther was excommunicated by the Pope that year, but Luther did not consider the Pope to be the supreme head of the Church any longer, and continued to preach even despite the danger to himself. Many of Luther's teachings found root in the hearts, minds and souls of people throughout Christendom. I had read Luther's works, and whilst I did not agree with him on all points, I liked many of his arguments. I was saddened to find that the reaction of the Church was as I had expected it to be. Rather than listen to the arguments of such a radical thinker, rather than think that to reform the Church and practises which had fallen into corruption would be a good thing, they moved against him. They banned and burned his books, as did many monarchs of the world. They moved against the followers of the new thought, and they encouraged attacks on Lutherans. Henry of England's book was such an attack.

Whilst the King had some help from his advisors Thomas More, and Richard Pace, in proofing the book, the sentiments and thoughts enclosed therein were entirely the work of the King, and it was violent in its language and expression. Luther was to respond to the King's book with a work of his own, which insulted the King, calling him a "*strumpet in a tantrum*" without knowledge or understanding of his subject, and accused the King of having had other men write the book for him; and so the battle lines were drawn. Henry could not bear to hear the name of Luther at his court, and sought to destroy all Luther's works that had crept into his lands. Luther's works were publicly burned, and the Pope gave Henry the title of *Fidei Defensor*, or *Defender of the Faith,* for writing his book against Luther. Although Henry came to alter some of his views later in life, he never truly lost his hatred for Luther, who had dared to insult him so, and he never gave up the title gifted to him for his defence of the Pope.

This was a time when there was much change in thought and action about us, and oftentimes I thanked my own fortune to be within the Court of France, where the protection of Marguerite meant that I could read both banned and authorised works by the great thinkers of our age, and not have to close my mind to any of them for fear of the Church.

But as change comes, it seems to spread and grow. There was change coming in my life too, which was to bring me much unhappiness.

In early December of the year 1521, I received a letter from my father, ordering me back to England, back to a homeland that I had not seen for years. It did not come wholly as a surprise. France and England were entering difficult times politically, and it seemed that there may well be war between them. The treaty of *The Field of the Cloth of Gold* was long since forgotten, it seemed, and now England looked to Spain for an ally. It was not a good idea for an English woman such as I to be at the court of the enemy of my country; I might be arrested or imprisoned as a spy, or held for ransom. My father wrote to urge me back home, before any problems with the English alliance with Spain occurred.

Although it was not wholly unexpected, I stared at the letter in horror. I did not want to leave the Court of France. It was my home. England was a country that I barely knew and had no wish to go to. I loved my life in France, so much of my life I had lived here. My friends were here, and I felt as though my future, too, was here… I felt I would not know or like England, not as I loved France.

And there was another message on this paper, another reason that I was being recalled from my position in France; my family had found me a husband. This was to be the official reason I was to give for leaving the French Court, as my father did not want to damage his personal relations with François. But it was also true; there was a match being seriously proposed for me in England. I did not know to whom I was being offered. My father did not embellish that letter with details; he obviously did not believe that the identity of my future husband was of huge significance to me.

I was simply commanded, as a daughter and a Boleyn, to get myself back to England as soon as possible.

I was going home… whether I liked it or not. I had no choice in the matter.

Claude was sad to see me leave, as I was full of sorrow to leave her. She had been a kind and generous mistress who had cultured my creative and artistic mind and helped me to hone it. She gave me strings of pearls and a dress of her own to take with me, and asked to keep the little miniature that I had had painted of myself when first I entered her service. I cried to leave Claude, but it was to Marguerite that I went with a truly heavy heart; it broke my soul to leave such a princess and such benevolence of company. She pressed her hands to mine and gave me a copy of her recent draft of *La Miroir l'ame Perechesse*. I was honoured, for Marguerite had not yet finished the work in entirety; this gift was a true mark of her favour and friendship.

"Remember well the lessons that God gives us," she said to me. "God only gives us as much as we can manage; the wise learn from those lessons and the foolish never do. You are no fool, Mistress Anne; I shall watch for you in court papers. You are not one to fade against the tapestries of the walls. I shall expect to read of your accomplishments often, and I would that you would write to me personally, when you are allowed to."

She smiled at me, as the beauty of her eyes made my throat clench and my heart sink. Would I see my great friend and mistress again? I knew not.

I nodded, and tears sprang into my eyes as I bowed to Marguerite for the last time. As I walked from the presence of that great princess, I felt my heart had drifted from my body and in its place was but an empty void. I clutched the volume she had given me to my breast, and swore that it should not be parted from me.

Later on, when I had long been living in England, Marguerite gave a finished copy of this work to my brother George to give to me. The little book had a plain black leather cover which masked the import of the weighty thoughts within. I had a gold chain made for the book and an outward cover to protect it from the English weather, bound in leather and jewels. I kept it with me as one of my most treasured possessions. I gave it to my daughter to hold, one sunlit afternoon many years later when we sat together in the gardens of Greenwich Palace. Elizabeth was too young to know what wonders it contained then; it was the sparkling jewels that she desired to touch with fat baby hands. I left the book in my chambers, on the day I was arrested. I know not where that book is now, but I hope somehow, some way, it has made its way back to the hands of my daughter. Perhaps it is in her possession now. Perhaps it will serve as a memory of me in the years left to come without me. Perhaps these are but desperate hopes and dreams, and yet somehow, I know that book I loved so well will find its way to my daughter.

Françoise and I shed tears together when an entourage of riders, sent by my father, came to escort me to the coast. She gave me a measure of fine silk to bring back to England and I gave her one of my favourite pearl-rimmed hoods, to remind her of me.

Through the tears she laughed suddenly. "François is most annoyed that you should be leaving his court!" There was a slight note, I thought, of recrimination in her voice, and I realised that although I was leaving and she should miss me as a friend, perhaps she would not miss me as a potential rival for the affections of her King. She had never seemed jealous of her lover's admiration for me before... something had changed.

"Bah!" I said wiping my eyes and my streaming nose. "His admiration for me was like his admiration for the Italian dresses he gave us, do you remember? We were jewels for the King to bedeck himself in. That is all I am to the King of France. There is but one lady with whom he chose to share his heart, and that was you. You have his heart, Françoise, of this I am sure."

She nodded and laughed, but saying goodbye to her then, I could see doubt in her eyes. Perhaps it was that François was waning in his affections to her? I did not believe it, not then at least.

I cried for a long time to leave these great women, these great friends in the country I loved so; it was torture to me. And now, I must go back to England.

What did I know of England? I was more French than a French-born woman! I was resentful and unhappy. I had to do my duty to my father and my family, but I did it with a heavy and aggrieved heart.

Every moment of the long journey to the English port of Calais, I longed to turn my horse and gallop as fast as I could to return to my own home, the Court of France. When I stood on the deck of the great ship that took me from France, my eyes were fixed on the disappearing shore, as I fought an urge to jump from the sides of the ship, and swim back to the court I loved so well. I was leaving all that I knew; my friends, the court… for a new life in England. For a husband whom I knew nothing of… not even his name! I wanted none of it. I wanted to go home, to France, to Claude, to Françoise, to Marguerite. I stood on the deck of the ship holding back tears and holding in fury. I felt I should never forgive my father for bringing me back to the land of my birth, and I knew that I would never be as happy in England as I had been in France.

I was returning to England; a stranger in a strange land.

Epilogue

17th May, 1536
The Tower of London

The wind whips past the window, startling me from memories of the past. I jump a little from my stool, causing a single knock from its wooden leg to sound heavily about the chamber. I look to the maids on the floor about me, but they do not wake. I have become calm, thinking on the past rather than on the present. But the past has disappeared from me with the shriek of the winds, and now I am in the present once again. And now, now I think on this day just passed within the Tower, the day my brother left this world.

They led me from these chambers to a cold room; to the Devilin Tower overlooking Tower Hill. I watched them lead out the prisoners, those men accused with me of crimes they know we did not commit. My brother stood with them, brought out from the Beauchamp Tower. They walked out slowly, with eyes blinking in the harsh, bright sun, after days in the gloom of their prisons. Guards surrounded them; their presence almost laughable, as if there were anywhere to which these prisoners could flee now.

I pressed my hand to the window as I saw my brother walk out from his prison. He looked around him, at the final sights his warm brown eyes would see. His clothing was his best, he was freshly shaved; even in death my brother was the picture of a gentleman.

My warm hand imprinted its sweat onto the window as I cried out to him silently; my eyes awash with tears of grief. As though he heard my silent cry to him, George looked up, and our eyes locked in one last goodbye in this world. He inclined his head to me and then bowed; the guards did not move to hold him. The others, standing near him, saw his actions and bowed to me also; Weston, Norris, Brereton…. all but Smeaton, who stood snivelling, wiping his nose on his sleeve, with his face turned from mine. He knew that his coward words have condemned us; that is the punishment he has taken to his maker. He has brought death to us all with his lies.

I watched them walk through the crowds. Thousands had gathered to watch them die; a national pastime, an entertainment… Such is our grief, such are our deaths… an hour's diversion for the low of this land, and the high.

There were swarms of people on that hill, come to watch the high brought lower than they and rejoice in the spectacle of death. My hand still at the window I felt panic rise in me as it must have risen in the men walking up the platform on Tower Hill, trying to keep their dignity as they walked towards Death himself.

I watched George, my little brother, my greatest friend as he climbed the steps to the platform amidst the roaring of the crowds. He stepped forward, and started to speak. I was too far away to hear him, but the crowds listened closely to him and there was a dull hush in the air as he spoke. Tears rolled down my face and a noise, not quite a scream and not quite a whisper, escaped my throat as I watched his distant figure kneel before the executioner and bow his head in prayer. He lowered his head, and held out his hands.

Then there was the flash of the axe in the day's light, and then there was blood. George's body fell sideways from the platform. The roar of the crowd signalled that my brother's life had been extinguished from this world.

My throat cried out again, the hollow, raw dark noise of sorrow.

They pulled his body, heavy with death, rudely from the platform and another figure stood where George had so lately been. Norris, my sweet friend, stood to make his speech now. I watched him die, too.

They took note, these women, these spies set around me, watching and analysing my grief to use against me still. I knelt, weak with grief and sick with fear for my own death. I cared little for what they thought of me now. I watched this pageant of death continue.

Weston, that handsome young man, came next; the platform was red, shining, sticky and slippery with blood that I could see even from this distance. All I could think of was the time when he and I had danced together in my apartments only a few weeks before. Weston was such an elegant dancer.

His head took some time to chop from his body. Perhaps the handle of the axe had grown slippery with the blood of the others. I watched each rise and fall of the axe, feeling as though I might vomit, but I could not stop watching.

Then there was Brereton, such an old rouge. His face was pale but his limbs stood true and still as he faced the crowds. He knelt in the blood of those who fell before him, and his head came off clean.

Then Mark Smeaton, snivelling still like the worm he is, stood to die the death of a noble man. He was to die like the others, by the axe rather than strung from a rope, although he deserved no such grace. He sold his soul for an easier death than his station allowed. He should have been hanged, and yet he was to die the death of a noble man. He would dip his head in the blood of those better than he; his blood would finally mix with those he had envied. In his death, in his last moments, finally Smeaton was where he had always desired to be; in the company of great men.

His lips muttered prayers as he died. I hope he prayed to God for forgiveness for all the death, for all the pain he has brought to this world.

I slid to the floor, weak and overwhelmed; my friends... my supporters... my brother...all dead. Tears would not come to me now. I sat and stared at my hands, listening to the roaring of the crowds; their fine entertainment now over, they went back to their everyday lives, happy to have seen death. Happy to have watched those greater than them fall from grace. But of course the common people do not know that they have been told lies. They rejoice for the deaths of traitors, and for me, the evil Jezebel, who soon will taste death herself.

One of the women, Cromwell's beast, came over to me. For a moment I thought she sought to comfort me as her arm reached around the back of my slim shoulders, but instead she leaned in close. "Master Wyatt watched this also," she whispered to me.

I raised my eyes slowly to hers; I saw a gleam of excitement in her pale eyes. Suddenly I felt more tired than I had ever felt before. Here, at the point where so much grief met with so much destruction in my life, here, this woman sought to trap me. To trick me into expressing something that might harm Tom Wyatt, as though enough death had not already come with the light of this day.

"Why do you say this to me?" I asked in a clear voice, anger flooding past the weary sorrow of my heart. "Do you seek some rich pickings of flesh to take to your master the wolf?"

I stood up and faced her, my lip curled in derision. "I have watched friends and kin die innocent this day; great men, greater than you or your master should ever hope to know or understand. Soon I shall be held in the great and gentle hand of God with them, for He knows the truth that you all seek to ignore. Take *those* words to your master, leech, and seek not to spill the blood of more innocents than you are guilty of already."

I walked to the door, turned and pointed at her. Her crafty face stalled as my eyes, always my greatest weapons, glinted at her.

"God watches all that you do," I said pointing at her, "and he will reward or punish all you have done in this life." I lowered my hand. "I will pray for you," I said and turned to leave.

"Pray for yourself, my lady," she said.

I looked at her and I smiled. "Although I am closer to death, you are more in need of prayer than I." I turned to be taken back to my apartments.

There I sat on a window seat and there I watched the bodies brought back and buried in the churchyard behind the Chapel of St Peter's on the Tower green.

As I watched their lifeless bodies, wrapped in cloth stained with blood, being immured in the ground, I began to laugh. Not from any humour within my heart, but from desperation, fear, from the terror of what awaited me.

"Soon I shall be Queen *sans-tete*.... the Lady Anne *lack-head*," I said, and the strange laughter that infected me during my first days in the Tower welled up inside me again. "I shall be the first Queen to rule without her head... perhaps that will serve me better, for trying to rule *with* a head did me no good".

I started to laugh wildly, my fine eyes afire with desperation and fear, cheeks flushed with unusual colour. My laughter bounced and echoed around the rooms. They stared at me. They have all looked at me in that way since we came here; these women who are not my women, not my friends. Agents of my enemies, their loyalty bought, their compassion dead. I probably wronged all their families in many ways I remember not now, and they are glad to see the proud, shrill Queen fall.

They stared at me, wondering if I had finally lost my senses, and I laughed louder still to see their fearful expressions, to watch them shrink back in fear from my glorious eyes, wicked and sparkling with hysteria and fear. My piercing laughter bounced from the walls and from the beautiful tapestries put here for my coronation. This laughter is the sound of the witch they have all been told that I am; the laughter of the whore, the temptress… the devil's concubine. They watch me all the time, slyly, carefully, through the sides of their little eyes to see what I am doing. It is as though they think I shall turn into a hare and flee this place.

They are afraid I shall curse them perhaps… as though I have access to those types of powers! As though I have access to any of even my earthly powers here. What are my talents now? What are my skills, my accomplishments? Who is there that I can charm here? Who is there that I can dance for or sing for… for my life?

Where is the King, my husband, whom I once could control with a single word or glance? Where is my great power now? I know now that there was never any such thing; it was all an illusion.

My laughter falters, and I return to stare from the window.

New ghosts walk amongst the old in the Tower compound this night. I see them from my seat at the window. I look out again, at the platform on which I am to die, and I feel panic rise in me once more.

I must think less wildly. I must think less on the present, for surely, here, I will lose my mind. In the past is where I will find my peace. In my memories I will find the strength to make my end with grace, and dignity.

I look from the window, but I do not see the green before me. I see the past. I see a girl standing on the deck of a ship, watching the land she loves disappear on the horizon, and turning herself with a heavy heart to face a new world. She knows not what will come to her, but I do. She knows not that the heart within her that she thinks broken for leaving all that she knew and loved, will come to know another love... a love I once thought could win over any obstacle or opposition. I see her, and I envy her. For soon, she will have what all of us long for in this life; to have another's heart beat only for yours, to know the overwhelming power love can bring to a soul... to feel, even for the briefest of moments, that you are adored, wanted and held above all others.

That girl who stands so restless and proud on that ship... would I tell her to go back, if I could? To flee to France as she wishes to? I know not. Her story will lead her to where I sit now, waiting for death. But if she had taken another path, would her life have ever been as miraculous, as strange and wonderful, as my life has been?

These questions cannot be answered. They will never be known. All that can be known are the steps that brought me to this place, and I will continue to walk them, even though I know the darkness towards which they lead me.

The past calls to me, and I give myself up to memories.

This is the end of *La Petite Boulain, Part One* of *Above All Others, The Lady Anne*.

In Part Two; *The Lady Anne*, Anne Boleyn returns to the lands of England, and to the court of Henry VIII.

About the Author

I find people talking about themselves in the third person to be entirely unsettling, so, since this section is written by me, I will use my own voice rather than try to make you believe that another person is writing about me to make me sound terribly important.

I am an independent author, publishing my books by myself, with the help of my lovely editor. I write in all the spare time I have. I briefly tried entering into the realm of 'traditional' publishing but, to be honest, found the process so time consuming and convoluted that I quickly decided to go it alone and self-publish.

My passion for history, in particular perhaps the era of the Tudors, began early in life. As a child I lived in Croydon, near London, and my schools were lucky enough to be close to such glorious places as Hampton Court and the Tower of London to mean that field trips often took us to those castles. I think it's hard not to find the Tudors infectious when you hear their stories, especially when surrounded by the bricks and mortar they built their reigns within. There is heroism and scandal, betrayal and belief, politics and passion and a seemingly never-ending cast list of truly fascinating people. So when I sat down to start writing, I could think of no better place to start than somewhere and sometime I loved and was slightly obsessed with.

Expect *many* books from me, but do not necessarily expect them all to be of the Tudor era. I write as many of you read, I suspect; in many genres. My own bookshelves are weighted down with historical volumes and biographies, but they also contain dystopias, sci-fi, horror, humour, children's books, fairy tales, romance and adventure. I can't promise I'll manage to write in *all* the areas I've mentioned there, but I'd love to give it a go. If anything I've published isn't your thing, that's fine, I just hope you like the ones I write which *are* your thing!

The majority of my books *are* historical fiction however, so I hope that if you liked this volume you will give the others in this series (and perhaps not in this series), a look. I want to divert you as readers, to please you with my writing and to have you join me on these adventures.

A book is nothing without a reader.

As to the rest of me; I am in my thirties and live in Cornwall with a rescued dog, a rescued cat and my partner (who wasn't rescued, but may well have rescued me). I studied Literature at University after I fell in love with books as a small child. When I was little I could often be found nestled half-way up the stairs with a pile of books and my head lost in another world between the pages. There is nothing more satisfying to me than finding a new book I adore, to place next to the multitudes I own and love… and nothing more disappointing to me to find a book I am willing to never open again. I do hope that this book was not a disappointment to you; I loved writing it and I hope that showed through the pages.

This is only one in a large selection of titles coming to you on Amazon. I hope you will try the others.

If you would like to contact me, please do so.

On twitter, I am @TudorTweep and am more than happy to follow back and reply to any and all messages. I may avoid you if you decide to say anything worrying or anything abusive, but I figure that's acceptable.

Via email, I am tudortweep@gmail.com a dedicated email account for my readers to reach me on. I'll try and reply within a few days.

I publish some first drafts and short stories on Wattpad where I can be found at www.wattpad.com/user/GemmaLawrence31 . Wattpad was the first place I ever showed my stories, *to anyone*, and in many ways its readers and their response to my works were the influence which pushed me into self-publishing. If you have never been on the site I recommend you try it out. Its free, its fun and its chock-full of real emerging talent. I love Wattpad because its members and their encouragement gave me the boost I needed as a fearful waif to get some confidence in myself and make a go of a life as a real, published writer.

Thank you for taking a risk with an unknown author and reading my book. I do hope now that you've read one you'll want to read more. If you'd like to leave me a review, that would be very much appreciated also!

Gemma Lawrence
Cornwall
2016

Thank You

...to so many people for helping me make this book possible... to my editor Brooke who entered into this with me and gave me her time, her wonderful guidance and also her encouragement. To my partner Matthew, who will be the first to admit that history is not his thing, and yet is willing to listen to me extol the virtues and vices of the Tudors and every other time period, repeatedly, to him and pushed me to publish even when I feared to. To my family for their ongoing love and support; this includes not only my own blood in my mother and father, sister and brother, but also their families, their partners and all my nieces who I am sure are set to take the world by storm as they grow. To Matthew's family, for their support, and for the extended family I have found myself welcomed to within them. To my friend Petra who took a tour of Tudor palaces and places with me back in 2010 which helped me to prepare for this book and others; her enthusiasm for that strange but amazing holiday brought an early ally to the idea I could actually write a book... And lastly, to the people who wrote all the books I read in order to write this book... all the historical biographers and masters of their craft who brought Elizabeth, and her times, to life in my head.

Thank you to all of you; you'll never know how much you've helped me, but I know what I owe to you.

Gemma
Cornwall
2016

Printed in Great Britain
by Amazon

13139659R00174